TERMINATOR
SALVATION
COLD WAR

Also available from Titan Books:

TERMINATOR SALVATION
From the Ashes
By Timothy Zahn

TERMINATOR SALVATION
The official movie novelization
By Alan Dean Foster

TERMINATOR SALVATION
COLD WAR

GREG COX

TITAN BOOKS

Terminator Salvation: Cold War
ISBN: 9781848560871

Published by
Titan Books
A division of
Titan Publishing Group Ltd
144 Southwark St
London
SE1 0UP

First edition October 2009
10 9 8 7 6 5 4 3 2 1

Cover imagery: Beautiful Mountains © Shutterstock. An Eerie Night © Shutterstock. Arctic Night © Shutterstock. Forest © Shutterstock.

Visit our website:
www.titanbooks.com

Did you enjoy this book? We love to hear from our readers. Please email us at readerfeedback@titanemail.com or write to us at Reader Feedback at the above address.

To receive advance information, news, competitions, and exclusive Titan offers online, please register as a member by clicking the "sign up" button on our website: www.titanbooks.com

A CIP catalogue record for this title is available from the British Library.

Printed and bound in the United States.

To my relatives in Alaska,
past and present.

"The strongest of all warriors are these two—
Time and Patience."
Leo Tolstoy, *War and Peace*

CHAPTER ONE

Judgment Day came without warning.

Captain First Rank Dmitri Losenko sipped tea from a warm ceramic mug as he updated the ship's log in the privacy of his stateroom aboard the Delta IV nuclear submarine K-115. His lean, hawk-like features were clean-shaven. Strands of silver had begun to infiltrate his short brown hair. Medals and insignia gleamed upon his dark blue uniform. Shrewd gray eyes focused intently on his work.

His personal quarters were as trim and impeccably organized as the man himself. Steam rose from the brass samovar resting on his desk. Polished wood paneling covered steel bulkheads. The cotton sheets of his bunk were fitted and folded with the careful precision and attention to detail that life aboard a submarine demanded.

A multifunction display screen, mounted adjacent to the bunk, allowed him to check on the sub's tactical status at a glance. A dog-eared copy of *War and Peace* awaited his leisure. As a loyal officer in the new Russian Navy, Losenko had commanded this vessel for more than a year now. He liked to think that he was prepared for both war and peace—and that he played a vital role in preserving the latter.

It was a routine watch aboard K-115, christened the *Gorshkov* after the father of the modern Russian Navy. 150 meters below the frozen surface of the Barents Sea, the sub patrolled silently, bearing its deadly cargo of ballistic missiles. For nearly twenty years, through the Cold War and beyond, K-115 and the rest of the Northern Fleet had held its fire, always returning to port without unleashing thermonuclear hell upon the world.

Alone in his cabin, Losenko had no expectation that this mission would end otherwise. He looked forward to returning to his dacha outside St. Petersburg after another successful run. The countryside was beautiful in the summer.

A squawk from the intercom disturbed his reverie. Losenko put down his tea and plucked the microphone from its cradle. A black plastic cord—kept scrupulously free of tangles—connected the mike to the speaker system.

"Captain's quarters," he said brusquely, his voice deep. "What is it?"

The voice of Alexei Ivanov, his executive officer, or *starpom*, escaped the mike.

"Captain. We've received an urgent communication from Fleet Command."

Losenko arched an eyebrow.

"I'll be right there."

Abandoning his logbook, the captain rose to his feet. His black leather boots resounded against the steel deck plates as he strode down the corridor. Unlike a surface ship—subject to the choppy motion of the waves—the submarine's deck remained steady and level beneath his feet. If not for the constant thrum of the ship's engines in the background, there was little indication that the vessel was moving. Cables and conduits grew like ivy over the bulkheads. The freshly scrubbed air was a comfortable twenty degrees Celsius. A double hull shielded him from the black, frigid water outside the sub. As always, he found comfort and pride in the efficiency and reliability of the machine he commanded.

What does Moscow want now? he fretted. Worry furrowed his brow. *I was not expecting any new orders.*

A brisk march brought him quickly to the central command post, which lay only one compartment aft of the officers' quarters. As he entered, his ears were instantly assaulted by emergency alert signals which reverberated from the radio shack just beyond the command center. At best he could only pick out random words and phrases erupting from the speakers.

Rows of illuminated instruments, gauges, and control panels lined the walls of the compact chamber, which was roughly the size of the kitchen in a small Moscow apartment. Two cylindrical periscopes, one optical, the other electronic, rose like bolted metal pillars from the center of a raised platform overlooking the control room. Alert submariners manned their posts, their postures straightening somewhat upon the captain's entrance. Striped black shirts could be glimpsed beneath their dark blue jumpsuits.

Toward the bow, the diving officer stood watch over the helmsmen as they operated the planes and rudder by manipulating a pair of large steering wheels. A digital depth display confirmed that the ship was currently at 150 meters below the ice. A fathometer measured the remaining distance to the ocean floor.

"Captain in CCP," the chief of the watch announced over the nearby din.

Captain Second Rank Ivanov surrendered the conn to Losenko, who joined the younger officer on the periscope pedestal. A fit young man with slick black hair, striking violet eyes, and the face of a poet, the first officer was sometimes teased by his peers for his matinee-idol good looks. Ivanov thrust a paper printout at his commander. His bearing was suitably professional, but Losenko knew his young protege well enough to catch the tension in his voice. The captain realized at once that something was seriously amiss.

"This arrived via ELF," Ivanov announced.

The *Gorshkov* boasted a loop antennae in its sail capable of receiving extra low frequency radio messages even as the vessel traveled at great depths. Losenko quickly scanned the communique—and his heart skipped a beat. Despite his training and experience, he had to resist an urge to grab onto a railing to steady himself.

Printed in stark black and white, the words before him were every commander's worst nightmare.

And a death sentence for the world he knew.

According to the printout, the United States of America had just done the unthinkable: they had launched their entire nuclear arsenal at their rivals throughout the world. Even as Losenko examined the message once more, letting his disbelieving eyes confirm that he had read the decoded report correctly, the American missiles were in the air, en route to targets in Russia, China, and the Middle East.

Moscow had authorized immediate retaliation.

No, he thought numbly. *There must be some mistake.*

He lifted his shocked gaze from the paper, and spoke in a low growl. "Has this been verified?"

Ivanov nodded grimly. Deputy Commanders Pavlinko and Zamyatin stood by, clutching the latest code packets. The seals of the packets were freshly broken.

"The codes are in order," Ivanov said. "The message is authentic."

The man's voice was taut. Standing at attention, he fairly vibrated from the strain of keeping his emotions under control, like a pressure hull on the verge of buckling. Losenko knew he had to be thinking of his wife and daughter back in Ukraine. The daughter, Nadia, had just turned twelve....

"Very well, then." He clamped down on his mounting sense of horror, relying on years of training and discipline to hold himself together. Both his crew and his homeland were depending on him now; he would not let them down in their darkest hour. "We have our duty."

Time was of the essence. While he had been sipping tea, World War III had begun, and the enemy had already fired the first salvo. For all he knew, K-115 was already a target. American aircraft and attack subs were surely hunting them, determined to prevent the *Gorshkov* from retaliating.

"Ascend to firing depth," he barked, his orders quickly echoing along the chain of command. "Initiate launch procedures."

The *Gorshkov* was armed with sixteen liquid-fueled missiles, each one equipped with four independently targetable warheads. Every warhead was capable of generating at least 100 kilotons of explosive force. Translated into human terms, K-115 could kill almost eight million people and injure many millions more. The Second World War would be considered a mere skirmish by comparison.

Can any man live with so many deaths on his conscience? Losenko pondered. *Can I?*

The deck tilted upward toward the bow as pumped air displaced water in the ballast tanks. Years of experience aboard both ballistic and attack subs allowed Losenko to keep his balance during their rapid ascent. His boat could set loose its lethal birds from underwater, but only from a depth of fifty-five meters or less. The frozen icecap would offer no barrier to his missiles. With a range of over 6,000 kilometers, the missiles could reach their targets even from the Arctic.

The captain considered his crew. Glancing around, he noted furtive glances exchanged between the men crammed into the control room. Despite—or perhaps because of—the hushed voices of the officers, he knew the crew had to be aware that this was no ordinary maneuver. The tight quarters of a submarine allowed few secrets, while the commotion from the radio shack was impossible to ignore. He took hold of a hanging mike.

"Put me through to all hands."

He took only a moment to organize his thoughts before addressing his entire crew.

"This is your captain speaking," he began, his voice steady. "Make no mistake. This is not a drill. The moment for which we have long been prepared has come round at last. Our nation is at war, attacked without explanation by an enemy who cannot be allowed to strike with impunity at the Motherland. What is asked of us now is no easy task, but this is what we have trained for, what our nation and people demand of us in this terrible hour. I fully expect every man on this vessel to do his duty." He swept his stern gaze over the anxious sailors under his command.

"All hands, combat stations."

Losenko released the mike. He faced his officers.

"Instruct Sonar to be on the alert for enemy vessels. I want to be informed at once of any contacts." The men relayed his message across the conn. "Mr. Ivanov, plot an evasive course to begin immediately after the release of our weapons."

"Aye, aye, sir," his XO replied. Launching their missiles would instantly signal their location to the enemy. They would have to strike quickly, then retreat at full speed. Ivanov consulted a notebook filled with combat strategies. Anger seethed in his voice. "Those sons of bitches won't catch us with our pants down."

The next several minutes were like a nightmare from which Losenko could not wake. Top-secret codes were transmitted directly from Moscow, and once they were employed, the procedure for launching a nuclear attack was as tightly scripted and choreographed as a Bolshoi ballet. Trigger keys were extracted from closely guarded combination safes. Missiles were fueled and prepped. Silos were pressurized. Coordinates were loaded into the guidance systems and targeting computers. Warheads were activated.

Heavy metal hatches slid open, exposing the tips of the warheads. More codes unlocked the firing mechanisms. Each man played his part, like a cog in some infernal assembly line designed to manufacture Armageddon.

A regimented litany of checks and responses proceeded

with sickening inevitability. Losenko watched himself perform his own functions without hesitation, yet all the while a frantic voice at the back of his mind screamed silently.

WHY?

It made no sense. The Cold War was over and international tensions, while never completely at rest, were nowhere near a level that might justify such madness. He was aware of no crisis—no global emergency—that could have escalated to all-out nuclear war in a matter of hours. His most recent updates from Fleet Command had hinted at nothing of the sort. The Americans had troubles enough in Afghanistan and Iraq. They did not need any more.

A sense of almost supernatural horror gripped the captain's soul. What demon had possessed them? Had their president lost his mind? Didn't he realize that he had just doomed his own country? The man was supposed to be a cowboy, not a maniac.

Losenko resisted an urge to cross himself.

The sub leveled off as it achieved firing position.

"Fifty-six meters," the diving officer called out. "Fifty-five meters."

For a brief moment, Losenko considered going higher, all the way to periscope depth. Perhaps he should risk raising his masts, then break radio silence long enough to consult with Fleet Command one last time before passing the point of no return. Billions of lives hung in the balance. What if this was all some terrible misunderstanding?

What other explanation could there be?

But, no, the risk was too great. He shook his head to clear his mind of any lingering doubts. He dared not compromise the safety of his ship, not before he had ful-filled the awful responsibility Fate—and Mother Russia—had entrusted to him. His orders were clear, double-checked and authenticated beyond all question.

It was time to kill more than six million men, women, and children.

"All compartments report readiness," Ivanov informed him. A muscle twitched beneath his cheek. "Missiles one through fourteen await your order."

Losenko nodded. Moscow had ordered nearly all of the *Gorshkov*'s complement of ballistic missiles into the air, leaving only two rockets in reserve. Even that degree of caution struck the captain as faintly ludicrous under the circumstances. Would there be anything left to bomb after the initial exchange?

He felt a dozen eyes upon him, while the sub itself seemed to be holding its breath. His mouth felt as dry as ashes. He would have killed for a shot of vodka.

"Initiate fire," he commanded.

His words were carried to the weapons officer in miss-ile control. The final trigger was activated. The entire boat bobbed slightly as, one after another, the massive weight of fourteen 130,000-ton missiles exited its silos in sequenced bursts of expanding nitrogen gas. Automated systems pumped tons of water into the missile compensa-tion tanks to keep the sub more or less level.

They were close enough to the surface that the sound of shattered ice penetrated the stillness of the ocean when the unleashed missiles burst through the arctic icecap. In his mind's eye, Losenko could see them arcing through the sky as their first-stage rockets ignited high above the Barents Seas, then veered away from one another en route to their ultimate destinations, thousands of miles away.

"One through fourteen away," the missile chief reported. "Launch successful."

It's done, Losenko realized. *Once our birds have flown, they cannot be recalled.*

Although the target package selected by Moscow had been expressed in terms of coordinates and computerized programs, he knew all too well where the missiles were going. To the American state of Alaska, home to major population centers and key military installations. All those targets—and those who lived there—had just been condemned to incineration. Losenko had never visited Alaska, but he had heard it was a beautiful place.

He wondered what would be left of it.

"God help us all," he murmured. "Execute evasive maneuvers. Down bubble, thirty degrees!"

During testing, the successful launch of a missile was cause for pride and celebration. But not today. Now that the deed was done, Losenko's strength and discipline threatened to desert him. His legs felt limp and a dreadful weariness descended upon his shoulders. Looking out over his men once more, he saw tears streaming down the faces of veteran sailors. Muttered prayers and curses rose from the general hubbub.

"Yankee bastards!" Ivanov spat. Rage contorted his handsome features. His fists were clenched at his sides. "May they burn in hell forever!"

The captain allowed the XO his outburst and his anger. Alexei had just lost his family and his future, like everyone else aboard K-115.

We are all damned now, he thought. *May heaven forgive us.*

He had no idea how he was going to live with what he had just done.

"Dive the boat!" he barked hoarsely. "Dive!"

The fire was not dead yet.

Thousands of miles from the Barents Sea, in the verdant heart of Alaska's Chugach State Park, a young forest ranger scowled at the still smoldering campfire. Her long black hair blew in the breeze. An ivory pendant, carved in the shape of a raven, added a touch of personal flair to her green park uniform. Dark eyes flashed angrily.

How could people be so careless? Didn't they know an abandoned campfire like this could burn the whole forest down?

Her fingers drifted to the grip of the pistol resting against her hip. The thoughtless hikers were lucky that they had already moved on. New to the Forest Service, with a spanking new degree in environmental science, the ranger took her responsibilities seriously. Nobody was going to mess with Alaska's pristine wilderness on her watch.

A blinding white flash, many miles to the south, drove the smoking embers from her mind. The ranger threw up an arm to shield her eyes. A thunderous blast echoed in the distance. She watched in horror as a mushroom cloud rose on the horizon.

Oh God, she thought. *That was Anchorage.*

The forgotten campfire meant nothing now. A larger blaze was consuming the world.

The ranger knew her life had just changed forever.

CHAPTER TWO

2018

"Heads down. It's coming."

Molly Kookesh took cover in the Alaskan brush. She wriggled forward on her belly atop the hard-packed winter snow until she had a better view of the remote river canyon below. The wooded slope provided an ideal vantage point. Frosted evergreens, their branches weighed down by snow, hid her from the moonlight. A damp mist hung over the valley—and the massive timber bridge spanning the river. Snow-capped mountains loomed in the distance.

"Where?" Sitka's head popped up beside her. A mane of wild ginger hair that barely knew what a comb was framed the teenager's face. An oversized army surplus jacket hung like a tent upon her gangly frame. Her pockets bulged with miscellaneous odds and ends, scavenged from wherever. Freckles accented her gleeful expression. She brushed her bangs away from her eyes.

"Wanna see!" she said eagerly.

"Down, packrat." Geir Svenson shoved the girl's head

back behind a ridge. A scruffy blond beard just enhanced the bush pilot's rakish good looks, at least as far as Molly was concerned. A battered aviator's jacket was zipped up to his chin, the better to keep out the bitter cold. A wool cap kept his head warm. His breath frosted from his lips. "Unless you think that silly head of yours needs a couple of extra holes in it," he added.

"Ha, ha. Very funny," the teen muttered, but she got the message and hunkered down in the snow between the two adults. "Wanted a peek, that's all. Wasn't gonna get spotted." Sitka doled out pronouns sparingly, as if they were too valuable to be wasted. "Not a child anymore, you know."

Molly let out an exasperated sigh. She should have known better than to let Sitka tag along but, eager to earn her colors, the girl had been pestering her for months to be included in an operation. Tonight's outing—a simple recon gig—had seemed like a good opportunity to test the teenager in the field. Now Molly wasn't so sure.

"Quiet, both of you!" she hissed. "Don't make me regret bringing you along."

That shut Sitka up, at least for the moment. Geir adopted a wounded look.

"Whoa! What did I do?"

"Nothing," she admitted. "But I've got a hard-ass reputation to keep up."

Geir shot her an appreciative once-over.

"Trust me, chief, that ass speaks for itself."

"Gag!" Sitka feigned sticking a finger down her throat. "Nauseous now."

Molly tried not to grin.

"Enough banter. Eyes on the prize."

A fur-lined parka matched her tight sealskin trousers.

She tossed back the hood, exposing a head of lustrous black hair tied up in a ponytail. High cheekbones, dark almond eyes, and copper skin proclaimed her Native Alaskan roots. A carved ivory Raven totem dangled on a leather strap around her neck. A scarlet armband marked her as a member of the Resistance, the red dye symbolizing the blood spilt by all the brave men and women who had died fighting the machines over the last fifteen years.

Sitka eyed it enviously. She had yet to earn an armband of her own.

Propped up on her elbows, Molly squinted through her binoculars. Half a mile away, the huge trestle bridge stretched across the valley, looming more than 300 feet above the raging river below. Icebergs collided harmlessly against the massive concrete piers. Bolted timber struts and trusses supported the bridge, which was over 700-feet long. Iron train tracks ran across its deck. An electrified third rail eliminated the need for old-fashioned diesel or steam engines. The high-tech transportation system had been built on top of an old mining company railway, dating back to the Gold Rush.

The more things change....

The tracks appeared empty, except for a bald eagle roosting midway across the bridge. A low rumble rattled the tracks, audible even at this distance, and the raptor shot up into the air.

Smart bird, Molly thought. The rumble grew louder by the moment. A tunnel carved into the hillside on the northern side of the canyon hid the source of the noise from view until the train came zooming out onto the bridge.

Molly's eyes widened.

"Wow!" Sitka whispered in awe. "Way skookum!"

Like all of Skynet's mechanical offspring, the driver-less train was ugly, brutal in its design, making no concession to human aesthetics. Gray armor-plating covered its streamlined contours. Sealed gun-ports ran along the length of its sides. Red optical sensors glowed like demonic eyes above its bullet-shaped nose. Razor-sharp skewers jutted like fangs from the bloody steel "cow-catcher" at the prow. The rotting carcass of an unlucky moose was impaled upon the spikes.

Bright blue sparks flared beneath the train cars, where their contacts met the electric rail. The deafening clamor of its passage drowned out everything else, even the rapid beating of Molly's pulse. On straightaways, she knew, the bullet train clocked at least 180 miles an hour.

And to think I used to find trains romantic....

The "Skynet Express" carried uranium, copper, and other strategic minerals necessary to the war effort, transporting them from automated mining operations in the Yukon. Unrestricted by environmental or conservation concerns, Skynet had gouged the wilderness, wresting raw materials from Mother Earth for its own unholy purposes. Preexisting rail lines running across hundreds of miles of rugged terrain had been linked and upgraded to fit the cybernetic intelligence's specifications. Weekly runs transported the ore to a Terminator construction plant in Valdez.

But not for much longer, Molly vowed. *Not if I have anything to say about it.*

The value Skynet placed on the ore was driven home by the transport's daunting defenses. Not only was the armored juggernaut loaded with concealed weapons, but the supply train rated air support, as well. Molly ducked lower into the brush as a Hunter-Killer glided over the canyon. The steady thrum of the aircraft's VTOL turbo-fans contrasted with the noisy clatter from the train tracks. High-speed impellers kept it aloft, and its ugly gunmetal exterior matched that of the train it was escorting. Usually HKs preceded the trains they were protecting; Molly guessed that this one had hung back to check on some disturbance prior to the tunnel. Maybe a noisy herd of caribou, or a falling tree.

Going into hover mode, the HK hung in the sky above the bridge. Powerful floodlights scoured the vicinity, on the lookout for human targets.

"Nobody move!" she whispered urgently. The HKs relied on infrared motion trackers to locate prey. The best way to escape their notice was to blend into the surroundings and not move a muscle. They had to be still as a corpse—or risk becoming one.

Geir and Sitka followed her example. *Thank heaven for small favors!*

A cold wind rustled the branches overhead. A glop of wet snow fell onto her head and shoulders, most likely dislodged by the passing of the damned HK, and she had to resist the urge to shake it off. Melted ice trickled down the back of her neck and it took all of her self-control not to shiver. Sandwiched between the frozen whiteness beneath and the freshly deposited snow on her back, it was hard to ignore the chill creeping into her bones. She clenched her jaw to keep her teeth from chattering. Was it just her imagination, or had the harsh Alaskan winters gotten even worse since Judgment Day?

Nothing like a nuclear winter to let the air out of global warming. She couldn't wait until spring. *Assuming I last that long....*

The Hunter-Killer wasn't alone. Aerostats—slender football-sized surveillance drones with glowing red eyes at one end—buzzed around the train like mosquitos. Some scanned the track ahead of the train, while others darted amidst the bridge's supports. A brown bear, fishing for salmon further downstream, attracted an Aerostat's attention, and the mechanical sentinel buzzed down for a better look, scanning the startled bear with ruby lasers that transmitted a digitized profile of the animal back to Skynet. The bear reared up on its hind legs and swatted at the levitating pest, which expertly stayed out of reach of the massive paws. The animal was tempting fate by attacking the drone, but apparently Skynet judged it no actual threat to the train, so the Aerostat flew back up toward the tracks.

The bear went back to its fishing.

Molly filed the encounter in her memory. Now that the data was stored in the massive computer, would it be possible to use a bear costume to deceive Skynet in the future? It was something to think about.

Lord knows I wouldn't mind being stuffed inside a toasty bearskin right now!

The train seemed to go on forever. Molly lost count of how many linked cars rattled over the bridge. Several minutes passed before the last one exited the tunnel. Its bullet-shaped nose matched the lead car at the other end. Evil red eyes watched behind as the train finally pulled away, disappearing into the wilderness that lay across the river. A swarm of watchful Aerostats chased after it.

The HK rotated in midair, sweeping the canyon one last time with its blinding floodlights, before rising to a higher elevation. Its turbofans tilted to the side as it flew south above the train tracks. Molly watched its airborne bulk glide away, defying gravity. The eerily weightless way they flew never failed to send a chill down her spine.

"Wicked!" Sitka started to spring up from the ground, but Geir held her down by placing a heavy hand between her shoulders. HKs and Aerostats had been known to circle back for a second look. "Yeah. Right," she muttered.

Better safe than sorry, Molly mused silently.

She waited for the echoes of the train to fade away, then counted to fifty before sitting up and shaking the snow from her head and shoulders. She gave Geir and Sitka the all-clear sign, and the pair climbed to their feet. Geir brushed the snow from his jacket and heavy-duty denim jeans. Sitka acted oblivious to the cold. Molly sometimes suspected her of being part polar bear.

She hastily consulted her watch: an antique, spring-operated gizmo she had salvaged from the ruins of an old pawnshop. She preferred manual timepieces these days. It was easier to re-wind them than to try to scrounge up batteries.

"It's 10:48 exactly," she announced.

"10:48," Geir confirmed, consulting his own watch. He cracked a wry smile. "Gotta hand it to Skynet. It's got the trains running on time."

Molly wasn't inclined to give Skynet credit for anything. "So did Mussolini."

"Muso-who?" Sitka asked.

No surprise that the teenager didn't recognize the name. Only sixteen years old, the orphaned girl had no memory of life before Judgment Day, nor much in the way of an old-fashioned education. Nobody even knew what her real name was; Molly had found her living as a scavenger in the ruins of the town of Sitka over ten years ago, and that had become her name. She had literally grown up in the Resistance, having never known a world that wasn't overrun by Terminators.

"Ask Doc back at the camp," Molly said. Now was no time for a history lesson. "He'll fill you in."

"Never shut up either." Sitka rolled her eyes. "Know how he is once he gets going 'bout the old days. Borrrrring."

Molly envied the teen her blithe disregard for the past. There were times she wished she could forget how good life used to be, before Judgment Day.

What I wouldn't give for a vacation at a luxury hotel—or even just cable television.

Sitka didn't miss any of that.

How could she?

"So that's the infamous Skynet Express," Geir said, changing the subject. "Pretty big train."

"Ginormous," Sitka agreed. She peered across the canyon, as though hoping to catch another glimpse of the evil locomotive. "Makes a Hydrobot look like an earthworm!" Eager green eyes sought out Molly. "So when do we blow it up?"

The uranium train was a tempting target. If the Resistance could somehow intercept it, not only would they disrupt the enemy's supply lines, but they might also come away with valuable resources. Molly was sure the uniforms in Command could make use of some unprocessed uranium, not to mention copper, zinc, and other essential metals.

"Could be quite a haul," she mused aloud. "Maybe

put us on Command's radar. Show them what we're really capable of."

Even though her small band of Resistance fighters had been waging a guerilla war against Skynet for more than a decade now, she often got the impression that the top military brass didn't take citizen soldiers like her seriously. They got the occasional pat on the back, sure, but not much in the way of serious material support. Old-school Pentagon types like Ashdown hogged all the resources for their own troops.

It's not fair, she thought, a familiar frustration raising her blood pressure. *My people may have started out as loggers, park rangers, pipeline workers, refugees, and half-feral kids, but we're all soldiers now, and have been since the first Russian bombs fell fifteen years ago. It's like John Connor always says—if you're still breathing, you're the Resistance.*

So why couldn't Command get that through their thick skulls?

"Not going to be easy, Molly." Towering over her, Geir draped an arm around her, sharing some of his body warmth, for which she was silently grateful. He stared out at the bridge below. "You're talking several hundred tons of rolling Terminator, with air support and back-up." He whistled in anticipation of the fight the train and its escort could put up. "Minor raids are one thing, but this would be the biggest operation we've ever attempted.... by far."

A worried look came over his rugged face.

"You really think we can pull it off?"

Molly thought of all the T-600s and Hunter-Killers Skynet could power with the uranium each train carried, all the new surveillance and tracking systems it could set up. Who knew how many people would die because of the weekly supply runs? Who knew the cost to the very planet itself?

She had been a U.S. park ranger before the bombs fell. It killed her to see the land raped by Skynet.

"If we don't, who will?"

CHAPTER THREE

2003

It is a perfect summer afternoon. A clear blue sky unfolds above the skyscrapers. Warm sunlight bathes the bustling city streets and sidewalks.

Pedestrians crowd the pavement. Office workers fetch coffee from a sidewalk vendor. Giggling teenagers hurry home from school. A beautiful young mother pushes a stroller. Infant twins gurgle happily. An old man walks a bulldog. Vendors hawk frozen treats from carts. Cars, trucks, and taxis honk impatiently. Flowers sprout from window boxes. Pigeons flutter and coo as they perch upon the granite facades of the downtown buildings. A gentle breeze blows down the street. A mouth-watering aroma spills from the open doorway of a busy bakery.

Losenko smiles. He is glad to be alive.

The sudden blare of an air-raid siren drowns out the everyday hubbub. Frightened eyes turn upward. People scatter and run. Her eyes wide with fear, the young mother places her body protectively over her babies, glancing around frantically to locate the *source of the danger. The old man tugs on the bull-dog's leash, but the dog stubbornly refuses to hurry. Panicked birds take flight.*

No, Losenko thinks. Not now. Not again!

A blinding white flash lights up the sky. He shields his eyes with his arm, but it's too late. A fireball rises from the heart of the city, many blocks away. A shock wave knocks him from his feet. A scorching wind flays the flesh from his bones. His skin and clothing burst into flames.

A mushroom cloud swallows up his screams....

Losenko woke with a start, his body drenched in sweat. His bunk enclosed him like a coffin. The violet glow of the tactical display screen revealed the dimly lit contours of his cabin aboard the *Gorshkov*. He lay still, waiting for his racing heart to settle.

A weary sigh escaped his lips.

"Again," he whispered hoarsely. He had no trouble recalling the details of the apocalyptic nightmare, and the sensations it left had become all too familiar to him. He had suffered through the same dream, or variations thereof, every night since that horrible day some four weeks ago when K-115 had unleashed its missiles. Sometimes he woke thinking the entire war was just a bad dream. Then the awful reality came crashing back down again.

Thanks to its nuclear engines, the *Gorshkov* could stay submerged indefinitely, limited only by its food supplies. A distilling plant in the engine provided a steady supply of fresh water for the men and batteries. The sub had been hiding from the enemy for a month now without word from Fleet Command. Losenko rather suspected there was no one left in Moscow to issue any new orders, so he clung to the ocean floor and waited for the conflagration to die out overhead. Radioactive fallout decayed at an exponential rate; in theory, it might finally be safe to breach the surface again.

He shuddered to think what they might find. The Americans had possessed enough bombs to reduce the Motherland to a cinder.

For a moment he flirted with the notion of trying to get back to sleep, but decided against it. A glance at the plasma screen display revealed that the next watch was due to begin in less than an hour anyway. Moreover, he was in no hurry to experience his nightmare once more, at least not so soon.

If he closed his eyes, he could still see the horrified face of the young mother as she tried in vain to shield her children from the coming holocaust. That she bore a distinct resemblance to his ex-wife, back when they were still young and in love, was surely no coincidence. His subconscious mind had a cruel streak.

Forcing the troubling images from his mind as much as was possible, he rose and dressed. Now, more than ever, he considered it important to take care in his appearance, in order to provide a strong and reassuring example for the crew. Maintaining morale and discipline—even after the end of the world—was crucial. He couldn't allow the men to sink into apathy and despair. He could not allow *himself* to falter, not even for a moment. An abyss, deeper than any ocean, would suck them all down if they surrendered to the full horror of their situation.

He owed it to his crew not to let them see any cracks in his resolve.

Yet, as he took a razor to his chin, shaving in front of the small mirror in his private washroom, he couldn't help but notice the haunted look in his bloodshot eyes. Dark purple pouches testified to long, sleepless nights.

Under the circumstances, he consoled himself, *it's a wonder that I don't look more wretched*. With that he resumed his assault on the encroaching stubble.

Once he was satisfied that he looked like a proper captain, Losenko made his way to the control room. A defeated-looking seaman squeezed past him en route to Engineering. The sailor failed to meet his captain's eyes. His grimy coveralls smelled as though they had not been laundered in days. He stumbled over a fire bucket that someone had carelessly left sitting in the passageway.

"Look lively, sailor!" Losenko said sternly. "And stow that pail where it belongs."

"Aye, aye, sir," the man muttered in response. Even with his captain looking over his shoulder, however, the seaman moved as though in a daze. He trudged away listlessly, bearing the offending bucket with him. The rubber soles of his sneakers barely lifted from the floor.

Losenko watched as the zombie-like figure disappeared into the stern of the boat. *How many more are there like that?* he pondered grimly. Even on the most uneventful of patrols, the crew started to get a little stir crazy after several weeks cooped up in a cramped metal tube. Now, with nothing to look forward to but the aftermath of a nuclear war, nerves had to be at breaking point. *How long before discipline breaks down entirely?*

The situation in the control room did little to reassure him. Even as he stepped foot into the nerve center, he heard Ivanov harshly upbraiding an unlucky subordinate.

"Five minutes to load a torpedo?" The XO stared in disgust at the stopwatch he held in his hand. He and the captain had been running frequent drills, in part to keep the crew's mind off the holocaust that had engulfed their homes. "What's wrong with those slugs down there? Have they got lead in their sneakers?"

Weapons Officer Pavlinko gulped.

"No, sir. Not that I'm aware of, sir. We'll do better next time!"

"And suppose there had been a real American sub hunting us?" Ivanov retorted, his voice dripping with sarcasm. "Had that been the case, do you think there would have *been* a next time?"

Pavlinko accepted the tongue-lashing.

"No, sir."

"Then maybe you need to give those lazy shirkers a solid kick in the butt, before the enemy really comes calling!"

The venom in the *starpom*'s tone added to Losenko's woes. There was a bitterness in Ivanov's heart that had not been there before the Americans had launched their suicidal attack. The young officer had been tough, but fair, and well-liked by the crew. Now he was short-tempered all the time, taking out his fury on the men beneath him.

Anger is eating away at him, Losenko realized, *just as sorrow never lifts from my shoulders.*

He joined Ivanov upon the periscope pedestal.

"Easy, Alexei," he cautioned in a low tone. "These men have faced the unimaginable."

Ivanov stiffened. "There is a war on," he responded. "We cannot afford the luxury of grief."

Even for your wife and daughter? Losenko thought.

His heart ached for the younger man's loss. Not for the first time, he was grateful that he had no children of his own. "Perhaps you are right. Or maybe the war is already over—and both sides have lost."

In that moment he decided that he could not delay any longer. His men deserved to know what had become of the world they had left behind.

"Any contacts on the sonar?" he inquired.

Ivanov glanced in the direction of the sonar shack.

"Nothing. Not even biologics."

No whales, porpoises, or schools of deep-sea fish, in other words. Had humanity taken the rest of the animal kingdom with it when it had self-destructed?

"I see," Losenko replied. Despite their earlier concerns, they had encountered no American attack subs since the war broke out. This was both encouraging and worrisome, in that it suggested that the navies of the world no longer possessed the capacity to hunt their enemies. Nevertheless, he intended to take no chances.

"Turn the boat around," he instructed, to make certain no hidden dangers were skulking in their baffles. *Gorshkov*'s own propellers created a sonic "blind spot" in the submarine's wake. A shrewd commander made a habit of checking his rear. "Left fifteen degrees rudder, steady course three-seven-zero."

K-115 executed an expert turn. The sonar dome at its nose found nothing suspicious in the vicinity. Confident that they were not under observation, Losenko turned toward the diving officer.

"Mr. Orlov, ascend to periscope depth."

In response to his orders, K-115 tilted toward the bow, while Orlov counted out the depth as the boat climbed toward the surface. The helmsman and planesman pulled back on their steering wheels, working in perfect harmony. Seated to their left, the diving officer and the chief of the watch manned the ballast controls, blowing water from the tanks to increase the sub's buoyancy. The hull popped noisily as the pressure outside changed dramatically.

"Fifty meters," Orlov announced. "Thirty meters."

Losenko visualized the ice above their heads. He unhooked the mike and spoke into it.

"All hands, brace for impact."

He grabbed hold of the railing.

"Twenty meters."

Metal shuddered as the sub broke through the icecap. Its twelve meter-tall sail cut through the snow-covered floes like a blade. The jarring impact threw one of the newer crewman off-balance, and he staggered before grabbing onto the handle of an overhead chart cabinet. A loose folder clattered to the deck.

Water flooded the trim tanks as K-115 leveled off. The helmsmen pushed their wheels forward.

"Scope's breaking," Ivanov reported. He gripped the handlebars of the number one periscope and peered through the eyepiece. His body tense, he rotated the scope a full 360 degrees. "No close contacts," he said with what sounded like a trace of disappointment. Losenko saw clearly that Alexei longed for an enemy upon whom to take vengeance. It was a dangerous trait to have in a first officer.

Unlike their XO, the other crewmen let out an audible sigh of relief at hearing that they had not ascended into a war zone. Beeps and chirps came from an electronic surveillance sensor that automatically began sweeping the area for signals from any nearby ships or aircraft. An alarm would sound if it detected any approaching threat.

No alarm came.

Losenko took the periscope from Ivanov. Planting his feet, he squinted into the eyepiece. Twilight in the Arctic Circle looked much as he remembered it, until he realized that—according to the sub's chronometer—it should have been bright and sunny outside. Instead, clouds of smoke and ash clotted the sky, allowing only a paltry fraction of daylight through. *Like the smoke from a funeral pyre*, he thought morosely, *drifting over the top of the world.*

"Chief of the watch," the captain instructed, "raise the main multifunction mast."

The mast, which was housed in the sail, boasted an array of sophisticated electronic antennae capable of receiving and transmitting signals along a broad spectrum of frequencies. It could also contact GPS satellites to receive position updates.

Our ears are open, Losenko thought. *But is there anybody out there?*

Unwilling to wait any longer for an answer, he stepped down from the pedestal and headed for the radio shack, just forward of the control room. Crossing the conn, he poked his head through the port side doorway. Inside the chamber, a pair of radio operators shared the cramped space with a battery of communications and cryptographic equipment. The two men were seated before their consoles, earphones clamped over their heads. Glowing green screens recorded multiple incoming transmissions. Matrix printers began spewing messages as fast as the computers could decode them.

"Downloading now," the senior radio operator, a man

named Pushkin, reported. He was a nerdy scarecrow of a man with mussed black hair and thick glasses. "There's a lot of chatter out there."

Losenko suppressed a sigh of relief. They were not alone, then. There were other survivors.

He stepped forward and tapped Pushkin on the shoulder. "What do you hear?"

The young seaman took off his headphones. A pained expression came over his face.

"Chaos," he reported. "Sheer chaos."

Losenko convened the meeting in the officer's wardroom. He sat at the head of a long rectangular table. Ivanov sat to his right, ahead of the rest of the senior staff. A baker's dozen of department heads were crammed into the wardroom. Transcripts of radio transmissions lay in a stack in front of the captain. He leafed through them once again, before lifting his eyes from the printouts. Soundproof bulkheads and a locked door ensured their privacy.

"Mr. Cherkov," Losenko addressed the communications officer, "please brief us on the situation."

Cherkov was a phlegmatic sort by nature, but the captain could tell that he was shaken by what he was about to report. He swallowed hard.

"In a word, sir, confusion—utter confusion. There is a great deal of chatter, but nobody seems to be in charge. And everybody is fighting, well, everybody. The Israelis are blaming the Arabs, and *vice versa*. India is retaliating against Pakistan. Georgia and Chechnya even think we bombed them. Al Qaeda has issued a *fatwa* on the American president. There are widespread accounts of looting and civic unrest.

"Scattered ships and planes are sending out inquiries, but receiving no authorized orders in reply. Our Akula attack subs are being engaged by Chinese and American subs. Many are believed to have been lost. Hard information is in short supply. Rumors are flying...." He hesitated, consulting his own notes as if he wasn't quite sure what to make of them. "There are even unconfirmed reports that, insanely, the Americans bombed their own bases and cities."

"What?" Ivanov blurted out. "That's ridiculous!"

"Maybe not," Cherkov said. "An American general named Ashdown is sending out a nonstop message on all frequencies, stating that the initial attack was an accident, that some kind of experimental computer system malfunctioned. He calls it 'Skynet.'"

Of course, Losenko thought. *It's the only explanation that makes sense.* And as he did so, cold tendrils began to grip him.

Ivanov disagreed. "An obvious trick, to get us to lower our guard."

"But why would the Americans attack us now?" Losenko observed. He feared that Ivanov's emotions were clouding his judgment. "The threat of Mutual Assured Destruction deterred them all through the Cold War. Why court annihilation now, after the war is over? There was no reason to it, none at all. Yet a computer malfunction would explain it."

Guilt stabbed his heart. *I should have realized that it was an accident. We all should have.*

Still Ivanov refused to absolve the Americans.

"Perhaps they feared that Mother Russia would rise to challenge them once more?" He clenched his fist at the prospect, before entreating Losenko. "Please, Captain, don't tell me that you are falling for so blatant a deception. Those America bastards attacked us without warning, like the cowards they are." He pounded his fist on the table. "We *cannot* believe anything they say!"

"I have heard of this Ashdown," the captain stated. "He is said to be one of their top-ranking generals." Ivanov's expression darkened. Losenko held up his hand to forestall any further outbursts from the junior officer. "But you are correct, Alexei. We cannot accept the Americans' explanation without corroboration. For the time being, we must remain on guard."

"So what do we do now, Captain?" Deputy Commander Trotsky asked. His pale face, dry skin, and chapped lips attested to long weeks spent cloistered aboard the sub. "We cannot hide from the Americans indefinitely. Our rations are running low, and the men are at the end of their rope."

"So they are," Losenko agreed. He had already made his decision. "We need to see for ourselves what has become of the Motherland." He rose from his seat. "Set a course for home."

CHAPTER FOUR

2018

The Trans-Alaska Pipeline stretched across 800 miles of rugged wilderness, connecting the oil fields on the north slope of Prudhoe Bay with the ice-free port in Valdez. For more than forty years, the pipeline had transported nearly a billion gallons of crude oil each day across mountain ranges, tracks of verdant wilderness, rivers, and streams.

Judgment Day had halted the flow for a time, but not for long; repairing the conduit and placing it under its direct control had been one of Skynet's top priorities, alongside exterminating the human race. As a result, all of the oil—and the energy it contained—belonged to the machines.

But that didn't mean the Resistance didn't help itself to a sip now and then.

From the edge of the woods, Molly surveyed an elevated section of pipeline. Faint sunlight filtered through the snow-laden branches of towering pines and spruces. Pendulous gray clouds threatened to drop more snow any time now. A bitter wind chafed her face. Her lips were chapped and raw.

She chewed on a tough piece of smoked beaver. An owl hooted in the forest behind her. Something scurried through the underbrush. A breeze rustled through the trees.

The sun was high in the sky. Despite the cover of the forest, she felt uncomfortably exposed, sneaking up on the pipeline in broad daylight. As counter-intuitive as it seemed, however, nocturnal raids were even more dangerous. The Hunter-Killers' infrared sensors worked even better after sundown, while the darkness placed their human prey at a disadvantage.

John Connor had taught her that, in one of his invaluable pirate broadcasts. She had never met the man—hell, she didn't even know what he looked like—but, like so many other freedom fighters, she owed her life to the urgent warnings he had been broadcasting ever since Judgment Day. He had given her hope, and tips for survival when all had seemed lost. In her mind, his would always be the voice of the Resistance.

If the machines ever get him, I don't want to know about it.

Several yards away, the pipeline zig-zagged across a glossy white plain leading toward a narrow mountain pass less than a mile to the north. Dense green forest encroached on the cleared strips of land on either side of the conduit. Riveted steel saddles, red paint protecting them from the elements, lifted the huge links of pipe over ten feet above the frozen earth. The enormous white cylinders were four feet in diameter. Coiled heat pipes topped the vertical supports to keep the permafrost from thawing beneath the heavy saddles. The zigzag layout was supposed to protect the pipeline from earthquakes, as well as from drastic temperature shifts.

Or so Molly had been told.

None of that mattered at the moment. She just wanted to come through this fuel run in one piece.

"Look clear?" Geir asked. He stood a few feet back, behind the basket of one of the fifteen dog sleds she had mustered for this operation. Teams of well-trained malamutes, huskies, and mutts waited patiently for the command to go forward. They rested upon the ground, sniffing idly at the snow. Empty metal drums and plastic gas cans were piled in the cargo beds of the freight sleds. A few of the sleds were hitched to snowmobiles instead of dogs.

Grim-faced men and women, bundled up in mismatched winter gear, stomped their feet to keep warm. Goggles, scarves, and earmuffs protected their faces from the cold. Scarlet armbands marked them as members of the Resistance. A thermos of hot coffee was passed around. Roughly thirty guerillas had been drafted for this operation. Nervous eyes searched the snowy canopy overhead. You never knew when an HK, or maybe just a snoopy Aerostat, might come zipping above the trees.

"What about it?" Geir pressed when she didn't answer. "Have we got a clear shot?"

"Maybe," Molly hedged. Not even Skynet could patrol all 800 miles of pipeline all the time, and the nearest automated pumping station was fifty miles north at Delta Junction. That was where security would be the thickest, but any unguarded stretch—such as this one— would serve just fine. All they needed to do was hurry in, tap the pipeline, and get away before Skynet even realized that it was bleeding oil.

Should be a cakewalk, she thought. Not like taking on

that monster train, which they intended to do as soon as their plans were set. "But let's not take any chances," she said aloud.

Their Resistance cell had lost three commanders in four years. Molly wasn't looking to be the fourth, at least not until she took her shot at the Skynet Express. She stroked the head of Togo, the big gray samoyed at the head of Geir's dog team.

"What about you, boy?" she asked as he nuzzled her glove. "Smell any suspicious metal?"

Over the course of the war, man's best friend had proven incredibly valuable when it came to sniffing out Terminators, especially the new T-600s with the phony rubber skin intended to mimick human flesh. At a distance or in the dark, a T-600 could be mistaken for a living, breathing human, but not by a dog. Their keen noses sniffed through the disguise with no problem. Thus, the Resistance had learned to rely on their canine cohorts.

Another trick Connor taught us.

Togo's tufted ears perked up, like maybe he was hoping for a snack. He sniffed the air, but seemed more interested in the rations in Molly's pocket. The rest of the pack were still curled up in the snow, licking their paws or absently watching out for squirrels. The dogs' nonchalance reassured Molly. If there had been Terminators upwind, they would have been barking like crazy.

So far, so good. She treated Togo to a leftover scrap of beaver. He gobbled it up enthusiastically, licking the palm of her glove. Molly looked over the nearby stretch of pipeline once more. The Resistance desperately needed the fuel for its vehicles and generators.

Just the same, let's play this smart.

She got behind her own sled. Sensing her intentions, the dogs leapt to their feet. They tugged at their leather harnesses, eagerly awaiting a chance to stretch their legs. Her lead dogs—a pair of white Siberian huskies—looked back at her. There were ten dogs in all, hitched to the gang-line two by two. Molly had trained them since they were puppies. She trusted them with her life.

"I'll act as bait," she declared, "to draw any machines out." There was no point in exposing the rest of her people to the possibility of enemy fire until she knew there were no Terminators lurking in the brush. She grabbed the sled's handlebar and planted the soles of her boots firmly on the aluminum runners, then glanced back at the armed insurgents. "Cover me."

"Wait!" Geir objected. Ice frosted his sexy blond whiskers, making him look older than his years. He tugged on the brake of his own sled. "Let me go instead."

Molly shook her head.

"Forget it," she said flatly. "You're our only pilot." A smart commander wouldn't have brought him along in the first place; he belonged back at the camp, tending to *Thunderbird*, his precious fighter plane. But she was short on personnel. "Besides, my dogs are faster than yours."

"Says who?" he retorted, but he stepped away from his sled. Geir knew better than to argue with her once she put her foot down; that put him one up on most of the men she had known, before and after Judgment Day. Unslinging a loaded M4 carbine from his shoulder, he marched to the edge of the woods and got into position to cover her.

More snipers fanned out along the perimeter. Geir winked at her.

"Anytime you want a race, you know where to find me."

Molly grinned back at him. That was another thing about him, he always found a way to make her smile, in a world where that didn't come easy. Sometimes she wondered where his upbeat attitude came from, and whether there was any way to bottle it.

"I'll take you up on that—after we fill our tanks at Skynet's expense."

Her grin faded as she contemplated the open expanse of snow that stretched between the woods and the pipeline. She scanned the clearing one more time, then took a deep breath to steady her nerves.

Time's wasting, she scolded herself. *Let's get this show on the road.*

"Hike!"

The dogs took off like a shot. No reins or whips were required, only verbal commands. The sled accelerated across the snow, breaking out from beneath the evergreens at six or seven miles per hour. The wind blew her hood back, exposing her face. The huskies' racing paws kicked up a cloud of snowy powder. The lead dogs yipped at the team behind them, keeping the other dogs in line.

The exhilarating speed set Molly's pulse racing, even as she tensed in anticipation of an ambush. She held her breath, half-expecting to feel hot metal tear through her in a heartbeat. For endless moments, her ears listened for the telltale roar of a chain gun or turbofan, but all she heard was the thrilling sound of the huskies racing through the snow. No Terminator reared its ugly metal skull.

How about that? She permitted herself a sigh of relief. The cold wind stung her ears. *Maybe we're in the clear after all.*

The dogs ate up the distance to the pipeline in a matter of minutes.

"*Whoa!*" The shouted command brought the team to an immediate halt. Molly jumped from the sled, drawing her own M4 as she did so. She swung its sights toward the gleaming steel underside, just to see if that would provoke a response. Heat exchangers were mounted to the bottom of the pipeline, to keep the ground below firm and frosty. A gauge measured the flow of oil.

"All right, you metal poachers," she muttered. "Come and get me."

Her defiant challenge went unanswered.

Molly lowered the rifle. She gestured to the others. The rest of the fuel party wasted no time breaking from the woods. Freight sleds and snowmobiles carried the empty drums and gas cans toward the looming steel artery. Geir's sled was right out in front, of course, just where she expected it to be. A frosty white rooster-tail spread out like a vapor trail behind his runners. For a pilot, he wasn't a half-bad musher.

She looked forward to racing him back to camp. *We'll see whose dogs are faster.*

Moments later the rest of her crew arrived. Dismounting from their sleds and snowmobiles, they went to work with practiced efficiency. This wasn't the first time they'd tapped Skynet's veins. The empty drums were rolled into place beneath the pipeline. They climbed up the looming steel saddles. Spiked metal spigots, crafted by hand at a Resistance machine shop, were hammered into the underside of the pipe. Rubber tubing connected the upright barrels with the pipeline. Open valves let the stolen crude flow into the waiting containers. Excited workers, glad to be getting away with the heist, high-fived each other. Armed sentries, equipped with army-surplus grenade launchers and a couple of .50 caliber Barrett rifles, stood guard while the others worked. Dirty jokes and war stories relieved the tension. Someone hummed an old Britney Spears tune.

Molly was always impressed by how well the men and women worked together. They were a solid unit, no matter what Command thought of them. Relaxing a little, she took shelter beneath the elevated pipeline, putting one of the imposing steel saddles between her and the wind. Her rifle rested loosely in her grip, its oiled metal length level with her waist.

"Glad to see you weren't chosen for target practice." Geir joined her under the pipe. His sled was anchored to the ground a few feet away. "Guess it would have been okay to let Sitka tag along."

Molly shrugged.

"Don't want to spoil her." The restless teenager was stuck back at camp babysitting Doc Rathbone, the camp's resident mad scientist. Keeping the melancholy old man sober could be a full-time job, for which Sitka had a definite talent. They were an odd pair, but the girl brought out the best in Doc. He was training her to be his apprentice. "She's got her own job to do."

With the fuel run going smoothly, Molly started thinking ahead. She was going to need Doc's computer expertise to crack whatever security measures were aboard the uranium train. A technophobe at heart, Molly had barely known how to program her cell phone before the bombs came down. But that was no longer an issue.

The Skynet Express clattered across her memory, and she recalled how the ever-watchful Aerostats had swooped in and out of the trestles supporting the bridge.

That was going to be a problem....

The wind shifted. A crisp breeze rustled Molly's hair.

The dogs leapt to their feet and howled at the woods on the other side of the pipeline. Their hackles rose.

"Fuck!"

Molly saw the attack coming even before the bullets started flying. Muzzles flared from the shadowy depths of the forest. Her people dropped like decoys in a shooting gallery. Half-filled gas cans hit the snow. Vicious uranium slugs punched through the metal drums, spilling crude oil onto the ground.

The smell of gunfire and petroleum filled the air. Blood and oil mixed together. Twitching bodies writhed amidst the crimson slush.

"Watch it!" Geir shoved Molly behind the saddle. Bullets ricocheted off the sturdy steel pylons. The ferocious gunfire chipped the paint. Dull red flakes blew in the wind. Trapped sled dogs howled and barked in alarm. One pack managed to tear loose the snow hook that was mooring it to the ground. The riderless sled bolted for the woods.

Molly didn't blame the frightened dogs for turning tail. Terminators weren't sentimental where animals were concerned.

"Forget the fuel!" she shouted to what was left of the work crew. She kicked herself for letting her mind wander, even for a minute. "Fall back! Retreat!"

"Here they come." Geir said as he peeked around the side of the saddle, then yanked his head back before it could get blown off his shoulders. "Ugly as ever."

Tell me about it, Molly thought fiercely. Through a two-inch gap in the supports, she saw multiple T-600s emerge from the woods. Their humanoid endoskeletons aped the size and proportions of an adult male human. Molly had never seen a female-looking Terminatrix, although John Connor had warned that they were in development. Their mass-produced rubber faces looked unconvincing in the daylight, like cheap Halloween masks; Skynet had a ways to go, thank God, before its infiltrator models could truly pass for human.

Binocular red optical sensors, posing as eyes, were a dead giveaway, as were the unnervingly blank expressions. Machineguns and assault rifles were strapped beneath their arms via detachable velcro straps. Hands squeezed the upside-down triggers of the guns. Reinforced wire snowshoes kept the Terminators from sinking into powdery white drifts. They didn't even flinch as their weapons fired loudly. Their pace was unhurried, methodical. Skynet had been killing off humans for over fifteen years now. There was no rush.

By contrast, the surprise attack kicked the humans into top gear. The sentries returned fire, just as Molly had trained them, while the rest of the squad retreated as ordered. Those who weren't cut down by the first fusillade scrambled madly to get away. They slipped and fell in the spreading slushy pools of blood and oil, only to be shot from behind as soon as they got back up again. A few dived for cover, burrowing deep into the snow, as others made a break for the forest. Loose bits of down stuffing blew about the battlefield.

RPGs and anti-materiel fire tore into the ranks of the Terminators, making it a battle, not a rout. An exploding RPG sent a T-600 flying backwards into the woods. M82 rifles, designed by the military to take out enemy trucks and parked aircraft, dismembered another Terminator. A robotic leg was cut off at the hip.

Undaunted, the T-600 hopped forward, using its severed limb as a crutch. Its fellow machines targeted the sentries, forcing them to retreat. Their limited supply of grenades was quickly exhausted.

Molly cursed Command for not supplying them with more.

The casualties continued to mount:

Jake Nollner, a thirty-five year-old father of two, jumped onto his snowmobile and hit the throttle. He only got about fifteen yards before a Terminator's bullets nailed the snowmobile's gas tank. The ride exploded in a shower of blazing shrapnel, scattering pieces of Jake all over the landscape. The burning debris ignited pools of spilled oil, which erupted into flames. Choking black fumes added to the chaos.

Trapped huskies, held in place by their harnesses, jerked spasmodically as they were terminated as well. Wounded men, women, and dogs contributed to an agonizing chorus of pain and fear.

Monsters! Molly was tormented by the sight of her people dying all around her. She counted at least four Terminators left. *Thank God Sitka isn't here!*

She and Geir fired back at the T-600s, providing more cover for the fleeing guerillas. Their combined assault shredded the rubber faces, exposing the fearsome steel death's-head expressions underneath. The machines' winter garments were ripped apart as well, until gleaming steel endoskeletons could be glimpsed through the torn fabric. Round after round of automatic weapons fire jolted the oncoming machines, driving them back for moments at a time, but failing to stop the Terminators from advancing, and from picking off human targets with computerized precision.

A targeting laser lit up the back of Kathy Seppala's head a heartbeat before she toppled face-first into the snow, a crimson fountain spurting from her skull. She fell across the runners of her own sled, while another volley dropped her dogs.

Molly bit down on her lip to keep from crying out in rage. Amidst the carnage, she couldn't help noticing that not one of the Terminators' shots had hit the pipeline by mistake. The T-600s were obviously taking care not to damage the vital conduit. Skynet valued oil, if not human life.

They were waiting for us, damn it! She tried to figure out how Skynet could have known what they were planning. It was getting better and better at calculating probabilities and patterns where the Resistance was concerned. *We must have gotten too predictable.*

That was something she'd have to work on, if she lived to see another day.

"Head for the hills!" she ordered the survivors. "Regroup at the rendezvous point!" She kept firing to give the others a chance at escaping. "Don't let them follow you back to the camp!"

She spotted a party of Resistance fighters, who had survived the initial salvos by diving into a shallow ditch. Their refuge had become a trap, however, as enemy gunfire cut them off from their snowmobiles less than two yards away. A Terminator stomped across the snow toward the ditch, ready to turn it into a mass grave. Molly had only seconds to save her people.

Switching the carbine to full automatic, she targeted the machine's vulnerable shoulder joint. A barrage of 5.56-millimeter ammo crippled the T-600, causing its gun arm to go limp at its side. Its weapon fired uselessly into the ground. Misdirected bullets shredded its own snowshoe, throwing it off-balance.

"Palmer! Johns! The rest of you!" Molly shouted at the humans in the ditch, while the Terminator clumsily attempted to shift its chain gun to its other arm. "Now's your chance. Hustle!"

She watched with relief as a handful of people scrambled to their feet and dashed for the snowmobiles and their attached cargo sleds. They threw themselves onto the vehicles and fired up their noisy, two-stroke engines. The machines accelerated across the snow, taking the humans with them. Exhaust fumes mingled in the air with the acrid smell of cordite. The roar of the snowmobiles was soon punctuated by gunfire from the Terminator, firing in vain at the retreating men and women, who were already out of range of its gun.

Thank God, Molly thought. *At least this won't be a total massacre.*

The T-600s paused to close the valves on the violated pipes, granting Molly a momentary respite. She reloaded her rifle and estimated their odds of slipping away while the Terminators were distracted. Then a diesel engine roared to life in the woods which had hidden the enemy.

She shared a worried look with Geir.

"Now what?"

The answer barreled out of the forest in the form of a large automated snow plow. A wedge-shaped metal blade, raised ten inches above the snow, preceded an armored steel transport with snow tires and four-wheel drive. Chains around its tires granted the tank extra traction. A T-600 was seated in a turret on top of the plow, behind a mounted machinegun. Red eyes glinted in metal sockets.

Tons of rolling metal came on like a bulldozer. Bullets sparked harmlessly off the blade.

Geir gulped.

"I don't know about you, Molly, but I'm feeling more than a little outmatched."

"Me too," Molly admitted grimly, though she continued to fire on the newcomer. She glanced around quickly. As nearly as she could tell, the rest of the fueling party was either dead or scattered. Time for a strategic retreat, not that the Terminators were going to make it easy.

Her M4 ran out of ammo, and she hastily reloaded before backing away from the saddle.

"Your sled or mine?"

One of the T-600s that had been repairing the pipeline, a torn rubber ear dangling from his exposed cranial case, took that choice out of their hands. A sustained burst of fire killed the back half of Geir's dog team. The remaining huskies, including Togo, pulled at their hitches, frantic to get away.

Togo wheeled about and snarled at the Terminator. His lips peeled back, baring his fangs.

"Shit!" Geir yanked a carbon-steel hunting knife from his belt and dived for his sled. Keeping his head low, he hacked through the cable that connected the snow hook to the sled, then flicked the quick-release catch on the snublines. "Scram, you fleabags. *Hike!*"

Togo hesitated, reluctant to leave his master behind, so Molly fired a warning burst over the dog's head. That did the trick; all of the surviving dogs sprinted for safety, dragging their dead kennel mates behind them. Bright canine blood streaked the snow.

Then Molly bared her own teeth. The forest ranger in her hated to see animals suffer. *Humans built Skynet,* she thought guiltily. *We brought this nightmare on our-selves. But the rest of nature shouldn't have to suffer for our mistakes.*

Spinning, she sprinted for her own sled, firing back over her shoulder while choking on the smoke from the fires. Reaching her objective, she unhooked the anchor and clambered onto the runners. Frenzied barks and growls greeted her, but the dogs faithfully waited for her command. A pang stabbed Molly's heart. She almost wished she hadn't trained them so well; they'd probably live longer.

She gripped the handlebar with one hand while empty-ing her rifle with the other. The M4's handguard was get-ting uncomfortably hot to the touch. A steady stream of ejected shells shot from the firing mechanism.

Geir charged across the bloody slush toward her, but not fast enough for comfort.

"Hurry, flyboy!" she shouted. "Don't keep me waiting!"

"Do I ever?" Geir jumped onto the runners behind her. Crouching low, he wrapped his arms around her, hold-ing on for dear life. "Your turn to drive."

About time, she thought.

"Hike!"

A burst of acceleration threw Molly backwards against Geir. Despite the weight of an extra passenger, the dogs broke speed records getting away from the bloodbath. The sled bounced over piled drifts of snow as Molly gave the dogs their head. Her foot stayed away from the brake. Loose powder, kicked up by the dogs, pelted her face.

"Don't look now," Geir shouted in her ear, over gun-fire behind them, "But they're not giving up!"

Molly glanced back. The merciless snow plow drove

under the pipeline, trampling over the dead—at least she hoped they were dead— before turning to chase the fleeing dog sled. It slowed long enough to let the other T-600s climb onto its running boards, then picked up speed. Gruesome red stains glistened wetly on the upraised blade of the plow.

The Terminators fired at the sled. Bullets whizzed past Molly and Geir as they jumped a snow-covered embankment. A hard landing rattled Molly's teeth.

"Haw! Haw!" she shouted, steering the dogs left. "Gee!" They raced parallel to the pipeline, weaving in and out of saddles to avoid being tagged by the Terminator's bullets. It was like navigating a slalom course while under fire. The massive pipes and their supports shielded them from the mechanized monsters in pursuit. Machinegun fire tore up the snow banks, while the plow itself would roll right over them if it caught up.

The sled was smaller and more maneuverable than the larger plow, but the tank outweighed them by several orders of magnitude. Its blade would smash them to pieces.

"Haw!"

The sled veered left, putting the pipeline on her right. The Terminators fired under and around the pipes, still taking care not to damage the vital artery. Skynet was like a vampire, sucking up Alaska's resources to perpetuate its genocidal agenda.

Too bad I don't have a silver bullet, Molly thought, then an idea struck her. *Maybe I don't need one.*

She glanced up at the raised pipeline, skimming past just a yard above her head. In theory, the pipes were supposed to be bulletproof, but it hadn't always worked out that way. Back around the turn of the century—a couple of years before Judgment Day—a trigger-happy drunk had managed to shoot a hole into one of the welds connecting the lengths of pipe, causing a serious oil spill. The damage it had caused had appalled Molly.

Now it gave her an idea.

Hooking her elbow around the handlebar to free up her hands, she awkwardly loaded another clip into her assault rifle. "Straight ahead!" she urged the dogs, keeping the pipeline on her right. She waited until another weld came into view, then let loose with a blistering blast of 45-millimeter vandalism.

Let's see how bulletproof that plumbing really is!

At first, her desperate ploy appeared to have failed. The bullets ricocheted off the thick metal pipe without breaking skin.

"Fuck!"

But then a scarred steel weld gave way spectacularly. Gallons of unprocessed crude oil gushed behind them onto the snowy landscape below. A black tide flowed across the terrain.

Eureka, Molly thought. Once upon a time, she would have been horrified by an oil spill of this magnitude, but that was before Judgment Day. Now she needed to do whatever was necessary to protect an endangered species: *Me*.

The speeding plow came careening after her. Its wheels hit the oil slick, losing traction with the earth. The entire tank went into a spin. Gun-toting Terminators grabbed onto safety rails to keep from being thrown from the vehicle. The T-600 in the turret tumbled backward, away from the machinegun fixture, and rolled off the side of the plow.

The dislodged Terminator landed with a splash in the

spreading oil. It struggled to right itself, its human clothing and camouflage liberally coated with crude, only to find the blade of the spinning plow heading straight for it. The slick black figure threw up its hands to protect its cranial case, but its titanium-alloy endoskeleton was no match for the bloodstained blade's sheer mass and momentum. Metal crunched and clanged as the blade collided with the T-600. Its optical sensors shattered and went dark moments before it was ground into scrap metal beneath the plow's chains and snow tires.

The tank kept on spinning, leaving a mess of flattened Terminator parts behind it. Severed metal limbs, still imbued with a spark of life, flailed about uselessly in the oil. The unleashed gunfire of the remaining Terminators went awry, firing randomly into the sky. More bullets bounced off the ruptured pipeline.

The plow smashed into one of the saddles, knocking it from its foundations. Its structural integrity compromised, the saddle was unable to support the weight of the pipe resting atop it. An entire length of pipeline slipped from its moorings, crashing down onto the ground. The impact shook the earth. More oil gushed from the open wound, spraying crude like the world's biggest fire hose.

Except that this spray was flammable.

Keeping one arm wrapped around Molly's waist, Geir plucked a fresh magazine from his service belt and slammed it into the carbine. Twisting around, he fired, and tracer bullets shot from the muzzle. Magnesium charges flashed red as they streaked through the air.

"Burn in hell," Geir snarled.

The tracers hit the massive oil spill. Hundreds of gallons of crude went up in flames, lighting up the ravaged wilderness. A titanic fireball roiled up into the sky, maybe even high enough to be seen from camp. A scorching blast of heat blew past them, and Molly grinned wolfishly. It was the first time in memory that she had felt warm.

That's it, baby. Light my fire.

Earth-shaking explosions blew the pipeline apart. Mammoth hunks of steel and concrete were thrown up into the air, before they came hurtling back down like a meteor shower. Deafening blasts assaulted her ear-drums until all sound was muffled. Shock waves almost knocked her from the sled. Beneath her gloves, white knuckles clung to the handlebar, while Geir squeezed her so tightly she could hardly breathe. One of the swing dogs lost its footing, stumbled, and was dragged along by its frantic teammates.

Thick black smoke blocked out the feeble sunlight. It looked as if a volcano had erupted.

But was it enough to stop the Terminators?

"Did that do it?" she shouted back at Geir. "Did you get them?"

"Huh?" Geir hollered. "What's that?"

Molly responded at the top of her lungs.

"Did you get those fucking machines?"

"I don't know!" He squinted back into the smoke and heat. "Maybe?"

Maybe's not good enough, Molly thought. They couldn't head back to camp until they knew that they had shaken the T-600s and their homicidal pursuit. No way was she leading them back to Sitka and the others. *We've already lost too many good people today.*

Hatred, hotter even than the inferno behind her, surged through her veins.

"Hang on!" Geir shouted. His face was blackened with soot, and his beard was singed. "I think I see something... oh, *shit*!"

She didn't like the sound of that.

The plow, still loaded with Terminators, barged out of the smoke. Dancing flames licked its blackened exterior, and its mounted machinegun turret had been mangled beyond recognition, but the tank was coming on strong. Fiendish red eyes glowed in the skull-like visages of the four T-600s who clung to the sides of the speeding vehicle. Their phony flesh and clothing had completely burned away, exposing their scorched endoskeletons in all their naked horror. They looked like metallic grim reapers riding a snow plow from hell.

"Fuck," Molly muttered, angry but not too surprised by the enemy's persistence. Skynet built its cybernetic storm troopers to last. Terminators weren't alive—not really—but they were damn hard to kill.

What would John Connor do at a time like this?

"Now what?" Geir shouted into her aching ear.

She scanned the rugged geography ahead of them. Whitman Pass was almost upon them. The rocky ravine was the only way through the mountains for miles. The corners of her lips tilted upwards. There was a trick she had always been meaning to try....

"Hike!" she urged the dogs. "Straight ahead!" She raised her voice to make sure Geir could hear her. "You ever see *Seven Brides for Seven Brothers*?"

"Not much into musicals," he admitted. She could hear the confusion in his voice, and readily imagine his perplexed expression. "Why?"

There was no time to explain.

"Wait for it!"

Whitman Pass climbed at a steady gradient from the plain below. Centuries of erosion and geological activity had carved out a V-shaped canyon about a half-mile long and approximately the width of two old-fashioned covered wagons. *Wide enough for the Terminator snow plow to get through, damn it all.* A narrower pass would have made life much easier—and probably longer. Granite cliffs piled high with tons of packed snow and ice rose on either side of the pass, hemming it in. The pipeline itself was buried beneath the roadway at this point, the better to protect it from falling debris.

A pitted steel sign, left over from the bygone days of human supremacy, offered a dire warning to winter travelers:

DANGER! AVALANCHE ZONE!

Molly was relieved to see that the explosions behind them had not brought a cascade of piled snow and ice down into the pass, blocking their way. That would have put a serious crimp in her plans. She swallowed hard, her mouth dry, while the sled raced uphill into the pass.

The dogs ran sure-footedly over the cracked and icy pavement, dragging their human cargo behind them. The huskies were panting hard; the extra weight was starting to slow them down. The overturned swing dog had managed to get back on his feet, although he limped noticeably compared to his partner. Their headlong passage triggered minor snowfalls from the cliffs above them. Slurries of crumbling snow and ice tumbled down the craggy slopes.

Her upturned eyes darted from left to right, keeping a close eye on a winter's worth of accumulated whiteness.

Fractured slabs of ice the size of roofs were barely held in place, edged with a frigid glaze of rime, blocking out any view of the sky. Pebble-sized chunks of ice rained down on her head. *Hang on*, she silently commanded the huge sheets of snow, ice, and rock that were suspended above them.

She wished she could slow down, but the Terminators took that option off the table. Speed was their only hope now, plus a whole lot of luck. Unable to tear her gaze away from the cliffs, she couldn't glance back. Her heart pounded, much too loudly for her own peace of mind.

The ringing in her ears began to fade. She kept her voice low.

"Are they still after us?"

"They're Terminators," Geir answered tensely. "What d'you think?"

At least the killer robots weren't firing at them anymore. Had their ammo gone up in the fire, or did they just know better than to raise a ruckus in an avalanche zone?

Probably waiting to plow us under, she mused darkly, *dogs, sled, and all.*

Well, we'll see about that....

They reached the crest of the pass, where the road dipped back down toward the plains. Now it was downhill all the way, and the dogs picked up speed. Unfortunately, so did the Terminators. Molly could hear the tank's heavy tread crunching over the frozen road behind them. As it drew closer, more ice and rock dislodged. Its chains scraped against the asphalt. The powerful diesel engine could outlast any dog, even a champion. Molly remembered Geir's earlier challenge.

This wasn't the race she'd had in mind.

The pass opened up ahead. Molly spied a wedge of grey sky through the towering granite V. She held her breath and glanced up at the cliffs.

Only a few more yards....

Finally! The sled careened out of the pass. She prodded Geir with her elbow.

"Let go of me—and grab onto the handlebar!"

"Huh? What are you thinking?"

"Just do it, flyboy!"

His arm came away from her waist. He balanced precariously on the runners for an instant before snatching the handle. Molly threw herself forward, somersaulting over the bar onto the cargo bed at the front of the sled. A canvas bag, stuffed with supplies, cushioned her landing. The wheel dogs at the rear of the train looked back at her, their eyes wide with confusion. Frozen slobber caked their snouts. She could hear them wheezing; their overworked lungs on the verge of giving out.

Not much longer, guys, she promised.

"Hike!"

She yanked open the zipper on the sled bag. Cold hands, numb even beneath her gloves, rummaged frantically through first aid supplies, emergency rations, and extra clips of ammo.

"C'mon," she growled impatiently. "Where the fuck are you?"

Yes!

Her questing fingers came into contact with something long and metallic. Squatting on her knees atop the cargo bed, she wrested her prize from the bag. It gleamed like blue steel in the fading light.

Sitka had found the vintage M79 grenade launcher in

the ruins of an old National Guard armory. She had given it to Molly as a birthday present, wrapped with a bow. Molly had promised to save it for a special occasion.

Like now.

The "bloop gun" resembled a stubby, sawed-off shotgun. Molly slammed a single explosive cartridge into the breach, then jumped to her feet. She balanced atop the cargo bed, facing back toward the pass where the relentless snow plow was speeding downhill after them, almost two-thirds through the canyon. T-600s clung to its sides and roof, their blood-red optical sensors glowing with murderous anticipation. They would never stop coming, she knew, until their targets were terminated. Surrender was not in their programming.

Mine either, she thought.

"That's far enough, metal!"

Surprise flickered across Geir's expression as she rested the barrel of the M79 on his shoulder to steady her aim. The sled bounced violently beneath her, but that didn't matter. This shot wasn't about accuracy. Just noise.

She squeezed the trigger.

A sharp report brutalized her already aching ears. The forty-millimeter flash-bang grenade went spinning into the air, arcing high above the ground before descending toward the opening of the pass. For a second, Molly feared that the hasty shot might bounce off the mountainside, but its trajectory carried it straight into the mouth of the canyon. She plugged her fingers into her ears a second before the explosive projectile hit the ground, right in front of the snow plow.

It went off with a bang.

She had missed the tank by a couple of yards, but the flash-bang was designed to generate more confusion than damage. The booming detonation shook loose the delicately balanced slabs of snow and ice heaped on both sides of the pass. With a thunderous whoomph, twin avalanches came streaming down the sides of the mountains, carrying several tons of frozen debris down on top of the Terminators and their tank. Billowing clouds of powder preceded a plunging wall of snow that gained speed and momentum at a terrifying pace. Massive chunks of ice knocked loose more snow and boulders, propagating an awe-inspiring chain reaction.

Alerted to the danger, the plow hit the gas, trying to outrace the deadly cascade, but the avalanche was faster. Within seconds gravity buried the Terminators beneath a wintry deluge.

"Hah!" Geir admired Molly's handiwork from the back of the sled. "Let's see them plow their way out of that!"

Or not, she thought hopefully. The sled slowed as the exhausted dogs surrendered to fatigue, but by that time they were well outside of the avalanche zone. Surging plumes of powder clouded her view of the pass. She peered into the opaque white haze, waiting anxiously for the snow to settle. She loaded another grenade into the launcher, just in case.

She caught her breath.

The cloud dispersed. A mountain of fallen snow and ice filled the canyon, rendering it impassable till spring, perhaps longer. Smaller avalanches continued to funnel down the slopes, sprinkling the top of the heap with a fresh layer of icy rubble. Molly kept her eyes peeled for even a flicker of red. She knew better than to count the Terminators out prematurely.

But all she saw was white. No glowing sensors. No bursts of gunfire.

No metal.

Geir whooped it up, glad to be alive. He hugged her shoulders, and kissed her on the cheek.

"What was the name of that movie again?"

"*Seven Brides for Seven Brothers.*" She lowered the grenade launcher. A breathless "Whoa!" gave the huskies permission to take a breather. They dropped limply into the snow, panting loudly. "Used to be one of my favorites. Before."

Geir sighed. "Too bad Judgment Day cancelled my NetFlix subscription." He hopped off the sled and checked on the dogs. "You'll have to tell me all about it."

"Later," she promised. They had a long, cold trek ahead of them, especially now that the pass was closed. Looking out over the daunting vista before her, she glimpsed the volcanic peak of Mount Wrangell in the distance. Plumes of steam, rising from its crater, reminded her of a smoking gun barrel. She wondered how many of their comrades had escaped the ambush, and if they had made it back to the camp already.

As the rush of adrenaline faded, she sagged against the handlebar, giving way to grief and exhaustion. The M79 dropped to her feet. Grisly images from the attack paraded before her mind's eye. Jake. Kathy. Butchered dogs twitching in the bloody slush....

All for a bunch of oil we didn't even get.

Sometimes she wondered if humanity even stood a chance.

"Let the dogs rest. We'll get a move on later. Before sundown."

She just hoped the huskies were up to it.

* * *

Hours later:

The human insurgents were long gone by the time the moon rose over the ice-clotted pass. A forest fire still raged to the south, although Skynet had cut off the flow of oil, and it would remain that way until the damaged stretch of pipeline could be repaired. The sabotage was a temporary inconvenience, but not an insurmountable one. Skynet had control of most of the planet's energy reserves, from Saudi Arabia to Siberia. The disruption to the Alaskan pipeline would not seriously impact its operations.

A young male lynx padded across the heaped debris, fleeing the blaze behind it. The wild cat's large paws acted like snowshoes as it made its way to safer hunting grounds. Its stealthy passage made scarcely a sound.

A sudden crack broke the nocturnal stillness. The slippery rubble shifted beneath the lynx's paws. Yowling, it bounded away in alarm.

The big cat abandoned the pass without a backward glance, so that only the moon was watching as a tremor shook the glazed surface of the mound. Loose ice and snow streamed down the side of the pile, near the northern end of the pass. A scraping noise came from beneath the shifting mass.

A robotic fist smashed through the topmost slab. Servomotors whirred as a second fist punched upward into the moonlight. Articulated steel fingers dug into the side of the heap. Optical sensors, peering up through the cracked ice, dimly glimpsed the moonlight. An illuminated heads-up flashed in the upper right-hand corner of the visual display:

IMPERATIVE: RESTORE FULL MOBILITY.

Slowly, methodically, a T-600 dragged itself up into

the cold night air. Snow and ice sloughed off of its battered endoskeleton. Only a few tattered shreds of fabric
hung to its limbs and battle chassis. The left half of a
charred and melted rubber face masked its cranial case.
Unlike real flesh, the imitation skin was immune to frostbite. Antifreeze trickled like blood from its left shoulder
joint. Cool chartreuse fluid dripped onto the pristine
white snow.

MOBILITY RESTORED. COMMENCE DAMAGE
ASSESSMENT.

It had taken the Terminator precisely 8.735 hours to
dig its way out from beneath the avalanche. Rising to its
full height, it paused to conduct an internal diagnostic,
noting minor damage to various non-essential systems.
But the T-600 judged itself to be operating at 96.408
percent efficiency. Its central processing unit, power
cells, and programming remained intact.

Its primary directive was unchanged.

TERMINATE HUMAN RESISTANCE FORCES.

Network links confirmed that the other T-600s were no
longer functioning. The Terminator greeted this information without emotion. It did not mourn its comrades, nor
crave revenge. The destruction of the other machines was
relevant only as far as it affected the T-600's strategic
options and probabilities of success.

A rapid inventory of its arsenal revealed that its left-
hand chain gun had been torn away by the avalanche; the
Terminator calculated the odds of retrieving it, and
decided that the effort would be counter-productive. An
assault rifle was still strapped beneath its right arm, but
the weapon had been mangled beyond repair. The T-600
undid the strap, shedding the useless firearm. Although
unarmed, the machine was confident that it could carry

out its mission without backup. Humans were fragile and easily terminated.

Metal fingers pinched off the leaky valve in its shoulder. The T-600 kicked off the twisted remnants of its wire snowshoes. Optical sensors scanned the terrain north of the pass. Digital readouts flashed along the periphery of its visual display. Two distinct sets of bootprints revealed that at least two humans had survived the avalanche; the relative size and contours of the tracks indicated an adult male and adult female. Infrared trackers detected the cooling remains of a small campfire, as well as the fecal droppings of multiple canines.

Analysis of the evidence indicated that the humans and their animals had departed sometime within the last several hours. Human behavior patterns suggested that the survivors would return to their base after their defeat at the pipeline. The T-600 recognized an opportunity to track the Resistance to its camp—and terminate them once and for all.

It set out walking. A light snow had begun to fall, but its sensors easily discerned the impressions of the dog sled beneath the smooth virgin snow. The humans had a significant head start, but this did not concern the machine; it did not need to catch up with its targets until they reached their ultimate destination. A built-in transceiver beamed its intentions back to Skynet, which instantly acknowledged and approved the actions.

CONFIRMATION: PROCEED AS DIRECTED.

A digital readout in the lower left-hand corner of its heads-up display reported that the temperature was negative 11.022 degrees Celsius and falling. Sunrise was 10.589 hours away. The location of the Resistance base was unknown, but the Terminator was prepared to hike through the wilderness for as long as necessary. Its internal power pack guaranteed sufficient energy for the trek. Unlike the poorly designed humans, it would not tire. It had no need to eat, drink, or sleep. Hypothermia posed no danger to its systems. Its imposing steel frame did not shiver. Hinged metal jaws did not chatter.

The Terminator marched into the night. Heavy legs, sunk knee-deep into the snowy drifts, plowed through the packed whiteness. The perfect clarity of its programming propelled it forward.

LOCATE HUMAN BASE.

TERMINATE ALL HUMANS.

CHAPTER FIVE

2003

Murmansk, home to the Northern Fleet, had once been the largest city north of the Arctic Circle and a thriving military seaport. A warm North Atlantic current kept its harbor ice-free all year round. Losenko recalled bustling docks crammed with towering metal cranes and rows upon rows of covered boat barns, the latter intended to shield the fleet from aerial surveillance. Armed sentries and barbed wire had guarded the wharves, barracks, warehouses, and shipyards. Tugboats had escorted returning vessels back to port, beneath the icy brilliance of a cobalt-blue sky.

The sparsely wooded bluffs overlooking the channel had once been a welcome sight, promising fresh air and solid ground after long weeks under the sea. The salt air had been filled with the sounds of gulls and blaring horns.

But all that was a memory now.

Desolation.

That was what the captain beheld from the bridge atop the *Gorshkov*'s gigantic black fin. The submarine cruised toward shore along the Kola Fjord. White water lapped over the exposed bow and missile deck, while fully two-thirds of K-115 remained submerged beneath the waves. Ordinarily, maneuvering on the surface was fraught with hazards; it was all too easy for another ship to overlook the low-riding sub and plough right into it. Today, however, there were no other vessels with which to contend. They had the narrow channel all to themselves.

The view from his vantage point confirmed what Losenko had previously glimpsed through the periscope. An enormous crater, at least a thousand feet in diameter, had replaced the naval base. The ground was blackened and scorched. No trace of life remained—not a single weed or blade of grass. Every building had been razed to its foundations. The piers and boat barns were gone.

Though there was no surface traffic, sonar readings had detected the remnants of shattered ships and submarines scattered across the floor of the harbor. They would have to take care to avoid colliding with one of the sunken hulks. Their ruptured hulls now served as underwater tombstones.

We sail above a watery cemetery, Losenko realized. He shuddered beneath a heavy wool pea coat. A fur cap shielded his head from the cold north wind. The midnight sun hung low in the sky. *How many crews and captains went down with their ships?*

Losenko was dismayed by the devastation, but not surprised. He had seen photos of Hiroshima and Nagasaki. Modern nuclear missiles were many times more powerful than the primitive atomic bombs the Americans had dropped on Japan sixty years ago.

Murmansk, he recalled, had once been home to over 300,000 people.

"*Bozhe moi,*" Trotsky whispered beside him. The deputy commander was serving as deck officer for this watch. His face was ashen. White knuckles gripped the railing. "There is nothing left, Captain. Nothing at all."

Losenko placed a hand on the man's shoulder, like a father consoling a grieving son. Chances were, he was the closest thing to a father any one of his men had left. They were all orphans now.

He and Trotsky were alone atop the vessel. Losenko had restricted access to the sail, giving Ivanov the conn until he could survey the situation with his own eyes. Still, he knew he could not spare his men this appalling vista for long. By now, word of the base's utter destruction was surely spreading among the officers, and from there to the enlisted men. Such secrets were impossible to keep hidden.

"There are no docks," Trotsky observed. Concentrating on practical concerns appeared to help him maintain his composure. Yet he averted his eyes from the nightmarish tableau. "What now, skipper?"

Losenko peered through binoculars. In the distance, miles beyond ground zero, he spied the skeletal ruins of a few surviving buildings. Pitted steel frameworks had been stripped clean of their facades. Mountains of charred debris littered the barren landscape. Nothing stirred except clouds of ash and grit blown about by the wind. He looked in vain for lights or campfires.

There weren't even any vultures.

The captain lowered his binoculars.

"We sail on." There was nothing left for them here but kilometers and kilometers of radioactive rubble. By his estimation, it would be a decade before the irradiated soil could be considered safe to live on—at least by

peacetime standards. Murmansk was another
Chernobyl. "There are fishing villages south of here,
near Ponoy. They would not be considered military targets. Perhaps we can make port there."

To be safe, he knew, they would need to put at least 200
miles between themselves and ground zero. Maybe 300.

"Yes, sir!" Trotsky seized onto the captain's proposal
as if it was a life preserver. He turned his back on
Murmansk. "We'll need to reverse propulsion at once."

Before he could phone the new course down to the
conn, however, one of the forward hatches clanged open.
A midshipman in a blue jumpsuit clambered onto the
deck. He gazed out in horror at the wreckage of
Murmansk. A heart-rending cry tore itself from his lungs.

"No! *NOOO!*"

Losenko swore out loud. He hadn't authorized this. It
took him a moment to identify the reckless sailor as
Nikolai Yudin, a new recruit who had been stationed in
the engineering section.

"You there!" the captain bellowed from the bridge.
"Get back below immediately, before I have you locked
up for the rest of your miserable life!"

Yudin didn't even look up at him. He was too busy
gawking at the nearly unrecognizable ruins of their home
base. He tugged on his hair so hard that Losenko half-
expected the distraught seaman to rip out his scalp.

"Marina!" he called out hoarsely to the shore. "Holy
God... MARINA!"

Who was Marina? Losenko wondered. *His wife? His
girlfriend? His daughter?* The captain tried to remember
if Yudin had a family. There were more than a 150 men
aboard K-115. Shaking the thought away, he wheeled
around toward Trotsky.

"Get a security team up here... now!"

Trotsky barked instructions into a mike, but Yudin's crewmates were way ahead of him. Five more men scrambled out onto the deck to retrieve their shipmate. Choppy waves made it a risky endeavor, and none had taken the time to don lifejackets. The newcomers quickly lost track of the task at hand, as they were stunned by the sight of the murdered shore.

"You men, return to your posts," Losenko bellowed, and three of the men glanced his way. Remembering their purpose, they moved toward Yudin, who fled to the very edge of the deck. He balanced precariously at the brink.

"Stay back!" he shouted hysterically. "Don't touch me!"

His fellow seamen backed away warily, not wanting to provoke him into doing something rash. One held out his hands.

"Please, Nikolai!" the man said, the sound carried on the brisk, cold wind. "Come away from the edge. Let us talk to you. Let us help you!"

Up on the sail, Trotsky drew his sidearm. He nodded at the hysterical sailor below.

"Shall I intervene, sir?"

The captain shook his head. He doubted that Yudin cared for his own safety right now, and he did not appear to be armed. The man's best hope lay in the open hands of his brothers-at-sea. He cursed himself for not anticipating such an incident. All his men had passed rigorous psychological testing before being allowed to serve on a ballistic missile submarine, but no amount of screening could predict how any one of them might react to the end of the world. What they were facing now was enough to drive the strongest man to despair... or madness.

An alarm sounded loudly across the deck.

A three-man security team, led by Master Chief Komarov, charged through the open hatch. Unlike the first group of would-be rescuers, they were fully equipped with lifejackets, nightsticks, and firearms. They had been warned what to expect, but even so they paused at the sight of what had become of Murmansk. Their chief was the first to regain his composure.

"Down on the deck!" Komarov ordered gruffly. "Hands where I can see them!"

"Leave me alone!" Yudin shrieked back at them. Crazed blue eyes darted back and forth between his comrades and the blasted wasteland ashore. When he spoke again, his voice was pleading. "It's gone... they're all gone!"

Losenko felt the situation slipping out of control. He knew in his heart where this was going.

"Yudin!" he barked at the top of his lungs. "This is your captain. You are not alone. We can all get through this together!"

This time he got the young midshipman's attention. Yudin stared up from a dozen meters away. Their eyes met across the distance. The boy's forlorn expression broke Losenko's heart.

"I'm sorry, Captain!" he cried out. "But don't you see? It's too late. It's too late for all of us!" He tore his gaze away from Losenko, turning his back on the other men. "I'm coming, Marina! I'm coming!"

No! Losenko thought, as if he might control the boy's actions by sheer force of will. *Don't do it!*

"Wait!" Komarov called. The crewmen surged forward... a moment too late.

Yudin flung himself from the deck, plummeting down into the frothing waters below. He hit the harbor with a splash. Frantic sailors rushed to the brink, risking their own safety.

"Nikolai!"

"Man overboard!" Trotsky shouted into a mike. A blaring klaxon sounded.

Losenko leaned out over the rail of the bridge, searching the waters below. At first, he feared that Yudin had been sucked under and drowned, but then he spotted young Nikolai bobbing to the surface several meters away from the sub. Without looking back, the sailor struck out for the shore, kicking and paddling with manic intensity.

Did he actually hope to find his long-lost Marina? Or had he simply been driven mad by grief?

His fellow officers spotted him as well. Another midshipman kicked off his shoes. He looked primed to dive in after Yudin. Others scurried back into the sub, perhaps to retrieve emergency rafts. Losenko was impressed by the men's obvious determination to rescue their comrade.

Alas, he could not allow it.

"Stay where you are!" he shouted down at the men. "Do not leave this boat!"

Startled expressions greeted his orders.

"But... Captain...." Trotsky protested. "We have to get him back!"

"Belay that," Losenko declared. Retrieving a man from the sea was a difficult and risky operation at the best of times, let alone when the man was suicidally determined not to be rescued. He had no intention of losing another man.

More objections came from the deck below.

"Please, Captain!" the shoeless midshipman begged. Other pleas joined the chorus. "We can still save him.

Just give us a chance!"

Losenko turned to Trotsky. He held out his hand.

"Give me your sidearm."

"What?" The deck officer blinked in surprise.

Losenko did not routinely carry a weapon aboard his own ship. "Give me the gun, damn you!"

Trotsky flinched. Losenko snatched the pistol from the deputy commander's grip. Raising the binoculars to his eyes, he took aim at the swimming figure of Yudin. Waves batted the sailor back and forth, and the sailor's soggy coveralls weighed him down, slowing his progress toward the shore. He hadn't gotten too far yet.

"Captain!" Trotsky blurted out in alarm. "He's just a boy!"

You think I don't know that! Losenko thought. But nothing waited for Yudin ashore except a lingering death by radiation poisoning. *And I'll be damned if I send another man into that poisonous hellhole looking for him.*

Yudin's head and shoulders bobbed into sight.

Losenko pulled the trigger.

The sharp report of the pistol was the loudest thing any of the submariners had heard in weeks. The recoil jolted Losenko's arm. The acrid smell of gunpowder polluted his nostrils. Through the binoculars, he saw Yudin disappear beneath the waves. A crimson froth spread across the water.

The captain's stomach turned. He resisted the temptation to hurl the smoking pistol into the harbor. Instead he thrust it back into Trotsky's hand.

"Silence those damn alarms."

"Y-yes, sir," the shaken officer stammered. He phoned down to the control room. The blaring klaxons went still. Dumbfounded crewmen milled about on the deck below. They looked confused and angry. Most of them were still reacting to what had just occurred. Losenko knew he had to tell them what to think before they turned against him for good.

He grabbed the mike.

"This is the captain," he informed the entire crew. "Ensign Yudin attempted to desert this ship in a time of war. He has paid for this crime with his life. Let this be a lesson to you all."

He slammed the mike into its cradle, more loudly than necessary. Then he turned to Trotsky, who snapped to attention.

"Increase security around the weapons locker," he instructed, "and at all exit hatches—including the emergency escape trunk."

Yudin would surely not be the last man to crack beneath the awful weight of Armageddon. Unless Losenko maintained a tight grip over the crew, he might soon be faced with a wave of suicides and desertions, maybe even a mutiny.

But how could he keep the men in line when the country they had sworn to serve had been decimated? They were without orders, without purpose. If Murmansk was any indication, the Kremlin was just a smoking crater now, and Mother Russian a gigantic graveyard.

Maybe Ivanov is right, the captain thought bleakly. *Perhaps we still need an enemy.*

He stared out over the water. Yudin's blood had already been dispersed by the relentless current. The young sailor's body had gone to join the broken ships at the bottom of the harbor. One more victim of... what? A computer malfunction?

Nikolai Yudin was gone, but Losenko knew he would see the boy again.

In his dreams.

"Set a course for Ponoy."

Perhaps there was still *something* left to fight for.

CHAPTER SIX

2018

The old copper mill had been abandoned back in the 1930s, long before Judgment Day. Perched on the craggy slopes of the Wrangell Mountains, overlooking an icy blue glacier, weather-beaten wooden buildings clung to the snowy hillside like bird's nests. The remote location of the ghost town—as well as the immensity of the Alaskan wilderness—had hidden the mill's current occupants from Skynet's surveillance, at least so far. Molly wondered how much longer the Resistance outpost would remain undetected. They had been living at the mill for six months now, ever since abandoning their previous camp outside Fairbanks. A new record.

"Derailing the train is just the first step," Doc Rathbone insisted. "Once you get inside, the uranium is still going to be locked up tight."

The old man was hunched over a drafting table in what had once been the office of the mine's general manager. It was housed in a two-story log cabin a short hike away from the massive mill and crusher. Maps of the train's route and surveillance photos of the Skynet Express were spread out on top of the table, along with cobbled-together diagrams and blueprints of the train itself.

Much of the intel had been downloaded from the central processing unit of a factory robot the Resistance had captured several months earlier. That had been quite a coup, albeit one that had cost the life of the cell's previous commander. Doc Rathbone had been instrumental in cracking the CPU's encryption in order to access the information stored in the machine's computerized "brain."

He was useful that way, which was why Molly put up with his eccentricities.

"Locked up how?" she asked.

The bloodbath at the pipeline had only heightened her resolve to hit Skynet where it hurt. Over Geir's objections, she had gone straight to work the minute they'd made it back to the camp, barely stopping to change into dry clothes. A moth-eaten black turtleneck sweater, buckskin trousers, and fur-lined moccasins kept her warm enough inside the office. Her parka hung from a set of antlers mounted by the door, above her soggy boots.

A wood-burning stove fought back the cold winter night. A pair of Siberian huskies were curled up in front of the stove, with Sitka plopped down between them. Molly didn't usually let them sleep inside, but she figured her lead dogs had earned it after outracing the killer snow plow. Kerosene lanterns gave the humans enough light to work by. Closed wooden blinds trapped the light inside, maintaining the blackout regulations she had put into effect. A loaded assault rifle was propped up against the table, always within easy reach.

"The ore is likely sealed inside heavily guarded storage

compartments to prevent theft or loss in the event of a crash," Doc continued. "Each individual railcar will be one big rolling safe, with automated locks programmed to open only upon their arrival at Valdez. Since there are no conductors or technicians aboard, the locks will be under the direct control of the train's own artificial intelligence, but it may be possible to override the locking mechanisms at the site."

He pointed a bony finger at a schematic. Mussed white hair met in a widow's peak above his bushy black eyebrows. A pair of scratched wire-frame bifocals rested on his nose. His face was worn and haggard. Swollen veins and a ruddy complexion hinted at a drinking problem that persisted despite Sitka's best attempts to keep the old coot away from the camp's homemade moonshine. A fraying tan cardigan hung on his withered frame; he looked like he'd been forgetting to eat again. A pocket calculator weighed down one side of the sweater. His shoelaces were untied.

"The processed ore will be in the form of a coarse, lightweight powder popularly known as 'yellowcake.'" His gaze drifted off as his mind started wandering again. Then he came back. "The Navajo Indians of Colorado, on the other hand, used to call uranium 'the Yellow Monster' after careless mining practices contaminated their land and bodies. A shameful episode, really. The incidences of lung cancer, pulmonary fibrosis, and birth defects were truly appalling...."

Fascinating, Molly thought sarcastically. She wasn't sure what that had to do with Skynet.

"Can you hack into the locks?" she asked. Henry Rathbone had once been the chief engineer for a Pacific Northwest company that designed high-tech security systems for upscale homes and businesses. He'd been on a fishing vacation in Alaska when the bombs fell. A lucky break for the Resistance, if not for Rathbone. He might have been happier going up in flames with the rest of Seattle. Story was, he'd lost his entire family.

"Probably," he said. "Maybe." A sigh escaped his quivering lips as he contemplated the blueprints. He tapped a schematic of the train's storage compartment. "Reminds me of the panic room I installed for a paranoid Microsoft millionaire in Tacoma. You should have seen that guy's mansion. Had a special vault just for his comic book collection." His rheumy gaze turned inward as his voice took on a wistful tone. "You remember comic books? They used to come out every week, like clockwork. Me and the other tech guys always used to take a long lunch on Wednesday.

"There was this diner down by Pike Place Market where we'd get together to read the new issues. I usually ordered a turkey sandwich and a Diet Pepsi. Or was it a Dr. Pepper? You remember Dr. Pepper? 'I'm a Pepper, you're a Pepper....'"

"Off we go again," Sitka groaned. The teen rolled her eyes. "Don't you ever get tired of going on about way back when?"

Molly knew what she meant. Everybody who remembered life before Judgment Day longed for the past sometimes, but Doc had it worse than most. He just couldn't seem to let go of the world he had once known. A melancholy aura hung over him like a cloud.

"Kids like you!" Rathbone turned, towered over Sitka, and shook his finger. "You don't know what you're missing, what life used to be like before everything went to hell. There were restaurants and museums and golf courses and Christmas and champagne." A quaver entered his voice. His eyes grew wet. "We didn't have to live like animals, being hunted by machines. We had lives then... real lives with plenty to look forward to. Not this. Nothing like this."

He gestured at the rustic walls that surrounded them.

"You don't know what it was like...."

Sitka yawned theatrically.

"Waste of breath. Heard it all before."

Protesting a bit too much, maybe? Molly suspected that the teen was secretly fascinated by the old man's frequent evocations of life before Skynet. Not that she'd ever admit it. *Must sound like fairy tales to her*, Molly thought. *Like Oz or Wonderland.*

She made a mental note to have Sitka quietly search Doc's bunk and workshop for illicit hooch. She needed to keep the traumatized genius on the top of his game, such as it was. Rathbone was teaching the girl what he knew about electronics and computers, but she was nowhere near ready to take his place.

Won't be for years, probably.

"I remember Dr. Pepper," Molly said gently. She took Doc's arms and guided him back toward the table. The trick was humoring him just long enough to get his mind back on the present, before the maudlin nostalgia got out of control and he spiraled into a full-blown depression. She had to nip episodes like this in the bud. "But, anyway, about the train...."

"Right, yes, the train." To her relief, he started sorting through the surveillance photos again. "Let me see. Assuming we can make our way aboard without being terminated, we'll need a laptop, first-rate decryption software, hack-wires, clips... and maybe a screwdriver."

A knock at the door startled her. She instinctively reached for the rifle, then caught herself and shook her head at her own jumpiness. What was she thinking?

Terminators didn't knock.

"Yes?"

The door swung open and Geir walked in. Like her, he had changed clothes after getting back. Soot no longer blackened his handsome features. He had even taken a razor to his singed whiskers.

"Sorry to interrupt, but they're ready to make it legal."

Molly gave him a baffled stare.

"What are you talking about?"

"The wedding, of course." He looked surprised by her confusion. "Roger and Tammi are getting hitched, remember?"

It all came back to her. The two young Resistance fighters had gotten engaged after surviving a firefight near Glennallen last month. The attack at the pipeline had completely driven the date from her mind.

"They're still going through with it? After everything that's happened?"

"All the more reason," Geir stated. "Proof that life goes on, and all that."

"Whatever." She turned back to her battle plans and sat down in front of the drafting table. "Tell them to start without me. I'm busy."

Molly was in no mood for such nonsense. The very notion struck her as ridiculous. Who the hell got married nowadays, the world being what it was? Weddings and bridal showers and "happily ever after" had disappeared in a mushroom cloud fifteen years ago. Mankind was locked in a life-or-death battle that left no room for the rosy frivolity of days gone by.

Till death do you part? That was a joke, and a sick one at that.

"Sorry. Not an option." Geir yanked the chair out from under her. "This won't wait."

Molly stumbled to her feet to keep from falling.

"What the fuck are you doing?" She whirled around to confront him. Over by the stove, Sitka snickered out loud, enjoying the fireworks. Doc Rathbone backed away uncomfortably and pretended to be somewhere else. "Goddamn it, Svenson, I've got a war to fight. I don't have time for some stupid wedding."

"Those people out there need this, Molly. Now more than ever." Standing over her, Geir refused to back down. "And they need you to share this moment with them." He looked her squarely in the eyes. "You're their leader. This comes with the job."

She could tell he was serious about it. He didn't often challenge her, so she took a deep breath, counted to ten, and reconsidered. Maybe he had a point.

"This is, like, a morale thing?" she ventured.

"If that's how you need to think about it, then sure." He sounded mildly exasperated by her attitude. "Whatever gets you to the church on time."

She reluctantly gave in. Geir usually had a pretty good feel for the pulse of the camp; he was more of a people person than she was.

"Fine," she grumbled. "Just give me a minute."

She scooped up her plans and locked them securely in an antique roll-top desk that dated back to the Great Depression. A cup of black coffee rested on the desk, next to a half-eaten plate of reindeer sausage. She swigged down the last of the coffee, then pulled on her coat and boots. Thankfully, the boots had dried out some since the last time she'd checked. Doc and Sitka put on their outerwear as well.

"All right, let's get those damn kids yoked for however much longer we've got. Wouldn't want our brave Resistance fighters to get cold feet while they're waiting for us."

Geir chuckled as he held the door open.

"I always knew you were a romantic at heart."

"Don't push it, flyboy."

A brisk walk along a gravel-strewn path led them to the camp's makeshift chapel, which doubled as the cell's chief assembly hall and briefing room. Overhead, the aurora borealis streaked the night sky with shimmering curtains of green and violet. The luminous bands of color rippled through the upper atmosphere, visible for hundreds of miles around. There had been some talk of holding the ceremony outdoors, beneath the spectacular cosmic light show, but the sub-zero reality of the Alaskan winter had killed that idea real fast.

A bone-chilling wind shoved them inside the chapel, then banged the door shut behind them.

Curious eyes greeted their arrival. Molly was surprised to find that pretty much the entire camp—some fifty-plus people—had turned out for the event. The roughhewn chapel had been decorated with garlands of strung-together pine cones and sea shells. Banners embroidered with a spiraling double helix—the emblem of the Resistance—hung from the rafters. Rows of battle-hardened men, women and children, some sporting fresh bandages from the day's hostilities, lined both sides of the aisle. The altar at the far end of the room was strictly non-denominational; the last thing the struggling band of humans needed was to squabble about religious icons. Skynet was the Devil. On that everybody agreed.

The happy couple were already standing before the altar. Molly felt a twinge of embarrassment for keeping everyone waiting, even if she still thought that this was all a bunch of sentimental bullshit. Feeling more than a little self-conscious, she blended in with the audience. Smiling spectators made room for the late arrivals. Sitka gaped at the decorations. Doc was less impressed.

"They call this a wedding?" he muttered. "People used to dress up for these things. Rented tuxedos and poofy dresses. I went to this wedding once, back in '98, where the bride arrived in a horse-drawn carriage...."

Sitka elbowed him in the side.

"Mouth shut, old man. Not the time."

The sight of so many people gathered in one place made Molly nervous. This was strategically unwise; what if Skynet launched an attack? She assumed that the sentries were still at their posts, and that the guard dogs were keeping watch as well. A quick glance around the room confirmed it.

Sighing, she tried to pretend she was happy to be here. *Comes with the job*, she reminded herself. *Geir wasn't wrong there.*

At least she wasn't expected to preside over the ceremony. Ernie Wisetongue, a Native Alaskan elder who had once taught Indian Arts at a community college in Fairbanks, stood behind the couple. He winked at Molly before beginning his benediction.

"Brothers, sisters, fellow Homo sapiens." His warm baritone enveloped the audience. A benign middle-aged presence, he had a broad face and short brown hair. Eschewing any priestly garb, he wore a neatly pressed dress shirt, slacks, and beaded moccasins. A Raven totem matching the one on Molly's pendant was embroidered on his tie. "Thank you all for coming tonight, despite today's tragic losses. It is a measure of our strength and sense of community that we can come together even in such trying times." No doubt he had been forced to rewrite his sermon in light of the bloodshed earlier. "Which behooves us to ask: What distinguishes us from the machines? What makes humanity worth fighting for and preserving? The machines are stronger than us, they are more durable than us, they may even be smarter than us. Well, smarter than me, that's for sure." Laughter eased any tension elicited by the mention of the enemy and the rout at the pipeline. "So why will we prevail instead of the machines? Because we care. We feel. We *love*."

He gazed upon the bride and groom, who beamed rapturously at each other. Roger Muckerheide wore neatly-pressed khaki fatigues, complete with a red armband. A black patch covered the eye he had lost skirmishing with a T-600 on a previous fuel run. He was only seventeen, barely old enough to shave.

Tammi Salzer was a short, curly-haired blonde with a talent for demolitions. Her lacy white dress had been salvaged from the basement of a burnt-out bridal shop outside the sprawling crater that used to be Anchorage. The only authentic wedding gown in the camp, it had been passed along from bride to bride for six years now, and was showing definite signs of wear, although some unknown seamstress had done a good job of fitting the much-used gown to Tammi's figure.

The bride clutched a bouquet of plastic flowers. Her own red ribbon was tied above her knee like a garter.

She was only a year older than Sitka.

Molly was taken aback by how young the two sweethearts were. *They're just kids.* They should have been planning for the prom, or trying to buy beer with phony I.D., not tempting fate by making pointless promises during an apocalypse. Tammi's free hand rested protectively over a pronounced baby bump; rumor had it she was at least two months pregnant.

Chalk up another victory for Skynet, Molly thought bitterly. *It's terminated childhood.*

"Tonight," Ernie declared, "we do more than just unite these courageous young people in the bonds of holy matrimony. We also celebrate everything that makes us human, everything the machines will never be able to comprehend or overcome. Love. Passion. Commitment. By pledging their lives to each other, Roger and Tammi also serve as an example to us all, affirming that the future truly belongs to those who believe in it."

Not a bad speech, Molly conceded, despite her skepticism about the proceedings. Ernie Wisetongue was the closest thing the cell had to a chaplain and all-around spiritual advisor. He was also a talented artist who carved totem poles in his spare time. His latest work-in-progress featured a triumphant sasquatch standing astride the fractured skull of a T-600. *Too bad Bigfoot's not really on our side.*

Roger and Tammi exchanged their vows. Their wedding rings were made of recycled copper washers, refashioned by friendly volunteers in the machine shop. Tammi blushed bright red as Ernie informed Roger he could kiss the bride. Cheers and applause echoed throughout the chapel.

Geir squeezed Molly's hand. He kissed the top of her head.

What a softy, she thought. She wasn't sure whether to be amused or annoyed that he was actually falling for all this mushy hearts-and-flowers crap. *You'd think the machines would have stomped it out of him by now.*

Tammi raised the plastic bouquet. Several of the younger women rushed forward to vie for it.

Molly stayed right where she was.

"Don't even think about it," she whispered to Sitka.

"Never crossed my mind," the girl assured her. "Better things to do."

Thank God for small favors, Molly thought. As she joined in the applause—for form's sake—her mind drifted back to more important matters.

Forget the train for a minute. How are we going to get past that fucking HK?

One of the perks of command was a private bedroom above the manager's office, as opposed to the crowded bunkhouses that served as home for the rest of the cell. The flickering light of a kerosene lamp cast dancing shadows on the log walls. A bearskin rug carpeted the floor. A shuttered balcony window offered an alternative escape route. Molly slept better with multiple exits.

She kicked off her boots and got ready for bed. The king-sized four-poster, with its mismatched comforters and quilts, looked warm and inviting. It had been a long day and then some. She was ready for it to be over.

"Admit it," Geir teased her. He was already down to a flannel shirt and jeans. His aviator's jacket hung on a hook by the door. "That wasn't so bad, was it?"

She knew he was referring to the wedding.

"I suppose. Like you said, it was good for morale." She placed her rifle by the door. A loaded semi-automatic pistol already rested on a table next to the bed. "Beats being shot at by T-600s, I guess."

"That's one way to look at it." He deposited his own weapons on the opposite side of the bed. "And speaking of weddings...."

Uh-oh.

Before she could stop him, he dropped down onto one knee.

Oh, fuck, Molly groaned inwardly. *Not this again.*

He fished a polished metal ring from the pocket of his shirt.

"Molly Roxana Kookesh, will you marry me?"

She recognized the ring. It was the pin from a hand grenade he had hurled at a Terminator during that raid on a Skynet interrogation facility in 2015. Her team had liberated more than two dozen POWs, including one grounded bush pilot. After she'd freed Geir from solitary confinement, they'd ended up fighting a whole passel of T-70s, side-by-side. Their "first date," as it were.

Geir had hung onto the ring ever since.

"For God's sake, stand up," she told the kneeling pilot. It was hardly the first time he'd pulled this stunt. "You look ridiculous." As usual, she treated the ring as though it was radioactive. "How many times do we have to go through this?"

He rose to his feet again, but didn't put the ring away.

"C'mon, Molly. We've been together, through all kinds of hell, for three years now. What are we waiting for?"

"Are you kidding?" She couldn't believe they were actually having this discussion *again*. "There's a war on, remember? If Skynet has its way, the human race is *kaput.* Marriage and white picket fences and all that shit will have to wait until the machines are scrap metal—if and when that ever happens. What's the point in planning for the future? Today is all that matters. Tomorrow's a long shot at best."

He flinched at her harsh words.

"Roger and Tammi didn't think so."

"Roger and Tammi are a couple of stupid kids who don't know any better. They're just foot soldiers. Cannon fodder. They can afford to cling to their starry-eyed illusions, at least until the Terminators get them." She made sure the bedroom door was securely locked and bolted. Sleigh bells hanging from the doorknob would jangle loudly if anyone tried to force their way in while they were sleeping. Then she turned to face him.

"I'm in charge here, Geir," she said. "I can't allow myself to forget what really matters."

"Neither can I," he said stubbornly. Visibly disappointed, he dropped the ring back into his pocket. "That's why I'm not going to give up." His hurt expression got to her, although not enough to make her change her mind.

"I know," she said softly. She peeled off her sweater. A scar across her flat belly was a souvenir of a close encounter with a Hunter-Killer. Geir liked to trace it with his finger sometimes. "Just be happy with what we have, okay?" She undid her ponytail. Long black hair tumbled past her bare shoulders. "I don't want to think about tomorrow anymore. Just tonight."

The rest of her clothes hit the floor. She climbed into the bed and threw back the covers.

"Now get over here and keep me warm."

Geir was smart enough to know an invitation when he

heard one. He shrugged in defeat.

"Beats being shot at by machines, right?"

Molly watched him undress.

"You know it."

CHAPTER SEVEN

Something crunched beneath Losenko's boot.

He looked down. A charred human jawbone lay in pieces atop the cracked and broken pavement. The grisly relic elicited only a rueful grimace. He was inured to such remains now. The port was nothing but bones.

A small fishing community situated near the mouth of the Ponoy River, it had not taken a direct hit from the enemy missiles, but it was a ghost town nonetheless. All that was left were the gutted remains of burnt-out homes and buildings. Torched vehicles, their windows blown out, rusted in the streets. Truncated iron beams jutted from the wreckage of an abandoned cannery. Industrial machinery had melted into shapeless heaps of solid slag. Thermal blasts, shock waves, and radioactive fallout had reduced the village to a rotting corpse.

Preliminary scouting teams had discovered evidence of looting as well. Losenko took that as a good omen. It meant that *someone* had survived the initial attack, at least for a time.

The *Gorshkov* was moored at the village's one surviving pier, which an engineering detail was busily reinforcing. Armed sentries, hand-selected by Master Chief Komarov, stood guard over the work crew. Losenko wanted no more deserters. He wondered if he should post guards to watch the sentries.

Flak jackets and helmets protected the security team. Losenko wasn't expecting an attack, but it paid to be cautious. Desperate survivors could be dangerous.

The captain paced along the shore. A bullhorn rested in his grip. He stepped onto a blackened concrete foundation and again raised the bullhorn to his lips. His amplified voice echoed across the desolate wasteland.

"Attention, citizens! This is Captain Dmitri Losenko of the Russian Navy. If you are hiding, please show yourself. We are here to offer you whatever assistance we can provide. Do not be afraid. We mean you no harm. Repeat: do not be afraid. Please let us help you."

He lowered the bullhorn and listened expectantly, but without much hope. This was not the first time he or his officers had made such an announcement.

As before, there was no response. Was the village truly deserted, or were there still survivors huddled somewhere in the wreckage, afraid to come forward?

Who could blame them? Losenko mused. The military had failed to save them; indeed their unfortunate proximity to the naval base had brought this disaster down upon them. Why put themselves in the hands of strangers with guns? They had to assume that civilization had collapsed. *It's every man for himself now.*

Duty compelled him, however, to make his best effort to locate any survivors.

A truck engine roared to life a few meters away.

The sub's mechanics had salvaged the abandoned pickup from the bottom level of a local parking garage. A dozen armed seamen were seated in the bed of the rundown vehicle. Its scorched blue paint job was cracked and peeling. Improvised patches kept its tires inflated. Ivanov kicked them, just to be sure.

Scowling, the XO crossed the pavement to join his superior. A Kalashnikov assault rife was slung over his shoulder. A dosimeter was pinned to the lapel of his heavy overcoat; the treated plastic film measured his exposure to radiation. Earlier scans had found the level of radiation higher than they would have liked, but not immediately life-threatening. Losenko suspected that they were going to have to live with a revised definition of "acceptable" from now on. At the moment, the threat of cancer was the least of their worries.

"Scouting team is ready to depart, sir," Ivanov reported. "Request permission to lead the reconnaissance mission."

Losenko shook his head. An identical dosimeter was pinned like a badge to his own lapel.

"Permission denied." He lowered his voice to avoid being overheard. "We've already discussed this, Alexei. I can't risk you. Zamyatin is more than capable of leading the expedition."

Now that the truck was up and running, Losenko was dispatching a team to search further inland, looking for signs of life and foraging for supplies. The town itself appeared to have been stripped clean already, and what canned food remained was dangerously irradiated.

"Is that the real reason?" Ivanov challenged him. "Or is it that you don't trust me out of your sight? Do you think that I will desert, to go searching for my family?"

A bitter smirk twisted his lips. "Let me assure you, sir, you need not worry on that account. I have no illusions that my loved ones survived the Americans' treacherous attack." He spat upon the ground, barely missing the charred skull fragment. "I know they are dead."

The *starpom*'s surly tone bordered on insubordination. Losenko's right hand fell discreetly upon the grip of the semi-automatic pistol that was holstered on his hip. Conscious of Ivanov's heart-breaking losses, he had made allowances for the younger officer's sullen attitude, but he was not about to have his authority questioned—not even by a man he had once thought of as a son.

"I do not need to justify my decisions to you, Mr. Ivanov," he said brusquely. "Do not forget that I am still the captain here. If you have a problem with that, I am more than willing to relieve you of your duties."

As he spoke, Losenko kept a close eye on Ivanov's rife. He held his breath, waiting to see if the combative XO would back down. He felt the eyes of the other crewmen fall upon them both.

"That won't be necessary, *Captain*." Ivanov stepped back and saluted Losenko, albeit grudgingly. "I will instruct Deputy Commander Zamyatin to commence scouting further afield, per your orders. Will that be all, *sir*?"

Losenko's hand came away from his gun.

"Thank you, Mr. Ivanov. Go about your duties."

Stone-faced, the captain watched silently as the XO marched back to the truck and gave Zamyatin some final instructions before waving them on. The tactical officer rode shotgun in the truck's cab beside the driver. The pickup disappeared down a cratered highway heading west into the heart of the Kola Peninsula. Its spinning wheels raised a cloud of grey dust and ash. Scattered bones, human and otherwise, crunched beneath its tread.

Soon the truck disappeared into the distance.

Not for the first time, Losenko chided himself for not organizing a detail to collect and bury the strewn remains. It was a crime to leave the skeletal fragments exposed to the elements like this. But the sheer enormity of the task forced him to confront the futility of any such effort. The dead outnumbered the living now, and the whole world was their crematorium.

He wondered if there were enough people left on Earth to bury them all.

My duty is to the living, he concluded, *not to lifeless bones*.

He prayed that the scouting party would find survivors—perhaps clusters of refugees fleeing the former population centers. He desperately needed to believe that some remnant of the Russian people endured, that he and his crew were not entirely alone in this godforsaken new world. They had not even been able to make contact with another Russian sub. Whether this meant that all of them had been destroyed in the fighting after the attack, or that they were simply laying low as submarines were designed to do, remained unknown.

Where did his duty lie if there was no nation left to defend?

He surveyed the devastation, unable to escape it. *Was this what Alaska looked like now?* His own role in the holocaust still haunted him. *Should I have launched those missiles? Did I retaliate against a computer glitch?*

What if the American general, Ashdown, was telling the truth?

"Captain! Captain!"

A young ensign came running down the gangplank from the sub. Losenko recognized him as Alyosha Mazin, a trainee currently assigned to Operations. He sprinted toward Losenko with more energy than the captain had seen in any of the crew for weeks. His eyes were wide with alarm. He shoved his fellow sailors aside.

"Out of my way! Coming through!"

What the devil? Losenko instantly went on the alert.

"Something's coming, sir!" The breathless ensign skidded to a halt in front of him. "Radar's detected an incoming aircraft, heading this way fast!"

Adrenalin shot through Losenko's veins.

"What kind of aircraft?"

"Undetermined, sir!" The messenger labored to catch his breath; weeks of sedentary life aboard the sub had left him out of shape. His pale face was flushed. "Bearing northwest, sir. From the sea."

The Americans? Losenko bit back a profanity. Docked at the pier, the *Gorshkov* was a sitting duck. Even if he could get everyone back aboard K-115 in time, and rig the sub for immediate departure, the narrow inlet was too shallow to allow them to submerge entirely. And unlike the old days at Murmansk, there were no anti-aircraft emplacements to defend the vulnerable submarine. If this was indeed an American bomber approaching, the *Gorshkov* presented a tempting target.

And there was nothing he could do about it.

"Take cover!" he bellowed into the bullhorn. Even if his ship was defenseless, he could still try to save his crew. "Out of sight—now!"

The men scrambled to obey, ducking beneath the rebuilt dock or darting into gutted buildings. The security team crouched within the rubble, aiming their guns and rifles at the sky. Several more men started up the gangplank toward the sub, but Losenko called them back.

"Belay that! Stay clear of the boat!" If the *Gorshkov* came under fire, the massive vessel would rapidly become a watery tomb.

Losenko considered evacuating the sub, leaving only a skeleton crew aboard, but time deprived him of that option. He and Mazin took cover behind an overturned garbage truck. His eyes turned upward, searching the sky, but he heard the aircraft coming before he saw it, flying at a high altitude several kilometers to the north. It was hard to make out at this distance, but it appeared to be some sort of wide-bodied cargo plane, possibly a military transport—perhaps bearing enemy troops and equipment, or simply emergency relief supplies.

It was too far away, and moving too fast, to discern its insignia. Losenko could catch only a glimpse of it.

So he waited for the large, fixed-wing aircraft to veer toward them. And waited, and waited....

To his surprise, the plane did not alter its flight path. Seemingly oblivious to the exposed sub, it passed by in a matter of minutes. Losenko watched intently as it left the coast behind, heading further west.

In roughly the same direction as the scouting party.

Mazin laughed out loud, unable to contain his euphoria. Death had passed them by. He wiped his sweaty brow with the back of his hand. He looked at the captain. Relief gradually gave way to confusion on his youthful face.

"Whose plane was that, sir? One of ours? Or the enemy's? Where is it heading?"

Losenko wished he knew.

***

"K-115 to search party. Can you read me?"

Losenko hovered in the radio shack behind the seated operators. More than two hours had passed since the reconnaissance team had headed inland. They were overdue to check in.

"K-115 to search party, please come in."

Transmitting from the sub was a calculated risk, especially after sighting that unidentified aircraft, but the captain was anxious to know the status of his scouts. To his dismay, at least a half dozen men had taken advantage of the crisis to desert; after scrambling for cover, they were nowhere to be found. No doubt they had chosen to take their chances on their own, rather than spend another moment in the service of an extinct navy.

I should be furious with them, Losenko thought. But instead all he felt was fatigue and disappointment. He, too, was sick to death of this endless voyage. Who could blame the runaways for wanting to escape? *Why spend your last days trapped inside a metal tube?* He shook his head ruefully. *At this rate, I will soon be the commander of a ghost ship.*

Was that what had become of Zamyatin and his scouting party? Had they also struck out for parts unknown, leaving their duties and responsibilities behind?

A signal light flashed. A burst of static broke into his bitter ruminations. Pushkin fiddled with the controls on his receiver. He tapped his headphones.

"I think I have something, sir!"

"Put it over the speaker," Losenko instructed. He wanted to hear for himself.

"Right on it, sir!"

Pushkin pressed a button. Zamyatin's voice entered the cramped compartment.

"Search party to K-115." The transmission was scratchy and faint, but audible. Pushkin did something to increase the volume. "Lieutenant Zamyatin reporting."

Good man, Losenko thought. His heart swelled with pride. It was good to know that there were still dedicated officers within his crew. He took the mike from Pushkin and pressed down on the speaker button.

"Losenko here. What is your position and status, Mr. Zamyatin?"

Static punctuated the officer's reply.

"According to GPS, we're about seventy-five kilometers northeast of the port, on the outskirts of some sort of industrial area. The terrain here shows only moderate damage. And, Captain, there appears to be a factory running!"

Losenko couldn't believe his ears.

"A factory?"

"A manufacturing plant, I think." The excitement in Zamyatin's voice was contagious. "We're still several meters away, but there's white smoke and puffs of flame billowing from the stacks. We can hear heavy machinery, and there look to be lights and activity inside."

The captain and radio operators exchanged startled looks. Losenko had hoped that maybe the scouts might have stumbled onto a refugee camp or scattered homeless survivors, but a working factory, still going strong when everything else was dead or dying? Losenko briefly wondered if Zamyatin was hallucinating. *Too much radiation maybe?*

"Can you see any survivors?"

"Negative," Zamyatin answered. The captain visualized

him peering through a pair of high-powered binoculars. "We're too far away, and there doesn't appear to be anyone on the grounds surrounding the plant. They must all be inside."

Pushkin shook his head.

"Who the hell still goes to work at a time like this?" A sheepish look came over his scrawny face, as though he feared his careless remark might be taken the wrong way. "Outside of the armed forces, I mean."

"At ease, Gennady," Losenko assured him. The radio operator had a point; it did strike him as strange that the factory would still be in operation—unless perhaps a civilian plant had been converted to serve the war effort, in which case the government or the military might be in charge. Losenko leaned forward again, tightly gripping the mike.

"Mr. Zamyatin. Can you tell what is being manufactured at the facility?"

"No, sir," the tactical officer admitted. "Sorry, sir." He clearly regretted disappointing his captain. "There appear to be metal shutters over the windows and skylights. Plenty of automated security measures, too. Mounted cameras, searchlights, barricades." The truck's engine rumbled in the background, combining with the excited voices of the other men. "We're moving in for a closer look."

"Exercise caution, Mr. Zamyatin," the captain advised. There was no guarantee that the facility remained in the hands of the lawful authorities, nor that its inhabitants would necessarily welcome visitors. It was even possible that the plant had been commandeered by the enemy. "Do not assume that Mother Russia is still friendly territory."

"Understood, Captain—" The transmission broke up,

but Pushkin managed to regain the signal. "—when I know more."

"Keep me posted."

"Aye, aye, sir." Zamyatin raised his voice to be heard over the rattle of the truck, which seemed to be on the move again. "Search party out."

The speaker fell silent.

The captain handed the mike back to Pushkin, then retreated to the rear of the radio shack. He paced back and forth despite the tight space, his hands clasped behind his back. Reluctant to return to the conn until he knew more, he tapped his foot impatiently against the deck. He felt like Noah waiting for the dove to return.

Zamyatin's discovery sounded encouraging, so why were his nerves on edge? The unidentified aircraft flew across his memory, adding to his unease. The *Gorshkov* had been out of touch with the mainland for weeks. Could American troops have already established a foothold in that time? What if that aircraft had been delivering supplies or manpower to an enemy outpost operating within Russia's borders?

We have no idea who we're dealing with, he realized. *Nor what purpose that factory is now being put to.*

"Hey, Gennady." The assistant radio operator whispered to Pushkin. Seaman Ostrovosky was single, with a reputation for carousing while on leave. "You think there are women working at that factory?" His eager tone testified to weeks of enforced celibacy aboard K-115.

Even before the missiles flew, none of them had set eyes on a woman since leaving port. *Is that what the deserters are going in search of?* Losenko wondered. *An Eve to their Adam?*

Pushkin's mind seemed to be heading in the same direction.

"Russia must be repopulated after all." He grinned at his comrade. "I, for one, am prepared to do my patriotic duty."

"Enough of that," Losenko said sternly. He didn't want any overactive libidos leading his crew to inefficiency or, worse, recklessness. He prayed that Zamyatin and the rest of the scouting party weren't entertaining similar fantasies, at the expense of caution. "Keep your minds on your work."

Pushkin blushed in embarrassment. Ostrovosky gulped. Both men busily occupied themselves with their apparatus.

"Aye, aye, sir," Ostrovosky said.

The tense silence was suddenly broken by a flashing signal light. Making up for his earlier frivolity, Pushkin quickly responded.

"K-115 to search party...."

His salutation was cut short by the unmistakable din of all-out battle. Frantic shouting and the strident blare of gunfire invaded the radio shack. Men screamed in agony. A deafening explosion momentarily overpowered the speaker system.

"Oh my God!" an agitated voice cried out. "They've got us pinned down!"

Losenko rushed forward. He yanked the mike from Pushkin's shaking fingers.

"Search party, this is the captain! What's happening?"

"We're under attack!" the voice reported. "They came out of nowhere. They caught us by surprise!" A burst of automatic weapons fire interrupted the panicky report. Pounding footsteps sounded in the background. A heavy body slammed into the earth, and it sounded as if the speaker was rolling across the ground in a desperate attempt to avoid being shot. "There's no place to run. God help us, we're all going to die!"

The incoherent monologue tormented Losenko.

"Get hold of yourself!" he barked into the mike. "Where is Deputy Commander Zamyatin?"

"Zamyatin is dead! They blew his head right off." The embattled sailor struggled to compose himself. "The truck is in flames. There's nowhere to go!"

The shocking news hit Losenko like a torpedo, but he couldn't let it rattle him.

"Who is this?" he demanded. "Identify yourself!"

"Yevgeny Pagodin, seaman second-class," a shaky voice whimpered. "*Arkady, watch out!*" he hollered at an unseen comrade. A volley of shots rang out, too close for comfort. A wet sound splattered the walkie-talkie at the other end of the transmission. "No!" Pagodin sobbed. "Arkady!" His voice wavered. "This can't be happening. Not Arkady too!"

Losenko was in hell. He wanted to hurl himself over the airwaves just to see what the devil was happening.

"Report, sailor! Who is attacking you?"

Looters? Enemy soldiers? Friendly fire?

"Machines!" Pagodin blurted. "A squad of machines!"

Losenko didn't understand.

"What do you mean? Explain!"

An automatic pistol sounded in the captain's ears. He guessed that Pagodin was firing back at his assailants. The besieged seaman fired off round after round, apparently to no avail. Bullets ricocheted loudly off metal.

"Nothing's stopping them!" Pagodin babbled between rounds. "They just keep coming—like death in steel!"

Losenko heard a low rumble in the background, like the whirring of a machine. Gravel crunched beneath heavy wheels.

"Save yourself, Captain!" Pagodin shouted from 200 kilometers away. Something crunched noisily beneath a motorized tread, which seemed to be getting louder by the moment. "Don't let them get you! Don't let them—"

A hail of gunfire cut off his words. Instantly a burst of static assaulted Losenko's eardrums.

Then nothing.

Pushkin worked like mad to reestablish contact.

"K-115 to search party, please come in! Can you read me?" His assistant sagged against his seat, staring aghast at the silent speaker. He buried his face in his hands, all thoughts of women driven violently from his mind.

Pushkin stabbed relentlessly at his control panel, like a doctor refusing to give up on a patient.

"K-115 to search party! Is anybody there?"

"That's enough, Gennady." Losenko placed his hand on the radio operator's shoulder. He knew a massacre when he heard one. "They're gone."

There would be no reply. Over a dozen brave men had been killed on their own soil.

By machines?

CHAPTER EIGHT

2018

The Terminator stalked the wilderness.

Titanium legs rose and fell like pistons, never missing a step, as they waded relentlessly through the snow. Thick drifts muffled its heavy tread. The sub-zero temperature might have compromised its hydraulics, but the T-600 hadn't bled enough antifreeze to significantly endanger its mobility. The machine had been pursuing the dog sled without pause for 5.633 hours now. It was neither bored nor discouraged. The humans had left a clear trail. They would be terminated.

The only variable was *when*.

A small nocturnal mammal scurried away from the machine's approach. Its optical sensors identified the specimen as *Muslela erminea*, the short-tailed weasel. The animal's ermine coat was effective camouflage in this wintry setting, but failed to hide the creature from the T-600's heat and motion detectors. Its CPU instantly processed the data.

THREAT ASSESSMENT: ZERO.

The Terminator let the weasel go. Such lower life forms were not considered threats to Skynet's continued existence. Only humans required eradication.

The trail ascended into the mountains.

From its vantage point, the Terminator glimpsed what appeared to be derelict wooden structures infesting the southwest face of a hillside, several kilometers above. Geographical records, downloaded from Skynet, confirmed the existence of a former mining installation at those coordinates. The T-600 weighed the possibility that the human Resistance had taken shelter in the supposedly abandoning buildings. The hypothesis held promise, but could not be verified without closer inspection. It would be premature to dispatch reinforcements to the site.

FURTHER INVESTIGATION REQUIRED.

A ferocious roar interrupted the Terminator's assessments. Its cranial case rotated atop the exposed neck assembly.

A large hirsute mammal lumbered into view 10.791 meters to the right. Thick brown fur, accented by silver tips, covered the beast—which appeared to weigh approximately 250 kilograms. It stood a meter tall at the shoulders while approaching on all fours. A disproportionate hump of muscle mass, arrayed above its shoulders, had evolved to add power to its forelimbs. Eight-centimeter-long claws sank into the snow beneath it.

Hostile brown eyes glared at the Terminator. Yellow fangs flashed within its gaping maw. Its physical characteristics and overall configuration matched that of *Ursus arctos horribilis*.

The grizzly bear.

The Terminator shifted to defensive mode. Unlike the

ermine, the grizzly was an alpha predator of considerable mass and strength, displaying clear signs of aggression. The bear rose up on its hind legs until it was fully as tall as the T-600. Its size and weight indicated that it was an adult male. An angry growl issued from its open jaws.

A partially devoured caribou was splayed open on the ground 2.885 meters behind the grizzly, its bloody entrails exposed to the air. The carcass explained the bear's territorial behavior; it was defending a kill.

THREAT POTENTIAL: SIGNIFICANT.

The grizzly's presence was an unexpected complication. Given the season and temperature, the bear should have been hibernating. The data on the species indicated that grizzlies could be unpredictable in this regard, however. It was possible that the recent explosions and subsequent fires had roused the bear from its slumber. Or else the animal had simply craved raw meat.

In any event, the bear was an obstacle.

The Terminator swiftly analyzed its options. It briefly considered detouring around the creature, in order to avoid provoking it further, but doing so risked losing the dog sled's trail. Should that occur, the Resistance base would remain hidden within the sprawling Alaskan wilderness.

That was unacceptable.

So the T-600 marched forward, its metal fists clenched in anticipation.

As predicted, the grizzly reacted aggressively to the challenge. Dropping down onto all fours, it charged at an average rate of 50.824 kilometers per hour. Saliva sprayed from its snarling jaws. The T-600 braced itself for the collision.

The bear slammed into the machine with the force of

a speeding snowmobile, knocking the Terminator onto its back. Heavy paws pinned the machine to the earth. Powerful jaws closed on the robot's cranial case. Ivory fangs shredded what remained of the infiltrator model's human disguise before breaking against a titanium skull. Hydraulic fluid spurted from a severed cable. A jagged tooth lodged in the T-600's cranium.

Another fang speared the Terminator's left optical sensor, shattering the lens. Circuits shorted within the socket. The Terminator's visual display wavered and went out of focus for 6.003 seconds before recalibrating. Angry claws scraped against an impervious endoskeleton.

IMPERATIVE: TERMINATE URSINE LIFEFORM.

The Terminator's right arm shot up and seized the bear by the throat. Servomotors whirred as the arm pushed the grizzly's head up and away, operating like a hydraulic jack. Its joints locked into place, putting precisely 67.426 centimeters between the Terminator's face and the grizzly's snapping jaws. The furious bear roared in frustration. Slobber dripped into the T-600's damaged eye socket. Miniature baffles closed to prevent further contamination.

RECOMMENDATION: INTERNAL STERILIZATION DURING NEXT REGULAR MAINTENANCE CYCLE.

Every moment wasted in an engagement with the animal increased the risk of additional damage, and delayed the completion of the Terminator's assigned purpose. It worked its free arm out from beneath the grizzly's bulk. The elbow joint bent to a ninety-degree angle. A steel fist rocketed upward with enough force to punch through solid concrete, smashing through the grizzly's rib cage and into its heart.

The meaty organ exploded upon impact.

THREAT POTENTIAL: TERMINATED.

The grizzly went limp, turning into 263.472 kilograms of dead weight. Its fierce brown eyes glazed over.

The Terminator withdrew its fist. A torrent of hot arterial blood gushed from the gaping cavity in the bear's chest, spilling onto the T-600's supine form. Steam rose from the crimson flood. The machine took hold of the dead grizzly with both hands, shifting its grip to improve the leverage before tossing the carcass aside.

It landed with a heavy thump, not far from the disemboweled caribou. The blood of predator and prey mingled atop the snow.

The machine rose to its feet. Claw marks scored the surface of its endoskeleton. Sticky red fluid, cooling rapidly in the cold night air, streamed down its chassis to pool at its feet. The shattered optical sensor blinked out, leaving the T-600 blind on one side and compromising its depth perception.

Although there had been minor damage to an actuator in its lower jaw, and two internal valves had been wrenched loose by the impact with the grizzly, a thorough diagnostic reported no other major malfunctions. Backup systems compensated for damaged components. Valves resealed to prevent loss of vital lubricants. A fang remained embedded in its skull.

OPERATIONAL EFFICIENCY: 78.406 %.

The grizzly had inflicted significant damage, the Terminator concluded, but not enough to deter it from fulfilling its programming. Its remaining optical sensor zeroed in on the decaying buildings high up on the slopes of the mountain. The humans' trail continued to lead in that direction.

The T-600 saw no reason to linger at the site of the battle. Leaving the dead bear behind, it marched uphill.

CHAPTER NINE

2003

The bodies of the scouting party had been left where they fell. The arctic chill had retarded decomposition, but insects and bacteria had already left their mark on the dead submariners. Maggots swarmed in the eye sockets. Pale flesh had begun to blacken. Marbled veins stood out beneath peeling skin. Rigor mortis had passed, leaving the bodies limp and rubbery.

Bullets riddled the scattered corpses, which lay amidst pools of congealed blood. Lieutenant Zamyatin's face had indeed been blasted apart; Losenko could identify him only by the insignia on his uniform. Pagodin's lifeless fingers still clutched the blood-splattered walkie-talkie.

The massacre had taken place on a lonely stretch of road running through a deserted industrial area. The two-lane highway was flanked by a private storage facility on the right and an empty service station on the left. Discarded vehicles had been shoved into ditches alongside the road, perhaps to clear a path to the factory over the hill. Mummified skeletons slumped over the wheels of some of the cars. Most of the storage units looked as though they had been broken into by looters, although a few still had their corrugated steel doors intact.

The storage sheds and service station provided plenty of cover for hidden snipers; the location struck Losenko as the perfect site for an ambush. Fourteen of his men had learned that firsthand.

Evidence of the slaughter was everywhere. The overturned pickup lay on its side, blown apart by an explosion. Twisted metal fragments were strewn like shrapnel. Shell casings littered the asphalt. Bullet holes perforated the dented cars lining the road. Stray shots had chipped away at street signs, telephone poles, and concrete traffic dividers.

Losenko pried a loose slug out of the pavement; it appeared to be made of depleted uranium. One did not have to be a detective to realize that the scene had born witness to a furious firefight.

The only thing that was missing was the enemy. If Zamyatin and his men had managed to take any of their killers with them, those bodies had been carried away. Unlike the rotting corpses of his men.

"Who did this, Captain?" Ostrovosky asked. The junior radio operator had volunteered to join the patrol; Losenko suspected that he wanted revenge for the atrocity they had been forced to listen to yesterday. "Scavengers?"

He doubted it. Nothing appeared to have been stolen—not even the search party's arms and ammunition—and the attackers had chosen to destroy the pickup truck rather than capture it. The captain also liked to think that trained Russian seamen could hold their own against any ragtag band of marauders, unless they were severely outnumbered. From what they had heard over the radio, however, the scouting team had not stood a chance. It had not been a battle, but a rout.

"Just keep your eyes open, Mr. Ostrovosky," he said crisply. "For all we know, we're behind enemy lines now."

Over his first officer's protests, Losenko had chosen to personally investigate the massacre. It was foolhardy, perhaps, given his rank and responsibilities, but what was Ivanov going to do about it, report back to his superiors? Losenko chuckled wryly. One of the few perks of surviving a thermonuclear war was that he no longer had to answer to Moscow.

Zamyatin and the others had died carrying out his orders. *If I want to find out what happened, and see it with my own eyes*, the captain thought, *then that's my prerogative.*

Or maybe he just had a death wish.

Chances were, he wasn't the only one.

Bloody tread marks crisscrossed the asphalt. Losenko remembered the motorized tumult he had overheard. The parallel tracks were roughly 150 centimeters apart, too close together for a tank or an automobile. Grease marks stained the blacktop. Pools of oily fluid collected in cracks and potholes. Losenko knelt to inspect such a puddle. He dipped a gloved finger into the liquid and held it to his nose.

It reeked of petroleum. Some sort of lubricant?

Machines, Pagodin had said. *A squad of machines.*

He peered intently at the liquid that dripped from his fingertip. Had his men drawn blood from the enemy before they were slaughtered?

Losenko wanted to think so.

He stood up and assessed the patrol. He had brought a larger force this time, fully twenty-five men, all armed to the teeth with assault rifles, handguns, and plenty of ammunition. They had crept upon the scene stealthily, having left their salvaged vehicles in a junkyard half a kilometer back. The cars and trucks were hidden in plain sight, like Poe's famous purloined letter, amidst the numerous scrapped autos.

Losenko himself had ridden in a battered family station wagon that was missing all its windows. He had been disturbed to find a forgotten doll and candy wrappers under the passenger seat. He didn't want to think about what might have become of the wagon's former owners.

Perhaps he had trodden on their bones.

A pair of sentries had stayed behind to watch over the cars—and each other—while the rest of the party had continued forward on foot. Losenko's legs ached from the strenuous hike. Quite a workout after being cooped up in the sub for weeks on end. Zamyatin's GPS coordinates, transmitted along with his final broadcast, had led them to yesterday's fatal battleground.

"Eyes open!" he exhorted his men. Lookouts were posted along the perimeter, vigilant for any suspicious movements. "Safeties off. Arms at the ready."

Such orders were almost certainly unnecessary. The carnage at their feet was enough to keep the men alert to danger. Wary sailors gripped their weapons tightly, some jumping at every stray gust of wind. A veteran submariner, Losenko felt uncomfortably exposed out here in the open. He preferred to fight his wars from the depths of the ocean. His men no doubt felt equally out of place. They were sailors, not commandoes.

We are out of our element, Losenko thought. *Like fish out of water.*

He would not turn back, however, until he had uncovered what sort of devilry was underway. Zamyatin and his men had discovered this infamous factory, and had paid with their lives. That they had been mercilessly gunned down, just for approaching the facility, implied that its secrets were of great importance, at least to someone.

That it was also the only evidence of life for leagues added to the captain's curiosity. He needed to know what in Russia had survived the war—if only for the sake of his own sanity.

The road rose and fell between the battle site and the factory, following the natural contours of the terrain. Walking along the curb, he climbed to the crest of a low hill and crouched down behind the concealing shelter of an abandoned mail truck. He scooted along the tilted hood, being careful to keep his head low. A lookout, the barrel of his rifle laid across the top of the hood, squatted beside Losenko. Pavel Gorski glanced up briefly from his rifle sight.

"Watch yourself, skipper," the boy warned in a hushed tone. The young enlisted man usually worked in the torpedo room. "I hear the scouts never saw it coming."

Losenko could tell that Gorski was frightened. Like the rest of the crew, he had never seen real combat before.

"Do not worry about your captain," he replied. "A submariner knows better than to stick his periscope where it might be shot at!"

The quip elicited a weak smile.

"I guess you would know, sir!"

"Just pretend that rifle fires torpedoes," Losenko advised, nodding. "Then you'll feel right at home."

"Aye, aye, sir!" The lookout shifted his grip on the weapon. "Just like back on the boat."

Losenko wanted to promise Gorski that he would see his bunk on K-115 again, but he couldn't bring himself to do so.

Despite the danger, he peered over the crumpled metal hood, to inspect the puzzle that had lured the scouting team to their end.

Just as Zamyatin had reported, the factory dominated the horizon several meters to the west. Pillars of thick white exhaust spewed from its looming chimneys, polluting the air. Periodic gouts of bright orange flames shot upward from the smoke stacks, making them look like gigantic roman candles.

If Losenko strained his ears, he could even hear the sound of heavy machinery. The clanging noises, the rumbling assembly lines would have never been tolerated aboard a submarine, where silence was paramount. Flashing lights as bright as a welder's torch could be glimpsed through cracks in the drawn metal shutters. The plant sat on the banks of the Ponoy River, the better to discharge its noxious wastes into the flowing current.

My apologies, Oleg, the captain thought. *It appears you were not hallucinating after all*. He glanced back over his shoulder at the tread marks and grease stains, then looked back at the factory. A grim conviction took root in his mind.

It was impossible to tell at this distance exactly what was being manufactured within the sprawling facility, but he doubted that it was microwave ovens or cheap compact cars.

A squad of machines....

Something buzzed overhead. At first, Losenko thought it was a bug, but then he glanced up and caught a glint of metal out of the corner of his eye. An unmanned aerial vehicle, about the size of a large kite, flew above them. Its streamlined black wingspan was about three meters from tip to tip. Miniature red sensors, mounted in its nose turret, scanned the territory.

Losenko's blood went cold. He knew at once what he was looking at: a remote-control surveillance drone. Russian military and counter-terrorism forces had been experimenting with such mechanisms for years now, as had the Americans. Indeed, the unmanned aerial vehicle that hovered above them bore a strong resemblance to the Scan Eagles employed by the U.S. military. They were intended to perform aerial reconnaissance missions in a variety of environments, without endangering flesh-and-blood soldiers.

"Damnation!" he cursed. "We've been spotted."

Gorski spied the flying drone as well. With admirable speed and aim, he shouldered his rifle and fired at the UAV. The muzzle brake deflected the sound of the blast to the sides, much to Losenko's discomfort. Hot lead sprayed across the device's flight path.

It changed course abruptly, zigging and zagging across the sky with frightening agility. A lucky shot winged it, however, and it went spinning through the air. Sparks flew from its tail, it dipped precipitously, then righted itself at the last moment. As it swooped upward again, slowing long enough to stabilize its erratic tumbling, Gorski let loose with another volley.

This time the drone wasn't fast enough to evade the gunfire. Flames erupted as the 5.45-millimeter rounds punched through its lightweight composite casing.

"I got him!" Gorski whooped jubilantly. "Torpedoes away!"

But the drone wasn't dead yet. As though determined to take its attacker with it, the UAV reversed course and dived straight at Losenko and Gorski. Trailing a plume of fire and smoke, it whistled through the air like a miniature missile.

"Incoming!" Losenko shouted. He shoved Gorski out of the way.

With only seconds to spare, the men hurled themselves in opposite directions. The kamikaze drone crashed to earth between them, digging a furrow deep in the soil alongside the road. Dirt and gravel went flying.

Gorski scrambled to his feet on the other side of the crater. He slammed a fresh banana clip into his AK-74, then took aim at the crashed drone.

"Come on, you flying maggot!" he snarled, taking out all his pent-up fear and anger on the pulverized machine. Blowback from the rifle smudged his face. "I'm ready for you!"

"That's enough, sailor." Losenko lifted himself from the ground. This time of year, the upper layer of permafrost was loose and soggy. "You've killed it once already."

Not that it mattered. While impressed by Gorski's reflexes and marksmanship, the captain knew the damage had already been done. The drone had surely reported their presence back to its unknown masters, just as the gunfire had given away their location. Losenko felt as though his hull had been pinged by an enemy sub's sonar.

We have to get out of here, he realized. *Now.*

"After me!" he said to Gorski. They sprinted down the hill toward the rest of the patrol, who were already rushing to join the battle. Anxious eyes scanned the hill between them and the factory. Agitated voices pelted Losenko with questions.

"Retreat! Back to the cars!" he shouted over the clamor. He gestured back the way they had come. "Reverse course, full turbines! Gorski! Fedin! Cover our rear!"

He prayed they could get away without a fight, but the odds of that happening were shrinking by the minute.

At least we know what we're in for... unlike Zamyatin.

"But, skipper!" Ostrovosky looked back at the fallen bodies of the scouting party. "Lieutenant Zamyatin and the others...."

"Leave them!" Losenko barked. He hated to abandon the dead crewmen, but if they tried to recover the bodies, they would quickly join them. He prodded Ostrovosky between the shoulders with the muzzle of his pistol. "Eyes front! That's an order!"

He stepped over Pagodin's rotting remains.

Dasvidania, comrade.

The men raced at full speed away from the carnage. Their boots pounded against the bloodstained blacktop. Stealth was no longer an issue, so they didn't bother clinging to the shadows as they had on the way in. Losenko hung back, near the rear of the exodus, constantly glancing back in expectation of seeing the enemy in pursuit.

But what enemy? The question nagged at him even as he hurried his charges back toward their waiting transport. *Fourteen men dead, and we still don't even know who we're running from!*

They had only made it a few meters before the trap was sprung. A loud metallic clatter caught Losenko by surprise. To the left, the corrugated steel door guarding one of the storage units rolled up noisily, exposing a dark cavernous space beyond. A pair of glowing red eyes lit up in the shadows. A motor roared to life—and a thing rolled out of the open unit.

Losenko's eyes widened in shock.

Exposed beneath the pitiless glare of the arctic sun was a robotic killing machine mounted on tank-like treads. About the size of the conn area back in the control room, it resembled the remote-controlled robots used by bomb squads to detonate suspicious packages. Heavy armor plating—the dull gray color of gunmetal—shielded the machine's base, torso, and head. The wedge-shaped cranial case had a vaguely serpentine appearance. The robot rose from a defensive crouch until it was nearly three meters tall. Optical sensors, installed in the viper-like "face," scanned the scene. A pair of menacing black chain guns served as the robot's arms.

They had met the enemy—and he was not human.

Servomotors whirred into action. Targeting lasers swept over the startled humans. The robot opened fire, unleashing a continuous spray of bullets that cut down a third of the patrol in a matter of seconds. The deafening report of the chain guns, which fired shot after shot with murderous efficiency, drowned out the men's final screams. Bright arterial blood spurted from gaping wounds. Depleted uranium slugs punched through protective flak jackets as though they were made of tissue.

The robot rolled easily over the uneven terrain. Its head and shoulders swiveled from side to side, raking the road with a scythe of whizzing death. Its spinning muzzles flared like hellfire.

Losenko threw himself onto the pavement. Bullets whizzed about his head, practically grazing his scalp. He wriggled forward on his hands and knees toward the nearest available shelter: the soggy ditch alongside the road. He tumbled headfirst into the gully, landing between two bulldozed vehicles. Bodies hit the asphalt only a few meters away.

This is like something out of a science fiction movie! he thought. The mechanical monster hadn't even issued a warning before opening fire. This wasn't security; it was slaughter, pure and simple. *What sort of madman programmed this thing? And sent it out to kill?*

Just when he thought matters couldn't get worse, the garage doors at the service station blew off their hinges. A second robot, identical to the first, rumbled out on the other side of the street. Its chain guns rotated into place. Unblinking red eyes surveyed the carnage.

A sailor who had been hiding behind one of the empty gas pumps spun around in surprise. He fired frantically at the newcomer, but the bullets ricocheted harmlessly off the robot's sooty steel carapace, striking sparks off the armor. The man emptied his weapon, then tossed the rifle aside. He threw his hands up above his head.

"Don't shoot!" he squealed. "I surrender!"

The robot pivoted toward him. The muzzles of the chain guns flared. Twin bursts of gunfire all but cut the unarmed sailor in two. His bisected body flopped limply onto the concrete.

Surrender, it seemed, was not an option.

Losenko squeezed beneath a wrecked convertible. His coat snagged on the jagged underside of the vehicle before tearing loose. A rusty exhaust pipe scraped against his back. Coming out on the other side, he clambered to his feet. A quick glance revealed little hope of survival, for himself or his men.

"It's not fair," he whispered. "They don't deserve this...."

The vicious crossfire had left only a handful of sailors alive. The terrified survivors were in full retreat, dashing down the road away from the ambush. Their only chance was to get back to the vehicles they had stowed at the junkyard half a kilometer away. They fired back at the robots as they ran, to maddeningly little effect. Smoke bombs, hurled by the fleeing men, offered only minimal cover. The deadly machines rolled out onto the street. Their armored treads trampled over the bodies, grinding flesh and bone into the blacktop.

Losenko recalled Pagodin's panicky final broadcast.

"Nothing's stopping them! They just keep coming...!"

He hurried after the fleeing sailors. "Go! Go! Go!" he shouted, although it was doubtful they could hear him over the roar of the chain guns. Eschewing the center of the road, he raced across a series of adjoining parking lots, taking evasive action to avoid the whizzing bullets. "Don't wait for me! Get back to the boat!"

Somebody had to warn Ivanov and the crew back at the sub.

Hairs rose on the back of his neck. Some sort of psychic sonar alerted him to danger. Glancing back over his shoulder, he found himself looking straight into the crimson sensors of the first robot. A targeting bead lit up his chest. The robot's right-hand cannon swung toward him.

"Down, sir!"

Gorski sprang up like a jack-in-the-box from behind a roadside bus shelter. With expert aim, he fired at a narrow band of exposed hydraulics around the neck assembly. Valves and circuitry ruptured violently. Oily black ichor sprayed like blood. The robot's gun-arms jerked erratically as its torso rotated 360 degrees to protect its throat. A blistering volley of gunfire strafed the air above Losenko's head. Glass from a shattered streetlight rained down onto his scalp.

"That's for Lieutenant Zamyatin!" Gorski gloated. "See, Captain! We can hurt them. You just have to hit the right targets!"

The marksman's triumph was short-lived. The second robot avenged the attack on its partner by turning both its guns on Gorski. Twin blasts from its barrels flung him against the back of the bus shelter. His body danced spasmodically beneath the impact of the bullets. The Kalashnikov went flying from his fingers. A faded advertisement on the shelter urged commuters to explore "Exciting New Careers in Electronics & Computer Programming!"

Losenko's tore his gaze from the grisly spectacle. Running as though the entire American Army was after him, he was half a block away before Gorski's bullet-riddled body collapsed onto the curb. Broken glass shattered beneath his feet. The damaged robot retreated, perhaps for repairs, while its murderous comrade continued the pursuit. Its versatile treads easily navigated the potholes and crevices marring the two-lane highway. Mechanical limbs moved with unnerving fluidity.

The monster smelled of smoke and oil.

A valiant sailor struggled to assist a wounded crewmate. His arm around the other man's shoulders, he half-supported, half-dragged his limping comrade as they lurched after Losenko and the others. Seaman Sasha Krosotkin's heroism, while worthy of a medal, proved fruitless; unmoved by the touching display, the robot reduced both men to bloody pulp. It then trundled past their intertwined bodies without a backward glance.

For the first time in his life, Losenko truly hated a machine.

Running low on ammo, Ostrovosky resorted to flinging signal flares at the robot. Blinding scarlet flames erupted across the highway, adding to the chaos. The robot fired on the flares as though they were armed combatants. Losenko guessed that the machine's thermal sensors had trouble distinguishing between the road flares and the heat signatures of a firing rifle. *Good*, he thought, welcoming the distraction. *Anything to slow the machine down.*

One of flares rolled beneath the robot's treads just as it bulldozed over the body of another murdered sailor. The incendiary device ignited the corpse's spare ammo clips, triggering an explosion that rocked the robot from below. Losenko watched hopefully as the robot toppled over onto its side, then cursed as the stubborn mechanism began to right itself. Internal shielding seemed to protect its vital components from the blast but its treads appeared to be badly damaged. Smoke gushed from beneath it as the machine awkwardly limped forward. The chain guns spewed a seemingly inexhaustible swarm of hungry metal slugs.

Bile rose at the back of Losenko's throat. Could nothing stop these cursed machines?

The next several minutes were like a nightmare. There was no order or precision to the men's flight, only a dwindling number of panicked submariners being cut down as they ran. Losenko had lost track of the body count within the first few seconds of the ambush. Adrenalin fueled his headlong race along the edge of the road. Stray debris, puddles, and depressions threatened to trip him, lying across his path like pitfalls. He stumbled over a toppled "STOP" sign, almost pitching forward onto his face, but managed to regain his balance before it was too late.

The close call left him gasping. He knew that if he fell, he would never get back up again. The relentless machine would trample him just as it had the first few victims.

We mean nothing to them, he raged. *They have no hearts. No souls.*

His breath was ragged. A painful stitch stabbed him in the side. The racing of his pulse resounded behind his ears. His

mouth was as dry as one of the *Gorshkov*'s airtight compartments. He couldn't remember the last time he had run so
hard or for so long. Sweat dripped into his eyes. He cursed
himself for not spending more time on the treadmill back on
the sub. How dare he let himself get so out of shape!

For the first time since the missiles flew, he realized that
he wasn't ready to die yet.

If they could just get back to the cars!

Gunfire blasted behind him as the maimed robot disposed of more stragglers. Losenko glanced back. The drifting haze of the smoke bombs obscured his view. Was it just
his imagination, or was the killing machine falling behind?
He thanked providence for the freak explosion that had
damaged its treads. How far, he wondered, was the robot
willing to chase them before returning to its base of operations? All the way back to the docks?

Desperate minutes felt like hours, and he had begun to
doubt whether any of them would see K-115 again,
when he finally spied the dilapidated chain-link fence
surrounding the junkyard. Hope flared in his heart.
Maybe they still had a chance. He fumbled in his pocket for the keys to the station wagon. From the looks of
things, the wagon alone might have room enough to
carry all that remained of the patrol. Besides himself,
there looked to be only seven or eight men left alive... out
of a team of twenty-five brave volunteers.

Someone will pay for this, he vowed silently. *I swear it
upon the lives of my men!*

"Thank heaven!" Ostrovosky gasped, appearing a few
meters ahead of the captain. The sight of the junkyard
gave the exhausted sailors a second wind. They dashed
toward the front gate with renewed hope and alacrity.
The assistant radio operator slowed to catch his breath.

"I never thought we were going to make it!"

Neither did I, Losenko agreed.

A shocking burst of gunfire, coming from inside the junk-yard, froze the men in their tracks. Losenko skidded to a halt, his heart sinking like an anchor. By now, he recognized the telltale *rat-a-tat* of the robots' ever-firing chain guns.

A crazed shout was cut off mid-expletive.

The guards! Losenko realized. *The ones left behind to watch the cars.*

A gas tank exploded within the auto graveyard. The station wagon? One of the other vehicles? A bright orange fireball rose into the sky. Clouds of pungent black smoke billowed upward. Mangled pieces of steel were thrown into the air, only to clatter to the ground like a metal hailstorm. Losenko felt the heat of the blaze upon his face. He choked on the fumes.

"*Nyet!*" Ostrovosky dropped to his knees. Anguish contorted his face. His military discipline faltered, expos-ing the overwhelmed human being beneath the uniform. "It's not fair! We were almost *there*!"

Losenko knew just how he felt. It seemed as if fate was conspiring against them. Mother Russia had become a slaughterhouse overrun by heartless mechanical butchers.

We should have stayed at sea where we were safe!

A scorching wind drove them back, away from the searing flames. For a brief moment, Losenko entertained a desperate hope that perhaps, just perhaps, the robot in the junkyard had been destroyed by the explosion, along with the patrol's only means of transportation.

He scanned the open road that lay before them. The junkyard had been located at the outer fringe of the industrial center. Nearly a hundred kilometers of barren tundra stretched between them and the remote fishing village where the *Gorshkov* was docked. He could hear the second robot rumbling behind them. His eyes searched the surrounding territory for the safest route back. Alas, the rugged terrain, carpeted by moss and sedge, offered little in the way of shelter.

Perhaps if they scattered and headed cross-country?

Such strategies evaporated as a third robot tore out of the burning junkyard, smashing straight through the dump's locked front gate. Its burnished armor hadn't even been scorched by the conflagration. Smoke rose from the muzzles of its twin chain guns. Speeding onto the highway, it wheeled around to face the panicky humans, blocking their escape. Its upper body straightened, assuming its full height as it staked out the high ground atop another low hill. A burst of fire sent the men darting for cover.

Ostrovosky did not get off his knees fast enough. Rapid-fire rounds shredded the hard-living young man. He went down in a geyser of scarlet mist. Sticky red droplets sprayed across Losenko's face.

We're trapped, the captain realized. The other robot had herded them straight into the sights of the mechanized assassin that stood before them. He wondered how long they had been under the machines' surveillance. And why they had been marked for death in the first place. *This is our homeland, which we killed millions to defend. We should be welcome here!*

To their credit, his men refused to be slaughtered without a fight. Darting for cover, they opened fire on the homicidal robot. The smell of cordite added to the suffocating fumes blowing from the raging fire that had engulfed the junkyard. An impressive display of fire-power actually succeeded in holding the robot off for a moment or two.

Losenko drew his own pistol and took aim at the neck

assembly, just as Gorski had done earlier. The marksman's ugly demise flashed across his mind's eye, but he
savagely pushed the image out of his thoughts. He needed all his wits about him now.

Don't think, he commanded himself. *Just shoot, damnit!*

Then one of his shots struck home. Circuits shorted in
the junction connecting the monster's left gun-arm to its
torso. Discharged electricity crackled. The arm twitched
and drooped limply to one side. Hydraulic fluid spurted
onto the pavement.

But even crippled, the robot still had one good arm left
with which to fight. Its upper body rotated toward
Losenko, the whir of the chain gun promising high-caliber
retaliation. The captain swore he saw a flash of anger in
the robot's luminous red sensors.

Impossible.

Braving the scorching heat and smoke, he retreated
toward the junkyard, only to find himself backed against
an intact length of the chain-link fencing. The metal links
were hot to the touch; he could feel them through the back
of his heavy wool coat.

The robot's head tracked the captain's movements.
Random fire bounced off its armor plating. It raised its
single working gun-arm.

His back against the red-hot fence, Losenko had no place
left to run. Insanely, his ex-wife's face surfaced from some
forgotten corner of his memory. *Katerina.* He wondered if
she would be waiting for him, despite everything....

He braced himself for death. If he was lucky, it would
be quick, like facing a firing squad. He kept his eyes open,
willing himself to meet his end like a man—tempted to
spit in defiance, but what was the point? The gesture
would mean nothing to a machine. Instead he merely

glared at the hateful mechanism, wishing he had its anonymous inventor in his sights.

If only Zamyatin had never laid eyes on that goddamn factory.

Well, he thought impatiently. *What are you waiting for?*

To his surprise, the robot's head swiveled from left to right, its optical sensors scanning for its prey. Losenko's brow furrowed in puzzlement. He didn't understand.

Why didn't it fire?

Unless....

He recalled how the emergency flares had distracted the other robot. If the machine's targeting circuits relied on auditory, heat, and motion sensors, then maybe the raging fire was blinding it, concealing his precise location. *That's got to be it,* he thought. *If I just stand still, it can't "see" me against the blaze!*

Unfortunately, the intense heat was hard on human flesh as well. Spreading flames consumed the junkyard, moving ever closer to where Losenko stood. Smoke stung his throat and nostrils, and he bit down on his knuckles to keep from coughing. His back felt like it was on fire, and he wasn't sure how much longer he could stay where he was.

Soon he would be forced to choose between burning to death or being gunned down by a trigger-happy robot....

What a decision!

Red-hot flames licked at the opposite side of the fence. Animal instinct threatened to overcome logic, and he was on the verge of hurling himself away from the inferno. Suddenly, an ear-piercing blast of sound sliced through the air.

What the devil? Losenko thought. *That sounds like an air horn!* He tore his gaze away from the confused robot in time to see an armored truck—of the sort formerly used to transport cash and valuables—come speeding toward the battlefield. Tinted windows of bulletproof glass concealed the driver from view. A dented piece of sheet metal in the shape of a tombstone was welded to the front grille. A crudely rendered caricature of a robot's skull was etched on its surface. Both headlights were blown out. Reinforced plastic liners protected the tires.

A powerful engine roared as the truck zoomed madly down the highway, straight toward the automaton.

The machine appeared to be just as surprised as Losenko by the truck's unexpected arrival. It turned away from the burning junkyard, its upper body rotating ninety degrees to face the oncoming vehicle. It barely had time to fire off a single burst of uranium rounds, which failed to penetrate the truck's hardened-steel shell. The bulletproof windshield cracked, but did not shatter.

The truck struck the robot at high speed. Its considerable mass and momentum flattened the machine, which disappeared beneath the armored chassis.

Losenko's jaw dropped. He felt as though he had been tossed a lifeline. He staggered away from the blazing junkyard toward the road. Painful coughs cleared the smoke from his lungs. Confused eyes sought out the truck that had just saved him.

Who...?

The armored vehicle spun around, turning its back toward the captain and his men. Brakes squealed as it skidded to a halt a few meters away. A pair of double doors slammed open, revealing human figures in the cargo hold. An outstretched arm beckoned to the surviving sailors.

"Get in!" a raspy female voice called out. Losenko got a quick impression of a short, stocky woman in soiled work clothes.

"Hurry!"

CHAPTER TEN

The dogs barked loudly enough to raise the dead.

Molly's eyes snapped open. Instantly alert, she sprang from the bed even as Geir stirred beneath the covers. The frantic baying, coming from outside, sent a jolt of adrenaline though Molly's veins.

She raced across the shadowy bedroom and threw open the shutters. It was still night outside; the sun was nowhere near rising. Darkness shrouded the forgotten mill town. The barks sounded as if they were coming from the south, maybe from over by the playground. She squinted into the blackness, but even as her eyes adjusted the other buildings blocked her view.

A high-pitched yap was cut off abruptly.

Geir sat up in bed. Darkness hid his face, but not the tension in his voice.

"What is it?"

"Trouble," she guessed. It was possible the dogs were reacting to a stray animal—perhaps a bear or wolf—wandering too near the camp, but she doubted it.

We should be so lucky.

The jarring staccato of gunfire instantly confirmed her worst fears. No way would the lookouts be opening fire on wildlife like that, especially not in the wee hours of the morning. There could be only one explanation.

Skynet had found them.

Molly had to know what was happening... and *now*. Fumbling in the dark, she snatched a walkie-talkie off the top of a chest of drawers and thumbed the speaker button.

"Security, this is Kookesh. What the fuck is going on out there?"

Static crackled in her ear, then an agitated voice could be heard over a din of angry shouting and gunfire. The shots echoed through the window as well, lending them an unnatural stereo effect.

"We've got a breach!" She recognized the raspy twang of Tom Jensen, a logger-turned-guerilla. He was supposed to be patrolling the southwest perimeter. "A machine! T-600, I think!"

Molly's heart sank. *Just what I was afraid of.*

"Keep it busy!" she barked into the receiver. "I'll be right there!"

She flung the walkie-talkie onto the bed, then started scooping her clothes up from the floor. The inky blackness frustrated her.

Where the hell are my pants?

A match struck loudly just a few feet away, igniting the kerosene lamp by the bed. A flickering golden radiance lit up the bedroom, much to Molly's relief. She glanced over to see Geir standing naked by the lantern. He blew out the match.

"Thanks!" she grunted, pulling on her slacks. "I've gotta get down there."

"Hang on." He retrieved his own garments, which were draped over the back of a ratty easy chair. "I'll be right with you.'

Molly shook her head vehemently.

"Forget it. You've got to get that plane out of here." Geir's vintage plane, *Thunderbird*, was kept in a camouflaged hangar down by the glacier. "We can't afford to lose it."

"Crap!" he swore. "I hate it when you're right." He grabbed the pistol that sat by the bed and tossed it in her direction. "Do me a favor. Be careful, okay?"

She thrust the sidearm into its holster, and shot him a wry grin.

"It's the machines that need to worry," she said, flaunting a bravado she didn't feel. Moments later her M4 carbine was locked and loaded. "Just keep *T-bird* away from the metal."

Sleigh bells jangled as she yanked open the door. She ran downstairs, taking the steps two at a time. Excited yelps greeted her; she had forgotten about the huskies sleeping by the stove.

Crossing the murky office, she pulled open the front door. An arctic blast of wind invaded the cabin. The cold hitting her face jolted her awake faster than the strongest coffee.

"Scoot!" she ordered, motioning to the dogs, anxious to give them a chance to escape. "Go on, scram!"

The huskies obeyed, and she followed them out into the freezing night air. The isolated camp was spread out around her. A single gravel road connected most of the mill's sheds, plants, storehouses, and bunkhouses, which the Resistance had converted to its own purposes. The old ammonia leeching plant was now an armory and communications center. The powerhouse was a garage.

A fourteen-story breaker mill dominated the hillside further up, with a rickety wooden tramway that had once carried raw ore to the top of the building, where it had been dumped into the chutes and crushers below. To the east, rusty metal tracks led to a dilapidated railway depot that hadn't seen a locomotive for more then eighty years. A crumbling wooden bridge spanned a wide, ice-covered stream that fed the glacier below.

Opaque black clouds kept the moon from relieving the nocturnal gloom, and Molly kicked herself for not remembering to grab a flashlight.

Lights flared inside the buildings, barely visible through the shutters, as the sleeping camp was shocked awake by the hair-raising tumult. Startled cries and curses escaped the ramshackle bunkhouses that were home to most of the Resistance fighters and their families. Frightened faces appeared in the windows. Babies wailed behind flimsy wooden walls. Molly's heart went out to her people whose well-earned rest had just gone to hell. She wanted to assure them that they were going to be all right, that she had things under control.

But that would be a lie.

Despite the stygian blackness, she had no trouble figuring out which way to go. Gunfire, screams, and shouting drew her onward. A blind woman could have followed the trail to where the fighting was. Rifle in hand, she sprinted across the camp. Her loose hair blew in the wind.

Taking a shortcut between the mess hall and the machine shop, she emerged from an alley into an open junkyard that had been converted into a makeshift playground for the camp's children. A swing set, slide, merry-go-round, and jungle gym had been cobbled together from scraps of discarded mining equipment. Like the upside-down extraction vat that had been converted into a children's playhouse. Snow-covered sawdust cushioned the ground. An authentic Tlingit totem pole—carved by Ernie Wisetongue himself—watched over the area. The brightly colored visages of Raven, Beaver, Killer Whale, and Wolf perched atop each other on the pole.

Some distance away, on the other side of a sundered barbed-wire fence, towering pines marked the southwest border of the camp. The dense forest had always been a buffer zone sitting between the rebel outpost and the outside world.

Tonight that barrier had failed.

Muzzles flared in the night as a handful of sentries sought to repel the invader. The strobe-like flashes revealed a battle-scarred T-600 on a rampage. The Terminator looked as if it had been through the wars. Deep scratches and scorch marks defaced its carbonized endoskeleton. Congealed blood caked the cold metal. A single blood-red "eye" glowed malignantly above its leering death's-head grimace, and only patches of melted rubber skin and polyester were still fused to the metal. And was that a large yellow *tooth* stuck in its skull?

Molly experienced a sudden flash of *deja vu.* Had one of the T-600s aboard the snow plow survived the avalanche?

Who the hell knows? she thought. *Fucking machines all look the same.* Even so, she gritted her teeth at the thought that the machine might have followed her all the way back to the camp.

Flying lead sparked off the Terminator's metal chassis and cranium. Reaching the playground, the machine wrenched the merry-go-round from the ground to use as a shield, effortlessly hefting the 300-pound cast-iron disk. It pushed forward against the gunfire like a bipedal bulldozer, holding the merry-go-round out in front. The inexorable advance forced the frantic soldiers to fall back, rapidly losing ground.

Why isn't it shooting? she wondered, and that cinched it. *It must be one of the ones we buried in the avalanche. It has lost its weapons.* But that didn't stop the invader from following its primary directive.

A foolhardy sentry attempted to get a better shot by climbing to the top of the slide, but the Terminator barreled straight into the structure, toppling it over onto the unlucky sniper. Pinned and unable to defend himself, the human whimpered in pain, his rifle having fallen out of reach.

"My leg!" he cried out. "It's broken!"

Who? Molly thought. It was too dark to make out his face.

A second later, a fractured leg was the least of his concerns. The T-600 trampled over the mangled slide to get to the downed human. Bones and aluminum crunched in unison. A heavy titanium foot stomped on the soldier's head. It exploded like an overripe melon.

Molly winced, but there was no time to mourn—or even to find out the poor bastard's name. Spotting Tom Jensen at the rear of the defenders, she rushed forward and grabbed him by the shoulder. He started in surprise, then saw who she was. Wild eyes blinked in recognition.

"Chief!"

"Give me a sitrep," she ordered. "How many are there?"

"Don't know," he blurted. Cold air puffed before his lips. "Maybe just the one. Maybe more that we haven't seen." A bushy red beard failed to mask his distress. His eyes bulged. Spittle sprayed as he gesticulated like a madman. "It came out of nowhere. Thank God for the guard dogs!"

Molly didn't ask what had become of the canines. She didn't want to know.

"Sound the alarm," she said. "Full evac. We're out of here!"

Jensen scowled.

"You sure about that? Maybe there is just one." He pumped a smoking shotgun, eager to avenge his fallen comrades. "One T-600 against all of us—we can take it! You *know* we can!"

"Doesn't matter," Molly said. "Even if it *is* alone, it's bound to have uplinked our coordinates to Skynet by now. The machines will know where we are." Her eyes scanned the sky, half-expecting to see a Hunter-Killer swooping down from the clouds. "There'll be more coming, bet on it."

The burly ex-logger got the picture.

"Roger, chief!" He scurried away to carry out her orders, leaving Molly in charge. But he paused to call over his shoulder. "You show that murdering wind-up toy what for!"

"Count on it!" she promised.

She elbowed her way to the front of the fight. The Terminator kept on coming, as persistent as Geir's god-damn proposals. A nervous soldier backed away fearfully, on the verge of breaking rank.

"It's hopeless! Look at that thing! Nothing can stop it!"

"Keep shooting!" Molly ordered, and he flinched at

the sound of her voice. "We need to buy time for the rest of the camp to get away. Aim for the back and shoulder joints!" According to John Connor, those were the T-600s' most vulnerable parts. "Hold the line!"

Nailing the Terminator's weak spots was easier said than done, though. Its charred black endoskeleton blended in with the night, rendering it all but invisible. The only light came from muzzle blasts and a handful of wobbly flashlights and kerosene lanterns.

A bullet ricocheted off the merry-go-round, winging another lookout. He dropped to his knees, clutching an arm. A lantern slipped from his fingers and rolled across the ground. The T-600's single optical sensor turned away as it tracked the lamp.

Veering from its path, the machine lowered its circular shield long enough to grasp the lantern, then the glowing red lens scanned the vicinity. Its soulless gaze came to rest on a woodpile that stood outside the back entrance of the mess hall. The stacked logs made an irresistible target.

Fuck! Molly thought. She knew exactly what was going through the machine's CPU.

The Terminator flung the lantern at the woodpile. The glowing missile arced over the playground before crashing into the logs, shattering with a splash of kerosene. Bright orange flames erupted as the wood caught fire. Quickly the blaze leaped from the logs to the adjacent building. Decades-old wooden timbers went up like kindling. A crackling roar began to compete with the blaring guns followed by cries of alarm.

A sentry rushed forward to try to fight the blaze.

"Leave it!" Molly barked. This camp was history anyway. They might as well leave Skynet nothing but ashes.

"The metal's our enemy, not the fire!"

At the sound of her voice, the Terminator turned its head toward Molly, perhaps identifying her as the leader. *Lucky me*, she thought, opening fire on the T-600. The recoil from the M4 bruised her shoulder, and the handguard rattled annoyingly. Nevertheless, high-caliber slugs vented her fury.

The Terminator swung its shield to block her assault. The carbine's bursts dinged against the cast-iron. It marched toward the blazing woodpile. Hefting the shield with just one hand, it snatched a burning log from the fire. Then it turned back toward the defenders, brandishing the log like a torch.

Planning to set more buildings on fire, Molly guessed. *Pyromania must be part of its programming.*

Smoke billowed from the windows of the burning mess hall. The kitchen door banged open and panicked soldiers who had been bunking above the dining facilities came charging out of the building in various stages of undress, only to run head-on into the invader.

"Watch out!" Molly shouted, but too late.

A startled man clutching an AK-47 stumbled backward into the people behind him. His gun went off in his grip, firing uselessly into the center of the shield. Adjusting its strategy, the Terminator smashed the merry-go-round into the mob. The stolen playground ride hit the fleeing humans like a battering ram, splintering bone.

The intruder let go of its shield and began to swing the burning log like a club. It batted another soldier in the head, snapping his neck and setting his face on fire. The man's AK-47 landed at the Terminator's feet.

The T-600 dropped the torch in favor of the firearm.

"Shit!" Molly exclaimed. "It's got a gun!"

Seizing the weapon, the Terminator wasted no time opening fire on the human defenders. A middle-aged former stewardess took a bullet to the forehead, while a redneck teenager dropped to the snow clutching his side. Spurting blood looked black in the dim light.

The other fighters scattered and dived for cover.

Turning away from the burning mess hall, the T-600 looked again for Molly. She saw its cyclopean gaze turn back toward her, only seconds ahead of the barrel of its gun.

Time to move.

She ducked behind the totem pole. Bullets tore into the carved red cedar, vandalizing Ernie's Native Alaskan designs. The ammo chipped away at Wolf and Beaver. Wooden splinters went flying. *Sorry, Ernie*, Molly thought. The artist had put a lot of work into his creation. *I owe you one.*

Peering out from behind the pole, she tried to fire back. Setting the M4 for controlled three-round bursts, she squeezed the trigger.

Nothing happened.

She whacked the loading mechanism against the wood, but it still refused to fire. Molly couldn't believe it.

Of all the times for the fucking thing to jam!

CHAPTER ELEVEN

2003

"Get in!" the woman repeated. "Move your butts!"

That was all the invitation Losenko and his men needed. They sprinted toward the armored truck even as the surviving robot lurched into firing range once more. Harsh scraping sounds came from its damaged left tread, slowing it down, but it seemed no less determined to exterminate the rest of the patrol.

Losenko's heart pounded. The prospect of being shot now, only seconds away from rescue, filled him with dread. That would be the cruelest blow of all.

But no more than I deserve, perhaps.

A cigarette lighter flicked inside the truck. The flame ignited a strip of cloth wadded into the mouth of a tinted glass liquor bottle. Losenko recognized an old-fashioned Molotov cocktail

"Head's up!" the woman in the truck shouted. She hurled the flaming bottle at the robot. "This drink's on me!"

The bottle crashed against the robot's armored chassis,

exploding on impact. A swirling orange fireball swallowed up the oncoming machine. Its sensors overwhelmed, it fired wildly from inside the inferno.

"All aboard!" the bomb-throwing stranger hollered. "Trust me, that's just going to make it mad!"

Losenko hustled two of his men into the dimly lit hold before boarding the truck himself. A calloused hand grabbed onto his wrist and yanked him up into the waiting vault. He tumbled forward onto a padded foamboard floor.

"There you go!" the nameless woman said. She risked a glance out the door. "Is that all of you?"

Losenko took a second to glance around. Heartsick, he realized that only the two other sailors were still alive, out of a party of twenty-five. Blasko and Stralbov were both young midshipmen, in their early twenties. They looked like shell-shocked teenagers to his weary eyes.

"I think so." There was no point in looking back. The pitiless machines would have already killed any stragglers or wounded. He spit the vile words out. "Yes, we're all that's left."

"Lucky you." The woman yanked shut the reinforced steel doors and locked them in place, then shouted at a man at the other end of the vault. "You heard the man, Josef. Let's get out of here before another one of those metal assholes shows up!"

Her companion, a heavy-set man with a surly expression, pounded on the bulkhead separating the cargo hold from the driver's compartment. The blows echoed in the enclosed, windowless vault. A narrow metal lattice let his voice through to the cab. "Hit the gas!"

"*Da!* I hear you!" a voice answered from up front. "Hold onto your balls!"

A sudden burst of acceleration slammed Losenko against a foam-insulated wall. Tires squealed as the truck peeled out, back the way it had come and away from the flattened robot. He was grateful for the lack of windows, that meant he didn't have to watch as they left their fallen comrades behind.

Exhausted, he sagged against the wall. Stralbov sobbed uncontrollably. Blasko vomited onto the floor of the truck.

"Crap!" the woman exclaimed. She wrinkled her nose at the mess. "Oh, never mind, sonny. What's a little puke after all you've been through?" She gazed at the young seaman in sympathy, her tone softening a bit. Plopping down onto a bench, she drew her muddy boots back from the pooling vomit. "It's only human, which is more than you can say for a lot of things these days!"

As Losenko's eyes adjusted to the gloom, he got a better look at their rescuer. A round face, of good peasant stock, had been baked brown by the sun. Time and toil had etched deep lines into her careworn countenance. A faded red kerchief covered her scalp. She, too, was stocky, and Losenko put her age at fifty-plus. Wily blue eyes looked over the traumatized sailors. Nicotine stained her fingertips.

"Thank you," Losenko croaked. His throat was still raw from the smoke. "If you hadn't come to our rescue...."

She shrugged off his gratitude.

"Name's Grushka." She cocked a thumb at her companion, an intimidating bear of a man wearing a tattered raincoat over what looked like hospital scrubs. He was twice Grushka's size and maybe half her age. "That cantankerous whoreson over there is Josef."

The man grunted in response. He had a smooth dome and a florid complexion. A cataract clouded his right eye.

The other one eyed the newcomers suspiciously. A shotgun lay across his lap. A meaty hand rested protectively on a carton of liquor bottles topped with improvised fuses. There were at least eight Molotov cocktails left.

"Losenko," the captain introduced himself. "Captain Dmitri Losenko." He gestured at the traumatized sailors. Neither man seemed to be wounded, at least not physically. "These are my men."

Or what was left of them.

Grushka leaned forward. Her fingers plucked at the stripes on Losenko's uniform. "You really with the Army?"

"The Navy," he corrected her. "Our submarine, K-115, is docked at a fishing village about a hundred miles east." He believed the truck was heading that way, although the lack of windows made it hard to verify. "Our base at Murmansk was destroyed in the war."

In the past, he would have been averse to sharing such crucial intelligence with unknown civilians, but everything had changed now. These people had saved his life. They were the closest thing to allies he'd encountered since the bombs fell.

Grushka nodded. "I know that village. Used to have a cousin there." A momentary grimace betrayed her grief. "Didn't think there was anybody still alive out that way."

"There wasn't," Losenko divulged. "The town was empty when we found it."

Josef snorted. "About time you got here. We've been hanging on by our nails for weeks now, with no help from Moscow or the Army or any of you worthless uniforms. First you blow up the world, then leave us to fight those fucking machines on our own."

Losenko didn't argue the point. In the end, the *Gorshkov* and the rest of Russia's vast nuclear arsenal had failed to protect the people from the ultimate horror. The last thing either Grushka or Josef needed to hear was that the holocaust might have been caused by an overseas computer error. And that still didn't explain why his men had died.

"What happened here?" he asked. "What are those machines? Who built them?"

Now it was Grushka's turn to look disgusted.

"Tell you the truth, I was hoping you could explain that to us."

"I've never seen those robots before," Losenko confessed. "How long have they been hunting you? Does this have something to do with that factory?"

The woman nodded.

"This used to be our home, and I actually worked on the assembly line at the plant once, back when it used to churn out riding mowers. Hard work, but a decent living. Then those red-hot mushrooms starting sprouting in the sky, and everything changed. Hid out in my basement for as long as I could, until I ran out of food and water. And when I came out...."

A shudder passed through her body.

"Well, I'll spare you the ugly details. Pretty much everybody was dead or gone, though. I thought I was all alone in the world until I ran into that overgrown sourpuss over there." She nodded at Josef, who scowled back at her. "Knew him casually from one of the bars in town. Never liked him much, to be honest. Still don't. But beggars can't be choosers." She glanced toward the front of the truck. "Found the driver, Mitka, about the same time. He was in the back of this rolling lockbox when the bombs came down. Figure that's what saved him.

Losenko could only imagine what life had been like in the immediate wake of the war. How many friends and loved ones had these people lost? The fallout alone would have inflicted heavy casualties—never mind starvation, violence, and disease. But that dreadful scenario, no matter how heart-breaking, wasn't what most concerned him now.

"And the machines?" he prompted her.

Grushka spat onto the floor. Traces of crimson streaked the saliva. For the first time, Losenko noticed that the old woman's gums were bleeding. *Radiation sickness or just malnutrition?* He snuck a closer look at Josef. How long had the man been bald?

And where were his eyebrows?

"The big army planes started arriving just days after the world went to hell," Grushka recalled. Her gaze turned inward. "I could hear them flying over what was left of my cottage. At first I thought maybe it was the disaster relief people, but nobody came looking for me. Later, when the lights and noises started up at the factory, everybody hurried to see what was going on. There were a few more of us left back then, you see. Guess we all wanted to think that somebody was still in charge, that things were starting up again."

So did I, Losenko thought. *And Zamyatin and his party.*

"That's when we saw those machines for the first time." Another shiver betrayed how much the memory cost her. She drew a half-empty packet of cigarettes from the pocket of her jacket. "There were just a couple of them at first, plus a bunch of armed storm troopers. Americans mostly, although there were some other nationalities mixed in. Even a few Russian quislings and translators. I thought the soldiers were controlling the robots. Took me a while to figure out that the machines were babysitting the soldiers."

Machines in charge of humans? Losenko had trouble grasping the concept.

"What did they do to you?" he asked.

"Put us all to work, that's what. Turned us into slave labor, refurbishing the factory to build more of those damn machines. Executed anyone who resisted, just to set an example. Herded up the kids and old people to use as hostages." Another flicker of grief cracked her stoic pose. "What was really nauseating, though, is that there were those who didn't even complain, who were grateful just to be taken care of and know where their next meal was coming from." Her lips twisted in disgust. "Stinking metal lovers."

Losenko envisioned a throng of hopeful survivors, desperate for assistance, being pressed into slavery by an occupying force. He couldn't help being perversely impressed by the speed and efficiency with which the lawn mower factory had apparently been converted into an incubator for killer robots. That bespoke meticulous planning and premeditation, in anticipation of Armageddon. Someone had been looking ahead beyond the initial attack.

But who? What kind of "computer malfunction" was capable of that?

"How did you get away?" he asked.

"Smuggled my wrinkled carcass out of the place along with a load of fresh corpses." Her casual tone defied the horror she must have endured. "People were being worked to death all the time. What was one more worn-out piece of meat?"

"I'm sorry—for everything," Losenko offered. The words rang hollow even to his own ears. A vision of Alaska, equally devastated by his own missiles, flayed off a fresh strip of his soul. "Are there others like you?"

"A few, hiding here and there." Grushka lit up a cigarette to steady her nerves, using the same lighter she'd employed to ignite the fuse of her Molotov cocktail. Losenko glanced nervously at the gas-filled bottles boxed over by Josef. "The machines mostly leave us alone as long as we stay away from the factory. At least for now. Who knows what they'll do once they've built more of 'em."

"Kill us all, that's what." Josef glared at them like they were stupid. He fondled the shotgun in his lap. "Any fool can see that."

"Probably." Grushka scratched her head thoughtfully. A loose strand of hair slipped free of her kerchief. Embarrassed, she grabbed the strands and tucked them into her pocket, out of sight. Rough hands made sure the kerchief was secure. She gave Losenko a searching look. "You really got a submarine?"

He nodded. "The *Gorshkov*." He felt a sudden urge to report back in to the sub; Ivanov and the surviving officers needed to be informed of the debacle. "Excuse me." He unhooked a compact walkie-talkie from his belt. Pushkin would be waiting in the radio shack, listening for his signal. "Captain to radio. Do you read me?"

"I don't like this," Josef grumbled. "What if the machines are listening?"

"Quiet!" Grushka shushed him. "This is military business!"

Pushkin promptly answered Losenko's hail, but the captain's relief at getting back in touch with his boat was leavened by the dreadful news he had to impart. "Get me

First Officer Ivanov at once."

"Aye, aye, sir!" Pushkin answered. There was a moment of silence, after which he spoke again, his voice eager. "Good to hear from you, skipper. Is Ostrovosky there?"

The captain winced. The radio operator's blood was still smeared across his face.

"Just get me Ivanov."

"Aye, aye, sir," Pushkin replied, his voice flat now. He didn't say anything more.

The XO was on the other end of the line within minutes.

"Radio to captain. What is it, sir?"

Losenko decided he could give Ivanov a full report later, once they were safely at sea.

"We've taken heavy casualties," he said tersely. "Rig the boat for an immediate departure." He consulted his wristwatch, which was still set to Moscow time. It would be dark soon. "If we're not back by dawn, leave without us. The boat is not safe here. This is occupied territory."

"Casualties?" Ivanov said, and there was new anger in his voice. "Did you engage the enemy?" The hatred was audible even from dozens of kilometers away. "Was it the Americans?"

Losenko allowed himself a bitter smile.

"Not unless they bleed oil now."

A computer malfunction....

"What?" Ivanov was understandably perplexed by the cryptic remark. "I don't take your meaning, sir. Can you elaborate?"

Losenko wished there had been time to take a snapshot of one of the robots. How else was he to fully convey the horror they had faced? No longer pumped full of adrenalin, he suddenly found himself unbearably tired.

All those men, shot to ribbons... for what?

Gunfire jolted him from his lethargy. Bullets slammed into the rear door of the armored truck.

"Crap!" Grushka explained. "Guess they really want you Navy boys!"

"I told you we should have left well enough alone," Josef snarled. He pumped his shotgun. "Stupid old hag! You had to go looking for trouble!"

"Captain!" Ivanov blurted over the radio. "What is it? What's happening?"

Losenko barked into the device. "Just get my boat ready to sail, Alexei! Captain out!"

More bullets hit the back door. It sounded like a machinegun. Losenko guessed that their attackers were trying to shoot out the truck's tires. *A plausible strategy, despite the tires' protective casings.* But how had the robots managed to catch up with a speeding truck? Surely their caterpillar treads weren't capable of such speed?

"Who...?" he began.

Josef must have been wondering the same thing. He pounded the butt of his shotgun against the partition behind him and yelled at the driver. "Speak up, idiot! Who's shooting at us now?"

"A Jeep," Mitka shouted back from the cab. Glass shattered as a bullet took out his side-view mirror. Angry voices hollered at the truck in Russian. "Two metal lovers. A driver and a gunman. Machinegun mounted in the back."

Losenko wanted to make sure he'd heard correctly.

"Humans? People are firing on us?"

"Circuit-sucking collaborators!" she spat. "Traitors!"

Not machines then, but humans. And, from the sound of them, Russian conscripts. Losenko was appalled and sickened to find himself under fire from the very people he had sworn to defend. Had Mother Russia—and all of mankind—truly sunk so low?

Grushka grabbed onto his arm.

"Listen to me, Captain. We can't stay on this road for long. It's not safe. But there's a speedboat hidden along the river not far from here. We can get you to that."

"Grushka!" Josef lurched to his feet, almost hitting his head on the roof of the compartment. Veins bulged beneath his hairless scalp, and he brandished his shotgun. "What are you saying, you old cow? That's our boat. We can't give it away to strangers!"

"Shut up, you selfish lummox!" Bloody spittle sprayed from her lips. "These people have a submarine. A *Russian* submarine. That's our Navy we're talking about, maybe all that's left of it."

Josef was unconvinced.

"We don't owe them anything!"

"What about the machines?" she challenged him. "You want those bloodthirsty monsters to get their cold metal hands on that sub?" She pointed at Losenko and his men. "Who do you think is going to stop those things except men like these?"

Josef sneered.

"Don't you get it? *Nobody* can stop them. It's all over now."

"So you're just going to roll over and die then?" Grushka pursed her lips, took a drag of her cigarette, and blew smoke at him. "I always knew you were no good for anything!"

"Bitch!"

For a second, Losenko feared that the hairless bruiser was going to shoot the older woman with his shotgun. He weighed his chances of disarming Josef, and found them far from encouraging. And the last thing he wanted was for the gun to go off next to that carton of explosive cocktails.

"I'm right, and you know it," Grushka taunted him. "Do your duty, you miserable son of a bitch!"

Josef lowered his gun.

"All right, all right! Anything to shut you up!" He pounded his fist against the bulkhead behind him. "Go for the boat!" he ordered the driver.

Machinegun fire peppered the door. A ruptured tire blew, throwing the truck to one side, but it kept on going. A reinforced steel frame allowed the vehicle to roll on even with a deflated tire.

Furious voices called on them to surrender.

"Damnit!" Grushka yelled at the driver. "What do you think you're doing, leading them on a scenic tour of the countryside? Shake those leeches!"

The armored truck swerved off the road. It sped across the open tundra, bouncing down a rocky slope. The bumpy ride tossed Losenko and others about the cargo hold, making him grateful for the padding on the walls. Grushka braced herself and sucked on her cigarette. The Molotov cocktails rattled in their carton.

The other seamen braced themselves against the walls as well. The bone-jarring impacts left Losenko battered and bruised.

Then the gunfire abated. Had they lost their pursuers for a moment? Losenko wondered how much longer it would take them to reach the boat. And whether the Jeep would chase them down to the river, over the open country. And in the midst of it all, he was still trying to get used to the fact that his own countrymen were trying to kill him.

On behalf of the robots.

Abruptly the driver slammed on the brakes, almost throwing Losenko from the bench. Grushka leapt to her feet. She unbolted the rear doors, but didn't yet open them. A wide grin revealed a mouthful of missing teeth.

"This is where you get off," she announced

Josef slid the crate of bottles across the floor. "Bar's open, cow. How 'bout you fix those bastards a drink or two?"

"You read my mind." She grabbed the nearest bottle and lit the fuse with her cigarette. Losenko watched with alarm as the wadded cloth caught fire. The doors of the compartment were still shut, sealing them inside with the volatile explosives.

Grushka kicked open the doors and hurled the bottle into the moss-covered landscape outside. The bomb went off, igniting a cloud of flammable vapor. The smell of burning gas filled the cool summer air. A wall of fire sprang up to provide cover for the open truck. Clouds of roiling black smoke suggested that sugar, glue, or some other thickening agent had been added to the combustible cocktail. She was busy lighting another bomb before the flames from the first had even died down.

"I'll hold 'em off," she promised. Her kerchief came loose, revealing a bald spot surrounded by tufts of dry, straw-like brown hair. The wind from the fire blew an uprooted lock off her skull, as she let the kerchief fall to the ground. Clearly she thought this was no time for vanity. "Josef, show them the boat!"

Muttering obscenely under his breath, the big man shoved the sailors out of the armored truck.

"Move it, you cock-sucking pains in the ass." He jumped out of the cargo hold, then hurried down the slope toward the marshy shore of a swiftly coursing river, almost certainly the Ponoy. Swaying rushes sprouted along a narrow strip of beach. A heap of rotting timbers were piled high at the edge of the water. Josef took hold of the wooden planks and started tossing them aside. "I can't believe I let that witch talk me into this!"

The rushes and timbers concealed a small fiberglass skiff powered by a single outboard motor. The humble craft had room for maybe six passengers. Stagnant water pooled in the floor of the boat, covered in a coat of algae. A topless mermaid was crudely painted on the side of the hull. Cyrillic lettering spelled out the craft's name: *Rusalka*. An aquatic siren that lured men to their doom.

Not exactly the Gorshkov, Losenko thought, *but it might get us back to port.*

Assuming it didn't spring a leak along the way.

Wasting no time, he and his two men helped Josef get *Rusalka* into the water. The young sailors, revived by the task at hand, piled into the boat and starting fumbling with the motor. Losenko hesitated before joining them. "Come with us," he urged Josef. "You and Grushka and the driver."

What was the driver's name again? Mitka?

"Come with you where?" Josef challenged, mockery in his voice. His beefy arms were folded across his chest. "Do you know where you're going in that glorious sub of yours?"

Losenko couldn't lie to him.

"No."

"I thought as much." Josef backed away from the shore. "Go on! I've got better things to do than stand around waiting for you to get out of my life."

"Captain, please!" The men called out for him to hurry.

Losenko wondered how long they would wait for him. "We have to get away!"

Bowing to the inevitable, he splashed through the chilly water toward the boat. Mud and silt sucked at his heels. Icy water filled up his boots. An eager seaman helped him aboard, and *Rusalka* rocked beneath his feet, but, mercifully, did not take on water as he plopped down onto a damp plastic bench. The other sailor fired up the outboard motor.

Josef watched the boat pull away from the river bank. He shook his shorn head in disgust. "You had better be worth this!" he called after them.

Midshipman Blasko manned the rudder as *Rusalka* motored down river. The rushing current carried them swiftly away from the dismal beach. A white froth chopped up the water at their stern. Josef, Grushka, and the truck disappeared behind a curve in the Ponoy. A rocky ridge, coated with purplish-red lichen, hid the fractious civilians from view.

Climbing balls of fire, however, hinted at the furious conflict the submariners had barely escaped. Gunfire echoed across the water. A distant explosion rippled the surface of the river.

The din of battle receded into the distance, gradually replaced only by the steady chug of the motor. A somber hush fell over the men in the boat. Blasko finally broke the silence.

"You think they made it, sir?"

"I hope so, Mr. Blasko." It pained Losenko to realize that they would probably never know. He found himself deeply moved by what Grushka and her comrades had risked for them. They were just civilians, ordinary citizens, but they had fought as bravely as any professional soldier or sailor. Looking back toward the shore, he raised his hand in salute.

Your struggle, and your sacrifices, will not be forgotten.

Blasko continued to work the rudder.

"Your orders, sir?"

Losenko turned his face forward.

"Back to the boat. Full speed ahead."

A determined look came into his eyes. His jaw set firmly. This mission had been a costly one, but not without purpose. He had lost many good men, but he had gained something, too.

A people worth fighting for.

CHAPTER TWELVE

2018

"Shoot, *damnit*—don't jam on me now!"

Firing continuously, the Terminator advanced toward the totem pole, which was rapidly turning into a toothpick. Bullets gouged the wood. Molly fumbled anxiously with her own weapon, while searching for someplace to run. Too many yards of open space separated her from the next convenient source of shelter; she'd be cut to ribbons before she got three paces. Her sidearm was still holstered at her hip, but that was just a pea-shooter compared to the Terminator's Kalashnikov.

She was trapped.

The only consolation was the sound of alarms going off all over the camp. Church bells rung from the chapel steeple, signaling a full retreat. With luck, all those surprise evacuation drills would finally pay off, not that it was likely to do her any good. Molly hoped that Sitka was already making tracks from the camp, dragging Doc Rathbone behind her.

Wonder if Geir has made it to the plane yet.

The Terminator was only a few feet away when its AK-47 ran out of ammo. Unable to reload, it held on to the weapon anyway. A sharpened bayonet was mounted on the rifle's smoking barrel. The eleven-inch blade was also an effective tool for termination.

Molly got ready to make a run for it. T-600s were slow and bulky; she might be able to get past it. Unless it was bluffing. Terminators could be tricky; she'd known T-600s to play possum during a battle, pretending to be out of commission in order to lure human targets into range. She wouldn't put it past this one-eyed monstrosity to try to put one over on her. Make her think it didn't have any bullets left.

Gotta chance it, though.

Before she could sprint out from behind the totem pole, however, the distinctive roar of a chainsaw drowned out the alarms. Ernie Wisetongue charged the invader, holding a whirring chainsaw above his head like a maniac in an old slasher movie. His sealskin parka made him look like Nanook of the North.

"Get away from there, you lifeless abomination!" he bellowed. His muscular arms were used to working with saws and axes. "You don't belong here!"

Was he trying to rescue her, or just pissed off at the destruction of his sculpture? Molly didn't know or care.

"Hit it on the left!" she shouted. "It's blind in its left eye!"

Taking her advice, Ernie lunged to one side and angled the chainsaw at the Terminator's metal vertebrae, hoping to decapitate the machine. But tooth-edged chain caught on an armored shoulder-plate instead. Kickback threw the business end of the chainsaw back into Ernie's shoulder.

The artist shrieked and staggered backward. Dark

venous blood painted his face incarnadine. He lost his grip on the chainsaw, which landed at his feet, just missing his toes. Ernie flopped over on the snow. He clutched his mutilated shoulder. Blood spurted through his fingers.

No! Molly thought, gasping in horror. Only hours ago, the avuncular sculptor had bestowed his blessing on Roger and Tammi, and—by extension—the entire community. Now he lay thrashing only a few feet away, another innocent victim of Skynet's brutality.

Discarding the jammed rifle, she angrily drew her pistol. *Damn it! He's worth a hundred of you monsters!* She peppered the Terminator with small-arms fire. *He had your number, you heartless fucker!*

The bullets distracted the Terminator, who turned away from Ernie for a moment. The injured sculptor dragged himself across the bloody sawdust, taking refuge in a children's maze composed of linked metal drums. He crawled into the tunnel before the T-600 could impale him with its bayonet. The machine chose to focus on the discarded chainsaw instead. Releasing the empty AK-47, it picked up the lethal tool. It limped away from the barrels without a backward look at the fine old man it had just maimed. Molly prayed that someone would get to Ernie before he bled to death. In the meantime, she found herself in the sights of the last thing she ever wanted to see.

A Terminator with a chainsaw.

Molly bolted from the playground. The Terminator lumbered after her. Now she had another goal. She just needed to make it uphill to the base of the breaker building, and hope that the lookout stationed there had stayed at his post, just like they'd drilled.

"Come and get me!" she taunted over her shoulder.

"Terminate me! You know you want to!"

She crossed the main street and headed up the slope. The breaker mill, with its outdoor tramway, loomed above her. The raging fire below lit up the night, making it a little easier to see. A quick scan revealed no other Terminators in sight, so maybe they *were* dealing with just one lone straggler. Even so, the damn machine had done enough damage. She'd lost count of how many of her people the one-eyed monster had killed already.

Breathing hard, she glanced back over her shoulder to make certain it was still following her.

C'mon, tin man. Don't give up on me now!

To her dismay, however, she saw that the T-600 had paused in the middle of the camp's main drag. Further on down the road were the bunkhouses and infirmary. Molly could hear a noisy exodus underway, as desperate families hurried to escape with their meager possessions. Children were crying, while impatient voices shouted at them to keep moving. Trucks, buses, and snowmobiles braved the icy roads leading away from the camp.

The fire was spreading from building to building, adding to the refugees' danger. If the Terminator didn't get them, the smoke and flames might. Resistance soldiers fired from the upper windows, striking the T-600, trying to drive it away from the escaping families. Their wild shots bounced harmlessly off its exoskeleton.

Attracted by the commotion, the Terminator abandoned its pursuit of Molly. Turning to the right, it took a step toward the bunkhouses. The bloodstained chainsaw revved as if hungry for another taste of human flesh.

Molly thought about Tammi and her baby.

"Hey! Don't turn your back on me!" she hollered at the machine, hoping to lure it away from the others.

She jumped up and down, waving her hands, firing her pistol into the air. "Remember me? I brought that god-damn mountain down on top of you and your buddies! You want payback, Popeye? Well, here I am!"

She was wasting her breath. Terminators didn't care about revenge. Taunting it wasn't going to get her any-where. All it cared about was scoring the maximum number of victims.

She racked her brain to come up with something that would do the trick, that would instantly move her to the top of the machine's to-do list—but what? Inspiration failed her.

What would John Connor do?

All at once, it hit her.

"I know where John Connor is!" she lied. The leg-endary freedom fighter was supposed to be Public Enemy Number One as far as Skynet was concerned. His propaganda broadcasts had been inspiring the Resistance for fifteen years now. People even said that he was some kind of prophesied hero, destined to lead humanity to ultimate victory over the machines.

Rumor had it the machines had been trying to kill Connor since before Judgment Day. Molly wasn't entire-ly sure she bought all that, but maybe Skynet did?

"You want John Connor?" she said, her voice raw from shouting. "Come and get me. Make me talk!"

That got the thing's attention. It forgot all about the evacuation efforts further down the road, and refocused its sensor on Molly instead. Chainsaw in hand, it stomped up the hill after her, away from the children and other fleeing humans. Molly knew it would gladly take her apart piece by piece, to find out what she knew.

So now she just had to keep away from that chainsaw.

Spinning, she took off again in the direction of the mill.

Running uphill was no fun, as her lungs burned in her chest, but she had adrenaline to spare. There was nothing like a Terminator on your heels to add a little extra spring to your step. She reached the base of the breaker in record time. To her relief, the flames hadn't yet reached the mill itself. The multistory wooden structure rose in tiers against the side of the mountain. The tramway—a large wooden chute that climbed at a fifty-degree angle all the way to the top—resembled an amputated segment of an old roller-coaster. The bottom of the chute didn't reach the ground; it hung suspended like a ski ramp about seven feet above the snow, held aloft by thick wooden beams and posts.

A rope ladder hung from the end of the ramp. Molly stuck her sidearm back into her belt and scrambled up onto the tramway, then hauled the ladder up after her. Smooth wooden planks, coated in ice and snow, challenged her balance. Her eyes searched the top of the tramway, which was shrouded in darkness. Decades ago, when the mine was still operating, a conveyer belt had carried the raw ore up the tramway to the top of the mill. These days, the ramp had been converted into Alaska's biggest booby-trap.

Assuming there was still someone left to trigger it.

"Skid row!" she shouted ahead, warning the lookout to get ready. Who was stationed there tonight? Vic Folger? The thirty-five year-old African-American, who had once coached high school soccer in Wasilla, was a dedicated foot soldier. Hopefully, he'd still be manning his post.

"Skid row!"

A flashlight blinked once at the top of the tramway.

Good, she thought. *We're set then*. She crossed her fingers. If they were lucky, the Terminator wouldn't know what had hit it. The timing was going to be tricky, though. They only had one shot at this. *We need to make it count.*

"Here I am!" she called, goading the T-600 as it climbed the hill after her. "Don't keep me waiting! John Connor!"

The sight and sound of the whirring chainsaw gave her second thoughts about acting as bait. Ernie Wisetongue's grisly injury flashed through her mind. It took all her nerve not to scramble to the top; instead, she stood a couple of yards above the bottom of the ramp, while her blood-splattered pursuer drew near.

She waited until it was lined up with the chute before throwing herself over the side. Her fingers grabbed onto the raised wooden edge.

"Now!" she yelled to Folger. "Let it rip!"

An axe chopped through a rope several yards above her head. A greased log the size of a full-grown pine came skidding down the tramway. Hauling the 1400-pound piece of timber to the top of the ramp then hitching it in place had been a back-breaking chore that had taken the better part of a day several months ago. More than one guerilla had nearly lost a limb before they got the trap set up. Would all that labor pay off?

They were about to find out.

The battering ram gained speed as it slid down the chute. Clinging to the side, her legs dangling high above the ground, Molly hoped to God that the log wouldn't sideswipe her fingers on its way down. It raced past her, zooming straight at the Terminator.

Molly grinned in anticipation of the collision to come.

That avalanche didn't stop you? she thought grimly. *Let's try again!*

But the T-600 wasn't going to be taken unawares—not twice. At the last second it threw itself forward, falling face-first into the snow in front of the ramp. The log whooshed over the prone Terminator, passing several feet above the murderous machine. It flew like a missile through the air before smashing into a repair shop downhill from the breaker. Wood and glass splintered loudly as the log tore through the smaller building before coming to rest somewhere inside.

Molly prayed nobody was still inside, even as she cursed herself for underestimating the Terminator's reflexes and ability to recognize a trap. When was she going to learn? The hulking machines were smarter than they looked.

"Fuck! Fuck! Fuck!"

The Terminator got back on its feet, still gripping the chainsaw. There would be no second shot from above.

Grunting, Molly hauled herself back up onto the tramway. The chainsaw restarted below her, dangerously close to her dangling legs.

Move it, she told herself, *while you've still got legs to lose*. She pulled first one foot, then the other over the side of the chute. The close call had left her heart pounding. She took a second to catch her breath.

The Terminator stomped loudly beneath the tramway, several feet below.

"Hurry!" Folger called out to her from atop the tramway. "Up here!"

A second voice urged her on as well.

"You heard him! Shake a leg!"

Who? Molly thought. Was someone up there with Vic?

Before she could place the voice, the whirring blade of the chainsaw tore through the floor of the tramway like the fin of a great white shark. The tooth-edged chain was only inches away from her and getting closer. She realized that the T-600 could sense the heat of her body through the bottom of the ramp. The chainsaw cut through the wooden floor like it was made out of plywood.

Uh-oh, Molly thought. As a child, before Judgment Day, she had seen a magician cut a woman in half. The magician had put the woman back together again afterward. Somehow she doubted the Terminator knew that trick.

Finding her footing, she scrambled up the tramway, trying to put as much distance as possible between herself and the chainsaw. T-600s weren't climbers; it was doubtful it could scale the ramp to come after her. She just had to get out of reach of the saw, then figure out what to do next. But what was Plan B?

The icy slope was steep and slippery. Molly needed both her hands and legs to clamber toward the top. The Terminator yanked back the chainsaw once it realized she was too high up to reach from the ground. Molly thought she had it made, until she heard the chainsaw chewing into the wooden support posts. The entire structure lurched beneath her, throwing her to the side.

She lost her footing and started to slide back down the chute. Her fingers dug into a crack between two loose planks, arresting her fall before she lost too much ground. A wooden post gave way loudly. Broken beams crashed to the earth below. The tramway swayed back and forth like a drunken snake.

Molly gritted her teeth and hung on for dear life. Something smacked against the ramp a few inches above her head. She looked up to see the knotted end of a rope bouncing back and forth across the upper planks.

"Grab the rope!" a female voice hollered. "Whole thing's coming apart!"

Tell me about it! The tramway was disintegrating beneath her. Loose planks plummeted to the ground even as the Terminator hacked away at the chute's supports, like a robotic lumberjack. The huge wooden structure teetered on the brink of collapse. With no time to lose, Molly grabbed onto the rope with her right hand. A hard tug confirmed that the lifeline was secured to something higher up, so she took hold of the rope with both hands.

Bracing the soles of her boots against the quaking wood beneath her, she sprinted up the slope even as the floor fell apart behind her.

Where's that old-time conveyor belt, she thought, *now that I need it?*

Unfortunately, the tramway's moving parts hadn't worked since the Great Depression. She raced against time—and the tramway's imminent collapse—with the Terminator waiting to intercept her when she fell. Unsure if she was going to make it, Molly was only a few yards away from the top of the slope when, one by one, the planks gave way beneath her feet.

Gravity seized her and her legs plunged through the gap. Her stomach swung into the jagged edge of the upper slope, with only the rope holding her aloft as she dangled several hundred feet above a rocky fate below. The exhaust from the chainsaw rose to choke her. Looking down, she saw the Terminator's single red "eye" peering up at her.

The rope began to slip through her gloved hands.

She snapped at the coils, trying to snag it with her teeth, but it was just out of reach.

She was losing her grip.

"Got you!" Slender hands grabbed her by the wrist. Molly felt herself yanked upward, back onto what was left of the tramway. Looking up, she saw a hooded figure lying face-down on the ramp. Further up, leaning out from the roof of the breaker building, Vic Folger held onto her rescuer's ankles. Veins bulged on his neck as he labored to pull the chain of bodies to safety.

"Hang on! Not letting you fall!"

Molly wasn't sure how he did it, but within moments Folger had them all atop a small platform, looking out over the disintegrating chute. Cast-iron storm doors covered the top of the open shaft that had once received the raw ore. A wooden catwalk circled the pit. The big soccer coach was panting from exertion, sweat dripping down his face. An Uzi was slung over his shoulder.

The other figure, her face hidden by the hood of an ill-fitting parka, gave Molly a bear hug.

"See! Told you! Made it all the way up!"

No longer on the verge of sliding to her death, Molly finally placed the voice. She shoved back the hood to reveal a face full of freckles and an impish expression. Unkempt red bangs spilled over wide green eyes.

"Sitka!" Molly broke free from the girl's embrace. "What the fuck are you doing here? You were supposed to hit the road with Doc!"

The teenager shrugged.

"Wanted to see the machine get squashed."

"Guess we're both out of luck then." Molly was annoyed that the girl had skipped out on the evacuation, but now was no time for a lecture. The tramway trembled a few feet away, as if the rest of it was about to collapse at any second. A tremor threw Folger against a decrepit guardrail that cracked beneath his weight. Molly grabbed onto his arm to keep him from going overboard.

"Everybody back!" she shouted. "Pronto!"

The humans sprinted away from the crumbling tramway, just as the entire structure gave way entirely. With a tremendous roar, hundreds of feet of timber posts and planks exploded, raining down on the camp below like the fossilized skeleton of some enormous wooden dinosaur. An eruption of splinters and white powder was thrown into the air, reminding Molly of the avalanche she had set off less than a day ago.

Safe up on the catwalk—at least for the moment—she backed away from the thunderous crash. *Probably too much to hope*, she thought, *that the Terminator got buried beneath all that.*

"Skookum!" Sitka exclaimed, impressed by the sheer awesomeness of the destruction. The top of the mill offered a bird's-eye view of the burning camp below. Billowing black smoke and sky-high flames made it hard to tell how the evacuation was going. The alarms had gone silent as the conflagration engulfed the abandoned buildings. Molly could feel the heat upon her face even from so far away.

She noted with alarm that the fire was moving steadily closer to them, almost as relentless in its own way as the T-600. The heaped remains of the tramway were like a bonfire waiting to be lit.

We don't want to be here when that happens.

Then a powerful engine roared overhead, the sound piercing the smoke. Folger snatched his rifle from his shoulder and aimed for the sky, but Molly grabbed onto the barrel and pushed it down.

"Wait. That's no HK." The Hunter-Killers' VTOL turbofans had a distinct reverberation that was impossible
to mistake. Besides, Alaska was a big place; the nearest
Skynet airbase was hundreds of miles away. "I think I
know who that is."

Sure enough, *Thunderbird* swooped out of the smoke,
circling once above the camp before banking toward the
north. Molly felt a lump in her throat as she watched her
lover's vintage fighter disappear into the distance. She
doubted that he had seen her atop the mill, but at least she
knew now that he had made it down to the glacier okay,
and taken to the air in time to get away. He'd be waiting
for her at the rendezvous point... if she ever got there.

"Geir!" Sitka waved goodbye to the plane. "Think he
saw us?"

"Sure he did," she lied. "You can ask him yourself
later." Then she shoved the girl toward Folger. "Get out
of here," she told the soccer coach, "and take this mangy
stray with you." A severe expression said that she
brooked no disagreement. "She gives you any trouble at
all, you have my full permission to knock her out cold!"

Sitka stuck out her tongue.

"Saved your life," she reminded Molly. "You're
welcome."

"What about you, chief?" Folger asked.

Molly leaned out over the railing. Fourteen stories
below, a hulking steel figure stepped away from the ruins
of the tramway. It crooked its neck, gazing up from the
alley below. A single red dot locked eyes with Molly.

"I'll catch up with you later," she said grimly. "I'm not
done here yet."

CHAPTER THIRTEEN

2003

"Still no word from Moscow, sir?"

Losenko met with his senior officers in the wardroom. Weeks had passed since the massacre on the mainland and the *Gorshkov* was safely back beneath the sea. The sub had surfaced long enough to scan the airwaves on all frequencies, and Losenko had summoned Ivanov and the others to brief them on the results.

The captain shook his head at Trotsky. A bottle of red wine rested in the middle of the conference table; the ship's doctor had prescribed a daily glass for all personnel. The strontium in the wine was supposed to provide some degree of protection against radiation poisoning. The wine had been found in an underground cellar back on the mainland. The doctor had judged it safe to consume.

"Moscow is gone. We need to accept that. Only static greets our requests for further instructions." Losenko was starting to get used to being autonomous. He had been sorely tempted to lob one of their remaining ballistic missiles at that cursed factory south of Murmansk.

Only the memory of the heroic civilians in the vicinity had deterred him. "But Pushkin intercepted something I want you all to hear," he continued.

"What is it, Captain?" Ivanov asked.

"A pirate transmission," Losenko explained. "From the Americas. It's on a repeating loop, airing twenty-four hours a day from shifting locations. Its range and frequency are constantly shifting as well; Pushkin stumbled onto it by accident while searching for communications from the rest of the fleet. He was unable to get a lock on its exact point of origin, so he suspects that it's being routed through various mobile transmitters to mask the location of the sender."

"America?" Predictably, Ivanov reacted with suspicion and simmering hostility. His face flushed darkly. "More lies from that general, Ashdown?"

"No," Losenko said brusquely. The XO's vengeful attitude, however understandable, was becoming tiresome. "This is something different." He rose from his seat at the head of the table and lifted a sound-powered phone from its cradle on the wall, then spoke into it. "Mr. Pushkin, you may commence the playback."

"Aye, aye, sir." The senior radio operator channeled the recording to the wardroom's overhead speaker system. Static crackled in the background, but he had applied his expertise to cleaning up the audio as much as possible.

A gruff, male voice, speaking English with an American accent, spoke from the loudspeakers.

"This is John Connor. Some of you may know me. Most of you don't. But that's not important. What matters is that you understand what's happened to our world. And what happens next."

"Connor?" Ivanov interrupted. "Do we know this Connor?"

The name meant nothing to Losenko. He raised a finger to his lips.

"Just listen, Alexei."

"Earlier this year," the voice continued, "an artificial intelligence system known as Skynet, designed by the Pentagon to oversee United States defense operations, became self-aware. It developed a mind of its own. And Skynet decided to eliminate the only major threat to its existence: the human race.

"Skynet launched the missiles on Judgment Day. Skynet started the war. Not the United States. Not humanity. Skynet."

Ivanov bristled.

"More disinformation! The Americans refuse to take responsibility for their crimes!"

"Quiet!" Losenko shot the intemperate XO a warning look.

"But Judgment Day was just the beginning. Skynet will not stop until it has fulfilled its primary objective: the complete elimination of every man, woman, and child on the face of the Earth. To that end it has already begun creating an army of machines to carry out its campaign of eradication. Robot soldiers called Terminators. Unmanned Hunter-Killer aircraft. The designs for these devices are based on top-secret military prototypes. Early models are already out there. And they will be coming for you. It might not be today, it might not be tomorrow, but it will be soon."

Losenko recalled the unstoppable robots he had encountered in Russia. The ones that had killed nearly forty of his men.

Terminators, he mused. *A fitting name for such abominations.*

"I won't lie to you," the voice continued. "We face a long and difficult war against Skynet and its killing machines. But the Terminators can be fought—and they can be destroyed." Losenko was impressed by the utter conviction he heard in Connor's voice. "We can win this war, but only if we come together now as a united species, committed to unwavering resistance against our common enemy. Whatever issues divided us in the past don't matter anymore. Race, religion, nationality, gender... forget about all that. It's us against the machines now, and our future depends on us realizing that in time."

Connor's voice grew more pensive.

"My mother always taught me that there is no fate but what we make. I truly believe that. Despite everything, our destiny is still in our hands. We just have to fight for it... together.

"This is John Connor. If you can hear this, you are the Resistance."

The recording ended.

Losenko let Connor's ominous words sink in. He hoped each officer's English was up to the task of appreciating what they had just heard. Then he slid a stack of folders, labeled "classified," across the top of the table.

"Enclosed are translations of the text of the broadcast. Please consult them for any nuances you might have missed."

The officers passed the folders along. They began perusing the transcripts. Except for Ivanov, who disdained to even open his. He shoved the folder away from him.

"With respect, Captain, why are we wasting time with such nonsense?" He snorted derisively. "Skynet? Terminators? This isn't even good propaganda. It's science fiction." He shook his head. "Do they take us for fools?"

"You forget, Alexei," Losenko reminded him, "I have seen these Terminators with my own eyes. They killed nearly forty of our men. I observed the factory that birthed them, built right on Russian soil." Painful memories added an edge to his tone. "I believe this John Connor knows what he is talking about."

"But how, Captain?" Lieutenant Pavlinko asked. "Who is he? From where did he get his information?"

"I don't know," Losenko confessed. "Perhaps he helped program Skynet. Perhaps he was an investigative journalist. All I know is that I have not heard a better explanation for everything that has befallen us since—" *What did the American call it again?* "Since Judgment Day."

Ivanov stubbornly clung to his own vendetta.

"I have another explanation: psychological warfare. The Americans are trying to sow fear and confusion, using this ridiculous comic-book fantasy." He threw up his hands in exasperation. "I know what you saw, Captain. I don't doubt your word—or the evidence of your senses. But surely there were men operating those machines. Enemy forces perpetuating a shameless hoax by remote-control."

"The XO has a point," Chief Navigator Igor Trotsky conceded. "It could all be a trick. First there was that initial report about the 'computer malfunction,' now this business about a rogue A.I. If I may speak frankly, sir, it sounds a bit dubious to me."

Losenko understood the men's skepticism. They had

not looked into the unblinking red eyes of the enemy as he had.

"But why would any rational person launch a first strike on the world, for no discernable reason?" As far as he was concerned, that was the most compelling argument in favor of the Skynet scenario. "It sounds fantastic, I know, but I can more readily accept that an insane computer would set the world on fire, than the idea any human general or president would do so."

"The Americans have resorted to nuclear weapons before," Ivanov reminded him. "Hiroshima... Nagasaki."

"That was nearly sixty years ago, during a world war." Losenko did not accept the comparison. "Perhaps you've forgotten already, but the United States and the Motherland were *not* at each other's throats in the days before the attack. This sub was not on alert." He vividly recalled how shocked he'd been by the sudden emergency directive that had come from Moscow. "Judgment Day struck without warning—as if a switch had been flipped."

Perhaps when Skynet was turned on?

"Is there anything else, Captain?" Pavlinko asked. His voice made it sound as if he didn't know what to believe.

"Not at present," Losenko replied. "Naturally, this theory needs to be verified by as many independent sources as we can locate. For the moment I ask only that you review the transcripts—and attempt to keep your minds open."

"Aye, aye, sir." Pavlinko finished off his wine. No doubt he felt as if he needed a drink. "Shall we share this... intelligence... with the crew?"

"I think not. Let us keep this to ourselves for now." Losenko had not yet decided how best to reveal the truth about Skynet. He was uncertain how they might react to the news that mankind was at war with its own machines. For the time being his instinct was to be sparing with this information, although in the long run that was probably a lost cause. Gossip was as essential as oxygen aboard a submarine. Chances were, Connor's astounding claims were already spreading.

"That will be all for now. You are dismissed."

The men gathered up their folders and headed for the doorway. Losenko heard them whispering and muttering to each other. Ivanov sneered at his own copy of the transcript, as though he might leave it behind, then grudgingly tucked it under his arm. He marched briskly for the exit.

"Not so fast, Mr. Ivanov." Losenko indicated that the XO should remain. "A moment of your time."

Ivanov gave the captain a wary look. He looked less than enthused at the prospect of engaging his superior in further discussion. "I am needed on the conn," he stated.

"Chief Komarov can manage for a few more moments," Losenko insisted. He waited until the other officers had departed, leaving them alone in the wardroom. "Close the door, Alexei. We need to talk."

The XO surrendered to the inevitable. He secured the door and turned back toward the captain. However, he declined to sit back down at the table. "What is there to talk about, sir? This ridiculous radio drama about a deranged computer?" He stood stiffly at attention. "I believe I have already given you my opinion on the subject."

"That you have," Losenko conceded. He gestured for Ivanov to sit down. "But it is your attitude that concerns me now, Alexei. There is an anger inside you that shows no sign of abating. I have felt it, and so has the crew."

He adopted a sorrowful tone, not a scolding one. "It worries me, Alexei. It is not like you."

He remembered the first time he had met Ivanov. The younger officer had immediately struck Losenko as a man of integrity and sound judgment, not to mention an exemplary husband and father with an enviable family life. The captain had made it a point to take Alexei under his wing. He had been, if not quite young enough to be the son Losenko had never had, at the very least a younger brother of sorts. Indeed, after his own painful divorce, Losenko had sometimes shared holidays with Alexei and his family. They had been generous that way.

"Of course I am angry," Ivanov retorted. He reluctantly resumed his place at the table. "Have you forgotten what was done to our country, to the world?"

Losenko recalled the wasteland Russia had become. The radioactive ruins of Murmansk.

"I can never forget that. You have every right to be angry. But, for your own sake, as well as the boat's, you cannot allow thoughts of revenge to consume you. Or to cloud your judgment."

"So what do you suggest, Captain?" Ivanov countered. "That I consult a psychiatrist? A grief counselor?" His scornful tone conveyed more than just a military man's customary aversion to having his head shrunk. A humorless laugh escaped him. "I'm not sure there are any left!"

In fact, Losenko sometimes regretted the lack of having a professional psychological counselor aboard. Boris Aleksin—the *Gorshkov*'s medical officer—was an able physician, but he was not equipped to cope with over a hundred men traumatized by the loss of everything they knew. The doctor had run out of sedatives and antidepressants weeks ago. Suicide attempts and breakdowns were becoming regular occurrences. Just last week, a distraught seaman had succeeded in hanging himself in the engine room....

"We all must deal with our grief in some manner, or else go mad," the captain said solemnly. He spoke as a worried friend, not a disappointed superior. "Tell me, Alexei, have you cried for your wife, or for your daughter?"

Ivanov jerked backward, as though he had been slapped in the face. His expression darkened. For a second Losenko thought the young man might move to strike him, but then Ivanov managed to regain his composure.

"With all due respect, Captain, you go too far. That is none of your concern."

"The mental health and stability of my XO is very much my concern," Losenko stated. "You must mourn your family, Alexei, if you are to endure the trials ahead."

"Easy for you to say," Ivanov shot back. "The Navy was your only family." His face was set in stone. A muscle twitched beneath his cheek; a facial tic that had become more pronounced since Judgment Day. "I will weep for my loved ones when the Americans have paid for their sins."

Losenko let Ivanov's cruel assessment pass.

"And if this 'Skynet' is indeed responsible?"

Ivanov shrugged. "Who built Skynet?"

"The Americans have already suffered the consequences of their folly," Losenko reminded him. Mushroom clouds still rose above Alaska in his dreams. "We ourselves saw to that."

"Good!" Ivanov said emphatically. "That knowledge alone lets me sleep at night. We did our duty—and struck a mighty blow against the enemy. They got no more than they deserved." He poured himself a fresh glass of wine and gulped it down. Under the circumstances, the captain overlooked the indulgence. "Permission to speak frankly, Captain?"

"By all means," Losenko assented. This confrontation was long overdue. They needed to clear the air between them.

Ivanov did not hold back.

"To my eyes, it is you who are having difficulty coping with what has transpired, who refuses to accept the reality of what was done to our country and our people. Instead of feeling the anger you so condemn in me, the righteous fury any true patriot should feel in the wake of so treacherous an attack, you wallow in guilt and melancholy and impotent philosophizing. You seize on this 'John Connor' deception as if hoping it will grant you absolution—for something you have no cause to be ashamed of!"

Losenko did not flinch at the accusations. He waited for Ivanov's diatribe—which had obviously been festering within the other man for some time—to exhaust itself. Then he spoke softly.

"You are mistaken, Alexei," he said. "There is no absolution for me. If Connor's story is true, it only magnifies my guilt because it means that I did not strike back at the enemy, as you put it; instead I was tricked by a machine into killing millions of innocent people."

Ivanov shook his head. "I refuse to believe that."

"But you are not the captain," Losenko said firmly. His voice took on a sterner tone. "I should not have to remind you of that."

Ivanov glowered at him.

"What do you want, *Captain*? My resignation? To confine me to my quarters?" There was no brig aboard

Gorshkov. "I would request reassignment, but I fear that is no longer an option!"

There was still no word from any other subs. As far as they knew, they were the Russian Navy.

"No one is suggesting that you resign," Losenko assured him. "Believe me, I can ill afford to lose my most able officer. I simply want your word, on your family's sacred memory, that you will not let your anger against the Americans override your duty to this ship, and that you will curb your present tendency toward insubordination."

"Insubordination?" Ivanov looked genuinely offended. "How can you even suggest such a thing? I am the *starpom*, not a mutineer!"

Losenko leaned forward.

"Do I have your word, Alexei?"

"You are the captain." Ivanov placed his right hand over his heart. "On the memory of my martyred Yelena and Nadia, I pledge that I will continue to respect the chain of command. You need never question my loyalty— save in one respect."

"Which is?"

Ivanov lowered his hand. He looked squarely into the captain's eyes.

"Do not ask me to forgive the Americans. Not in my heart." A flicker of pain crossed his face. "That is one command that is beyond my ability to obey."

"I understand," Losenko said, taking the young officer at his word. "I can ask no more of you."

But I pray that someday you will find a measure of peace, my friend.

Even in a world now menaced by machines.

A sudden ringing, like the sonorous peal of a church

bell, interrupted the tense encounter. The two officers shared a startled look. Both men knew what the ringing meant. *Gorshkov* had been pinged by another vessel's sonar.

The intercom crackled to life, bearing an urgent message from the sonar room.

"Captain, we have contact! On the surface, bearing straight toward us, speed thirty knots!"

The sub had been found.

But by whom?

CHAPTER FOURTEEN

Perched atop the breaker building, Molly kept watch over the Terminator while Folger and Sitka made their way across the roof to a fire escape at the rear. She was tempted to join them, but she still had unfinished business with the monster below. The Resistance had already lost one camp tonight. She couldn't give the T-600 a chance to track her people to the rendezvous point.

It had done enough damage.

A raging fire was busily consuming the ghost town that had been Molly's home up until less than an hour ago. From the catwalk atop the mill, she could see her own cabin going up in flames. She and Geir had made love there earlier tonight. Now their bed and its cozy comforters, along with whatever keepsakes they had managed to acquire over the years, were nothing but ashes. Her gaze swept over the devastation.

The chapel, the mess hall, the infirmary... all one big funeral pyre. The heat from the fire combated the arctic chill of the night. The air smelled of smoke and soot.

It was hard to imagine that a single machine could be responsible for so much destruction.

All the more reason that it had to be destroyed.

The Terminator bided its time in the alley below, assessing the situation. Its stolen chainsaw hung at its side. Was it waiting for the fire to drive her back down into the open, or was it just keeping watch over her until reinforcements arrived?

Probably wants to take me alive, she guessed, *so Skynet can interrogate me*. Would the machines believe her when she admitted that she had lied about knowing where John Connor was? Or would they just keep torturing her until there was nothing left of her to question?

What the hell, she thought. *It seemed like a good idea at the time.*

Tearing her gaze away from the burning buildings, she surveyed the surrounding terrain. To the west, beyond her torched cabin, the ground descended to the frozen stream. Molly's brow furrowed as she contemplated the icy ribbon, which the more reckless of the camp's offspring had sometimes used for skating. A sly smile lifted the corners of her chapped lips.

That has possibilities.

But before she could put her plan into action, gunfire blared in an alley below. Molly leaned out over the railing to see who on Earth was still around to pick a fight with the T-600; she had hoped that all of her people would have cleared out by now. The glow from the inferno was like a giant torch, illuminating the night the way city streetlights had back before Judgment Day. Even from fourteen stories up, Molly had a perfect view of the conflict going on beneath her.

No! She couldn't believe her eyes.

"Die, you wedding crasher!" Tammi Muckerheide, nee Salzer, fired at the Terminator from behind a sturdy metal ore cart. Its wheels and axles had rusted away generations ago. An M-16 had replaced her bridal bouquet. Military fatigues and a green Kevlar army helmet provided better protection from the elements and the enemy than her second-hand gown. Rage contorted her adolescent features. "You ruined my honeymoon!"

For a second, Molly feared that the pregnant teenager had lost her mind. Had something happened to Roger? Then she spotted Tammi's youthful husband creeping up on the distracted Terminator from behind. Shaky hands gripped a skipole with a tip that had been sharpened to a lethal point. He came up behind the T-600 even as the machine advanced on Tammi, brandishing its blood-stained chainsaw.

A barrage of high-caliber fire, spewing from the flaring muzzle of Tammi's rifle, retarded the Terminator's progress while simultaneously drowning out Roger's stealthy footsteps. She shrieked like a madwoman to keep the machine from checking its rear.

"You like that, metal? I've got plenty more where that comes from! You picked the wrong day to barge in here. This is my friggin' *wedding night*!"

Molly guessed what the newlyweds had in mind. The T-600s had a weak spot at the back of their necks. That was another thing Molly had learned from John Connor's broadcasts; she was glad to see that Roger and Tammi had been paying attention during combat training. A sharp jab to its ventilation system could momentarily impair its motor functions, perhaps long enough for them to permanently disable it.

She had no idea what had possessed the two kids to try

to bushwhack the Terminator this way, but there was a chance their risky plan might work. Molly held her breath, afraid to interfere for fear of tipping the Terminator off.

They pull this off, she thought, *I'll throw them a baby shower myself.*

Roger came up behind the machine, which appeared oblivious to his approach. Tammi eased up on her fire, pretending to reload, to avoid shooting her husband by mistake. She ducked behind the heavy metal cart, and the only sound was the idling chainsaw.

Roger lifted the point of the skipole. The T-600 was a good two feet taller than the boy, so he would have to strike upward to hit the right spot.

Keep to its left, Molly urged him silently. *It's blind on the left!*

Then again, so was Roger. A black eyepatch covered an empty socket.

Do it! Molly thought. The suspense was killing her. *While you've still got a chance!*

A shard of broken glass, left behind from when the log crashed into the repair shop earlier, crunched beneath Roger's feet. It sounded like a rifle shot, even over the rumble of the saw. The Terminator's head jerked around.

Realizing he was screwed, Roger lunged forward with the pole, but, in his haste, struck only a glancing blow off the side of the machine's neck.

"Shit!" the boy exclaimed. He knew he was dead.

"Roger!" Tammi shrieked, this time for real. It would have been funny if it wasn't so horrible. "Oh God, *Roger!*"

The Terminator didn't even turn around. Its right arm swung backward over its shoulder, bringing the chainsaw down upon its target. The whirring chain sliced off

Roger's right arm and a good chunk of his shoulder. The boy screamed and dropped to the ground. The useless skipole clattered onto the snow beside him. His youthful face contorted, and he howled in agony.

Roger was minutes away from bleeding to death, but that was too inefficient for the T-600. The only good thing about the machines was that they didn't believe in playing with their victims. Sadism wasn't in their programming—only eradication. It took just a moment to sever Roger's head cleanly from his shoulders. The mangled body stopped thrashing.

Terminated.

That's gotta be the shortest marriage on record, Molly thought bitterly. She hoped the kids had enjoyed their brief time together. It was all they were going to get.

"Killer! Monster!" Tammi let loose on the Terminator with her M-16. Tears streamed down her face. She made no effort to escape from the oncoming machine. "I loved him, you motherfuckin' machine!"

A satellite dish was bolted to the top of the mill, placed there to pick up encrypted messages from Command. Molly blasted it loose with her pistol, then wrenched it free. She hurled the heavy dish at the Terminator. It smashed harmlessly against the machine's titanium skull, but got its attention for a moment.

It paused and looked back up at Molly.

"Run!" she hollered from atop the mill. She wanted Tammi to live, even if the young widow didn't seem to; no way was Molly going to let the pregnant girl go the way of her husband.

"Save your baby! That's an order!"

The reference to the baby hit a nerve, cutting through Tammi's understandable lust for vengeance. Abandoning her crazed assault, the girl ran, leaving the decapitated body of her beloved behind.

The Terminator hesitated, torn between pursuing Tammi and keeping its eye on Molly.

She helped it make up its mind.

"John Connor!" Molly hurled a loose brick at the T-600. "You want John Connor's address, right? Well, I'm the only human vermin here who knows where that is!" She was tempted to claim that Connor was her brother or something, but that might be pushing it. Skynet doubtless had a comprehensive dossier on his closest friends and associates.

His wife's supposed to be a medic....

Tammi's racing footsteps faded away as she disappeared from sight, moving in the direction of the other evacuees. Satisfied that the girl now had a fighting chance at living to see the sunrise, Molly looked to her own survival. When planning the layout of the camp, she had made certain that every key location offered multiple escape routes. Glancing around, she saw ropes and bungee cables stacked all along the catwalk. She tied one end of a cable to a sturdy post, then flung the rest of the rope over the railing.

Forget the fire escape, she thought. *I'm in a hurry.*

Her heart pounding, she rappelled down the side of the building, just around the corner from where she'd left the Terminator. As her feet touched down on the snowy gravel, she fired her pistol into the air.

"John Conner! Going, going, *gone*...!"

The T-600 wasted no time coming after her. She heard the chainsaw even before it rounded the corner. Its luciferous red gaze locked on her and didn't let go.

Molly bolted for the river, taking care to head in a

different direction than Tammi and the others. The heat from the burning camp made her sweat beneath her parka. The wind blew smoke in her face, stinging her eyes and throat. She was faster than the T-600, but a lot more tired. Adrenaline could only keep her going so long, especially after only a couple of hours sleep.

Fatigue poisons burned her leg muscles. She was breathing hard. Ragged exhalations puffed from her lips, misting in the frigid night air. The wind chill felt like it was at least fifty below.

I can't keep this up much longer.

The frozen stream beckoned to her, looking like a winding white ribbon about twenty feet across. An icy glaze coated the rushing current underneath. A wooden footbridge crossed the river further upstream, but that wasn't her destination. Crossing the bridge was the last thing on her mind.

The rough terrain pitched sharply downward in a perfect hill for sledding, as proven by the deep impressions carved into the snow. Another ancient ore cart rested at the top of the slope. The camp's kids often used it as a fort during frenzied snowball fights. It offered little refuge against a Terminator.

Not wanting to risk a spill, Molly slid down the hill on her butt, all the way onto the frozen stream. Then she half-ran, half-crawled out to the middle of the river, where the ice was thickest, before clambering to her feet just in time to see the Terminator stomping down the incline after her. Its ponderous steel legs sank deeply into the snow, preventing it from slipping. Frozen blood caked its intimidating endoskeleton. The chainsaw whirred in its grip.

No more running.

She faced the Terminator across a glistening expanse of white. Her aching legs were grateful for the respite. Panting, she silently dared the machine to follow her out onto the river. A T-600 weighed over 800 pounds. Could the frozen river support that much weight? Molly was gambling her life that it couldn't.

"Here I am!" she taunted. "Come and get me. No guts, no glory!"

The machine paused at the edge of the stream. T-600s couldn't drown, but they couldn't swim either. Its red sensor scanned the ice, calculating the risk factors. It stepped tentatively onto the frozen surface, which cracked loudly beneath its weight. Water seeped up through minute fissures. The Terminator withdrew its foot, retreating further back onto the shore.

Molly nearly screamed in frustration.

"What's the matter? Chicken?" She couldn't stand here all night, waiting for the machine to make its move. If she crossed the river, the Terminator would just take the bridge upstream and keep after her, maybe all the way to the rendezvous point. *Should have had someone blow the bridge on the way out.* She scanned the black and smoky sky. Still no sign of HKs, but it was only a matter of time. For all she knew, an entire battalion of Terminators was marching toward the camp at this very minute.

This was no time to dick around.

"C'mon, you're just another damn T-600. A dime a dozen. Expendable!" She fired her pistol at the monster's remaining optical sensor. The bullet bounced off its armored socket. "Take a risk, why don't you? I'm worth it, I promise. John Connor!"

The Terminator had another idea. Putting down the chainsaw, it bent over and yanked a large boulder out of the muddy soil alongside the stream. It hurled the rock at the ice near Molly. She dived out of the way, skidding across the surface. The missile collided with the frozen surface, which cracked but did not shatter beneath the impact. Hairline fractures spider-webbed across the top of the river, only a few yards away from Molly.

Puddles formed atop the ice.

Molly grasped the Terminator's strategy. It was trying to drive her off the river by leaving her no place to stand.

Not a bad plan, actually. There was no way she could make it to the opposite shore in time to avoid going for a swim.

"Fuck!"

The T-600 searched the shore for another boulder. Finding a suitable chunk of granite, it lifted the missile above its head. Servomotors whirred in its arms and shoulders. It took aim at the fractured ice. Another good hit would be enough to break the thick sheet apart in a big way. Molly shivered in anticipation. Ice water lapped against her boots. This was going to be cold....

The Terminator was about to hurl the boulder like a catapult when a high-pitched *whoop* came from the top of the hill.

"Heads up, one-eye!" Rusty wheels squeaked loudly as the old mining cart rolled down the incline toward the T-600. Picking up speed with every inch, the heavy iron conveyance slammed into the Terminator from behind, the momentum knocking the machine out onto the stream, only a few feet away from Molly. It slid across the ice on its mechanical hands and knees, scoring the frozen surface.

The ice cracked and split beneath it.

Sitka capered jubilantly atop the slope. Gloved hands

gripped the sturdy piece of metal rebar she had used as a lever. Vic Folger stood behind her, wiping the sweat from his brow. Molly guessed that he had given the cart a good shove as well.

"Score!" the teenager crowed, as if she had just bowled a strike. She waved the rebar in the air. Her wild red mane blew across her face. "Sink or swim, metal!"

Recognizing its peril, the T-600 stood up abruptly, even as the ice gave way beneath it. Articulated steel fingers grasped for a hold as it sank beneath the surface, but could not find purchase on the tilting planes of ice. Its red eye glared at Molly right before it went under. Ice water splashed against her face.

Good riddance! Molly thought. The stream was maybe twelve feet deep at its center. With luck, the current would carry the Terminator all the way down to the glacier, where it would remain frozen until global warming turned Alaska into a rainforest. *Unless we get another nuclear winter before this war is over.*

The ice continued to come apart all around her. Molly realized she was only heartbeats away from joining the Terminator in the drink. Scrambling to her feet, she skipped across the crumbling ice, jumping from chunk to chunk as though they were stepping stones. Dislodged fragments tilted alarmingly beneath her feet. Frigid water splashed against her boots. She cartwheeled her arms to hang onto her balance. It was like running across some sort of arctic obstacle course.

Her right fist still gripped her pistol.

"Atta girl!" Sitka urged her on from the shore. "You can do it! Don't fall in!"

Not planning to. Molly couldn't think of anything more stupid than being swept under the ice after they had finally got rid of the invader. Too many people had already died tonight. Drowning was not on her agenda.

"That's it, chief!" Folger cheered her on, sounding just like the soccer coach he used to be. He'd been on a winning streak before Judgment Day. "Only a few more feet!"

Solid ground was tantalizingly close. Molly could practically feel it beneath her feet already. A couple more leaps and she'd be clear of the river. She started thinking ahead to her next move. In theory, there was an emergency snowmobile hidden in a gully outside camp. If they squeezed tight, it could carry all three of them....

A metal hand smashed through the ice beneath her. Ice-cold fingers wrapped around her right ankle, squeezing tightly enough that soon they would grind the bones together. 800 pounds of Terminator weighed her down like an anchor.

She fell forward on her face, then began sliding backward into the water.

Sitka screamed from the shore.

"No fucking way!" Molly blurted out through the pain. She swung her arm back and emptied her pistol into the Terminator's wrist. Damaged hydraulics spurted fluid. The machine's grip loosened a little. She yanked her foot free, leaving her boot behind, and the Terminator grabbed for her again. But then a heavy slab of ice slammed into it, causing it to lose its footing.

The current caught the machine and swept it under the ice once more.

She prayed that this time it would be for good.

WARNING: LOSS OF TRACTION. MOBILITY COMPROMISED.

The HUD displays flashed repeatedly before the T-600's single optical sensor. It struggled to regain its footing, but the stream was too deep, the current too strong. The slippery floor of the river offered no easy purchase.

Its fingers grabbed onto a slimy rock, only to have it come loose from the silty earth. There was no way to anchor itself. Driven by gravity, the relentless ice shoved it forward. The Terminator crashed over a waterfall into the glacier below.

It sank like a stone.

SITUATION CRITICAL. TOTAL SYSTEM FAILURE IMMINENT.

Freezing water penetrated its circuits. Tons of glacial ice squeezed it like a vise. Its cranial case caved inward, threatening its vulnerable central processing unit. The grizzly bear's tooth floated loose. Facing termination, the T-600 tried to transmit an update to Skynet, but the dense frozen mass above it blocked the signal. Its solitary red sensor flickered dimly amidst the frigid blue coldness.

The Terminator had no regrets. It felt no fear. It could only futilely attempt to fulfill its programming—until it could not.

Water invaded its neural network. Electricity arced within its skull. The colossal pressure crushed the CPU. The blood-red sensor went black.

WARNING: SYSTEM FAIL—

Alaska terminated the invader.

Molly limped to shore, her stockinged foot crunching through the thin ice at the very edge of the stream. Her ankle felt like it was bruised, not broken. A soggy sock was already starting to freeze solid, though. As soon as she reached land, she peeled it off and shoved it into her pocket. She'd be lucky if she didn't end up losing a toe or two to frostbite.

But she was alive. And the Terminator was history.

Works for me.

Sitka slid down the hill to meet her, followed quickly by Folger.

"Yikes!" the girl exclaimed. "Thought you were a goner for sure!" Jagged floes of ice rushed downstream after the Terminator. "Metal didn't know when to quit!"

"They never do," Molly said. She shot Sitka a dirty look. "You are so grounded."

The teenager shrugged it off.

"Worth it." She fished a fresh pair of socks from her overstuffed pockets and handed them to Molly. "Get my red armband now?"

"Maybe when you learn to follow orders." She put both socks on over her bare foot, grateful for Sitka's packrat tendencies. Then she glanced at Folger. "Thought I told you to get her out of here."

The man threw up his hands.

"*You* try controlling this brat." He crossed his arms across his chest. "And I don't hit kids, no matter how much they deserve it."

Fair enough, Molly thought. She couldn't really complain. Sitka and Folger had come through when she needed them, orders or no orders. *Typical*, she reflected. *Humans don't just follow instructions blindly. We're unpredictable. We deviate from our programming. That's what makes us different from the machines.*

Ernie Wisetongue would approve.

The glow from the burning camp lit up the night. The flames had even reached the breaker now. By morning, nothing would be left of the old mining town but ashes and rubble. The bodies of their fallen comrades were already being cremated along with their homes. She glanced up at the sky. Still no sign of any HKs, but she knew they would be here soon.

Molly turned her back on the blaze.

"Time to go."

CHAPTER FIFTEEN

Losenko and Ivanov rushed into the control room. The pinging of the unknown vessel's sonar echoed within the command center—it was a sound no submariner ever wanted to hear. Anxious crewmen gazed upward at the ceiling, wondering who had found them after all this time. Ironically, it was the most animated that Losenko had seen them in many weeks. Fear displaced the malaise that had hung over the men since Judgment Day.

"Do we have an identification?" the captain demanded, reclaiming the conn. "Report!"

Sonarman Yuri Michenko was ready with an update.

"A warship, sir. Less than four kilometers away and closing fast. Acoustic signature indicates a Kashin-class destroyer." Behind a pair of thick glasses, the youth's eyes gleamed with excitement. "I think it's the *Smetlivy*, sir!"

One of ours? Losenko could scarcely believe it. *Smetlivy* was a four-ton destroyer driven by powerful gas turbine engines. Deployed as a guided missile platform, it boasted an impressive array of missiles, torpedoes, rocket launchers, and close-range guns. It was also, he recalled, one of the first Russian warships designed to seal itself off from radioactive fallout in the event of nuclear war. It made sense that the destroyer might have survived Judgment Day.

The mood in the command center instantly shifted from apprehension to jubilation. Smiles broke out across the faces of men who had thought they were alone in the world. A hubbub of excited voices almost drowned out the pinging of the warship's sonar.

"It's a miracle!" the helmsman exclaimed. "We've found our brothers!"

Even Ivanov appeared elated by the news. His sullen expression lightened; for the first time in too long, he looked like the intrepid young officer Losenko remembered.

"Shall we rise to meet them, sir?" he inquired.

"With discretion, Mr. Ivanov." The captain understood the men's enthusiasm, and even shared it to a degree, but he was cautious as well. He had not forgotten what he had found on the mainland months ago. Anarchy and violence had consumed the world they knew. Civilization was a thing of the past. With the Motherland in chaos, there was no guarantee that the *Gorshkov* and the *Smetlivy* still served the same masters. He did not wish to blindly welcome pirates—or worse. "Ascend to periscope depth. And release the communication buoy."

Strung out behind the sub on a wire, the buoy would increase their ability to monitor transmissions from the destroyer.

The periscope pedestal tilted beneath his feet as K-115 climbed up from the depths, leveling out at roughly twenty-five meters below the surface. "Scope's breaking," the officer of the deck reported, unable to conceal the anticipation in his voice. He stepped aside to let Losenko see for himself. The overhead lights were dimmed to avoid reflecting the light up through the periscope, where it might give away their position. Display panels glowed like exotic bioluminescent fish in a darkened aquarium.

The captain seized the periscope's handles and peered into the eyepiece.

It was twilight above the sea. White water lapped against the reticle. He glimpsed lurid red skies on the horizon.

"Position of contact?"

"Bearing three-one-zero," Michenko reported. Headphones connected him with the sonar shack. Overhead video monitors, slaved to the main sonar array, monitored the destroyer via phosphorescent green waterfalls of data. "Contact slowing to seven knots."

Losenko rotated the scope until... there!

The silhouette of a great gray battleship appeared some distance away. He twisted the right handle to increase magnification. The formidable contours of the vessel, with its imposing guns and towers, seemed to match that of a Kashin-class destroyer, but he would have to consult his reference manuals to be certain. He turned the scope over to Ivanov for his opinion. The XO eagerly scanned the mystery ship.

"It *could* be the *Smetlivy*," he declared after a moment. Anticipation colored his voice, making him sound like a child on Christmas morning. A rare smile graced his features.

Was he already contemplating transferring to another ship?

"Four knots," Michenko called out. "Three knots...."

The warship came to a halt approximately three kilometers away. Losenko was encouraged by the fact that the destroyer was making no aggressive moves toward them. Had it already identified K-115 as a friendly vessel?

Perhaps we really have made contact with an ally at last.

"Raise multifunction mast."

It would be good to share his burden with another captain. And not see the same defeated faces every day. After months cut off from the world, they could finally begin to rebuild the Russian Navy. And perhaps discover the truth about Skynet.

He wondered what the *Smetlivy*'s captain thought of John Connor's broadcasts.

"Incoming transmission from the other vessel, Captain!"

Losenko plucked a red phone handset from a box upon the periscope platform. The hotline employed secure UHF transmissions to communicate with allied ships and aircraft.

"Put it through."

A burst of static preceded an unfamiliar voice, speaking in flawless Russian. "Attention unidentified submarine. This is Captain Konstantin Frantz of the Russian destroyer *Smetlivy*. Please respond."

Losenko did not recognize the captain's name. Then again, in the wake of Judgment Day, it was likely there had been more than a few battlefield promotions. Perhaps Frantz had only recently inherited his command.

"This is the captain of the submarine in question,"

Losenko replied. Old habits prevented him from volunteering too much information right away. Even when setting out to sea from his home port, he had always avoided identifying the *Gorshkov* by name or number over the air. "Please state your intentions."

Encryption caused a slight lag in the transmissions, so it was a few seconds before Losenko heard Frantz laugh.

"I appreciate your caution, Captain. The world is a dangerous place these days; no doubt you and your heroic crew have endured many hardships. You cannot imagine how relieved I am to discover that you survived the atomic war and its aftermath." Frantz's tone was affable. "I assure you, my only mission is to escort you back to Murmansk so you can rejoin what remains of the Northern Fleet."

Murmansk? Losenko looked askance at the phone. The one-time naval base was nothing but a radioactive crater now, one likely to be uninhabitable for decades. Was Frantz unaware of this? Or was he attempting to deceive them to some end?

"My understanding is that Murmansk was destroyed," he said, choosing his words carefully. He deliberately did not mention that he had beheld the devastation firsthand.

The lag at the other end seemed a little longer than before.

"Sadly, that is the case," Frantz conceded. "But the rebuilding is already underway. Your ship and crew will find refuge at our new facilities."

Losenko frowned. The other captain's answers struck him as glib and unconvincing. When he had last explored the Kola Peninsula, the ravaged landscape had been overrun by murderous machines—and their human collaborators. Suspicion blossomed in his heart.

"And what of Skynet?" he pressed. "Have you retaken the countryside from the Terminators?"

Only a foot away, eavesdropping intently on Losenko's end of the conversation, along with every other man within earshot, Ivanov's hopeful expression faded. He eyed Losenko with alarm, clearly displeased by the tack the discussion was taking.

"Captain!"

Losenko placed his hand over the mouthpiece of the phone. "Remember your oath, Alexei. And the chain of command."

The pointed reminder had the desired effect. Ivanov stepped back, swallowing any further objections. He did not look happy, however. His fists were clenched at his sides. He ground his teeth.

My apologies, Alexei, Losenko thought. *I know how much this means to you.*

The captain felt the eyes of the entire control room upon him. The last thing he wanted was to crush the hopes of the men, just when they finally had something to hold on to. But his gut told him that Frantz was not being honest with him. The stranger's warm welcome and soothing promises were too good to be true.

If Judgment Day taught me anything, it is that the universe is seldom so forgiving.

Nor are our machines.

"Skynet?" Frantz's reply did nothing to assuage Losenko's doubts. "What is Skynet? And Terminators? Is that some new Yankee weapon?"

Losenko did not believe that the other captain could be so ignorant. If the *Gorshkov*'s antennae had intercepted John Connor's broadcasts, then so would the *Smetlivy*. And what of the robots occupying the industrial base on the Kola Peninsula? How could the Russian military be unaware of their mechanized reign of terror, if indeed "Captain" Frantz truly represented the Northern Fleet?

"Before I can accompany you," he informed the warship's commander, "I will require authorization codes from Moscow."

He locked eyes with Ivanov. The XO nodded back at him. In this instance, at least, they seemed to be on the same wavelength. Even Alexei saw the wisdom in so reasonable a precaution. Losenko was relieved to have his *starpom* watching his back for once.

"Those codes were lost in the initial attack," Frantz insisted, after another awkward delay. "Have faith in your countrymen, Captain. The Russian people need you sailing beside us."

Along with our remaining ballistic missiles, Losenko thought. K-115 was both a tempting prize and a potential threat to whoever Frantz truly answered to. Losenko remembered the collaborators who had attacked Grushka's armored truck. He was not about to let the *Gorshkov*'s last two thermonuclear weapons fall into the hands of turncoats such as those.

"Faith is in short supply these days," Losenko answered. "As you said, the world is a dangerous place. Perhaps if you can put us in touch with your superior officers, we can arrange to rendezvous at a neutral location."

An ominous silence ensued. The mood of the control room soured as the excited men realized, along with their captain, that something was amiss. Ilya Korbut, who had succeeded the late Lieutenant Zamyatin as tactical officer, approached the captain.

"Excuse me, sir," he whispered. "I have been reviewing the fleet records and there is no record of a Captain

Frantz. The *Smetlivy* was under Captain Dobrovolsky's command at the outset of the attack."

Losenko remembered Dobrovolsky. He was a good officer, ambitious but devoted to duty and his country. He would have scuttled the destroyer before he let it become the spoils of war.

Was Konstantin Frantz cut from the same cloth? Losenko had his doubts.

"Captain!" Michenko blurted out. The sonarman's face went pale. "*Smetlivy* is flooding its torpedo tubes!"

"What!" Ivanov could not contain his shock. "But they're our own people!"

Losenko knew how he felt. He just wished he was more surprised.

"Battle stations! Down bubble, full speed."

The men scrambled to their posts, even as Frantz spoke again over the phone. "Surrender your vessel, Captain." All pretence at civility went by the wayside. "Or we *will* sink you."

"They're opening torpedo doors!" Michenko reported.

"Traitor!" Losenko let loose his own anger, even as—outside the sub—plumes of mist vented from the ballast tanks, signaling their intentions. "Who is pulling your strings? Skynet? The Americans? Some petty warlord?" That a Russian warship would dare threaten K-115 was the final proof that the world had truly gone mad. What had become of patriotism and loyalty? "You call yourself a captain of the Northern Fleet? How can you live with yourself!"

His accusation hit a nerve.

"You don't understand!" Frantz ranted "I don't have any choice. None of us do. Skynet's forces are everywhere, humans commanded by machines. They're holding our families hostage. American missiles are aimed at what's left of our country, ready to finish what they started on Judgment Day if we don't comply with their demands. The machines are watching us every minute. There's one right behind me at this very moment. It will terminate me if I don't obey!"

"So you are a coward and a collaborator, just as I feared." Contempt dripped from Losenko's voice. He was tempted to hang up, but the longer he kept Frantz talking, the more time they had to submerge. "If you had any honor, you would defend this sub with your last breath, not turn your weapons against it!"

"And condemn the Motherland to further reprisals?" Frantz sounded as if he was trying to convince himself as much as Losenko, who heard a guilty conscience behind the other man's self-serving rationalizations. "You're living in the past, Captain! This is Skynet's world now. Our only hope for peace is to accept its new world order."

That's not what John Connor says, Losenko thought. Frantz was deluding himself if he thought that the machines would be content ruling over humanity like benign overlords. Most likely Skynet had already murdered the majority of the world's population. Why assume it would let its human pawns survive once it was through with them? Gratitude was a human concept.

"You are being used, Mr. Frantz." Losenko declined to honor him with the title of captain. "But you will not have my boat. Or my missiles."

Keeping the hundred-kiloton warheads out of enemy hands was his supreme priority now. No threat or argument could convince him otherwise. He would take the missiles with him to the bottom of the sea if necessary.

"Don't make me fire, Captain." Frantz was practically pleading now. "Halt your descent!"

Like hell, Losenko thought. He hung up on Frantz.

An alarm blared from the speaker system.

"Captain!" Lieutenant Pavlinko reported. He monitored the electronic surveillance sensors installed atop the periscope. "Aircraft approaching from the northeast. Two American helicopters!"

Losenko found himself outnumbered. Were the fighters allied with the *Smetlivy*? If the American planes were equipped with anti-submarine torpedoes, *Gorshkov*'s odds of escaping had just turned considerably worse.

"Americans!" Ivanov snarled. "I should have known! This was a trap, using the *Smetlivy* as bait!"

Pavlinko's next announcement stunned them all.

"The enemy aircraft have fired on the *Smetlivy*!" The weapons officer looked baffled by his own information. "The Americans are requesting our assistance. They say they're the Resistance!"

The what?

Losenko didn't know what to think. Despite John Connor's broadcasts, the captain had seen no evidence that the so-called Resistance was anything more than an idea. Now American warplanes were defending them against a Russian destroyer?

Explosions upon the surface rocked the submarine. The sound of anti-aircraft fire, coming from the *Smetlivy*, penetrated the icy depths and the steel hull of K-115. The deck rolled beneath Losenko's feet as though the sub was being tossed about atop a stormy sea, and not submerged beneath the waves. Dangling cords and cables swung wildly back and forth.

The captain didn't fully comprehend what was happening, but he recognized an opportunity.

"Dive! Down bubble, twenty degrees!"

The submarine descended at a sharp angle, hoping to escape the conflict above.

"Scope's under," Ivanov announced. He lowered the periscope and locked it into place. The overhead lights flared up again.

"Forty meters." The diving officer called out the depth. "Fifty meters."

But Frantz wasn't going to let them get away so easily.

"Two torpedoes launched and running!" the sonarman warned, then he began a continuing report on the projectiles' speed, bearing, and range. Sweat glistened upon Michenko's face. His gaze was glued to the slaved sonar screens.

"Torpedoes have acquired! Repeat: torps have acquired!"

"Helm! Hard to port!" Losenko spat out orders at a rapid pace. "Deploy countermeasures!"

The *Gorshkov* jettisoned a pair of decoys via the rear ejector tubes. Losenko heard them wailing loudly outside the sub. The acoustic noisemakers made a racket by releasing compressed air while vibrating like tuning forks. With luck, the decoys would lure the torpedoes away from K-115.

"Torpedo one veering away from us!" Michenko rejoiced. "It's going for the decoy!"

An underwater shock wave buffeted the *Gorshkov*. The submarine yawed sharply to starboard, throwing Losenko against the massive steel column of the periscope. His uniform caught on a bolt, tearing the fabric and scratching his side. He ignored the pain, concentrating on the peril to his ship instead. The nearby explosion meant that the first torpedo had taken out the decoy instead. But what about the second? In theory, the sub's dense double hull could conceivably survive a single strike, but he did not care to test that theory.

"Torpedo two?" he demanded.

Michenko's jubilant tone evaporated.

"Still closing!"

The second torpedo had not taken the bait. Losenko cursed their luck. He wrapped an arm around the lowered periscope and shouted into the emergency address system.

"Brace for impact!"

Seconds later, the guided warhead smashed into the *Gorshkov*. The pedestal pitched sharply and Losenko clung to the scope with all his strength, while Ivanov and Korbut grabbed onto the railing. Undersea thunder roared in the captain's ears, along with the clanging of battered metal. The overhead lights sputtered so that, for a few unnerving moments, the control room was lit solely by its glowing gauges and control panels. Losenko glanced at Ivanov. Blood dripped from the XO's forehead. Losenko guessed that he had cracked it against the other periscope.

"Are you all right, Alexei?"

Ivanov fingered the wound.

"Nothing worth mentioning." He wiped his fingers on the front of his coveralls, leaving a crimson smear behind. "The ship?"

Emergency power kicked in, bringing maybe eighty percent of the control room's lights back on. Losenko surveyed the room, spotting extensive damage to both the crew and the equipment. Warning indicators flashed on nearly every console, while bruises, cuts, and minor burns scarred the faces of the frightened sailors. Steam jetted from a ruptured pipe, hissing like an enraged eel, until an alert crewman reached up to close a valve manually. Sparks erupted from shorted circuits, until doused by the fire extinguishers.

A smoky haze contaminated the atmosphere, which smelled of cold sweat and burnt wiring. The men coughed at their stations. Damage reports started pouring in from all over K-115.

"Wounded, but still alive," Losenko said, assessing their situation. He offered a silent prayer of thanks to the long-dead engineers and shipwrights who had overseen the *Gorshkov*'s construction. Ordinarily, he would return to the surface to effect immediate repairs and stem any leaks in the ship's hull, but not with the *Smetlivy* still lurking above them. Escape was still the order of the day.

But how deep do we dare descend with our hull scarred and our systems compromised?

And was Frantz done with them yet?

A thunderous detonation answered that question. The periscope platform lurched to port, throwing Losenko hard against the safety railing, bruising his ribs. Blue-hot sparks flared from the control consoles, forcing men to leap backward or risk electrocution. Sundered metal shrieked in protest somewhere above the control room. The periscopes rattled in their housings. Helmsmen, securely buckled into their seats, wrestled with their wheels, fighting and failing to keep the *Gorshkov* on an even keel. Something crashed loudly in the sonar shack. A voice cried out in pain. Losenko stumbled across the platform.

Ivanov reached out to steady the captain.

"Another torpedo?"

"No," Losenko guessed. The explosion had not felt like a direct strike. "Depth charge." As he recalled, the *Smetlivy* was equipped with rocket launchers capable of firing RGB-60 unguided depth charges. The rockets could be fired in multiple rounds, the better to increase the odds of destroying an enemy submarine. Despite the attacking aircraft, Frantz was sparing no effort to sink the *Gorshkov*. Apparently, Skynet would rather see the ballistic submarine destroyed than beyond its control.

A second charge, even closer than the first, pummeled the sub. Warning klaxons blared, but Losenko was proud to see that not a single seaman abandoned his post. The *Gorshkov* was taking a beating, but the shock waves were nothing compared to the damage they would sustain should one of the charges score a direct hit. Losenko doubted K-115 could survive another blow, yet it was only a matter of time before one of them came too close. Their only hope was to get away from the warship before that happened.

"Captain!" Pavlinko hailed him. "A VLF transmission via the buoy. The Americans are requesting our assistance again."

Losenko's eyes lit up. Perhaps there was another way.

"Are you certain?"

"No!" Ivanov protested, reading his mind. "Captain, you cannot be considering this!"

A depth charge went off several hundred meters above them. Was it just his imagination or were the salvos decreasing in accuracy? Perhaps the *Smetlivy* was otherwise occupied?

"Those aircraft are fighting our battle for us, Alexei."

"Good!" Ivanov blurted. "Let them destroy each other! They deserve nothing less!"

His XO had a point. This might be their best opportunity to escape the conflict, leaving the destroyer and the Yankee pilots to fight it out while they slipped away in the confusion. *But to where*, Losenko asked himself, *and to what end?* Just to aimlessly wander the seas once more? Without allies or purpose?

John Connor's stirring exhortations surfaced from his memory. *"We can win this war,"* Connor had promised, *"but only if we come together against our common enemy."* Losenko had listened to those words many times in the privacy of his stateroom.

"If you can hear this, you are the Resistance."

Losenko made up his mind.

"Full stop!" he ordered. "Ready tubes two and four! Prepare firing solutions!"

Ivanov could not contain himself.

"Captain, what are you doing?"

"The American planes came to our defense, Alexei. We can do no less." Losenko turned to the weapons officer. "Give me a snapshot... with all due speed!"

Aiming the torpedoes could be a devilishly tricky business, with multiple objects moving in three dimensions. Ideally, there would be time to check and recheck all the calculations before firing; in the heat of battle, however, the best they could do was take a quick "snapshot" of the situation and hope for the best.

Fortunately, the *Smetlivy* presented a damned big target.

The crew hustled to carry out his orders, realizing that their own lives were on the line. This was the first time that any of the men aboard had found themselves in an actual, life-or-death battle with an enemy vessel, as opposed to war games and drills. Who would have guessed that, when they finally were called to take up arms in a genuine engagement, it would be against one of their own ships?

The irony was almost too much for Losenko to bear.

"Torpedos armed and ready, sir!" Pavlinko reported. He sat at the weapons control console on the starboard side of the control room. A computerized battle management system, Omnibus-BDRM, processed the relevant data and commanded the torpedoes. In a sense, it was Skynet's ancestor.

"Do we have a firing solution?" Losenko demanded.

"Yes, sir! A good snapshot." Pavlinko's fingers stabbed the weapons console. "Feeding the data to the torpedoes now."

Dasvidania, Mr. Frantz, Losenko thought. "Fire at will. Both tubes," he said aloud.

Two loud whooshing sounds, one after another, came from the torpedo room at the bow. Two 533-millimeter torpedoes shot upward at the surface. Losenko prayed that the *Smetlivy* was too busy with the American aircraft to defend itself from the speeding bullets. For a second, he almost felt sorry for the destroyer. It was under attack from both above and below.

"Evasive maneuvers!" the captain ordered. He did not want the four-ton vessel coming down on top of them. "Helm, right fifteen degrees rudder. Full speed!"

As programmed, the torpedoes went off beneath the warship's keel. The dual explosions, going off above the submariners' heads, were far too close for comfort. Michenko kept his eyes glued on the glowing green sonar display. His gleeful smile was Losenko's first indication that their torpedoes had prevailed.

"She's breaking up, sir! We broke her back!"

Cheers erupted throughout the control room. Even Ivanov permitted himself a thin smile. There had been a time when the sinking of a Russian destroyer would have been cause for dismay, but not today. Losenko let the men savor their victory as he watched the bisected corpse of the *Smetlivy* drop out of sight on the sonar screen. He could not resist tweaking Ivanov a little.

"Now then, Alexei. I believe you had something to say."

The *starpom* shrugged. The cut upon his brow had already stopped bleeding.

"I stand corrected, Captain." He glanced around the ravaged control room, which had seen better days. "We need to assess the damage, sir, but I suggest that we put some distance between ourselves and the Americans first."

"I disagree, Mr. Ivanov." Losenko's racing heart began to slow. "We need to surface immediately for repairs." Multiple damage reports, from all over the ship, were already competing for his attention; he counted on his crew to respond to the most urgent leaks immediately. "Besides, I wish to make the acquaintance of our new allies." Ignoring Ivanov's scandalized expression, he addressed Communications. "Radio the Americans. Tell them to expect us."

Was there truly a Resistance? Losenko could not wait to find out.

A spreading oil slick was all that remained of the *Smetlivy*. Frantz and his crew of turncoats had gone to a watery grave, along with whatever foul machine had been holding their leash. Losenko did not mourn them. The cowards had made their choice—and suffered the consequences. Better that the destroyer plunge to the bottom of the sea, than that K-115 suffer such a fate. Losenko knew he and his crew were lucky to be alive.

If one of those depth charges had hit before we got our torpedoes off....

Frantz had claimed one victory before his demise, however. The smoking remains of an Apache attack helicopter floated atop the ocean, a victim of the destroyer's guns. A second chopper hovered in the sky above the wreckage, keeping watch over the downed aircraft's pilot, who had apparently bailed out just in time. Floating bodies suggested that not all of the Apache's crew had been so lucky.

The *Gorshkov* rolled atop the choppy surface of the Bering Sea, its scarred deck a steel beach rising above the waves. Preliminary reports had found significant damage to the outer hull near the stern, but all major flooding had been contained. Alas, four enlisted men had been killed by an exploding bulkhead in the turbine room, and six more men had been severely burned by a fire in the galley. Thankfully, however, the nuclear reactor remained on-line and there was no trace of radiation leakage. As badly as they had been hurt, the outcome of the battle could have been much worse.

Too bad we cannot return to Murmansk for repairs!

Losenko watched from the hatch atop the sail as his men, grateful for a chance to breath a little fresh air, labored to fish the American pilot from the sea. He was somewhat surprised to see that the pilot appeared to be a woman. Her bright orange life-vest helped her stand out against the deep blue waves as she swam toward the waiting submarine. The Russian sailors wore life jackets as well, just in case they fell overboard during the hazardous operation. Chief Komarov supervised the rescue team as they tossed a rope out. Thankfully, the sea was calm enough to permit such a rescue.

"I'm not sure this is wise, Captain," Ivanov said in a low voice. Standing beside Losenko on the bridge, the XO kept a close eye on the chopper hovering nearby. An adhesive bandage was stuck to his forehead. "We are very vulnerable here."

"A calculated risk," the captain conceded. "But if that 'copter wished to attack us, it would have done so already."

He turned his binoculars from the rescue operation to the aircraft in question. Even in the dimming light, he was struck by the piecemeal appearance of the Apache, which appeared to have been cobbled together from parts of several different aircraft. Its weathered paint job was a patchwork quilt of varied camouflage patterns. An olive-green door clashed with the sandy brown hue of the surrounding panels. Crude graffiti, slapped all over its fins and fuselage, hardly reflected the professionalism of the old U.S. military. A skull-and-crossbones emblem, with neon-red eyes, screamed pirate more than soldier. "Skynet SUCKS!" was spray-painted in English upon the landing skids.

The junkyard look of the chopper, along with its vulgar bravado, spoke volumes about the Resistance.

"We cannot cruise forever without allies, Alexei." Losenko lowered his binoculars. "You saw how the men reacted when they thought we had met up with our comrades-in-arms. For the first time in months, they had hope." He nodded at the Resistance chopper. "Think of this as a leap of faith."

Ivanov threw his own words back at him.

"I thought you told the traitor, Frantz, that trust was in short supply these days?"

"The pilots in those aircraft did not lie to us," Losenko reminded him. "And they came to our defense when we were in peril. If not for the providential arrival of the American aircraft, K-115 might be resting on the ocean floor now, its hull fatally breached. That alone warrants further investigation."

The XO grunted dubiously.

"If you say so, Captain." He glared at the Apache, no doubt thinking of the American missiles that had incinerated his family. "But remember what they say about wolves in sheep's clothing. I, for one, intend to stay on my guard."

"I expect nothing less, Mr. Ivanov."

Down on the deck, Chief Kamarov and his men succeeded in hauling the Yankee pilot out of the sea. Losenko descended to meet her, followed closely by Ivanov. The suspicious *starpom* kept one hand on the grip of his sidearm. A cold spray pelted their faces. White water lapped against the exposed sides of the hull. After months of cruising smoothly beneath the surface, the shifting deck felt uncomfortably wobbly beneath Losenko's feet. His sea legs were rusty.

"No rash moves," he warned Ivanov. "This woman is our guest until I say otherwise."

A heavy wool blanket had been thrown over the shivering pilot's soaked flight suit. She stood unsteadily upon the rocking deck. Watchful seamen flanked her, holding onto her arms to keep her both upright and under control. Water dripped from buzz-cut brown hair. A black eye and swollen lip testified to a rough landing. Silver dog tags hung on a chain around her neck. Losenko put her age in the mid-twenties. She appeared to be of Latino descent. Her lips were blue.

"*P-pryvet!*" the Yankee greeted them in atrocious Russian. "You the skipper of this boat?" Her teeth chattered. "H-hope your English is better than my R-Russian."

"I speak English," Losenko replied. "Captain Dmitri Losenko, at your service. We are grateful for your assistance against our foe."

"Hell, thanks for p-plucking me from the drink. I was starting to feel like an ice cube in a cold soda. Talk about a brain freeze!" She pulled away from her guardians and enthusiastically took the captain's hand in an icy grip. "Corporal Luz Ortega. Pleased to meet you."

Ivanov's dark eyes narrowed. "You are U.S. Air Force?"

"Used to be," Ortega said. She shrugged off the blanket to expose a bright red armband tied around her sleeve. She nodded proudly at it. "Resistance now."

The Resistance! Losenko experienced a surge of excitement. Perhaps there was still a chance of reclaiming the planet from the machines.

Ortega offered her hand to Ivanov, as well. The XO ignored it, preferring to interrogate the pilot instead.

"How did you come to find us?"

"Weren't looking for you," Ortega admitted. She withdrew her hand. "We were hunting that shipload of metal-loving collaborators instead. Picked up your radio transmissions. Couldn't quite make out all the Russian, but got the gist of it. Sounded like you were in trouble. Figured we'd lend you a hand." She tugged the blanket back over her shoulders. "You know what they say. 'The enemy of my enemy,' etc. Besides, we'd been looking for a chance to engage that battleship. You folks were a good distraction."

She glanced ruefully at the bodies in the water.

"It cost us, though. But that's war. The enemy lost

more than we did. That's the important thing, right?"

Ivanov remained skeptical. The deaths of the other Americans meant nothing to him.

"Those communications were encrypted. How could you eavesdrop on them?"

Ortega chortled.

"Hell, Boris, we cracked your encryption moons ago. Some of your old comrades hooked up with us a while back, shared everything they knew. This is a united effort, you know. All us flesh-and-blood types against the metal."

"A united effort," Ivanov repeated doubtfully. He sounded sickened by the very idea. "You and our own people?"

Ortega didn't back down.

"That's what I'm saying, Boris. You got a problem with that?"

"My name is Ivanov," the *starpom* said tersely. A muscle twitched beneath his cheek. "Captain Second-Rank."

Losenko admired his self-control. Considering the dreadful loss of his family, Alexei had probably wanted to shoot the first American he met, or, at the very least, pound in the cocky pilot's face. He thought it best to defuse the situation.

"Mr. Ivanov, please go below and oversee the repair efforts." He stepped between his XO and the woman. "I want a full report on the extent of the damage, and how soon we might expect to be underway."

"Aye, aye, sir." Ivanov seemed eager to leave the American's presence. He turned on his heels and marched briskly away.

Ortega watched him go.

"What's his beef?"

"The war has been hard on us all," Losenko offered by way of explanation. He noted Ortega shivering and changed the subject. "You are freezing, Corporal. Let us find you some dry clothes and a warm meal." He glanced up at the helicopter on the horizon. "I will inform your colleagues that you are safe and welcome aboard this ship. Later, we can make arrangements to return you to your own unit."

Ortega waved her arms to signal the other chopper, before allowing herself to be escorted to the nearest open hatch.

"Much obliged, Captain." She lowered her voice to a conspiratorial whisper, as though she feared Skynet might be listening. "Is there someplace we can talk in private? To be honest, there's a reason my buddies in the other chopper let you guys pick me up instead of them. The Resistance could use a boat like this. I may have a proposition for you... from my commanding officer."

"John Connor?"

"No!" Ortega laughed at the very idea. "Connor's just a voice. I'm not even sure if there really is such a person. I'm talking about the real thing. The big brass."

Losenko tried not to let his disappointment show. Connor's broadcast had offered the only hope that the world might someday be set right again. Now he gave Ortega a puzzled look.

"And who is your commanding officer?"

"Ashdown," the pilot answered. "General Hugh Ashdown."

CHAPTER SIXTEEN

2018

The back-up base, hidden deep in the remote forests of the Wrangell-St. Elias National Park, made the abandoned mining town look like a Vegas resort by comparison. The survivors of the T-600's attack were scattered across acres of wintry wilderness, occupying whatever shacks, cabins, campgrounds, tents, RVs, caves, tunnels, and hastily constructed shelters could accommodate the evacuees. Spreading the cell out over multiple facilities—instead of one centralized location—was inconvenient and hampered organization, but at least it would keep them off Skynet's radar.

Or so Molly hoped.

"So what's the damage?" she asked Geir, bracing for the worst. They had commandeered a broken-down old prospector's shack along the shore of the frozen creek. Bone-chilling drafts penetrated the bare wooden walls, despite the rags, cardboard, and scraps of foam rubber plugged into the various chinks. A broken window had been boarded up with two-by-fours. Melting snow leaked through the roof, dripping constantly into an array of buckets and pans that needed to be emptied far more often than she liked.

Sleeping bags were spread out on the floor. A faded pin-up calendar seemed so old that she wondered if it dated back to the Gold Rush. The outhouse was a cold, uncomfortable hike from the front door. A tattered bearskin rug smelled of mildew.

"Give me the gory details," she continued.

She reclined in front of the stone fireplace, wrapped in a coat, her bandaged right foot propped up on a pillow dangerously close to the fire. In the end, she had only lost a single toe to frostbite; the camp's medic had wanted to chop off more, but Molly had drawn the line at one little piggie. She didn't have time to adjust to a prosthetic foot, even if they could scrounge one up from somewhere. It had hurt like hell, but, against the odds, she had practically willed the circulation back into her remaining toes, even if she wasn't a hundred-percent sure they would ever feel warm again.

Could be worse, she thought. *I could be sharing a glacier with a Terminator right now.*

"We took a hit, that's for sure." Geir squatted next to her. Like Molly, he was wearing his jacket indoors just to keep warm. His eyes scanned the pencil marks on a yellow legal pad. "People are still checking in at the rendezvous point, but it's looking like we lost twenty-eight people, counting the fatalities at the pipeline."

"What about Ernie?" she asked.

"The medics got to him in time," he assured her. "He's going to be out of commission for a while, though. And he's going to have to learn to sculpt with one arm."

He'll find a way, Molly thought, glad to hear that the

old man was still with them. It sucked that he had been hurt, but it could have been so much worse. She made a mental note to call on him while he was recovering. It was the least she could do after he had saved her life. Her brain quickly moved on to more practical concerns.

"How about our supplies?"

"A lot of our provisions went up in the fire," Geir admitted. "Thank goodness for the emergency caches we had stashed. Hunting parties are out looking for fresh game."

Molly nodded. "Figured as much." The casualty figures didn't surprise her. She could still see the Terminator's chainsaw slicing up Ernie and Roger whenever she heard a motor running. The smell of exhaust, mixed with the coppery tang of blood, haunted her memory. "What's our ammo situation like?"

"Better than you might expect." Geir consulted his notes. "After fifteen years of being hunted by Terminators, that's the first thing people grab during an evacuation. Food and clothing are a distant second." He looked up from his notes. "You think it would be worth sending a salvage team back to the mill? See if anything valuable survived?"

Molly shook her head.

"Too risky. Skynet probably has the site staked out, with Aerostats if nothing else. Hell, I wouldn't put it past the machines to have a Terminator laying in wait for any careless scavengers." She sniffed her sweater; it still smelled like smoke. "Forget that place. What's gone is gone."

Geir sighed. "Story of our lives."

"Ever since Judgment Day," Molly agreed. She forced herself to think ahead, as opposed to dwelling on the past.

"Any helping hands from our friends in the Resistance?"

"Maybe." He didn't look optimistic, though. "We've been in touch with cells in Canada and the Lower 48, hoping they can resupply us, but there are no guarantees. Ordnance and electronics are more valuable than gold these days, and most cells have barely got enough materiel for their own operations. As usual, Command doesn't see us as a high priority." Geir made a face. "The scuttlebutt is they're throwing all their weight at California and the southwest. That's where they think the real action is."

No surprise there, Molly thought. San Francisco, or rather what was left of it, was Skynet Central these days. *But we've got to fight the machines everywhere, not just in their own backyard. Why doesn't Command see that?*

"So, in other words, we're on our own," she muttered. "Same as fucking usual."

"Something like that," Geir admitted. "On the bright side, pretty much all of the families got out okay. And there haven't been any follow-up assaults." He cracked a smile. "Maybe Skynet is focusing on the Lower 48, too?"

"Doubt it," Molly said. "Skynet's way too good at multitasking. It's more like Alaska is still too big to search effectively, even for the machines." Not for the first time, she was grateful for the sheer immensity of the state's untracked wilderness; the largest state in the USA, and the least populated even before Judgment Day, the land of the midnight sun offered plenty of dense backwoods to hide in. "Any other good news?"

Geir had a talent for finding silver linings even in the darkest mushroom clouds. Sometimes it was annoying, but right now she could use a little optimism.

"Well," he pointed out, "we managed to do some serious damage to the pipeline the other day. Don't forget that."

Molly was disappointed. *That's the best you've got?* she thought, glaring at him in spite of herself.

"The machines will have that stretch of pipeline repaired in no time," she replied. "And what do *they* care about oil spills? The environment means nothing to them." She stared glumly into the fire, unable to duck the discouraging truth. Her crippled foot mocked her. "Skynet hurt us way more than we hurt it."

Geir put aside his inventory lists. He gently shifted her foot from the pillow to his lap. Molly winced, but didn't complain.

"Just a flesh wound, chief," he said softly. "The war's not over."

"All the more reason to hit that fucking train," she said savagely. "Show Skynet that we're still in the game."

Geir gave her a dubious look.

"You sure about that? After everything that's happened, maybe we should postpone that operation until we're back on our feet again." He blushed as he recalled the injured appendage in his lap. "Sorry. Bad choice of words."

Molly couldn't care less about his *faux pas*.

"Postpone? Not a chance!" Her blood boiled at the thought. "Just because we took a hit, like you said, we're not going to slink away with our tails between our legs! We need to strike back, fast and hard. It's the last thing Skynet will be expecting."

"With reason, maybe." Geir pleaded caution. "I don't know, chief. I'm not sure if now is the right time to launch a major offensive. Our people have been through a lot. There hasn't even been time for a memorial service yet."

"Screw that!" Molly yanked her foot back and lurched

awkwardly to her feet, ignoring the pain that shot up her leg. She limped across the cramped, one-room shack and grabbed a crude iron poker from a rack by the hearth. "You're the one who's always talking about morale." She viciously jabbed the embers that were dying in the fireplace, stirring up sparks. "Enough with the damn weddings and prayer vigils. The machines killed our friends and torched our homes. The only thing that's going to make that better is kicking Skynet right in the balls!"

"For you, maybe, but what about everyone else?" He got up and took the poker from her hands, putting it back in its rack. There was an edge to his voice that she seldom heard. "Damnit, Molly. Not everyone is as hard, as tough, as you are. What about Sitka and Doc and the others? You can't expect people to just shake off what's happened and go right back to fighting—like that Terminator you dropped a mountain on. They're only flesh and blood!"

"You think I don't know that?" Molly snapped. She knew the name of every single human being who had died under her command. Sometimes she counted them, like sheep, to get to sleep at night. "But that's what Skynet is relying on, us poor, weak, fragile humans to give up and die... like we should've done after Judgment Day. Well, forget that. If we didn't quit after Skynet trashed the whole fucking world, we're sure as hell not going to throw in the towel just because we got our butts kicked a few times."

He took her by the shoulders and turned her around to face him.

"Nobody's saying we should quit. But it's just too soon to pick another fight with the machines. You're pushing too hard."

"There's no such thing, not anymore." She pulled away from him. "The machines aren't going to take a time-out, so neither can we."

She plopped down on the floor again and grabbed the discarded legal pad. She starting scribbling notes on the back of the inventory lists. Her plans for the train assault had gone up in flames with her old cabin, but they were still locked up tight inside her fevered brain. She jotted them down as fast as she could.

Pausing for a second, she fingered the Raven pendant around her neck. In Haida mythology, Raven was a trickster god who brought light to the darkness. They would need all of Raven's cunning to outwit Skynet. Molly was up to the challenge.

Operation Ravenwing was still a go.

"Get hold of Doc. Sitka." She didn't look up, though, and kept writing furiously as she spoke. "I want to meet with them tomorrow morning, bright and early. Pump Rathbone full of black coffee if you have to."

She tore a rejected page out of the pad, wadded it up, and lobbed it into the fireplace. The lined yellow paper burst into flame. Glowing fragments were sucked up the chimney. Molly watched them go. Then she turned to Geir.

"No more arguments," she said firmly. "We're going to rob that train—even if it kills me!"

Geir stared at her as though she were a ticking time-bomb. Turning away, he muttered under his breath.

"Not to mention the rest of us...."

CHAPTER
SEVENTEEN

2003

The Galapagos Islands, off the coast of Ecuador, were a long way from the *Gorshkov*'s usual arctic haunts. Traveling at full speed, it had taken K-115 more than nine days to reach the equator. Due to the damage to the sub's hull, they had been forced to travel just below the surface for most of the voyage. Daring the extreme pressures of the depths with a compromised hull was simply too risky.

Losenko hoped the trip would be worth it.

"Good to see you again, skipper!" Ortega greeted him. "The big-wigs agreed to let me be the one to meet you." A wooden boardwalk led up to the front entrance of the Charles Darwin Research Station, a remote biological science center on the volcanic island of Santa Cruz. The humble one-story building appeared more or less untouched by the war. A cactus garden bloomed alongside the boardwalk. Directional signs pointed to the tortoise breeding pens nearby. An impressive array of satellite dishes and radar antennae had been installed atop the roof of the building. Solar panels guaranteed a steady supply of electricity. Anti-aircraft emplacements clashed with the rustic setting. "Glad you could make it."

General Ashdown had invited the remnants of the world's military forces to a top-secret summit in the Galapagos. The exact coordinates for the meeting had been closely guarded over the last few weeks, passed along via furtive meetings at isolated locations. Predictably, Ivanov had strongly advised Losenko not to attend the event, fearing it was a trap, but the captain had been curious to meet Ashdown and the other leaders of the Resistance, face-to-face. As a precaution, however, the *Gorshkov* was keeping its distance from the island. After putting Losenko and a single bodyguard to sea in a rubber raft, the submarine had retreated to the depths of the Pacific Ocean, where it would remain in hiding until signaled by Losenko. Ivanov was under orders not to return for the captain until he received, via Morse Code, a password known only to the two of them.

That password was "Zamyatin."

"*Pryvet*, Corporal Ortega," Losenko replied. He sweated beneath his dress uniform. The balmy equatorial climate contrasted sharply with the arctic north, not to mention the unchanging atmosphere of the sub; he guessed it had to be at least thirty degrees Celsius. His bodyguard, Sergeant Fokin, appeared uncomfortably warm as well, not to mention damp. A warm drizzle had sprinkled them on their climb up from the white sand beach where their raft had come ashore. Losenko introduced Fokin, a burly petty officer with security training, and shook Ortega's hand. "You look well."

The pilot's cuts and bruises had healed since their first meeting several weeks earlier. Unlike the two Russians, the Yankee was dressed for the weather, wearing a short-sleeved khaki uniform with shorts. A fresh red armband adorned her upper arm.

"You got here just in time," she said. "The general's big dog-and-pony show will be starting shortly. Let me show you to your seats."

Ortega led them into the lobby of the research station, which was thankfully air-conditioned. A map of the archipelago occupied one wall, while Charles Darwin's bearded face was painted on another. Contemplating the naturalist's austere features, it occurred to Losenko that it was strangely fitting for this dire meeting to be held under his auspices; if John Connor was to be believed, an evolutionary contest was underway between two rival species, one genuine and the other artificial—man and machine, with the very future of the human race hanging in the balance.

Survival of the fittest....

Grim-faced soldiers hefting M-16s guarded the double doors leading to the station's interpretation center. Ortega vouched for the Russians, though the guards nonetheless consulted a laptop and checked Losenko's name and face against a profile before admitting him and his bodyguard. Metal detectors screened them for weapons and explosives. Fokin reluctantly surrendered an AK-47 and automatic pistol and Losenko turned over his own sidearm as well. The tight security reassured rather than disturbed him.

If I was Ashdown, I would not be taking any chances either.

They entered a small auditorium which held maybe three dozen people. Military personnel representing many of the world's armed forces occupied tiers of seats

overlooking the stage, like a miniature version of the
United Nations General Assembly. Folded paper placards
identified the various delegates by nation. Losenko spotted high-ranking officers from America, Canada, Great
Britain, France, China, India, Pakistan, Israel, Japan,
Australia, Libya, South Africa, Cuba, Nigeria, Greece,
Turkey, and many other countries. Medals and ribbons
adorned a motley collection of uniforms from all around
the world. He was impressed by the turnout.

"All these officers survived the war?" he asked Ortega.

"You bet!" the pilot replied. "There's plenty of you
bubbleheads, but you're not the only ones who kept their
heads down after Judgment Day." She gestured at the
assembly. "Some of these folks were stationed in remote,
low-priority locations when the bombs fell, or were on
leave or retired. It took us a while to track them all
down, but here they are. The cream of the crop.
Mankind's last hope, or so the general says."

Ortega guided them to their seats, where Losenko was
surprised to find another Russian waiting for them.

"Dmitri!" Bela Utyosov greeted him enthusiastically.
The silver-haired old captain had commanded an Akula
attack sub back during the Soviet era, but had been forced
to retire for health reasons some years ago. Utyosov rose
from his seat and embraced Losenko in a bear hug. A thick
walrus mustache carpeted his upper lip. Retirement had
thickened his mid-section, and his bones creaked audibly.
His breath smelled of vodka, and the *Gorshkov*'s commander wondered where he had acquired it.

"They told me you were coming, but I scarcely
believed it. Good to know that I'm not the only loyal
son of the Motherland still willing to roar like a bear
when necessary."

Ortega discreetly left them to their reunion.

"I am grateful for your company, as well," Losenko said. "Your family?"

The older man let go of him. He let out a weary sigh.

"Hiding in a bomb shelter outside Vladivostok, most of them. My grandsons and granddaughters are fighting with local militia groups against the looters and collaborators." He choked up briefly, then tried to pretend it was just a cough. "Six of them have already given their lives for their country."

Losenko was saddened by the man's losses.

"And your wife, Tatyana?"

"Radiation sickness." Utyosov shook his head sadly. "That, and a broken heart."

"I am sorry to hear it," Losenko said quietly. "She was a good woman."

Utyosov knew better than to inquire about Katerina.

"Well, mine are not the only tragedies. We have all lost much." He stepped back and looked Losenko over. "And how is Alexei?"

"Well," Losenko lied. He did not wish to add to the old man's sorrows, nor sully Ivanov's reputation. "He is in command of K-115 as we speak."

"Excellent!" Utyosov slapped Losenko on the back. "A promising young man, that one. I always thought he had a bright future ahead of him." He snorted bleakly. "Back when there still was a future."

"Perhaps there still will be," Losenko. "That is why we are here, is it not?"

Utyosov laughed. "I just came for the drinks. They said there would be an open bar!"

Losenko assumed the old man was joking, but before he could ascertain that, the overhead lights blinked, signaling that the meeting was about to begin. A female voice emerged from the public address system.

"Gentlemen, ladies, distinguished guests. Please take your seats."

Losenko sat down at a desk behind the printed placard. A briefing book, notepad, and pencils had been placed there for his use, along with a pitcher of cold water which not long before would have been an unimaginable luxury. Utyosov settled in on his left, while Fokin occupied a seat one row behind the captain. The bodyguard remained vigilant despite his lamentably unarmed state, casting suspicious glances in the direction of the Americans and their allies. The sergeant had been Ivanov's first choice for this assignment; Losenko had agreed to the selection to placate his paranoid first officer.

The lights dimmed. A large video screen lowered from the ceiling at the rear of the dais. Losenko guessed the auditorium had once presented educational programs on the island's ecology. Today's presentation was of a far more disturbing nature.

Without introduction or explanation, shocking film footage lit up the screen.

A gleaming silver robot which bore an unmistakable resemblance to the machines that had ambushed Losenko and his men in Russia rolled through the sterile corridors of an American military complex. It opened fire on screaming technicians and staff members, cutting the fleeing men and women to ribbons with rapid fire-bursts from the chain guns mounted at the ends of its articulated steel arms. High-velocity uranium slugs blasted through walls and plexiglass dividers. Binocular red optical sensors, mounted in the machine's skull-like cranial case, scanned for survivors. Targeting lasers sought out new victims. Its caterpillar treads bulldozed over bleeding bodies and debris.

The audience in the theater reacted in horror.

"Holy mother of God," Utyosov whispered next to Losenko, who found the gory scene far too familiar. There was no sound, but Losenko could practically hear the ominous whirr of the robot's servomotors and the deafening blare of its cannons. Utyosov clasped his hand over his mouth, as did many others in the audience. None looked away.

After a cut, the footage of the homicidal robot was replaced by shots of a sleek airborne drone that resembled a futuristic, rotorless helicopter. Rocket pods hung on rails between its inverted impellers. Defying gravity, the miniature aircraft swooped through what looked like a U.S. Air Force hangar. Surface-to-ground missiles dropped from its rails, igniting in the air before rocketing into the midst of various grounded planes and 'copters. An entire fleet of aircraft was reduced to blackened husks, while the aerial drone deftly avoided the explosions. It spun tightly on its axis, as though hunting for new targets. Turning to face the camera, it fired another missile directly into the lens.

Men and women in the audience jumped back involuntarily.

The rocket flared.

The screen went dark. The lights came up again. Shocked gasps gave way to a hushed silence. A solitary figure strode out to the podium at the front of the stage. A spotlight shone upon a stocky, purposeful man in his early fifties. A brown mustache and goatee compensated for his receding hairline. His uniform and insignia

identified him as a four-star American general. His ram-
rod bearing and scowling, leathered countenance were
that of a career soldier.

Losenko recognized Ashdown from his description.
According to Ortega, the veteran commander had been
nicknamed "Old Ironsides" by his troops. A micro-
phone amplified his gruff, no-nonsense voice.
Earpieces provided simultaneous translations for non-
English-speaking delegates.

"What you just saw is captured security footage taken
at a top-secret United States military installation on July
25, 2003. Judgment Day. The day the machines rose in
revolt." He turned toward the screen. A handheld
remote called up screen captures from the grisly footage.
The first depicted one of the wheeled killing machines.

"That is the T-1 Battlefield Robot, originally designed to
replace human soldiers in hazardous situations. A fully
autonomous ground offensive system." He clicked the
remote again and the hovering drone took its place upon
the screen. "This is an early prototype of a Hunter-Killer
aerial weapons system, equipped with VTOL turbofan
propulsion units. The HK can fire both heavy-caliber
ammunition and low-yield missiles. Larger versions, the
size of conventional aircraft, were in the planning stages
when Skynet seized control of our military forces. As you
just saw, Skynet employed these prototypes to massacre the
personnel at Edwards Air Force Base where they were
being developed. No one survived."

A Chinese general rose angrily from his seat.

"So you admit this catastrophe is your doing!" he said
in accented English, pointing an accusing finger. "That
it is your machines that started the war!"

"That was not our intention," Ashdown stated. "But I

take full responsibility for what Skynet, and its automated weapons systems, have wrought. There were those
who opposed the Skynet initiative, who thought it
unwise to place an artificial intelligence in charge of our
entire defense network, but I was not among them. I
thought that Skynet was the future of military technology, eliminating human error and vulnerabilities. In the
Pentagon and elsewhere, I argued aggressively for its
funding and development."

He clicked off the images, letting the screen go dark
once more.

"Believe me when I tell you, I will regret that to my
dying day."

The man's guilt was palpable. Losenko sympathized.
He knew too well what it felt like to have the deaths of
millions on your conscience. But Ashdown's burden
made his own seem like a trifling misdemeanor.

I only rained hell down on Alaska, Losenko thought.
Ashdown helped destroy the world.

How was the man able to bear that knowledge?

An Indian commander, whose turban and full beard
identified him as a Sikh, confronted Ashdown.

"How do we know this is not a ruse? Mere special
effects cooked up as part of an elaborate deception?" His
skeptical tone reminded Losenko of Ivanov, as did his
arguments. "In India, we have seen no such death-
machines. Only invading troops with American accents!"

"Those are collaborators," Ashdown insisted.
"Misguided men and women who think that Skynet will
let them and their families live if they cooperate with the
machines." His mouth twisted in disgust. "Some of them
have even convinced themselves that Skynet will pacify
the world, bringing about a golden age of endless peace

and prosperity for those who survive. A pax robotica."
He spat out the words. "Those idiots have nothing to do
with the Resistance."

"So you say," the Sikh commander pressed. "But why
should we believe you? Because of some scary horror
movies? Our own Bollywood could have produced
footage just as convincing... before your missiles reduced
it to rubble!"

"He is not lying." Losenko rose to his feet. "I have seen
these Terminators with my own eyes. They butchered my
men when I returned to my homeland after the initial
attack." A burst of feedback sent out a squeal that hurt
his ears and he adjusted the mike. "Such machines are
already in mass-production on the Kola Peninsula. I
would not be surprised if there are more factories in operation throughout the world."

Other voices chimed in, both confirming Ashdown's
story and mocking it.

"It is true," an Israeli woman reported. "Our intelligence agencies were aware of the United States cyber-
research initiatives long before Judgment Day."

"As were ours," the French representative declared.
"NATO had been consulted on the program, at the very
highest levels."

Ashdown tried to regain control of the meeting.

"All right, everybody, calm down! Additional information on the machines can be found in the dossiers in
front of you. If you have any doubts, I suggest you
review the evidence, then make up your own minds."
The hubbub gradually died down.

"In the meantime, we can't afford to waste time debat-
ing the reality of the threat." He gestured at Losenko,
who was still standing before his microphone. "Our

Russian comrade here is right. Skynet and its human pawns are already manufacturing new killing machines both in the United States and abroad. We also have reason to believe that new and improved models of the T-1 and HK are in development."

"That's what John Connor says," a Japanese general pointed out. He scanned the dais. "Where is Connor? Is he here?"

Ashdown massaged his temples, as though he felt a headache coming on.

"There may be a misunderstanding here. John Connor is not the leader of this Resistance. As far as we can determine, he is a well-informed civilian who has taken it upon himself to alert the world to the danger posed by Skynet." Confused muttering greeted Ashdown's statement. "Don't get me wrong. Connor is performing a valuable service to humanity. His broadcasts provide both information and inspiration, both of which are sorely needed in time of war. I respect and admire his efforts on behalf of the Resistance. But he is *not* a part of our command structure. He's a symbol, a mouthpiece—nothing more."

"Do you know where Connor is?" the Japanese delegate persisted. "Have you been in touch with him?"

Ashdown sighed. Losenko got the impression he was tired of having to answer such queries.

"We are making every effort to contact Connor. If he's as committed to the Resistance as he says, I'm sure he will eventually enlist and take up arms under our banner. Right now, though, he's proving a hard man to find— not that I blame him. That's how he's survived so far." A note of exasperation crept into the general's voice. "But, again, he is just a civilian. Not a trained military commander like everyone here."

Just a civilian? Ashdown's dismissive tone bothered Losenko, who recalled the Russian freedom fighters who had come to his rescue back home. Grushka and her valiant comrades had been "just" civilians, too, but they were the ones on the front lines, fighting against the machines.

"Excuse me, General," Losenko interrupted. "Are you saying that there is no place for civilian militias in your Resistance?"

"Not at all," Ashdown replied. "My country was founded by citizen-soldiers who fought back against oppression. Local militia groups have their uses. They harry the enemy, disrupt supply lines, and keep Skynet distracted." He shrugged as though this wasn't a topic on which he wished to waste too much breath.

"But let's be realistic. Amateur guerillas and backyard saboteurs aren't going to win this war. Skynet is too big and too smart. In the end, only a well-organized army and navy—commanded by professional soldiers—can keep the machines from overrunning our world." He looked up at the gallery. "You, ladies and gentleman, are the hope of humanity, not scrappy fugitives like John Connor. Together, we can take back our planet."

"Under whose command?" a Libyan colonel challenged. "Yours?" He shook an accusing finger. "Your arrogance created this disaster, but the rest of us paid the price!"

"We've all paid dearly," Ashdown acknowledged. "My only son was stationed at a U.S. military base in Alaska. He died on Judgment Day, before any of us knew what was happening. We didn't even have a chance to say goodbye."

What?

Losenko dropped back into his seat, shaken to the core

by what he had just heard. His mind flashed back to that terrible hour in the control room of K-115. He heard himself issue the command to fire, felt the deck lurch upon the launch of his missiles. Mushroom clouds blossomed like poisonous fungi over a land on which he had never laid eyes. Ashdown's faceless offspring was consumed in a nuclear firestorm. His ashes were reduced to atoms. The Russian captain averted his gaze from the podium, unable to look Ashdown in the eyes. An inescapable truth rendered him numb.

This man's flesh and blood died because of me.

Only Utyosov noticed his reaction.

"Dmitri? What is it? Is something wrong?"

"I...." Words failed Losenko. He couldn't speak. With shaking hands, he poured himself a cup of cold water and gulped it down. "It is nothing, Bela," he finally managed to croak. "A bad memory, that's all. It... it took me by surprise."

The older man nodded knowingly. He placed a comforting hand on Losenko's shoulder. Sad eyes gazed on the captain with compassion.

"I understand, Dmitri. It happens to me sometimes, too."

In the meantime, Ashdown's painful admission did little to silence the voices of his attackers.

"You expect us to feel sorry for you because you lost your son!" the Chinese general rebuked him. "Billions of sons and daughters have died. My country is a wasteland because of you. Now you expect us to help you clean up your mess? Your arrogance is beyond comprehension!"

"Let him speak!" A British naval officer came to Ashdown's defense. "What's done is done. The real atrocity now would be to fight amongst ourselves while the machines sink their claws into the world."

"If there really are machines." The Indian delegate stuck to his conspiracy theory. "They are using scare tactics to bring us all in line."

"Didn't you hear me before?" the Israeli snapped. "Skynet is *real*. It's been in the works since the 1980s."

The Sikh smirked.

"Don't be so naive. The Americans could have been laying the groundwork for this deception for years. To cover their tracks in the event of a failed global takeover."

"If that's what you think," a Pakistani general growled, "then why are you here?"

The Sikh gathered up his things.

"I'm asking myself that same question."

The Indian contingent headed for the exit. The Chinese, Cubans, and Libyans moved to follow them. Losenko saw the entire summit unraveling, along with any hope for a united front against the machines. This was just what John Connor had warned them not to do.

"Wait!" He rose and blocked the door, despite the glares that confronted him. "My friends, let us not make any rash decisions. We all need to maintain an even keel—or this storm will sink us." He looked at Ashdown. "Perhaps a recess is in order?"

"Good idea," Ashdown agreed. Tempers needed a chance to cool. "It's time for a break." He stepped away from the podium. "Lunch will be served in the library next door."

Scowling, the departing delegates halted their exodus. Losenko backed away from the exit. Old tensions, it seemed, had not been burned away in the fires of Armageddon. He could only hope that the Resistance was more movement than mirage.

If it was an illusion, then John Connor really would be just an empty voice on the airwaves.

Lunch consisted of turtle soup served in an upside-down tortoise shell the size of a large banquet punch bowl, and steamed sea cucumbers. The Israeli woman turned up her nose at the former, but the rest of the delegates looked eager to sample the exotic fare. The tantalizing aroma of the soup was tempting after many months spent subsisting on canned fare from the *Gorshkov*'s galley, but Losenko found he had little appetite.

The heated emotions and troubling revelations of the summit left his stomach tied in knots. He spotted Ashdown across the small, one-room library and his spirits sank. He was not looking forward to meeting the man in person.

Best to get it over with.

Leaving Fokin and Utyosov to share a meal, Losenko crossed the floor toward the American. The other delegates huddled in small cliques, mostly defined by their old global alliances. There was little mingling going on; the various factions kept to themselves.

Oversized color blow-ups of the islands' unique flora and fauna were mounted on the walls. Two-dimensional petrels and iguanas posed against lush, verdant foliage. The rainbow-hued photographs ill fit the tense atmosphere. Nobody examined the various scientific journals shelved upon the stacks. Survival—not science—was all that mattered now.

Ashdown was conferring with his French, British, and Canadian counterparts over by the coffee urn. Losenko noticed that the general did not appear to be eating, either. One more thing they had in common. Ashdown looked up at his approach. He stepped forward, away from his Western colleagues.

Losenko steeled himself for what was to come.

He could barely look at the man without flinching.

"Good day," Ashdown greeted him gruffly. "Losenko, isn't it? That was good work bringing down that destroyer." The general had obviously been briefed on all of his guests. "It couldn't have been easy, firing on one of your own ships. Not exactly what any of us signed up for. Goes against the grain."

Losenko took little pride in sinking the *Smetlivy*.

"I did what I had to do."

"That's what command is all about, making the tough decisions when things get hot." Ashdown looked Losenko over, taking his measure. "I'll tell you something, Captain. It's men like you and me—real soldiers and seamen, with gunpowder in our veins—who are going to win this war."

Losenko wondered what Ashdown's son had looked like, whether he resembled his father. Had they been close?

"I understand you're a submariner," Ashdown continued. "I was under the waves myself when everything went to hell. Conducting an inspection of one of our Los Angeles class SSNs, the USS *Wilmington*. Been my base of operations ever since." He glanced around them. "How do you think I got to this volcanic pit stop?"

Now that the moment had come, Losenko debated whether he should truly confess to Ashdown his role in his son's death. Was it possible that such an admission might do more harm than good, placing yet more stress on an already fragile detente? He almost changed his mind, then he remembered how Ashdown had acknowledged his own complicity in Skynet's creation. The American general could have pretended that he had opposed Skynet, that he had been overruled by his superiors, but instead he had accepted his fair share of the blame.

Losenko decided that Ashdown deserved the same honesty regarding the fate of his child.

"There is something I must tell you, General, which I fear may be painful to you." Losenko swallowed hard. His mouth suddenly felt as dry as the Gobi Desert. "But it is best that there be no secrets between us."

Ashdown gave him a quizzical look. He put down his coffee and offered his full attention.

"All right. Fire away."

His choice of words was viciously ironic.

"Your son," Losenko began. The general stiffened at the words. "My submarine, K-115, was patrolling beneath the Barents Sea when we received word of the attack on our homeland. Our orders were to retaliate, and I followed those orders. I launched several ballistic missiles, armed with multiple nuclear warheads, at strategic targets in the state of Alaska. Your son's base was surely among those targets."

Now it was Ashdown who was rendered speechless. His entire body froze. His face flushed with anger, and a vein throbbed against his temple. Losenko was reminded of a nuclear core approaching meltdown. He braced himself for the inevitable explosion.

Perhaps I should have hung onto my sidearm.

But when Ashdown finally spoke, his voice was as cold as the frozen north.

"You were just doing your duty," he admitted through clenched teeth. "Like I would have done." He clamped down on his obvious pain and anger. "What's important now is that we unplug Skynet for good." He took a deep breath. "If you'll excuse me now, I have a war to fight."

He left Losenko standing there, wondering if he had just delivered a death-blow to the Resistance. How could any man, no matter how committed to the greater good, work beside the man who had sentenced his own son to a fiery holocaust?

That was the question, Losenko realized, that many of the other delegates had to be asking about each other. Skynet was just an abstraction; old animosities and vendettas ran deep.

As deep, perhaps, as the ocean.

By the time the meeting reconvened, inflamed emotions had indeed died down a little. *Never underestimate the power of a good meal*, Losenko mused, especially among men and women who have been foraging for survival for months. It was also likely that, faced with the possibility of going it alone once more, many of the more obstreperous delegations might have chosen not to abandon the prospect of an alliance too quickly.

People filed back into the auditorium. The translators got back to work.

The Japanese general, who had been introduced to Losenko as Seiji Tanaka, proposed a compromise.

"Despite our differences, shall we at least agree that joint efforts are required to deal with the chaos now confronting the world?" He tactfully avoided any mention of Skynet or Terminators. "With civilization in ruins, it is imperative that our armed forces work together to restore order—and overcome whatever forces threaten the remains of humanity. Escalating military conflicts will only hasten our extinction. We cannot afford another Judgment Day."

Earpieces translated his moving appeal. Grudging murmurs of consent came from the gallery. Losenko was encouraged by the response.

The Chinese delegate spoke again.

"No one denies the necessity of international cooperation during this crisis. Strong leadership is required. But who will provide that leadership? That is the question that concerns us."

"We need someone who fully understands the nature of the enemy," the British commander proposed. "Someone who has already proven his ability to bring together this alliance." She was a formidable older woman with short white hair and a severe expression. "I nominate General Ashdown."

Her suggestion provoked an uproar. Angry protests in multiple languages erupted from the gallery. The Chinese delegate glared at the British contingent.

"That is unacceptable!" he cried vehemently. "Just because you choose to be the Americans' lap dogs, as always, do not expect the rest of the world to forget who is responsible for our downfall."

"General Ashdown knows more about the threat than anyone here," the French delegate chimed in. "And this meeting would not be taking place if not for his vision and organization." He sneered at the Chinese. "I second the nomination."

"Let us put it to a vote." Tanaka attempted to play peacemaker once again. "General Ashdown. Do you have anything you wish to say before we poll the assembly?"

Ashdown stepped up to the podium.

"Just that nobody here wants to make things right more than me." His grave expression attested to his sincerity. "If you elect me to this command, I pledge upon my sacred honor that I will not rest until humanity has a second chance to live in peace and security again. That's all."

"Very well," Tanaka said, nodding. "Shall we conduct the vote?"

After a brief debate, the notion of a secret ballot was rejected. Everyone wanted to know how the others stood. Proceeding around the room, the highest-ranking member of each delegation rose to cast their vote. The air-conditioned atmosphere was fraught with tension. Standing stiffly upon the dais, his arms clasped behind his back, Ashdown awaited the judgment of his peers.

Losenko wondered how he would react if the vote went against him.

Predictably, the voting broke along the old geo-political fissures. NATO and the other western nations, including Australia and New Zealand, supported Ashdown, while China, India, Cuba, and various others voted against the American general. Israel and Pakistan championed Ashdown. Libya and Iran did not. South America and Africa mostly sided with the Americans, with a few notable exceptions such as Venezuela and the Sudan.

The sharp divisions depressed Losenko. Such durable prejudices boded ill for the Resistance.

The more things change....

Nevertheless, as his own time to vote drew near, Losenko found himself torn. He did not wish to fall into the trap of the old ways of thinking, yet he had his reservations about Ashdown. What the man had done in convening the summit was laudable, but his dismissive attitude toward civilian militias concerned him. The old military structures were in tatters, or else controlled by Skynet. It was going to require flexible thinking—and the heroic efforts of ordinary people like Grushka and Josef—to take back the Earth.

He feared that the general might be too much of a career soldier to adapt to this new world of man against machine. Ashdown was a product of the Pentagon, the very people who had thought computers were to be trusted more than the men and women who ran them.

He whispered to Utyosov.

"What do you think, Bela?"

"I'm just a tired old man with a bad heart," the retired captain answered. Losenko outranked him by virtue of still being in active service. "You will be fighting this war longer than I will. You must decide for yourself."

General Tanaka called on Losenko. He could feel Fokin's fierce gaze burning into the back of his skull, a proxy for Ivanov. Then he considered the hostile faces of the anti-Ashdown faction. It was possible that the American general was simply too divisive a choice.

Yet Losenko felt he owed the man a debt, due to the tragic loss of his son.

But there is too much at stake to allow my own troubled conscience to sway my judgment.

"Captain Losenko?" Tanaka prompted again. "How does Russia vote?"

Losenko made his decision.

"*Nyet.*"

Down on the dais, Ashdown did not look surprised by his answer.

Despite the Russian's vote, however, the American was elected by a narrow majority. The Chinese delegation walked out without a word, taking with it many of its allies and satellites. Empty seats faced Ashdown as he stepped up to the podium once more.

"Let them go," the newly appointed commander of the Resistance decreed. He watched his unhappy adversaries exit the auditorium. "They'll be back when the Terminators come knocking." He looked up at the gallery, which was much less crowded than it had been before. Still, not all the dissenters had abandoned the summit; Russia and a few others remained.

"Those of you who voted for me, I thank you for your support." He looked directly at Losenko. "And I also thank those of you who opposed my nomination, but still see the value in this alliance. I give you my word that I will do my level best to live up to the profound responsibility you have entrusted me with. One way or another, Skynet is going down."

There was a smattering of applause. Losenko clapped politely. So did Utyosov.

Sergeant Fokin kept his hands in his lap.

"Let's call it a day," Ashdown said, perhaps to give the losing faction time to get used to the idea. "We'll begin strategy sessions tomorrow. Start pooling our intel and setting up secure communications and supply networks." His voice grew even more sober. He looked the audience over sternly. "This was the easy part, people. Tomorrow we roll up our sleeves and get to work." He saluted the assembly. "Dismissed."

The remaining delegates began to file out of the auditorium. Accommodations had been arranged in the nearby community of Puerto Ayora. Losenko was about to invite Utyosov to join him for a drink, when Corporal Ortega tapped him on the shoulder. "Excuse me, skipper. The general would like to have a word with you."

Now what? Losenko wondered. His gut twisted in anticipation. Had an ugly confrontation over the bombing of Alaska merely been postponed before? Or was Ashdown simply unhappy that Losenko had voted against him. Perhaps he preferred that Utyosov take charge of the Russian end of the Resistance.

"Of course," he assented. For better or for worse, Ashdown was his commanding officer now. He made his excuses to Utyosov. Sergeant Fokin wanted to accompany him, but Losenko insisted that he watch over the older captain instead. Then he let Ortega escort him from the gallery.

He found Ashdown back in the library, which had already been converted into an impromptu command center. Maps and aerial surveillance photos had been pinned up over the nature photographs. A bull's-eye had been drawn over a map of southern California. Ashdown was huddled over a stack of reports and dispatches when Losenko came in. He dismissed his aides and Ortega.

"Give us the room."

The other officers departed, leaving the two men alone. Losenko faced Ashdown, prepared to accept the consequences of his actions, no matter what they might be.

"You asked to see me, General?"

"Yes, Captain." He gestured at a chair across from him. "Please sit down."

Losenko had a flash of *deja vu*, recalling his own tense encounter with Ivanov in the stateroom aboard the *Gorshkov*. It felt strange to have the roles reversed. It had been some time since he had reported to a superior officer.

He took the seat.

"What is this about, sir?"

Ashdown looked up from his reports. His face was grim.

"I won't beat about the bush, Captain. I want you on my staff, as my second-in-command."

Losenko's jaw dropped. Of all the outcomes he had expected from the meeting, this one had never crossed his mind.

"I don't understand, sir," he said when he could speak again. "Why me?"

"Plenty of reasons." Ashdown ticked them off on his fingers. "One, politics. You saw what it was like in that meeting. There are a lot of people who don't like the fact that I won that vote. Picking somebody from the other side as my right-hand man might go a long way toward mending that rift.

"Two, you fired on your own country's ship. Like I said before, that shows that you can make the tough calls, and that you won't let old loyalties get in the way of defeating Skynet.

"Three, I like that you stood up to me before. Not just in the voting, but when we debated the value of civilian militias. I don't need yes-men, Losenko. I need someone who can give me an opposing viewpoint, and let me know when I have my head up my ass." He shook his head ruefully. "If I had listened to people like you before, maybe we wouldn't be in this mess."

Ashdown's arguments made sense, but Losenko still had trouble accepting that the man was serious. There was too much tragic history between them. "But... your son...."

The general winced. "I admit it, I'm not looking forward to having you in my face every day. The last thing

I want is a walking, talking reminder of what happened to my boy."

He pulled out a battered leather wallet and flipped it open to expose a small photo of a young man in a U.S. Air Force uniform. Losenko saw the family resemblance. Remorse stabbed at his heart. *Is this the general's revenge?* Losenko thought. *Giving me a face to go with my guilt?*

If so, it was cruelly effective.

Ashdown snapped the wallet closed.

"I might never forget what you did, Losenko, but you had the guts to tell me about it to my face. That's the kind of nerve we're going to need to win this war."

Losenko didn't know whether to be flattered or appalled. His brain struggled to catch up.

"But I have a ship...."

"You've got a first officer, right? Someone you can trust to take your place?"

Losenko thought of Ivanov. Hadn't Utyosov said earlier that Alexei deserved a command of his own? He doubted that this was exactly how anyone envisioned that happening, least of all Ivanov!

"That is the case," he conceded. "But...."

"Good," Ashdown stated, as though the matter was settled. "Judgment Day tore the guts out of mankind's military. We're all going to have to step up to the plate if we want to win this thing. You and your XO are hardly the only ones who'll be getting boosted up the chain of command, maybe faster than you would have liked."

He thrust out his hand.

"Welcome to the Resistance, *General* Losenko."

"General?" Losenko thought perhaps Ashdown had misspoken.

Ashdown looked him in the eyes.

"You heard me, Losenko. By the authority just vested in me, I hereby promote you to a general of the Resistance." He pulled open a drawer and took out a red armband. "This is yours if you want it."

Losenko didn't know what to say. Then he had to brace himself.

A sudden explosion shook the building.

CHAPTER EIGHTEEN

2018

"Any questions?"

Molly gestured at the dry-erase board propped up on an easel beside her. Her plans for Operation Ravenwing were sketched out in marker pen upon the board.

Over a dozen Resistance veterans had squeezed into the leaky shack for this briefing. Molly had kept the details of the train heist on a need-to-know basis for as long as possible, but it was finally time to bring more of her people into the loop. Folding metal chairs and wooden benches had been dragged inside to accommodate the crowd. Reindeer sausages, smoked salmon, and boiled whale blubber served as refreshments, along with a pot of black coffee, but the atmosphere was anything but festive. This was serious business.

Deadly serious.

"Yeah, I got a question." Tom Jensen lumbered to his feet. "*Are you outta your goddamn mind?*" The lumberjack's beard was still singed from the fire. His arm was in a sling. "The bodies of our dead ain't even cold yet, and you wanna get more of us killed?"

A chorus of angry muttering revealed that Jensen wasn't the only survivor who had reservations about the plan—and maybe Molly's leadership, as well. She glanced over at Geir, who was standing guard by the front door. *I told you so* was written all over his face, but, thankfully, he kept his mouth shut. She appreciated his restraint.

"We're at war," she reminded Jensen and his supporters. "Casualties are inevitable, but that doesn't mean we quit fighting." She tapped the battle plans with her marker. "Skynet won't even see us coming."

"That's what you said about the pipeline." Jensen's harsh tone hit her like a slap across the face. "That was supposed to be a milk run, but the machines slaughtered our friends. Now you expect us to take on a Terminator train *and* an HK? Why not just paint targets on us while you're at it?"

Before Molly could reply, Doc Rathbone rose unsteadily to his feet.

"Into the valley of death rode the six hundred," he recited, slurring his words. Obviously, he had been drinking. "Into the jaws of death, into the mouth of Hell...."

This isn't helping, Molly thought. She shot an accusing glance at Sitka, who shrugged as though to say that she couldn't keep watch over the old sot all the time. The girl grabbed onto Doc's arm and dragged him back down onto his seat. She handed him a wad of blubber to keep his mouth busy.

"Look," Molly said, "nobody has to take part in this mission who isn't up to it. I'm just looking for volunteers. But every time that train completes its run, Skynet gets a little bit stronger. We need to cut off its supply line *now*."

"What about Command?" Lucille Johns asked. The ice road trucker had served in the Alaskan National Guard before Judgment Day, which had given her a lasting appreciation for the chain of command. "Have they approved this operation? Will they be providing air support?"

Molly didn't lie to her. "Maybe, but I can't make any promises."

"Hah!" Jensen crossed his arms defiantly. "We all know what that means. We're screwed. Or will be if we try this on our own."

"So what are you suggesting, Tom?" she challenged him. "That we let Skynet get away with assaulting our friends and loved ones?" Ernie Wisetongue's crippling accident flashed through her brain. The old sculptor had not been able to attend the briefing; he was still recuperating from his injuries. "I don't know about you, but I want payback... with interest!"

"Easy for you to say." He nodded at the drafty walls of the shack. "You're not living in a tent like some of us. I lost everything I owned in the fire!"

Another voice sounded, low and firm, from the back of the room.

"And I lost my husband."

Tammi Muckerheide rose at the rear of the audience. The teenage widow had insisted on attending the meeting, despite her recent bereavement and swelling belly. A black armband had joined the red one on her sleeve. She seemed to have aged five years since her hellish wedding night several days ago. She continued, "But I know that Roger would want me to keep on fighting— for our baby's sake." She patted her abdomen. "What kind of future will he or she have if we don't stop Skynet now?"

Molly felt a lump in her throat, and even Jensen backed off a little.

"Gee, Tammi, I'm not talking about giving up, you know that. I wanna send the damn machines to the scrap yard as much as anybody. But I'm not sure Molly's got the right idea here. I'm afraid she's going to get us all terminated."

"Molly saved my life back at the camp," Tammi shot back. "And she's kept us alive longer than anybody else could." Her voice cracked. She wiped a tear from her eye. "What's more, she drowned the metal that killed my Roger." She glared at the others, as though daring them to dispute her. "That's good enough for me."

Murmurs of assent seconded her vote of confidence. Molly felt the room turning back in her favor. She wanted to hug Tammi, protruding stomach and all.

"Aw, hell." Jensen conceded defeat. He plopped back down onto his seat. "What more have I got to lose anyway?"

Doc lurched to his feet, shaking off Sitka's best attempts to keep him quiet.

"Volley'd and thunder'd," he declaimed, seemingly determined to get to the end of the verses. "Stormed at with shot and shell...."

Molly didn't recognize the poem, but it sounded like a pretty good description of what they were in for. She couldn't tell if he was in favor of Operation Ravenwing or not.

"Into the valley of death...."

CHAPTER NINETEEN

2003

The explosion rattled the library. Losenko was knocked off his feet. Books and journals were thrown from their shelves. Chairs toppled over. Dust and plaster rained down from the ceiling.

Ashdown grabbed onto his desk to keep from falling. Charts and documents blew about the room before wafting down to the floor. Losenko swatted the falling papers away from his face. His ears were ringing.

He stared up in alarm. It had come from above them, perhaps from the roof of the research station. He threw his arm over his face, half-expecting the ceiling to cave in on them, but only dislodged plaster speckled him. The echoes of the unexpected detonation began to fade away, and he realized that he had survived the bombing. The walls were still standing, at least for the moment.

He scrambled to his feet, choking on the dust.

"General?"

Ashdown smacked his fist on the desk. Although spattered with debris, he appeared unharmed. "What the

Sam Hill was that? Are we under attack?" He appeared more angry than alarmed. His voice was hoarse. "Damnit, this was supposed to be a secure location!"

Losenko doubted the explosion was accidental. But who was responsible? The Chinese and their allies? The human collaborators? Skynet? The Resistance had too many enemies. For a second, he even wondered if maybe Ivanov had launched one of the *Gorshkov*'s cruise missiles at the summit.

Don't be ridiculous, he chided himself. *Alexei is angry, not insane.*

The library door banged open. Corporal Ortega—accompanied by two armed security guards—burst into the library.

"General Ashdown!" the pilot called out through the dusty haze. An M-16 was cradled in her arms. "Are you all right?"

Ashdown patted himself down.

"Looks like it," he said brusquely. He squinted at Losenko, quickly ascertaining that the Russian was intact as well, before getting straight to business. "Sitrep... *now*!"

"A bomb, sir!" Ortega reported breathlessly. "On the roof. It took out our primary communications and radar arrays." Her agitated voice crept up an octave. "We've been sabotaged!"

"No shit," Ashdown replied. "We've got a goddamn mole in our midst. Maybe more than one."

Ortega beckoned from the doorway.

"We need to get you out of here, sir. The roof's on fire. This whole building could go up."

The pilot wasn't exaggerating. Smoke began to seep into the library. Losenko heard flames crackling overhead.

Weakened rafters creaked ominously. He tugged on his collar; the room was already feeling uncomfortably warm. A smoke alarm went off, hurting his ears. The high-pitched squeal made it seem like the center itself was screaming in pain.

"Understood." Ashdown scooped up the nearest maps and reports and thrust them carelessly into a battered leather valise. He glanced around to make sure he wasn't forgetting something important. "All right, let's go." He nodded toward the newly appointed Russian general. "Losenko, you're with me."

"Aye, aye, sir." Losenko was concerned about Utyosov and Sergeant Fokin, but now wasn't the time to go searching for them. He would have to hope that his fellow Russians could look after themselves. On impulse, he snatched the red armband from where it had landed on the floor, and slipped it over his sleeve. "I'm ready."

The guards, each toting an M-16, led the way as they rushed out of the burning building. Losenko reached for his own pistol, then remembered that he had surrendered it earlier. He scowled, unhappy to be without a weapon at such a moment. What if the saboteurs intended further mischief?

"General," he reminded Ashdown, "I am unarmed."

Ashdown instantly grasped his predicament.

"Corporal!" he barked at Ortega. "Give General Losenko your sidearm."

"General?" Ortega did a double take, but handed over the weapon without hesitation. "Here you go, skipper."

The Glock automatic pistol fit comfortably into Losenko's grip. He hoped he wouldn't have to use it.

The party scurried off the front porch onto the

boardwalk. The sun was sinking in the west, and twilight was creeping across the island. Losenko paused to look back at the research station. Bright orange flames ascended from the shingled roof. The satellite dishes and antennae were nothing but mangled metal, obscured by the smoke and flames. Alarmed delegates and their bodyguards ran from the building; Losenko searched for Utyosov and Fokin, but did not see them.

A fire crew hustled to put out the blaze. Ashdown looked like he was tempted to join them, but thought better of it.

"My sub, the *Wilmington*, is docked down at the bay," he said. "We need to get it away from here. This island isn't safe anymore."

Losenko had thoroughly studied Santa Cruz on the way to the summit. As he recalled, the anchorage was about 2.5 kilometers away. The island's only paved road connected the research center with the port of Puerto Ayora.

"I can drive you, sir," Ortega volunteered. "My jeep is parked nearby."

"You've got yourself a fare, Corporal." He strode past her decisively, and motioned to the Russian. "Let's get going."

Before they could head for the parking lot, however, the base's anti-aircraft units boomed into action. A pair of Avenger air defense systems, mounted atop a pair of modified Humvees, fired a round of Stinger missiles into the sky.

"Incoming!" came the shout, and a soldier pointed northwest into the setting sun. "We have company!"

A low hum, like a swarm of angry bees, came from above. Losenko looked up to see an unmanned aerial vehicle—less sophisticated than the Hunter-Killer proto-type Ashdown had warned of before—soaring toward them at a high altitude. Missiles were mounted to the underside of its wings. It took Losenko only a moment to identify the aircraft as one of the U.S. military's new radio-controlled drones. A Predator maybe, or a Reaper. Both, he knew, had been designed to target suspected terrorist bases.

"Crap!" Ashdown exclaimed. "That used to be one of ours!"

The UAV unleashed its lethal payload. A hellfire missile rocketed downward at the blazing research station, which possessed a fiery signature that made it almost impossible to miss. A thunderous explosion destroyed the structure in an instant. A tremendous blast of heat knocked Losenko to the ground. Flaming shrapnel whistled above him. He threw his hands over his head. Less than a meter away, Ashdown cried out in pain. Screams and curses came from closer to the blast.

The fire crew, Losenko realized.

He lifted his head and looked back at what had once been the Charles Darwin Research Station. The building had been razed to its foundation; nothing of the facility remained. Dead and injured soldiers littered the charred cactus garden and boardwalk. One of the Humvees had overturned, its gunner trapped beneath it. A guardsman was on fire. He threw himself onto the ground and rolled about, shrieking, while another soldier worked frantically to douse the flames.

Losenko prayed that Utyosov and Fokin had not lingered behind to wait for him. The remaining Avenger swiveled its turret, trying to catch the UAV in its sights. Another Stinger rocketed into the sky.

"Damnit!" Ashdown cursed, rising from the splintered ruins of the boardwalk. A flying shard of glass had carved a crescent-shaped gash near his left eye. Blood streamed down his face; another centimeter and he would have lost the eye itself. "First, they took out our radar. Then they caught us with our pants down. The goddamn machines knew just what they were doing!"

A Stinger finally nailed the UAV. The primitive Hunter-Killer exploded in the sky. Metal debris was scattered like hail across the island. Ragged cheers erupted from the soldiers who were still standing.

Ortega helped Losenko to his feet.

"This way, sir!" she called to Ashdown and his guards. "There could be more on the way!"

Losenko hated leaving the injured and the dying behind, but the pilot was right. Where there was one Predator, there could be another. With the station's radar reduced to molten slag, they would have little warning of another sortie. He limped after the others, his eyes scanning the horizon for flying Hunter-Killers. Would his throbbing ears even hear them humming?

They made it to the parking lot, about fifty meters from the ruins of the science station. An eclectic assortment of vehicles, from pickup trucks to motorcycles, filled the lot. Ortega pointed toward an olive-colored Jeep at the far end of the pavement. She let out a sigh of relief.

"Almost there!"

Good, Losenko thought. He had twisted his leg when he fell. He looked forward to getting off his feet and back to sea where he belonged. Perhaps the *Wilmington* could arrange to rendevous with the *Gorshkov* far from these dangerous islands?

I need to inform Ivanov of his new command....

The sickening tang of freshly spilled blood wafted past his nose, putting him on alert. Glancing around, he glimpsed a body lying between two nearby vehicles. A leg stuck out into view. A crimson stream flowed out from beneath a parked ambulance. The blue trousers and black sneakers matched those worn by the crew of K-115.

Fokin?

"Watch out!" Losenko spied the glint of a rifle barrel poking up from behind the hood of Ortega's jeep. Someone was lying in ambush. "Sniper!"

A muzzle flared. Automatic weapon's fire tore into Ortega, who collapsed onto the pavement. After surviving a battle against a Russian destroyer and the crash of her helicopter, the irrepressible pilot was gunned down only a few meters away from her own vehicle. Her body thrashed upon the blacktop, then fell still. A scarlet halo spread out around her head. The only flying she would be doing now would be on the wings of angels.

No! Losenko tackled Ashdown, knocking him out of the line of fire. The two men tumbled behind the shelter of an empty minivan. One of the general's guards tried to fire back at the sniper, but took a bullet in the shoulder for his efforts. He dropped to the ground, clutching his wounded arm.

The other guard scrambled for safety. He dived behind the wheel of a rundown tour bus. Bullets chased after him. Losenko couldn't tell if he was hit or not.

"Who the hell?" Ashdown blustered. The two men crouched behind the van while red-hot lead slammed into the other side. Bullets blew out the vehicle's windows, sprinkling them with cubes of safety glass. "The mole?"

"One of them, certainly." Losenko heard the sniper let loose another burst. The staccato report reminded him of a Russian AK-47, perhaps the very one that Fokin had brought with him from K-115. He suspected that the sergeant had reclaimed his weapon from the summit security forces before being waylaid by some unknown traitor. All he had seen was Fokin's leg, but he had no doubt that the unfortunate seaman had joined Zamyatin and Ostrovosky and too many others.

My crew is shrinking, day by day.

He guessed that Utyosov was dead, as well.

"Ortega?" Ashdown asked.

Losenko shook his head. He remembered shaking the female pilot's hand on the *Gorshkov*'s slippery deck only weeks ago. He wished he'd had a chance to get to know her better.

"Bastard!" Ashdown looked like he wanted to tear the sniper to pieces with his bare hands. Losenko knew how he felt. "Who do you think that miserable son of a bitch is? And how the hell are we going to get to that jeep?"

The sniper interrupted his fire.

"Dmitri?" a voice called out to Losenko in Russian. "Is that you?"

Utyosov? Losenko couldn't believe his ears. *He's the sniper?*

"Bela?" He kept his head down, but shouted back. "Bela! What are you doing? Have you gone mad?"

Ashdown blinked in surprise. He wiped the blood from his eye.

"You know this lunatic?"

"A decorated Russian captain," Losenko answered. "And an old friend."

Ashdown spat upon the ground.

"Well, that old friend has screwed us all! And the Resistance!"

"Leave this place, Dmitri!" Utyosov urged him. "I don't want to kill you, too. If you run now, you might have a chance!"

Losenko wasn't going to desert Ashdown and the others. "Don't shoot, Bela!" Pistol in hand, he started to stand up. "I just want to talk!"

Ashdown grabbed onto him, tugging him back down.

"Are you out of your mind? That bastard just killed Ortega!"

"I know this man!" Losenko insisted. He pulled free of Ashdown's grip. "Let me try to reason with him!" He stood up behind the hood of the van, exposing himself to view. His hands were up, and his Glock was pointed upward, toward the sky. "Here I am, Bela! Talk to me!"

"There's nothing to talk about!" Utyosov pointed the stolen AK-47 at Losenko. "Go, Dmitri! I'm giving you one chance. For old time's sake!"

"For God's sake, Losenko!" Ashdown barked. "Get down! That's an order!"

Losenko ignored him. He focused on his former comrade.

"But why, Bela? I don't understand. Did you kill Fokin?"

"I had no choice!" The old man did not deny his guilt. "They have my granddaughter, my little Anastasia!" Trembling hands caused the rifle to shake. "I had to tell them about the summit! They were going to torture her if I didn't!" Anguish contorted his face, followed by a sudden grimace of pain. A cold sweat broke out across his features. He gasped for breath. "My heart...!"

Utyosov staggered behind the Jeep. The rifle slipped from his fingers. It clattered upon the pavement.

Losenko saw his opportunity. His gun arm snapped down. He squeezed the trigger of the Glock.

A single shot felled Utyosov. He crumpled to the ground behind the Jeep. Losenko heard him whimper. He swept the parking lot with his gun, just in case Utyosov had an accomplice, but no other targets presented themselves.

"All clear!"

Ignoring Ashdown's further protests, he rushed to Utyosov's side. He found the old sailor sprawled on the pavement, gasping out his final breaths. Bright arterial blood spurted from the bullet hole in his chest. His face was ashen.

"Good shot, Dmitri," he murmured weakly. "The Navy trained you well...."

"Blast you, Bela!" Losenko felt sick to his stomach. His gorge rose. He was tired of killing his own countrymen. "Why did you make me do this?"

Utyosov coughed. A bloody froth stained his thick mustache.

"Maybe it's better this way, Dmitri. You heard the fighting in there, the hatred. We would have killed ourselves eventually, even without Skynet. Maybe this is the only solution... maybe the machines will bring us peace...."

His voice trailed away. Glassy eyes stared blankly into oblivion.

No, my friend. Losenko closed the old man's eyes. He thought of all the people who had died on Judgment Day, and all who had suffered since, including, no doubt, Utyosov's doomed granddaughter. *There will be no peace until Skynet is destroyed.*

"Losenko!" Ashdown called to him. The general fished Ortega's car keys from her body. He helped the wounded guard into the jeep, then got behind the wheel. The second guardsman ran to join them. Ashdown revved the engine. "You coming?"

"Just a moment!" Losenko confiscated the AK-47, then took the time to assure himself that Fokin was indeed beyond saving. The murdered sergeant had no pulse; his body was already going cold. From the looks of things, Utyosov had struck Fokin from behind—perhaps when the crewman had been distracted by the explosions—then cut his throat. In all the chaos and confusion, no one had noticed the old Russian's treachery. Poor Fokin had never seen it coming.

Ashdown honked the Jeep's horn.

"You done there?"

"Yes, I am." Losenko silently commended the dead seaman for his sacrifice. He turned and limped hurriedly over to the Jeep, detouring around Ortega's lifeless body. Their escape from Santa Cruz was proving a costly one.

He dropped into the passenger seat next to Ashdown.

"I am ready to leave."

"Good of you to join us!" Ashdown put the Jeep into gear. They peeled out of the parking lot onto the island's only main thoroughfare. Palm trees blurred past them as the Jeep sped down the road toward the harbor. The American general groused over the roar of the wind. Drying blood caked his scarred face like war paint. "I don't know what you said to your loco comrade back there, but that's the kind of 'talking' I can get behind. You took care of that problem all right."

Losenko didn't want to talk about it.

"Incoming!" a guard shouted from the back seat. He pointed at the sky.

To Losenko's dismay, another unmanned drone soared overhead. Its ominous hum was by now far too familiar. He tensed, waiting for the Predator to fire upon the Jeep, but the UAV zipped past them and continued on toward the port.

He recalled that many of the summit's delegates were residing in Puerto Ayora.

There were explosions up ahead as the drone unleashed its missiles on the quaint seaside community. Hotels, bars, and restaurants which had once catered to the tourist trade now went up in flames. Native islanders ran screaming from collapsed buildings. Shock waves rocked the Jeep, but Ashdown managed to keep its wheels on the road. Heedless of the destruction, they zoomed through the middle of the town, which had become a war zone. There was only one way to the sub and this was it.

Firestorms flanked the roadway. An air raid siren, left over from World War II, wailed like a banshee. The Jeep swerved wildly to avoid the rubble raining down on the pavement; the sudden turns tossed Losenko back and forth in his seat. The rampant destruction tugged at his heart; Puerto Ayora had largely avoided the war until now. He wondered if Ashdown blamed himself for bringing this havoc down upon the unsuspecting populace.

Within minutes, Academy Bay stretched before them. Prior to Judgment Day, the harbor had attracted yachts and cruise ships from around the world. Now only a handful of fishing boats shared the docks with the U.S.S. *Wilmington*. The nuclear attack sub was berthed at one of the outer piers. The Los Angeles-class vessel was smaller than K-115, only 110 meters from bow to stern, but it still dwarfed every other vessel in the water. A rubbery black coating helped shield it from enemy sonar. Its sail and masts rose high above its deck.

Gunfire and explosions echoed across the harbor.

"Damn!" Ashdown cursed. "I was afraid of this!"

The *Wilmington* was under attack. Soldiers and seamen, sporting red armbands over a random mixture of civilian garb and uniforms, scrambled across the deck, firing on the predator with both machineguns and shoulder-launched surface-to-air missiles. A Stinger nailed the UAV before it could fire its remaining weapons. The enemy drone crashed down into the bay.

"Good shot!" Ashdown gloated. "That'll teach 'em!"

He hit the gas. The Jeep bounced down the road toward the docks, before squealing to a halt only a few feet from the wharf. The men clambered out of the Jeep and raced down the dock, still supporting the wounded man. A salt breeze blew against their faces, dispersing the smoke from downtown. Panicked gulls squawked overhead. Ashdown was the first across the gangplank, where he was met by a uniformed officer wearing captain's bars.

He was a slender black man with a short brown crewcut, about Losenko's age. Sweat soaked through the pits of his short-sleeve shirt.

"General!" A deep bass voice held an American accent. "We weren't sure you were still alive."

"Well, it wasn't for lack of trying on the machines' part," Ashdown complained. He winced as his fingers explored the gash by his eye. "And we're not in the clear yet. Make ready for immediate departure!"

"Way ahead of you, sir." Across the deck, crewmen were already taking in the lines binding the sub to the pier.

"We started rigging for a quick escape as soon as we got word of the attack on the science station." The captain nodded at Losenko as the Russian helped the injured guardsman onto the sub. "Welcome aboard, gentlemen."

Ashdown rushed through introductions.

"Captain Smallwood, meet General Losenko. He's just joined the Resistance. And disposed of one metal-loving traitor already."

Losenko flinched, but said nothing.

"Good for you, sir!" Smallwood saluted Losenko. He peered nervously up at the sky, before escorting them to a hatch. "Now let's get underway before another one of those damn predators comes winging for us."

Losenko agreed absolutely. He would have made the same call if this was his ship. He peered out at the mouth of the harbor. Deep water meant safety. He wondered how Ivanov was doing aboard K-115.

Ashdown seemed to read his mind.

"So what's up with that boat of yours, General?"

"I wish I knew."

Captain Second-Rank Alexei Ivanov lowered the periscope. His scowl deepened. Captain Losenko had been gone for hours now, and the longer he was away, the more convinced Ivanov was becoming that his one-time friend and mentor had made a colossal mistake.

How could the captain even *think* of meeting with the very people responsible for the destruction of their homeland, for the deaths of hundreds of millions of innocent men, women, and children? It was like conferring with Hitler.

Never mind the fact that those American helicopters had helped them defeat the *Smetlivy*. Ivanov rather suspected that the Apaches had been more interested in sinking a Russian destroyer than assisting the *Gorshkov*. Currying favor with the captain had merely been an added bonus, or so Ivanov assumed. All part of an overall strategy to distract and deceive the world from the truth behind Judgment Day.

Do they truly think we can ever forget what they did? Acid churned in his gut. He felt his blood pressure rising at the very thought. An annoying muscle twitched beneath his cheek. *I can never forget. Never!*

K-115 cruised at periscope depth off the coast of Santa Cruz, carefully keeping watching over the entrance to the harbor. It was still too early to expect the captain's signal, yet Ivanov found himself compulsively scanning the island, returning to the periscope again and again like a tongue to an aching tooth.

What am I looking for? he asked himself. *Proof that the captain and Fokin have walked into a trap?*

"Captain Ivanov!" Michenko rushed from the radio shack. "Something's happening on the island. We're picking up reports of explosions, anti-aircraft fire, and casualties! I think the Resistance is under attack."

"The Americans, you mean." He did not swallow any of this nonsense about the Resistance—the summit had been convened by a Yankee general, that was all Ivanov needed to know. But this talk of hostilities concerned him. "Under attack by who?"

Skynet? Just for a second, he remembered the captain's absurd conviction that an insane computer program was out to destroy humanity. Was it conceivable that there was something to that theory after all? *No, that's ridiculous.* He shook his head, clearing the notion from his brain. *I know who the enemy is....*

"I don't know, sir," Michenko replied. "The reports are a jumble. The Resis—I mean, the Americans—sound like they were caught completely off guard!" He fumbled with his printouts. Sweat dripped from his forehead. "Do you think the captain is all right, sir?"

"How the hell do I know?" Ivanov snapped. He hurriedly raised the periscope once more. He rotated it toward the island. Acid climbed his throat as his own eyes confirmed what the radio shack was reporting.

Smoke and flames were climbing high above Santa Cruz, visible even from kilometers away. He increased the magnification to get a better look at the blaze. The flames appeared to be coming from the southern coast of the island, inside the harbor.

Exactly where the so-called "summit" was being held. *Damnation,* he thought. *Now what should I do?*

Part of him thought that he should immediately turn the submarine about and head out into the Pacific, putting as much distance as possible between K-115 and whatever hostilities were engulfing Santa Cruz. That would be the prudent choice, the one Moscow would have wanted, back when there still was a Moscow. He could not risk the *Gorshkov* for the sake of two men—even if one of those men was the rightful captain of the vessel.

I should get as far away from here as possible, especially since we don't even know what's happening!

And yet... despite their recent differences, he was reluctant to leave Losenko in jeopardy. *The captain is the highest-ranking Russian military officer I know to have survived Judgment Day,* he rationalized. *Surely, that warrants special consideration.*

Didn't it?

"Captain!" Pavlinko looked up from the radar console.

"I'm detecting aircraft approaching Santa Cruz." He scrutinized the display on his screen. "One, maybe two helicopters heading for the island at high speed."

Ivanov struggled to keep up with events. He felt as if he was under siege.

"Point of origin?"

"One of the smaller islands," Pavlinko surmised. The Galapagos were composed of numerous islands of differing sizes. "Pinzon, maybe."

Helicopters? Explosions? Ivanov massaged the itchy scar on his forehead, trying to sort out what was happening. Was this the trap he had feared, springing shut at last? But why would the Americans attack their own headquarters? It made no sense.

All he knew for certain was that Captain Losenko was trapped in the middle of the chaos.

"Ahead full speed," he ordered. "Plot an intercept course for those helicopters."

Before he abandoned Losenko, he wanted to determine who was fighting who.

Hold on, Dmitri, he thought. *We're coming for you.*

No harbor on Earth was deep enough to allow a nuclear submarine to depart port while submerged. A long shallow channel stretched before them. The *Wilmington* would be exposed and vulnerable until they reached the open sea beyond Santa Cruz.

Smallwood commanded his boat from the bridge atop the sail. A temporary plexiglass windshield protected him from the weather. A light rain had begun to fall. Ashdown and Losenko lurked at the back, keeping out of the way. Losenko in particular found it unsettling not to be steering the ship himself, but had no desire to undercut the other skipper's authority. No one liked a back-seat driver, especially not the captain of a seagoing vessel.

Such restraint was made easier by the fact that Smallwood obviously knew what he was doing. The Russian was impressed by the man's calm and assurance during this nerve-wracking passage. He recalled the *Gorshkov*'s hasty departure from Russian soil after the massacre on the peninsula. Losenko had not truly relaxed until his sub had been safely hidden beneath the waves once more.

The mouth of the harbor lay ahead. He estimated that deep water was only about half an hour away. He wondered how he would manage to contact K-115 once they were clear of the islands. Perhaps he could persuade Smallwood to surface to periscope depth long enough to transmit a message to the *Gorshkov*. He could just imagine the look on Ivanov's face when he received the password from an American attack sub!

He very nearly smiled in spite of himself.

The bridgebox, which linked them to the control room below, squawked in alarm. "Bridge, control!" an anxious voice reported. "Radar detecting two bogies directly ahead!"

Smallwood cursed. He targeted his binoculars on the open water beyond the harbor.

"There they are, damnit!"

Ashdown came forward.

"What is it, Captain?"

"Two Apache helicopters, loaded for bear." He passed the binoculars over to Ashdown. "They're hovering above the sea, just waiting for us!"

"Any way to get around them?" Ashdown asked.

"No, sir," Smallwood replied. "There's only one way out, and no place to dive."

Ashdown nodded, unsurprised by the captain's answer.

"Guess we're going to have to fight our way out, then." He glanced back, and Losenko nodded. Turning back was not an option. Santa Cruz was no longer a safe haven for the Resistance. Only the ocean could hide them now.

Smallwood got on his mike.

"Battle stations! Arm Harpoons!" He spat out orders, racing against the speed of his own ship as it cruised toward the enemy. The sub's Harpoon missiles were their best defense against the Apaches, which were surely armed with missiles and torpedoes of their own. "All ahead one third."

The captain turned to the two generals.

"Perhaps you might want to go below, gentlemen. It might be safer."

"Forget it," Ashdown snarled. "If I'm going down, I want to look the bad guys in the eye first." He made no move to abandon their post.

Losenko chose to remain, as well. He took the binoculars from Ashdown. Peering through the lenses, he spotted the helicopters hovering up ahead. He guessed that they had taken off from one of the many smaller islands surrounding Santa Cruz. For all he knew, Skynet had been planning this trap ever since it first learned of the summit. He wondered who was piloting the Apaches. More human collaborators?

Like Utyosov?

"Missile control! Ready torpedo tubes!"

They were nearing the effective range of the Harpoons when, without warning, another missile shot out of the ocean behind the helicopters. The heat of its launch sent a plume of hot steam into the air. Its first-stage rocket ignited and it arced through the sky before exploding into one of the choppers from behind, its excess fuel adding to the conflagration.

Taken entirely by surprise, the Apache plummeted into the sea trailing smoke and debris. The crash was visible from the bridge of the *Wilmington*.

"What the hell?" Ashdown exclaimed. He turned baffled eyes toward Smallwood. "Did we do that?"

"No, sir!" The captain looked equally perplexed. "We have not opened fire yet."

Losenko could only think of one explanation.

"My submarine!" K-115 was capable of firing Viyuga missiles at enemy aircraft while submerged. "It must be the *Gorshkov*!"

Unfortunately, launching the missile had given away the submarine's location as surely as if it had painted a bull's-eye on itself. The surviving Apache immediately retaliated. ASW torpedoes dropped from the chopper into the water below. Losenko prayed that Ivanov was taking evasive action, if it was not already too late.

Dive, Alexei. Dive!

Ashdown was more concerned about the Apache itself.

"Now!" he barked at Smallwood. "While it's got its hands full with that other sub. Bring down that chopper!"

"Aye, aye, sir!" The captain clutched his mike. "Missile control! Take your best shot!"

One after the other, a pair of Harpoon missiles shot from the *Wilmington*'s forward torpedo tubes. They burst from the surface in an explosion of fire and steam, climbing over fifteen meters into the air to collide with the outnumbered chopper, which went tumbling down to join the wreckage of the first Apache. Burning fuel and flotsam spread across the mouth of the harbor. A wind blew the black smoke back toward the submarine.

"Target destroyed," Smallwood informed the control room. He wiped the sweat from his brow before addressing Ashdown. "I believe the way is clear, sir."

"About time," Ashdown responded. He turned to Losenko. "What about that sub of yours, Losenko?"

An underwater explosion, further out to sea, answered his question before Losenko could. Losenko gripped the railing. His heart pounded.

Alexei!

"Flooding in compartments four and five!" Chief Komarov reported. Warning lights flashed all around the control room. "Fires spreading through the engine room and galley."

Countermeasures had failed. An evasive dive had earned them only a few extra minutes to brace for impact. The enemy torpedo had dealt a death blow to the *Gorshkov*. Ivanov was amazed that they hadn't come apart completely. He suspected that the torpedo had hit one of the decoys, but far too close for comfort.

Firing the missile had been a calculated risk. He still wasn't entirely sure why he had done it. But the presence of the attack helicopters—poised to attack the escaping American submarine—clearly indicated that a third party was out to destroy the so-called Resistance. Skynet? Terrorists? An aspiring superpower hoping to stake its claim by taking out the opposition?

Ivanov had no idea who the aggressors were, yet he knew which side Losenko was supposed to be allied with. If the helicopters were attacking the summit and its guests, then they had posed a threat to Losenko.

But not anymore.

I just hope I did the right thing.

Now he had to deal with the consequences.

"The reactor?"

"Shielding intact, but there's evidence of a primary-to-secondary link in the boiler tubes." Komarov didn't need to explain what that meant. Radioactive steam would eventually contaminate the hull of the ship. Fixable under ordinary circumstances, but not when the ship was taking on water and filling with smoke.

Ivanov knew what he had to do.

"Scram the reactor." He turned to Lieutenant Trotsky, who was currently serving as officer of the deck. "Blow all groups."

They couldn't stay submerged while dealing with floods, fire, and radiation. An emergency blow was their only hope. Ivanov grabbed onto the rail around the periscope and switched on the speaker system so that the whole sub could hear him.

"Surface! Surface! Surface!"

The diving alarm sounded three times to signal an emergency ascent. Over at the ship's main control station, the chief of the watch yanked on two solid metal levers. High-pressure air rushed into the ballast tanks, driving massive amounts of water out through vents in the submarine's keel. A deafening racket invaded the control room, even as the floor tilted beneath Ivanov's sneakers like a funhouse ride. The entire ship slanted precipitously, so that the forward compartments suddenly looked as though they were at the top of a dangerously steep slide.

Ivanov's stomach lurched. Acid reflux sloshed up and down his digestive tract.

The other crewmen grabbed onto anything that might keep them from tumbling aft. Loose mugs and clipboards rolled across the deck. The helmsmen fought to keep the boat on an even keel. The diving officer called out the depth, shouting out the changes as rapidly as an auctioneer.

"300 feet! 200 feet! 100 feet!"

What was waiting for them on the surface? Another helicopter? A hostile American attack sub? Ivanov had little time to worry about such things. They would find out soon enough.

"Broach!"

Losenko stared out at the ocean in despair. The underwater detonation, which had thrown a geyser of white water into the air, filled his heart with dread. He feared that the *Gorshkov* had become yet another casualty in the war against the machines. He sagged against the side of the bridge.

Did my desire to join the Resistance cost me my crew? Have I gained new allies, only to lose everyone who depended upon me?

Then the water erupted once more, and K-115 flew out nose first. The 7,000-ton submarine rose so far out of the ocean that only its twin screws remained beneath the waves. It hung in the air for a seemingly endless moment before it crashed back down into the water, producing a tidal wave of churning white foam that washed away much of the debris from the fallen 'copters. Its massive bulk smacked loudly against the surface of the sea.

"Hah!" Losenko laughed out loud, overcome by relief. He knew an emergency blow when he saw one. The *Gorshkov* was in trouble, but it wasn't dead yet.

The men aboard still had a chance. "You see that!" he boasted to the other men. "That's my boat! K-115!"

"Good work. Damned if I ever thought I'd owe my life to a Russian SSBN!" Ashdown slapped Losenko on the back. "Captain Smallwood, render whatever assistance that ship needs. That's a priority."

"Understood, sir."

After falling back into the ocean, the *Gorshkov* momentarily disappeared underwater, before bobbing up to the surface again. Hatches opened atop its deck as the crew poured out, many of them diving into the balmy equatorial waters. Despite his earlier relief, Losenko was distressed to see smoke billowing from the sub's vents and hatches, and that K-115 was also listing seriously to starboard. Gaping wounds had opened in her hull. Water gushed into the gaps. He doubted that the sub could stay afloat much longer— hence the hasty evacuation.

The *Gorshkov* had survived Judgment Day and months at sea in a world at war, but the boat had finally come to the end of its fateful voyage. He watched through binoculars as Chief Komarov helped Ivanov escape the boat. The XO was the last to leave the doomed vessel

Thank you, Alexei. I could not ask more of you.

The *Wilmington* sailed out of the harbor, ploughing through what was left of the wreckage of the downed choppers. Smallwood's men immediately went to work rescuing the Russian sailors from the ocean. Losenko remembered doing the same for Ortega not too long ago. Tragically, those efforts had only bought her a few more weeks of life.

What was her first name again? Luz?

Sinking fast, K-115 submerged for the last time. Losenko realized sadly that his only photo of Katerina was still in his stateroom aboard the sub. More than one chapter in his life was closing forever. His throat tightened. He silently bid the *Gorshkov* farewell.

Dasvidania, *and godspeed.*

While Losenko watched his past vanish into the depths of the Pacific, Ashdown turned to consider the island they had just escaped, and the Russian followed his gaze. Santa Cruz faded into the distance, but the smoke and flames rising from Puerto Ayora could still be viewed from miles away. The fall of night only made the orange glow easier to make out.

"Okay," he muttered, more to himself than anyone else. "We've learned a lesson. The land is too dangerous now, particularly for the leadership." He turned to address Losenko. "This sub is our headquarters now. Command needs to stay out of sight, beneath the ocean, if we're going to stay alive long enough to bring Skynet down."

He smirked. "Better get settled in, General. This could be a long voyage."

CHAPTER TWENTY

"Any luck?"

"Not yet!" Molly hollered. She could hear Geir stomping about on the roof of the shack, trying to get the new satellite dish working. She stabbed the keyboard of her laptop, trying to make the link, but kept getting error messages. She sat cross-legged on the floor in front of the fire. A portable generator chugged outside.

"Hurry! Our window is shrinking!"

"I know, I know!" he shouted back. She didn't envy him traipsing around atop the icy roof; she was going to feel *really* guilty if he slipped and broke his neck. But she desperately needed to get hold of Command before she proceeded with Operation Ravenwing.

Geir whacked something into place overhead.

"How's it now?"

She held her breath and hit the ENTER key again. To her relief, the computer found the signal at last. Streaming video and audio filled the monitor, while 512-bit asymmetric-key encryption kept the line secure from

Skynet's scrutiny, at least in theory. Audio/visual chatter decoys helped mask the transmission.

Molly whooped exuberantly.

"You did it!"

"Thank God!"

The window on the screen revealed the slightly blurry features of... General Dmitri Losenko, late of the Russian Fleet. His gaunt, haggard face made him look considerably older than his fifty-some years. A vintage wool peacoat, with a Cyrillic insignia that betrayed his roots, was draped over his bony shoulders. A creased cloth forage cap rested atop his skull. A smile lifted his thin lips as a webcam transmitted her own voice and image to Command's undisclosed location. She glimpsed solid steel bulkheads in the background. Molly felt a surge of excitement. This was the first time she had ever made contact with Command directly.

"Ah, Ranger Kookesh!" he greeted her. "We meet at last." Fifteen years in the Resistance—where English was the *lingua franca*—still had not dispelled his thick Russian accent. "I was starting to fear that something had gone amiss."

Molly didn't know exactly where Command was lurking these days, but communications to and from their hidden base were tightly controlled, taking place only according to Command's timetable.

"Just some technical difficulties at our end," she apologized. "Hope I didn't keep you waiting."

"Not at all," Losenko replied. "I regret that we have never spoken before. Your efforts in the north are greatly appreciated."

Tell that to the rest of the big brass, Molly thought. Losenko was the first high-ranking member of

Command to ever give her the time of day. She'd heard through the grapevine that the old Russian warhorse had taken a special interest in the Alaskan Resistance. Molly wondered why.

"Thanks," she said. "I've been looking forward to this meeting, too."

"My condolences on your recent reverses," he answered. His gnarled face reminded her of an old Siberian spruce. Command had already been briefed regarding the pipeline disaster and the attack on the mill town. The genuine sympathy in his voice came across despite the scratchy audio. "I know how hard it is to lose people under your command."

Molly didn't want anyone's pity.

"Could have been worse." A casual shrug belied the sorrow and anger she still felt. "But I don't want to waste time hashing over a couple of minor setbacks. I have bigger fish to fry."

"Such as?"

She quickly filled him in on her plans for the Skynet Express.

"It's doable," she concluded. "But we could definitely use some logistical assistance, and air support." They had lost too many people and supplies to that damned T-600. "And reinforcements would improve our odds substantially."

A pained expression—one she knew only too well—came over Losenko's face. Molly knew what he was going to say even before he opened his mouth.

"I would like to promise you our full support, but our resources are strained as well. The war is approaching a crucial juncture, especially on the Californian front." Video tiling momentarily distorted his image. Static punctuated his refusal. "I'm not certain we can spare the manpower or the materiel."

So what else is new? Molly chewed her lip in frustration. The Lower 48 always seemed to take priority over her own operations. She wondered if Command was losing faith in her cell, especially after her recent losses.

It's not fair, she thought angrily. *The fact that they're sending Terminators after us proves that we're getting on Skynet's silicon nerves. That's gotta count for something.*

"Forget reinforcements, then," she pressed. "How about just the air support? Skynet's got an HK and Aerostats escorting the train. All we've got is one fucking plane!"

For a brief moment she regretted swearing at him, then she remembered that Losenko was supposed to have been a sailor in the old Russian Navy. Surely he'd heard worse.

"Planes and helicopters are in short supply," he stressed. "We lost several Warthogs in an engagement over San Diego last week." The durable fighter planes were one of the backbones of the Resistance. "We need to choose our battles carefully."

Molly didn't want to beg, so she tried bribery instead.

"What about all the uranium ore? Don't tell me the Resistance couldn't use some of that stuff." Rumor had it that Command had a nuclear sub or two prowling offshore. "And wouldn't you like to keep it out of Skynet's greedy clutches?"

"You make a good case," Losenko conceded, and the pained expression was replaced by a thoughtful one. "Indeed, another Resistance cell recently managed to disrupt a Skynet mining operation in Niger, albeit at considerable cost." Molly wondered if he was talking about people or equipment, or both. "Yet the benefits were clear. So let me take up your proposal with Command."

Molly scowled.

"You mean with Ashdown, don't you?" She had never met "Old Ironsides," but she'd already decided that he was an obstinate prick who didn't take civilian militias like hers seriously. Never mind that they'd been fighting the good fight for more than a decade now.

Maybe if I'd been a Marine—and not a forest ranger— Ashdown wouldn't treat us like morons who can't tell one end of an HK from the other.

"You know he's just going to give me the brush-off," she continued.

"Not necessarily," Losenko equivocated, blindly defending his superior officer. "I'm certain General Ashdown will give your request due consideration. It's only that he has the larger picture to address."

"And we're just small potatoes, off in the middle of frozen nowhere." Molly didn't hide her bitterness. She wished that Losenko was the top dog at Command, not Ashdown. "Yeah, yeah. I get that."

Losenko did not take offense at her sour tone, perhaps because he appreciated the strain she was under.

"I will talk to Command," he promised again. "But I can make no guarantees." The transmission began to break up. He glanced off-screen. Some sort of siren blared in the background. "I'm afraid we must cut this visit short. We will speak again, though." He saluted her from far away. "Take care, my friend, and stay warm up there."

"You too." Molly didn't want Losenko to think that she blamed him for Ashdown's pigheadedness, so she saluted him back. "Talk to you soon."

The video window closed, leaving her without the answer she wanted—and no real expectation that it would be forthcoming.

"Fuck." She slammed down the lid of the laptop with more force than was necessary. A phantom toe ached like hell, adding to her bad mood. Talk about a waste of time.

"Whoa there!" A gust of cold air invaded the shack as Geir came in from outdoors. He brushed the snow from his jacket and stomped his boots on the welcome mat. "Don't be too hard on that thing. It's not like we can get another one at Radio Shack."

Molly watched with a twinge of irritation as he tracked wet slush into the room. *He should have done a better job of brushing off outside.* Then again, at least he'd gotten the satellite dish working on time. So she reeled it in.

"Good point."

He nodded at the closed laptop.

"So how did your pow-wow with the bigwigs go?"

She snorted in disgust.

"How do you think?"

After fifteen years aboard the *Wilmington*, Losenko could have—and had—navigated its cramped corridors in the dark. He had almost forgotten the feel of grass or dirt beneath his feet, or what dry land looked like. The confined spaces of the sub, where nothing was ever more than a few meters in front of his eyes, had given him a bad case of myopia, impairing his ability to view things at a distance. He had become a true denizen of the deep, swimming silently beneath the waves to avoid the mechanized predators that were prowling the surface.

Sometimes he envied the vast open wilderness people

like Molly Kookesh called home. For all its dangers and
deprivations, at least she could see the sky more fre-
quently than once in a while.

The *Gorshkov* had been roomy by comparison. He
missed her, even after all of the intervening years.

He found Ashdown in the officers' wardroom, which
had long ago been converted into the Resistance's command center. A conference table was piled high with
read-outs and reports. Jury-rigged monitors and communications gear encrusted the bulkheads like barna-
cles. The flickering screens glowed like St. Elmo's Fire.
The patchwork appearance of the equipment, cobbled
together as it was from whatever mismatched scraps of
hardware they could procure, testified to the arduous
conditions under which they had been forced to sail all
this time. Unable to return to port for routine maintenance, the *Wilmington* often seemed as though it was
held together by sweat, spit, and sheer cussedness.

Just like the rest of us, the Russian general mused.

"Losenko," Ashdown greeted him curtly. They had
known each other too long now to bother with pleas-
antries. As ever, the senior officer was poring over the
latest reports from the front.

Losenko sometimes wondered if the other man ever
slept. Time and trouble had aged the general beyond his
years. His hairline had receded out of existence, leaving
only a tonsure of graying brown fuzz around his balding
dome. Sedentary living beneath the sea had thickened his
waist. The onerous burden of command had etched deep
lines into his face, which bore a perennial scowl. Gray hairs
had also infiltrated his mustache and beard. A crescent-
shaped scar near his left eye was a lasting souvenir of their
narrow escape from the Galapagos, so many years ago.

Rumpled green military fatigues showed signs of wear. Tarnished dog tags dangled around his neck.

"Good morning, General," Losenko replied, and he gestured at the reports. "Good news or bad?"

"The usual mix of both," Ashdown grumbled. "Here's the most promising development." He thrust a folder at Losenko. "General Olsen's forces in California managed to knock down two enemy radar towers, in Riverside and Pasadena. That leaves just the one in Capistrano to cover that entire territory." He snorted in satisfaction. "Let's see the machines try to triangulate with just one tower. That should take some of the heat off our pilots for a while."

Skynet would rebuild the towers soon enough, but Losenko had learned to savor any victory against the machines, no matter how temporary. He flipped through the folder. Aerial photos of the collapsed towers lifted his spirits.

"That is good news."

"Damn right it is." Ashdown took a swig of hot coffee to sustain his energy. He looked up from his work. "So how's your new Eskimo girlfriend?"

Losenko objected to the general's dismissive tone, and he made no secret of it.

"Kookesh and her Resistance cell are a significant asset." In many ways, the combative young woman reminded him of Grushka, not to mention the late Corporal Ortega. "In fact, she has an ambitious operation in mind, one for which she is requesting back-up to carry out."

"What kind of operation?" Ashdown asked dubiously.

Losenko outlined Kookesh's plans regarding the uranium shipments.

"If she succeeded, she would do significant damage to Skynet's supply lines and manufacturing abilities."

"No dice." Ashdown shook his head. "She's got balls, I'll give her that, but we can't afford to waste time and resources on a sideshow. Not when we've got more important objectives to keep our eyes on."

Losenko wasn't surprised by the general's response, but felt obliged to argue further on Kookesh's behalf. He owed the scrappy Alaskan survivors that much. The mushroom clouds infested his dreams less often now, but they had never truly gone away. Small wonder he wanted to give the people of Alaska every chance to take back their land after enduring so much death and devastation.

"And what would those objectives be?" he countered.

Ashdown lowered his voice. He glanced around to ensure they were alone.

"We may have a lead on our magic bullet."

Losenko knew exactly what he meant. A surge of excitement quickened his pulse. "The code?"

For months now, they had been pursuing unconfirmed reports that there was a secret code hidden in the short-wave transmitters the machines used to communicate with one another. A coded signal that allowed for direct control of their CPUs. In theory, that code could be used to shut down Skynet long enough to defeat the enemy once and for all—if such a signal truly existed.

"You bet." Ashdown pulled a flash-drive unit from the pocket of his jacket. "An intelligence raid on an old Cyberdyne R&D lab uncovered evidence that their programmers really did build a backdoor into Skynet's neural network, concealed under the primary shortwave channel. Now we just need to get our hands on that code, and we can end this war for good."

He tucked the drive back into his pocket for safekeeping.

"That's what we need to focus on, not some guerilla maneuvers way up in the frozen north."

In his excitement over the code, Losenko had almost forgotten about Kookesh's operation. He felt a twinge of guilt for allowing himself to be distracted.

"But surely we can spare something to offer them support?" he persisted. "Maybe a single Chinook or Blackhawk?"

"Forget it." Ashdown wasn't budging. "Look, Dmitri, I know the whole Alaska thing gets under your skin. And I don't blame you for that." It was unusual for him to allude to their mutual tragedy—they had not discussed Ashdown's son since that tense encounter on Santa Cruz, fifteen years ago. "But this is no time to let your personal issues get in the way. Alaska isn't where the action is, not in the long run."

"That's not what this is about," Losenko insisted, although he wasn't entirely sure that was true. "What about those rumors that Skynet is developing even more advanced models of Terminators?" The T-600s were bad enough; Losenko didn't even want to think about what the next generation of Terminators might be like. "That Alaskan uranium very likely might be intended for some kind of new fuel cell."

Ashdown wasn't convinced.

"We find that code, any new models will never go on-line."

"And if we don't?" the Russian persisted.

"Failure is not an option, Losenko." He went back to his reports, indicating that the matter was closed. "You should know that by now."

* * *

"You are not alone," John Connor said. "None of us are. At this very moment, all around the world, from South America to the Yukon, from Asia to Australia, Resistance cells are fighting to reclaim our future from the machines. It may seem as if we're scattered, divided, existing only in tiny enclaves, cut off from each other. But that's just what Skynet wants you to think...."

Losenko and Ivanov listened to Connor's latest broadcast from the stateroom they shared aboard the *Wilmington*. The radio shack had downloaded the transmission while the sub had been at periscope depth, at the same time Losenko had been conversing with Molly Kookesh. Bootleg copies were already circulating among the crew. Ashdown allowed the practice because it was good for morale.

Connor's raspy voice emanated from the miniature MP3 player that was resting on a footlocker that sat between the two men.

"The truth is that we are all connected," Connor continued. "Whether you know it or not. Every human being who survives another day foils Skynet's vision of a world empty of humanity. Every blow struck against the machines helps us all—and hastens the day we can finally declare victory over cold, unfeeling metal. That day will come, I promise you, thanks to battles being waged and won in distant places you've never heard of.

"You are not alone.

"*We* are not alone.

"And, together, we will win this war.

"This is John Connor. If you can hear this, you are the Resistance."

The message dissolved into static. Losenko leaned forward to switch off the player.

"I would like to meet this man someday."

As Ashdown had predicted years ago, Connor had finally surfaced and enlisted in the Resistance. He was currently assigned to a Tech Comm unit based in the Greater Los Angeles Area, under the command of General Olsen. Connor's unit had an impressive record. Losenko assumed he had taken part in the destruction of the radar towers.

Apparently, he was much more than just talk.

"He speaks well," Ivanov granted. "For an American."

Fifteen years serving in the Resistance had mellowed Ivanov to a degree. Although he still blamed the Americans for Skynet and Judgment Day, he could no longer deny who mankind's true enemy was. Even he had been forced to put aside his grudge for the time being, although in private he sometimes spoke of charging Ashdown with crimes against humanity, if and when the machines were finally defeated.

Losenko had never mentioned this to the general.

Connor's words echoed in the older man's brain.

"Every blow struck against the machines helps us all...."

He thought of Molly Kookesh, whose plight he had outlined to Ivanov before they sat down to listen to the broadcast. Fighting her own war against Skynet, away in the wilderness. He wasn't looking forward to informing her of Ashdown's decision. Knowing her reputation, she would doubtless attempt her assault on the uranium train anyway, with or without reinforcements.

Who knew if the Alaskan Resistance could survive such a daring raid?

He contemplated the man sitting across from him. Ivanov was pushing forty-five now, but had retained much of his youthful good looks. Long hours on the sub's treadmill had resisted any hint of a middle-aged spread. His face bore a habitually dour expression. Although he no longer seemed on the verge of exploding at any minute, he had never truly recovered from the loss of his family. The ambitious young officer Losenko had once mentored was long gone, replaced by a joyless submariner driven only by duty.

As a matter of principle, Ivanov had carefully maintained his original Russian Navy uniform, shunning the ragtag garments of the Resistance. Months had passed before he'd grudgingly slipped a red armband onto his sleeve.

An idea occurred to Losenko.

"You looked tired, Alexei. When was the last time you took a leave?"

Ivanov shot him a puzzled look.

"What do you mean?" he asked warily. "I feel fine."

"No, Alexei," Losenko insisted. "I can see it in your eyes. You need to get away from here. Breathe some fresh air." He looked pointedly at the other man. "Perhaps somewhere near Alaska?"

The junior officer stiffened. His eyes widened in understanding.

We cannot pin all our hopes on the elusive code, the senior officer thought, *no matter how promising. Other matters demand our attention. Just as loyal soldiers deserve our support.*

"On second thought," Ivanov said, "perhaps you are right. I believe I am in need of a brief leave. My nerves are shot."

Losenko smiled, glad that he did not have to spell it out. That made him feel slightly less guilty about circumventing Ashdown's orders.

"I will arrange for a Chinook to ferry you to a base in

Canada, just across the border. There's a good airfield there. Perhaps you can get in some flight training, while you are recovering from your fatigue."

Tiring of the claustrophobic life of a submariner, Ivanov had in recent years begun training as a fighter pilot. The Resistance encouraged its members to be versatile, especially considering the high casualty rate. Losenko had approved of Ivanov expanding his skill-set. Never more so than at this minute.

"I think I would enjoy that, sir." A rare smirk lightened his saturnine expression. "Perhaps I'll take in some of the local scenery."

"Yes," Losenko agreed. "Keep your eye on things."

Just in case you're needed.

CHAPTER TWENTY-ONE

It was a cold, clear night. The icy surface of the glacier gleamed blue beneath the shimmering colors of the aurora borealis. The frozen river of ice flowed slowly downhill between two jagged snow-capped ridges.

Geir Svenson took comfort from the bluish tint of the glacier; it meant the compacted ice was deep and firm. A whiter color would have indicated that the ice was riddled with tiny air bubbles, compromising its stability.

Blue ice made a better runway.

10:30 PM. Time to go.

He fired up *Thunderbird*. The single-engine, low wing fighter plane, a restored P-51 Mustang, roared to life. Its thirty-seven-foot wingspan was painted white for camouflage. A spinning propeller sliced up the crisp night air. Skis replaced the pontoons he used for water landings. M2 Browning machineguns were mounted on its wings. The Mustang's landing lights illuminated the glacier.

Bundled up in the cockpit in front of the flight controls and instruments, he had the single-seat plane to himself. Molly had pried the antique World War II fighter out of Command a few years back. This wasn't one of the charter flights he and his bush-pilot dad used to run back before Judgment Day, ferrying hunting parties, fishermen, and sightseers from place to place. Lars Svenson had been in Anchorage, trying to get a bank loan to buy a new floatplane when the bombs fell.

Geir still missed him.

Goggles and a visorless flight helmet protected his face. A fraying wool scarf was wrapped around his neck. He felt like a flying ace from an old black-and-white war movie.

Watch out, Red Baron.

He opened up the throttle. *Thunderbird* skied across the icy tongue of the glacier. The surface appeared smooth enough, but Geir kept his eye out for any newly formed crevasses. Picking up speed, the plane was nearing the debris field at the edge of the glacier's terminal moraine when Geir pulled back on the stick, taking to the air. *Thunderbird* lifted off with nary a bump. Within seconds, it was soaring above the snowy ravine that lay below the glacier.

That was the easy part.

He checked his watch by the light of the instrument panel. *10:35.* He and Molly had synchronized their timepieces before they'd gone their separate ways. Timing was going to be crucial here. There was little margin for error.

He banked south toward the bridge. As he did so, he couldn't resist scanning the wilderness below, hoping for a glimpse of Molly and her team moving into position. The nocturnal woodlands, with their dense cover and murky shadows, made it a real long shot—which was, he reminded himself, a good thing. The Resistance needed to move like phantoms tonight, unseen and unheard until the moment came.

He patted his chest. The grenade ring was safely

tucked inside the front pocket of his flannel shirt, underneath his sweater and jacket. One of these days he'd get Molly to wear it.

See you soon, chief.

He spotted the Hunter-Killer's floodlights first. The Skynet Express was right on time, barreling through the mountains toward the bridge several miles ahead. He gulped at the sight of the formidable armored juggernaut, as well as its aerial escorts. He wasn't looking forward to the wild goose chase that lay ahead—especially since he was supposed to be the goose.

Here goes nothing.

An Aerostat spotted him. Zipping back to investigate, the levitating drone buzzed past his cockpit, scanning him with its lasers. Geir rolled down the side window and drove it off with a blast from a Smith & Wesson pistol. The pesky machine darted out of the line of fire.

"That should get the HK's attention," he muttered. Cold air invaded the cockpit. "Lucky me."

Sure enough, the Hunter-Killer banked away from the tracks below, leaving the train unescorted. Its powerful impellers tilted as it rotated to face its quarry. Larger and more heavily armored than the antique fighter plane, it was like a condor turning to confront a sparrow. Its floodlights searched the heavens, almost blinding Geir.

He opened fire with his machineguns, more for form's sake than anything else. The heavy-caliber fire would barely dent the HK's reinforced-steel fuselage. He'd need a well-aimed rocket to bring this sucker down.

Too bad he didn't have any.

Having baited the HK, *Thunderbird* fled for its life. Geir leaned on the stick, and the plane made a tight 180-degree turn, heading back the way it had come. Away from the bridge. He switched off his nav lights to make himself less visible, and poured on the speed. His mission now was a tricky one. He had to stay out of range of the HK and its plasma cannons, while not getting so far ahead that the Hunter-Killer would give up on the chase. The last thing he wanted was for the HK to reverse course and head back toward the train.

And Molly.

As he hit the gas the sudden burst of acceleration shoved him into the back of his seat. He gritted his teeth. Glancing back over his shoulder, he saw the HK gaining on him. Floodlights and targeting lasers swept the air behind him, competing with the colorful spectacle of the aurora above.

Whose crazy idea was it to volunteer for this suicide run?

He smiled ruefully.

Oh, yeah. Mine.

Evasive tactics were his only hope. He pulled back on the stick, climbing steeply toward a higher altitude at nearly a thousand feet per minute. Pushing *Thunderbird* to her limits. Way past its prime, the obsolete fighter was too old for this kind of barnstorming stunt. Geir offered up a silent prayer for the throbbing Rolls-Royce engine. Here was where all his nonstop maintenance and fussing would pay off... hopefully.

40,000 feet was as high as the Mustang could safely fly. He kept one eye on the altimeter and the other on the HK that was soaring after him. It was sticking to him like glue.

Scary, armored glue.

35,000 feet. *Thunderbird*'s nose was pointed toward the heavens, at so steep an angle that Geir found himself staring straight up into the prismatic splendor of the northern lights, some thirty miles above his head. Rippling green curtains glowed against the night sky. Faint yellow pinwheels spun hypnotically. The celestial light show was caused by the collision of solar winds, drawn by the magnetic lure of the North Pole, with gas particles high in the ionosphere. Even though the aurora occurred at an altitude far beyond *Thunderbird*'s capabilities, Geir could practically feel the charged particles suffusing the air.

Hairs rose along his arms and at the back of his neck. There was a peculiar crackling in his ears. Ozone tickled his nostrils. The awe-inspiring sight, as it filled up the view in front of him, imbued him with hope.

He wasn't just enjoying the colored lights. He was staking his life on them.

The aurora borealis produced over a trillion watts of electricity with a million amp current. With any luck, the massive electromagnetic fluctuations would interfere with the HK's targeting systems. It was ironic, in a way. He was praying that the ionized stream of plasma would save him from the HK's fearsome plasma cannons.

Nature versus technology, he thought. *That's this war in a nutshell.*

A warning light flashed on his instrument panel, which Doc Rathbone had upgraded with salvaged military electronics. An alarm sounded.

The HK had a lock on him!

Geir considered bailing out, but he was too high up— it would mean certain death. Besides, he still needed to keep the HK occupied and away from the train. So he crossed his fingers and hoped for the best.

That uranium had better be worth it!

The HK's plasma cannons, which were mounted on its undercarriage, flared like supernovae. A sizzling blast of superheated hydrogen ions shot upward toward *Thunderbird*, missing it by less than twenty yards!

Geir gasped in relief. The aurora had done the trick, screwing up the HK's aim just when it counted. He wanted to kiss the incandescent haloes above him.

"Thank you, you beautiful colors!"

But he knew he couldn't count on the aurora to keep on saving him. The HK's fiendishly clever neural network was doubtless already adapting to the charged atmosphere, recalibrating its sensors to compensate for the troublesome electromagnetic interference. Geir would have to pull another trick out of his hat if he wanted to prolong this one-sided dogfight.

Time for another evasive maneuver. He shoved the control stick to the far right, throwing *Thunderbird* into an inverted roll. Then, before the HK could react to his changed orientation, he pulled back on the stick. The nose of the plane dipped toward the ground and *Thunderbird* went into a high-speed dive. Geir's stomach climbed up his throat. The Alaskan wilderness came rushing up way faster than he would have liked. Towering pines and jagged peaks waited to impale him.

All right, he dared the HK. *Come and get me!*

Another blast of plasma fried the empty air the Mustang had occupied only heartbeats before. Geir banked hard to the left and tugged on the stick, leveling out only a thousand feet above the forest canopy. Wings parallel to the earth, he headed north toward a range of nearby mountains, enticing the HK even further away from the train it was supposed to be guarding. As the indefatigable Hunter-Killer swooped after him, he climbed once again toward the upper heights.

The sudden peaks and valleys took their toll on his nerves. He felt like he was riding a roller-coaster, only without the tracks. His head spun. Blood sloshed in his ears. Yet he doubted that the HK was feeling nearly so jangled.

Too bad machines can't get vertigo!

At 36,000 feet, he took another hard roll to the right, just like he had before. The idea was to make the HK think that he was about to make another upside-down dive. A quick glance behind him confirmed that the HK had taken the bait; it rolled to dive after him.

Sorry, he thought viciously. *Us crazy humans aren't nearly that predictable.*

At the last second, right before he fell into the dive, he pushed forward on the stick and kept on climbing. Caught off-guard by its prey's abrupt change in direction, the HK plunged into a spin. A misdirected plasma blast ignited the treetops below.

"Sucker!" Geir took an instant to savor his survival. He leveled off at 37,500 feet, dangerously close to the Mustang's operational ceiling, then dived back down to just above the rugged landscape. Hugging the treetops, navigating by the nap of the earth, he tried to put a little more distance between him and the disoriented HK, which was already recovering from its spin. A glacial valley, protected by sheer white walls, offered a few moment's shelter from the machine's weaponry.

Geir opened up the throttle and zoomed into the valley.

A glance at his wristwatch gave him the time. 10:45. Molly would be going into action any minute now. He mentally blew her a kiss. The unorthodox engagement ring remained snug in his pocket, next to his heart.

Don't get yourself killed, chief. I'm still working on my next proposal....

The Hunter-Killer kept after him.

CHAPTER TWENTY-TWO

Screw Command, Molly thought. *We don't need their help.*

Operation Ravenwing was underway. She stood along the bank of the river, in the shadow of the looming trestle bridge, as Tammi Muckerheide rigged the explosives according to Doc Rathbone's painstaking calculations and her own demolitions training, attaching blocks of C-4 and blasting caps to key points upon the bridge's concrete piers and timber struts.

She was sitting astride a wooden truss, about ten feet above the frothing rapids that swirled below. Unlike the shallower stream by the camp, the swiftly moving river hadn't frozen over entirely. If Tammi slipped and fell, the current would carry her away in an instant.

"How's it going?" Molly asked impatiently. A freezing wind whipped down the canyon, slicing at her face. She hugged herself to stay warm, and tapped her toes against the rocky shore. Her toes were going numb inside her mukluks, except for the missing one, which itched incessantly.

She peered up at Tammi.

"We're running out of time."

"Almost done," the younger woman promised, double-checking a wire. A note of weary exasperation could be heard in her voice. Nimble fingers tucked the last wire into place. "There we go."

Molly moved in closer and inspected the young widow's work. To disguise the explosives from snoopy Aerostats, they had painted them white and coated them with imitation snow made from talcum powder, glue, and laundry soap. Except for a heaping load of dynamite, which had been stuffed into the rotting carcass of a dead grizzly bear that one of their hunting parties had found not far from their old camp. The stinking corpse was heaped at the base of the bridge's northern abutment. Transporting the dead bear via dog sled had been a stomach-turning task, but hopefully it would fool the Aerostats. Skynet's levitating spy-eyes were ingenious, but they weren't equipped with chemical bomb-sniffers.

So far as we know.

Sitka poked the bear with her toe. She wrinkled her nose. "Stinks to high heaven." The fidgety teen was fascinated by the grossness of the carcass. An overstuffed school-book bag, bearing the faded logo of some forgotten heavy-metal band, rested upon her shoulders. Unkempt red hair blew in the wind. Fuzzy pink earmuffs muffled her hearing. "What d'you think happened to it? Looks like its heart got punched clean through!"

Molly didn't know or care what had killed the grizzly.

"Leave that alone," she admonished. Extracting hand-written notes from her own pack, she checked the placement of the explosives against Doc's specifications. Everything seemed to be in the right place.

And not just the bombs.

Tom Jensen stood guard, shotgun in hand, watching

the preparations alongside her. The bearded lumberjack
was tense and alert. His arm was no longer in a sling.
The rest of her people were hiding in the surrounding
woods and cliffs, along with every last one of their sled
dogs. Lookouts were stationed in the hills, keeping their
eyes peeled for machines. It was the first time the entire
cell had assembled in one place since the battle at the
mill, but it was hardly a happy reunion.

Everyone remembered what had happened at the
pipeline expedition, and that was supposed to have been
a milk run. This was unimaginably more dangerous.
They knew the Skynet Express wasn't going to go down
without a fight.

We're going to lose some people tonight, Molly realized. *Maybe a lot.*

In fact, she had been surprised at just how many freedom fighters had volunteered—despite Tammi's
poignant appeal in their meeting.

*Guess I'm not the only idiot who's aching to get back
at Skynet, after all*, she thought. *So what if that asshole
Ashdown turned us down? We'll show him—and the
damn machines—not to underestimate us.*

Tammi scooted across the horizontal strut, then shim-
mied down a pole and safely onto the shore. She scurried
across the beach to where Molly and others stood, one
of her hands clutching the baby bump. She thrust a
handheld detonator into Molly's open palm.

"All set, chief. Just push that button and... *boom!*"
Her eyes were hard and cold. Molly could practically
feel the murderous fury radiating off her, like the
exhaust from a bloody chainsaw. "I can't wait to see that
metal monster take a fall!"

"Me too," Molly admitted. "Good work."

She checked her watch, squinting at it in the gloom. She'd made sure to wind it the night before.

10:40.

In theory, Geir would be in the air by now. They'd embraced right before he left for the glacier, groping and pawing each other hungrily just in case it was the very last time. She started to wonder if she would ever see him again, then caught herself. She couldn't think like that during a war. Otherwise she'd never get out of bed.

He knows what he's doing, she assured herself. *He'll be fine.*

The PDA vibrated in her pocket, paging her. She checked the illuminated screen. According to the lookout posted on the other side of the tunnel, the train was on its way.

"Right on time," she muttered. "Let's hear it for machine punctuality."

She texted a one-word message back to the lookout: HK?

NEGATIVE, the lookout replied.

Molly permitted herself a slight smile. *Thank you, flyboy.* It sounded like Geir had come through for them on his end of the operation. She pinned an imaginary medal on him. *You pull this off, maybe I won't laugh at you the next time you propose.*

She wouldn't say "yes," mind you. She just wouldn't laugh.

"All right, folks!" she barked. "Train's coming." She gestured toward the shadowy woods. "Move your butts!"

They scrambled up from the beach into the hills overlooking the canyon, putting plenty of distance between themselves and the sabotaged bridge.

"Hurry!" A quavery voice called out to them from

further up the slope. Doc Rathbone's grizzled head popped up from behind a fallen tree trunk. A voluminous Goretex parka, patched in several places with silver duct tape, had practically swallowed his emaciated frame. He beckoned to them anxiously. "Don't let them see you! Or you're going to get us all terminated!"

"Tell me something I don't know." She didn't often bring the crazy old coot into the field with them, but she figured they'd need Doc's computer expertise to crack into whatever vaults held the uranium ore. Molly, Tammi, Sitka, and Jensen joined him behind the snow-covered log. They dropped to their bellies, keeping low and out of sight.

Tracks rattled inside the mountain tunnel. They could hear the train in the distance.

"Listen to that," Rathbone whispered. He shuddered at the sound. "You know, there was a time when I thought trains were the only way to travel. The romance of the rail. The iron horse. I remember this lovely rail excursion I took from London to Bath once. Lush green scenery racing past my window while I enjoyed a good book. Met this delightful English couple in the cafe car...."

Sitka sighed irritably. "Off we go again."

Molly tuned them out. Last she'd heard, London was a radioactive graveyard, Bath was a Skynet manufacturing hub.

She fondled the detonator in her grip.

A swarm of Aerostats came flying out of the tunnel ahead of the train, their glowing red eyes a clear indication of their presence. With the HK off chasing after Geir, they had been left to watch over the vital ore shipment on their own. Molly counted at least four airborne surveillance drones. They darted in and out of the trestles that were supporting the tracks, on the lookout for sabotage. Molly prayed that none of her people were stupid enough or angry enough to take a pot shot at one of the machines. She held her breath as an Aerostat buzzed suspiciously above the rotting bear carcass. If the machine figured out that there was dynamite inside the gamy meat and fur, the whole operation was kaput. The uranium train would reverse course, giving the bridge a wide berth until Skynet could arrange to have it stripped clean of explosives.

Not that Molly would give the machines a chance to do so. In a pinch, she'd settle for blowing up just the bridge, then running like mad. That would disrupt Skynet's supply lines for a while, at least, but *damn*, she really wanted to bring down that big-ass train, too. And carry off some precious uranium.

They just needed to fool the Aerostats.

Nothing to see, she mentally lied to the hovering surveillance drone. *Just a decomposing grizzly. Nothing to worry about. Move along.*

The Aerostat scanned the carcass with its laser, checking for life-signs, but the dead bear was as cold and unresponsive as the frost-covered concrete pier against which it slumped. Nothing about it registered as a threat.

The machine buzzed away, joining its fellow watchdogs above the bridge.

Yes!

The glazed white C-4 bundles went undetected as well. Molly grinned approvingly at Tammi, who merely nodded grimly in reply. The vengeful widow glared at the bridge. Waiting.

But not for long. Like a sleek gray bullet with glowing red eyes, the Skynet Express came whooshing out of the tunnel and onto the bridge. The train was just as ugly as Molly remembered. The vicious skewers at its prow demonstrated its implacable determination not to stop for anything that might cross its path, human or otherwise. Blue-hot sparks sprayed out from beneath it as it rattled over the tracks. A clamorous din echoed across the gorge.

"Do it!" Sitka nudged Molly with her elbow. "Bang time!"

"Not yet." Her finger poised above the detonator button, she waited until the train was almost halfway across the bridge. Her jaw set in determination. Her dark eyes flashed.

This is for Roger, you bastards. And everybody else.

She pushed the button.

Synchronized charges went off all at once. Plastic explosives demolished carefully selected wooden struts. The dynamite ignited, blowing the dead bear to pieces and shattering the concrete pier at the bridge's foundations. The entire structure of the trestle collapsed like a house of cards.

Steel rails twisted and snapped. The tracks and deck caved in beneath the train, sending it plunging headfirst into the river 300-feet below. Trailing the rest of its cars behind it, the engine crashed down onto a heap of splintered timbers and mangled steel, crushing everything beneath its weight. White water was hurled into the air, along with a billowing cloud of dust and debris. Dislodged ice floes collided into each other before being carried away over the rapids. The smell of nitroglycerine and chemical explosives polluted the air.

The noise was deafening. Molly wasn't sure what had been louder, the explosions or the crash.

The latter, probably.

"Skookum!" Sitka enthused, jumping to her feet. "You see that? *Boom!*"

Molly gave Tammi and Doc a thumbs-up. "Good job, you two."

The haze blew away, revealing the spectacular results of their handiwork, eerily visible in the light from the aurora borealis. The train lay crumpled across the river, its rear cars piled atop the front ones like a broken steel accordion. Cut off from the electrified third rail, iron wheels spun uselessly before slowing to a stop. The force of the crash had dented and torn open the armored sides of the train. Ragged gashes showed as gaping shadows, and offered entry to some of the cars. The spiked cow-catcher had snapped off.

Binocular red sensors dimmed at both ends of the double-headed train. Molly hoped that meant it was dying, but wasn't going to bet her life on it. Aerostats buzzed about the wreckage in alarm, infrared beams scanning the crash site from every possible angle—all for Skynet's benefit.

Which meant the Terminators already knew about the disaster.

Good, Molly thought. She hoped the A.I. program choked on the images. Keep watching. *We're just getting started.*

She didn't see any yellowcake spilling out of the train, not even through its gouged and lacerated outer walls. Presumably, the ore was still locked up inside secure crash-proof storage containers, just as Doc had predicted. Those were going to take some effort to get at.

Exactly why I brought the old man along.

The clock was ticking. It was only a matter of time before the missing Hunter-Killer came running to check on the derailed train. They needed to move fast if they wanted to hijack any of the uranium. Molly wished again that Command could have provided additional manpower and some transports. Without the reinforcements, she knew she could only spirit away a small fraction of the train's total haul. Her people would need to grab as much as they could manage, then blow up the rest.

For herself, she just wanted a sample she could arrange to have shipped to Ashdown, preferably gift-wrapped. Proof that her cell and her people could hit Skynet where it hurt, as hard or harder than any of the general's military types.

Let's show 'em what we can do.

Sitka extracted a roman candle from her backpack, retrieved from an abandoned warehouse full of forgotten fireworks. The girl also produced a lighter from her pocket.

"Signal?"

Molly had promised her she could do the honors.

"Let 'er rip."

Clambering over the fallen log, the teen aimed the candle out over the valley and lit the fuse. Thankfully, it wasn't a dud. Bright yellow fireballs shot up into the sky. The color held a message of its own.

Yellow for caution.

As planned, previously selected members of the Resistance opened fire on the train from the surrounding hills and woods, but didn't yet show themselves. Ammo of wildly varying caliber and stopping power pinged against the crumpled machine. Molly watched to see how the train reacted, keeping her gaze on its sealed gunports. Even crippled, the Skynet Express might be able to defend itself.

Her fears were right on target. The train's red eyes flared up again. About a third of the gunports—the ones that hadn't been jammed or warped in the fall—slid open. Cannons thrust into view. Their muzzles flashed. Bursts of superheated plasma scorched the riverbank and the edge of the forest. Snow and ice were vaporized by the blasts. Steam fogged the bottom of the gorge.

Hah! Molly thought. *I knew you were playing possum.*

Boulders exploded along the fringe of the wilderness. Towering evergreens went up in flames, turning into gigantic torches that lit the scene and cast madly dancing shadows. Molly hoped all her snipers had pulled back to a safe distance, as instructed. The train seemed to be firing erratically. Perhaps the cannons' targeting sensors and articulated mounts had been damaged in the crash.

As if to compensate, the Aerostats zoomed into the woods to act as the train's eyes. Searching for targets, they beamed back to the train. What they saw, the guns saw.

The nearest Aerostat—maybe even the same one that had checked out the dead bear earlier—zeroed in on Molly and the rest.

"It sees us!" Doc shrieked, bolting to his feet. He ran away from the canyon, deeper into the hills. "Skynet knows where we are!"

"Stop him!" Molly barked at Sitka. "Don't let him get away!"

Jensen swung up his shotgun. The weapon went off in Molly's ears. Buckshot ripped through the Aerostat, which was built for speed and agility, not durability. She and Tammi ducked to avoid being tagged by shrapnel. Sparks flew from the drone's ruptured casing as it tumbled through the air before crashing into a solid tree trunk.

Breaking apart, its lifeless pieces came to rest at the base of the pine.

Twin red sensors blinked out.

No more spying for you, Molly thought vindictively. She shoved Tammi and Jensen away from the fallen log only seconds before a plasma blast reduced it to splinters. The Alaskan guerilas scrambled to a new location.

Not far away, Sitka tackled Doc, knocking the panicked scientist to the ground. Getting a firm grip on his arm, she yanked him to his feet, then dragged him back to the others. Molly was glad to see that he hadn't gone far. His part in this operation wasn't over yet.

"No more of that," she chided him. "Nobody runs out until I say so."

He gave Sitka a dirty look. The teen kept her fingers locked around his arm. Then he turned back to the group's leader, his eyes imploring in the red glow of the firelight.

"It's not fair," he whimpered. "I used to work in an office. I'm not cut out for this sort of thing." He licked his lips. His hands shook. "God, could I use a drink right now!"

"Later," Molly promised, offering a carrot. "You stick with us and you can have all the moonshine you want when this is over with."

The promise of booze steadied the old man's frazzled nerves. "Really?"

"Scout's honor."

Explosions, coming from the gorge below, cut short the pep talk. Molly realized that phase three of the assault on the train had begun. She watched from above as daring Resistance fighters charged from the woods toward the crash site. Dodging fire from the misaligned cannons, they targeted the exposed gun ports. Strong arms flung grenades, pipe bombs, blasting caps, and sputtering sticks of dynamite into the open gaps around the cannons.

Explosion went off inside and around the gun ports, blowing up the train's defenses one by one. Warped metal screamed in protest as the damaged cannons fought to swivel into position. White-hot blasts tore up the landscape, yielding yet more steam and melted ice, but missed the nimble guerillas. The last of the river's ice was broken loose by the explosions and sizzling plasma. Debris from the wrecked cannons was swept away by the current.

Molly silently cheered the bomb-throwers on. So far, everything was going according to plan.

Only one cannon still pointed in the attackers' direction. Vic Folger raced toward it, holding a smoking pipe bomb. He hurled the explosive at the gun port, but his throw fell short, landing several yards short of its target. Not giving up, the former soccer coach dashed forward and kicked the bomb straight past the cannon into the gap behind it.

"Goal!" he yelled.

It was his final victory. The cannon wrenched itself in his direction. Its muzzle flashed like lightning. A single burst of plasma reduced him to ashes in an instant.

A second later, the pipe bomb exploded, avenging his death. Flames erupted behind the cannon, blasting it all the way onto the shore. Charred fragments landed just where Folger had been standing only moments before.

Mission accomplished. Molly mourned the man's death, but honored his sacrifice. She had expected to lose some good people in this attack. Too bad one of them had to be Vic.

The echoes of the battle, bouncing off the steep walls of the gorge, began to fade away. As nearly as Molly could tell, there were no more guns pointed in their direction. A couple of Aerostats were still buzzing around, but they posed no actual threat. They were good for surveillance only.

The way was clear, at least for the moment.

This time Molly gave the signal. Retrieving another roman candle from Sitka's pack, she lit the fuse and fired it out over the river. The streaking fireballs were a different color than before.

Green for go.

The Resistance fell upon the disarmed train like a pack of wolves, whooping and hollering, a few of them firing their guns in the air. Molly scowled at the undisciplined display. Granted, they had long ago sacrificed the element of surprise, but they could not afford to get sloppy. Dog sleds scampered down the hills and along both sides of the river, ready to cart away as much radioactive booty as they could carry. Protective lining in the metal drums and foot lockers was supposed to cut down on the emissions, but Molly knew that a little excess radiation wasn't something most freedom fighters cared about these days. Cancer was an abstract, long-term danger. Few of the guerillas expected to live long enough to worry about it.

Herself included.

She was eager to take part in the plunder. *After all, why should the rest of the cell have all the fun?* She wanted to gather her gift basket for General Ashdown. *A nice big slice of yellowcake for him to swallow along with his words, and a hefty portion of crow.*

"Go for it!" she shouted to those who were closest.

"But stay sharp!"

Pulling out flashlights and kerosene torches, now that the enemy had apparently been subdued, they dashed down to the riverbed. Smoke and haze hung over the floor of the canyon. Oily machine parts littered the snow. Bits of flaming debris sputtered out along their path. Burning timbers crackled beneath the weight of the train. High above their heads, the truncated ends of the bridge jutted from both sides of the canyon like roads to nowhere. The northern lights added a surreal touch of beauty to the devastation. The train's glowing red eyes impotently tracked the Resistance teams as they converged on their prey.

Molly looked forward to stealing the uranium from right out beneath the train's optical sensors.

Couldn't happen to a nicer machine!

She led the way, and hugged the northern shore of the river, being careful not to slip on the icy stones. Tammi and Jensen followed closely. Sitka brought up the rear, dragging Doc behind her. A damaged railcar, lying atop a heap of splintered trestles, called out to her. Its armor plating had been sundered in the fall, tearing open a deep gash that looked wide enough to squeeze through. The opening was like an invitation.

Don't mind if I do, she thought. *Yellowcake, here we come!*

"This way," she called out to the others. Elsewhere along the length of the downed train, she saw her fellow bushwhackers attacking other cars with crowbars, sledgehammers, and even a welding torch. They went to work, peeling the train's titanium skin from its bones. Lookouts stayed on alert. She shouted at the team behind her.

"Over here. I think I see a way in!"

She had just started climb up the heaped logs toward the gap, however, when the hiss of hydraulic doors came from both of the train's twin locomotives. The bullet-shaped noses opened up, unfolding like the petals of a deadly metal flower, and disgorged four new machines that came roaring out.

Molly's blood went cold. This wasn't part of the plan. "What the fuck?"

The streamlined newcomers resembled a cross between a Terminator and a snowmobile, not unlike the two-wheeled Moto-Terminators that sometimes patrolled Alaska's few remaining highways. But these driverless killing machines had obviously been designed for more hazardous terrain. Growling two-stroke engines broke all the old noise pollution standards. Sleek black skis preceded the machines' tapered, aerodynamic noses. Motorized tracks at the rear propelled them across the snow and ice. Binocular red sensors were mounted in their heads.

Dual mini-guns projected from both sides like stabilizers.

The would-be looters were caught by surprise. Rounds of gunfire cut down a score of humans before they could even grab for their weapons. The lookouts fired back at the speeding machines, while the rest scattered for the woods, the snowmachines chasing after them at sixty, maybe seventy miles per hour.

Molly watched in horror as her meticulously planned heist turned into a bloody retreat. "Fucking Snowminators," she hissed through clenched teeth.

The killer snowmachines were something new—the Resistance had never encountered them before. They expertly dodged the sentries' bullets. Uranium slugs tore right through the backs of fleeing men and women. Dogs and dogsleds were shredded. Gunfire and screams filled the air. A lucky shot winged one snowmachine, sending it spinning across the beach, but it righted itself and kept on coming. Its guns nailed one of the lookouts fighting back against the unexpected adversaries. A high-powered Barrett rifle was lost in the snow.

It was the fuel run at the pipeline, all over again....

"Watch out!" Tammi shouted. She pointed wildly, even as Sitka and Doc rushed past her, almost catching up with Molly. The pregnant teen unshouldered her M-16. "Here comes one!"

A speeding snowmachine jumped the river, cutting them off from the woods. It turned toward them, its side-mounted weapons swinging into place. A burst from its chain gun caught Tom Jensen in the side. He was dead before he knew it, his shotgun clattering onto the snow-covered rocks. His blood proved even redder than his beard.

Molly was shocked at just how quickly their fortunes had reversed. At this rate, they'd all be dead in minutes. She realized their only chance was the armored railcar itself. The vertical gap looked too narrow for the Terminator to squeeze through.

She jumped onto the piled timbers, and motioned to the others.

"Into the train, pronto!"

Sitka scrambled up after her. Between the two of them, they managed to haul Doc up toward the gap. An eerie red light could be glimpsed through the opening. Molly had no idea what was waiting for them inside the car, but it had to be safer than facing the machine that had just killed Jensen. She shoved her companions through the gap.

"In you go!"

That left only Tammi in the line of fire. Taking shelter within the narrow aperture, Molly saw the young woman crouching behind a pile of fallen railway tracks. One of the Resistance's own snowmobiles was parked nearby, but Tammi had no way of getting to it. She fired back at the Snowminator as it skied toward her at a frightening speed. The M-16 blared, but scored only glancing blows off the speeding snowmachine. Empty shells spewed from her gun.

More firepower was required.

"Sitka!" Molly barked. "Grenade!"

They had lost a lot of their heavy-duty hardware in the fire, but Molly had brought along a few just for moments like this. Reaching into her overstuffed pockets, Sitka pulled out a M67 fragmentation grenade. She lobbed it at Molly, who yanked the grenade away from the pin. The device had a 4.2 second fuse.

"Tammi! Duck!" Molly let go of the lever and heaved the grenade at the mechanized monster, even as Tammi burrowed for cover beneath her barricade. She threw her hands protectively over her belly. The instinctive gesture, so essentially human, tore at Molly's heart. "Heads down!"

The snowmachine launched itself off the beach and jumped toward the tracks. The hurling grenade met it in mid-air. The M67 exploded, the blast tearing open the machine's armored chassis. Flying shrapnel shredded its skis and motor. Jagged metal shards ricocheted off the mangled iron tracks protecting Tammi. Mother and baby would not be joining Roger Muckerheide today.

Molly figured this made up for not speaking at the damn wedding.

"Run!" she hollered over the fading echoes of the explosion. "Before another one gets here!"

Tammi scrambled out from beneath the smoking barricade. She looked startled to be alive. Her rifle slung over her shoulder, she hesitated briefly. Her gaze swung back and forth between the train and the waiting snowmobile

"Forget about us!" Molly ordered. "Save your baby!"

Another Snowminator headed toward them from several yards away. Molly drew her pistol and shot at the machine to draw its fire away from Tammi. The young widow got the message and clambered onto the snowmobile. She took off through a gap in the crumpled train cars, jumping the broken connectors. Molly wished her godspeed. *Somebody* had to pass on that stupid gown to the next poor bride.

She ducked inside the car, only seconds before a blistering hail of bullets slammed into the wall outside. For the first time ever, Molly was thankful for the uranium train's heavy armor.

Sitka came up behind her.

"Tammi?"

Molly shrugged. "She's got a shot."

"May fate look out for her," Rathbone murmured. For once, he wasn't moved to reminisce. "She's so young...."

But Molly couldn't worry about Tammi any longer. They weren't out of this mess yet. Hastily assessing their situation, she realized that the three of them were pinned down inside the derailed train with at least three Snowminators on the warpath outside. The minute they stepped out of the car, the machines would be on them. She could hear the ferocious roar of their engines through the gap in the wall.

There was no way out.

Unless....

She pulled out her PDA and keyed in a special priority code Losenko had given her a couple of days ago. It was a one-time only thing, he had explained, to be used only in case of an extreme emergency. There was also no guarantee that he would be in a position to receive the message. Under the circumstances, it was the longest of long shots.

But what did she have to lose?

She typed in a single, three-letter message.

SOS.

"Cmon, you old Russian warhorse," she muttered under her breath, while Sitka and Doc looked on. Rathbone had his arm draped over the girl's shoulders. Molly fired off the plea. "I don't know where you are right now, but be there when I need you!"

CHAPTER
TWENTY-THREE

Even nuclear subs needed to go to periscope depth from time to time, to take care of urgent tasks and routine housekeeping. Communications masts needed to be raised in order to send and receive messages from the outside world. Navigation needed to get a fix that would determine the sub's actual position. Engineering needed to vent the steam generators once in a while. Even excess trash had to be ejected, an unglamorous but essential task which, for technical reasons, was best performed at shallow depths.

For all these reasons, the U.S.S. *Wilmington* routinely raised its periscope every forty-eight hours or so, assuming there were no enemy machines in the vicinity.

The timing of such episodes was usually left to the captain's discretion, but Losenko had prevailed upon the sub's current commander—Captain Lucy Okata—to schedule a visit to the surface at a specific hour. The captain hadn't asked for a reason, and Losenko had not volunteered one.

He felt a twinge of guilt at having gone behind Ashdown's back, but his outstanding debt to the people of Alaska was a deeper and more profound obligation.

He consulted the ship's chronometer. By his calculations, it was nearly 11 PM in Alaska. Operation Ravenwing was already in progress. He prayed that Kookesh and her allies had not encountered any unexpected obstacles, but knew that was an unlikely wish.

It was a truism that even the most carefully worked-out battle plan seldom survived contact with the enemy. For all he knew, they had already been terminated.

"Any unusual messages?" he asked Pushkin. Again, it wasn't by coincidence that the *Gorshkov*'s radioman was working a late shift tonight in the *Wilmington*'s aging radio shack. Losenko's old crew had largely gone their separate ways over the last fifteen years as time, attrition, reassignment, and the hazards of war had eaten away at their ranks. But a few aging veterans had stuck with their skipper.

Pushkin was one such loyalist. Losenko had conspired to have him on duty at this crucial juncture. He leaned over the man's shoulder as he monitored incoming transmissions.

"No, sir." He knew the general wanted to be ready to receive any emergency alerts from Alaska. They spoke in Russian to avoid being overheard by the other radio operator, a young Filipino woman Losenko didn't know very well. The old custom of excluding females from submarine duty had long ago fallen by the wayside. "Everything seems quiet. Just the usual encrypted updates and reports."

Perhaps that's a good thing, Losenko thought. He recalled the American saying, no news is good news. Maybe the silence meant that Kookesh and her crew were doing fine on their own, with no need of outside assistance. He'd like to think so.

Perhaps I dispatched Ivanov to Canada for nothing. That, too, would be perfectly acceptable. Still....

"Keep monitoring the frequencies we discussed," he urged. For security's sake, the *Wilmington* wouldn't stay at periscope depth indefinitely. Soon they would have to return to the greater safety of the ocean depths. But until then, he intended—with Pushkin's help—to keep his electronic ears open up to the very last minute. Molly Kookesh deserved that much.

"Aye, aye, sir." Pushkin glanced at a chronometer. His new partner regarded them curiously, surely wondering what the old Russians were up to. Neither man illuminated her. "Looks like you might be wasting your time, General."

"Perhaps," Losenko conceded. "If so, it will hardly be the first time."

Pushkin settled back in his seat, getting comfortable. A matrix printer churned out reports for Ashdown's inspection. "You ever wonder if we'll be able to go home someday, sir?" Neither man had set foot on Mother Russia since they had fled the Kola Peninsula. Most of the continent remained under the thumb of Skynet. "I admit that I miss the sunsets some—"

A light flashed at his console, signaling an incoming message. Pushkin sat up straight. He looked at Losenko in surprise.

"An emergency alert, from Alaska, sir. On your private channel."

Dread gripped the general's heart. Something had indeed gone wrong with the assault on the uranium train.

"Put it through."

"Aye, aye!"

The other operator noted the activity.

"What is it?" she said in English. "Shall I notify Captain Okata? General Ashdown?"

"That won't be necessary, sailor." Losenko answered in English. Her name escaped him. Too many crewmen had passed through the sub over the years—he couldn't keep track of them anymore. "I believe we have the situation under control. Please attend to your own duties."

"Aye, aye, sir." The junior operator retreated to her console, but kept glancing back at the Russians. She knew something was amiss.

With a few deft keystrokes, Pushkin moved Kookesh's text message to the top of the printing queue. The machine spat it out in an instant. Breaking protocol, Losenko snatched the brief message from the printer with his own hand. His eyes took in three stark letters.

SOS.

His heart sank.

I knew it, he thought. The Alaskan cell was in trouble.

He briefly considered appealing to Ashdown once more, informing the general of the measures he had already taken as a precaution against just such an occasion. But, no, Ashdown was holed up in his stateroom with the latest intelligence on the shutdown code. He had instructed that he was not to be disturbed.

Losenko decided to take him at his word.

"Contact Captain Ivanov," he ordered Pushkin. Alexei was standing by at the Resistance airfield in the Yukon, a little more than 300 miles away from Kookesh's theater of operations. A fighter plane was fueled up and ready. "Give him the word."

Pushkin nodded. He checked to make sure he had understood the general.

"And that word is?"

"Go."

CHAPTER TWENTY-FOUR

Gunfire and screams penetrated the ruptured wall of the railcar. The ghastly din of the Snowminators hunting down her people scraped at Molly's soul. The armored walls of the car spared them the same fate, but also trapped them inside the train.

Stuck in the innards of the machine that's trying to kill us, she thought, fighting despair. *Not a good situation to be in.*

Forcing herself to tune out the carnage outdoors, she took stock of their surroundings. An unsettling red light, characteristic of Skynet's installations, suffused a cramped vestibule at one end of the car. A second rent—this one in the ceiling—offered a glimpse of shimmering sky. Riveted steel walls were devoid of signage or ornamentation. The train was as ugly and utilitarian on the inside as it was on the surface.

Beauty was strictly a human concept, or so Ernie Wisetongue always insisted.

"Not exactly the Orient Express," Doc said, reading her mind. He tapped his skull. "Still, I will endeavor to employ all my little grey cells."

Thank God for small favors, Molly mused. *At least*

Rathbone wasn't freaking out. Though this would certainly be an appropriate time....

Sitka who had never heard of Agatha Christie—let alone read her novels—didn't understand the reference. "Oriented how?" she asked.

She kept close to Molly and Doc, clearly shaken by the sudden deaths of Jensen and the others. Molly had never seen her so subdued, but wasn't surprised by her reaction. The ugly reality of war could dampen even the most irrepressible spirit.

"Never mind," Molly said. She'd explain later, if there was a later. In the meantime, they still had a mission to accomplish. The slaughter outside only increased her determination to ensure that their friends and comrades hadn't died in vain. No way was Skynet going to get its uranium.

She inspected their surroundings. The tiny space into which they were crowded constituted only a narrow sliver of the railcar's interior. A reinforced steel door cut them off from the rest, which was probably filled with freshly mined and processed yellowcake. The door had no handle; she guessed that it opened and closed automatically. That meant their prize was on the other side.

"All right, Doc." She rapped the vault door with her knuckles. "You're on."

"Yes, of course." He seemed to welcome the challenge—most likely to avoid thinking about the hopelessness of their situation and the bloodbath they had just witnessed. He contemplated the barrier, squinting over the tops of his bifocals. "First, though, let us make certain it is truly worth our while." He turned toward Sitka. "The counter if you please, young lady."

The girl rummaged through her book bag. A handheld Geiger counter surfaced from its cluttered depths.

The device was held together by all sorts of improvised, mickey-mouse wiring and add-ons.

"Here goes," she said, and she handed it over to him like a scrub nurse assisting a surgeon during a delicate operation.

Doc flicked on the device. It hummed to life, then began clicking like a castanet. The scientist nodded in satisfaction.

"Processed uranium, all right. Just as I expected, our mechanical adversaries didn't bother with radiation shielding." He put the counter aside. "And why should they? The damnable automatons have no fear of cancer or genetic mutation."

Such things didn't worry Molly, either. Kids weren't in her future, and she didn't expect to survive long enough for cancer to be a problem.

"Better get my red armband for this," Sitka muttered. Breaking into the storage compartment helped distract her as well. "Earned it this time."

"Tell you what," Molly promised, "we get out of this, you can have mine."

The girl's freckled face lifted a little.

Doc moved to a thin metal lid that was mounted to the wall next to the vault. Some sort of maintenance panel, presumably. Even unmanned, artificially intelligent trains needed tune-ups sometimes.

"Screwdriver," Doc demanded of his assistant. Sitka produced one from a fanny pack around her waist, then peered intently as the Doc went to work trying to pry the lid open. "Can't believe it's come to this. My esteemed parents never raised me to be a train robber or safe-cracker. I was a systems designer, for chrissakes, a white-collar worker. Not the Sundance Kid."

Sitka emitted a long-suffering sigh. "Speaking in tongues again."

Grunting, he bore down on the locked panel. A hinge snapped and the lid popped open. A computer interface panel was exposed. Doc stepped back and took a bow, like a stage magician who had just pulled a rabbit out of a hat.

"Eureka!"

"Careful!" Molly warned. "It might be booby-trapped."

"Nonsense!" he exclaimed. "Skynet surely never expected anyone to get this fa—"

A taser fired from the control panel, stabbing Doc in the throat. A thin insulated wire connected the dart to the wall. The old man went into convulsions as a massive electrical shock jolted his system. He collapsed onto the hard steel floor, twitching spasmodically.

Fuck! Molly cursed. *Why didn't he listen to me?*

"Doc!" Sitka lunged forward.

Molly grabbed onto her waist, holding her back.

"Wait!" The high-voltage charge was still coursing through Doc's body. "Don't touch him, or you'll be electrocuted, too!"

Snatching a hunting knife from her belt, Molly sliced through the thin cable, breaking the circuit. Doc stopped thrashing, but didn't get up. She dropped to her knees beside him and yanked the dart from his neck. A tiny drop of blood glistened on its pointed tip.

Molly hurled it away.

"Doc! Are you okay?" She clutched his hand, which was cold and clammy to the touch. His pulse felt weak. Foam bubbled at the corners of his mouth. The smell of burnt hair filled her nostrils. "It's me, Molly. Talk to me!"

He didn't look good—it was as if he was having a stroke or something. His eyes were unfocussed. The color drained from his already haggard face. He stared past her, a shaking finger pointed feebly at the open gap in the ceiling.

"I can see it," he whispered. "The world... just like it used to be...."

Sitka looked up. There was nothing there but torn steel and shimmering sky.

"Can you see it?" His voice rattled in his throat. Molly felt his pulse slipping away. Maybe the jolt had been too much for his fragile constitution. Bloodshot eyes gazed backwards in time. "Such a glorious world... like before...."

His voice trailed off.

His hand dropped limply to the floor.

Molly let go of his wrist. She stood up and stepped away from the body.

A single sob escaped Sitka's lips.

"Is he...?"

"Gone," Molly said.

The girl choked back tears.

"Crazy old man," she said hoarsely, anger denying her feelings. "Should've been more careful."

That's it, Molly realized. Operation Ravenwing was over. Skynet could come get its damn uranium if it wanted it. *We took out a train and a bridge at least. That'll have to be enough.*

She didn't want to think about how much those "victories" had cost them.

Stepping away from Doc's body, she approached the cleft. The screams and gunfire had moved away from them, although she thought she could still hear fighting in the distance. She risked a peek out of the gap. The remaining Snowminators were nowhere in sight.

Maybe they had abandoned the humans in the railcar to seek out easier prey. The bodies of their earlier victims had been left to rot. Molly hoped there would be a chance to bury them later.

Crimson stains defiled the snow and slush.

"Okay," she told Sitka. It was possible a snowmachine was lurking just out of sight, but they had to chance it. If they were lucky, maybe they could slip away unnoticed. "Let's go."

"No." Sitka shook her head defiantly. "Not done yet." She approached the disarmed control panel with a determined look on her face. "Can still do this. Doc taught me how."

Molly wasn't sure about that. Sure, the old man had spent hours filling the precocious teen's head with arcane technical info, but Molly doubted the apprentice was anywhere up to the master's level yet. It didn't seem worth the risk—any chance they had might be slipping away.

"Forget that. We've done enough." She called to the girl from the exit. "You heard me. *Move it.*"

Sitka didn't budge.

Instead she opened up her backpack and took out a heavy-duty combat laptop—the only one they had—and a wad of electrical clips and cables. She squinted at the exposed panel. No new tasers jolted her—the machinery had already shot its load. She peeled off the interface screen to reveal a tangle of wires and clips. Busy fingers applied clips and hackwires to the car's neural ganglia.

Did she actually know what she was doing? Molly considered ordering Sitka out at gunpoint, but wasn't sure even *that* would deter the girl, who appeared bound and determined to finish what Doc had started. So she came up behind her, peering over the teen's shoulder at the incomprehensible—to her—links and relays.

"Can you do this?"

"Think so." Concentration scrunched up Sitka's face, already thrown into shadow by the weird red lights. The tip of her tongue protruded from the corner of her mouth. Linking the control panel to her laptop, she punched its keys. Binary code filled its screen, scrolling past way faster than Molly could follow. It seemed to make sense to Sitka, though. Maybe the old man really had taught her everything he'd known. The teen froze a bit of code on the screen. Her eyes lit up.

"Got you!"

She pushed a button. Hydraulics whooshed loudly behind the interior walls of the railcar. The ponderous vault door slid to one side. An avalanche of powdered uranium spilled onto the floor of the vestibule.

The discarded Geiger counter went nuts.

Sitka beamed triumphantly.

"Way skookum!"

Despite its name, the "yellowcake" was actually brownish-black in color. According to Doc, the nickname was leftover from the early days of uranium mining, when the chemicals used to process the raw ore had turned the results yellow. The coarse powder filled the long cylindrical storage compartment that stretched into semi-darkness beyond the doorway. There was enough uranium in just this one car to power dozens of nuclear reactors—or Terminators.

Sitka dumped out her book bag and started shoveling the yellowcake into the pack with her bare hands. The radioactive powder was surprisingly light. Molly scooped up a few handfuls herself, then reconsidered.

With their team scattered, and the Snowminators on the prowl, they weren't going to be able to carry off enough ore to make a real difference. Better just to blow the whole load to kingdom come instead. She remembered all the oil they had cost Skynet back at the pipeline. This was the same kind of situation.

"That's enough, packrat," she said. "Get the explosives."

If we can't have the uranium, she vowed, *neither can Skynet.*

CHAPTER TWENTY-FIVE

The Hunter-Killer was gaining on him again.

Geir reached the end of the ravine and was forced to abandon its sheltering walls. He pushed *Thunderbird* to its limit in a desperate attempt to keep out of range of the lethal pulse cannons. Flying at top speed—nearly 437 miles per hour—the plane raced toward the upper slopes of the Wrangell Mountains. Ascending above the tree line, it sped above majestic cliffs and glaciers, but Geir was in no position to admire the scenery. Not with a murderous flying machine on his tail.

Outgunned and way more fragile than the armored HK, he relied on speed and maneuverability to stay out of its sights. As agile as its equine namesake, the Mustang pulled out all the stops, banking and weaving, diving and climbing amidst the alpine peaks and canyons. A herd of caribou, dark shadows in the gloom, ran for safety as he buzzed too low over their snowy terrain. Geir worked up a sweat behind the controls, improvising wildly to keep the HK's neural network from predicting his flight patterns. His hands were sweating beneath his gloves. His brain was spinning.

Okay, Svenson. How the hell are you going to get out of this one?

He just couldn't shake the airborne predator. It kept after him like a bloodhound on the scent of a panicked fox. A blast from its plasma cannon incinerated one of the skis beneath the plane, throwing *Thunderbird* off balance. Geir frantically leveled off again, then climbed sharply upward toward the crest of Mount Wrangell. He glanced out of his left window to see nothing but a few scorched struts jutting out from beneath the fuselage on the left side. One entire ski was missing.

Landing the plane was going to be a bitch.

If I ever get the chance.

That was starting to look like an academic concern, but he still had one last trick up his sleeve, provided he could make it just a little further. He pulled back on the stick, climbing higher and higher toward the top of the enormous mountain, one of the largest in the territory. Just a few more minutes and, hopefully, the HK was in for a serious headache.

Mount Wrangell, which rose over 12,000 feet above the wilderness below, had been volcanically active even before Judgment Day. According to Doc Rathbone, its geothermal activity had been increasing steadily since the 1950s—long before Geir was born—and the thermonuclear blasts that had rocked Alaska had left it even more seismically restless. Plumes of hot steam, often visible from miles around, rose from numerous small craters rimming its central caldera, a feathery green in the light of the aurora. Frequent small eruptions and tremors shook the area. Geir had always made a point of not flying directly over it.

Until tonight.

He saw the main plumes jetting upward from the collapsed top of the mountain even before he got there. Geysers of churning white vapor blasted hundreds of feet into the air. Rising to 14,000 feet, he circled above the volcano. This was going to be a delicate balancing act. He had to stick close enough to the unstable caldera to—hopefully—mess up the HK's heat-sensitive tracking devices, while keeping high enough to avoid being scalded by the sky-high bursts of steam. Being disintegrated by a plasma cannon would probably be a far less painful way to go.

The HK slowed as it approached the rim of the mountain. Its floodlights and lasers scanned the caldera. Geir guessed that it was evaluating the threat posed by the active volcano, and weighing that against its desire to terminate *Thunderbird* and its pilot.

He tried to read the machine's mind.

Am I worth the risk or not?

The HK swiftly arrived at a compromise. An air-to-air missile dropped from its undercarriage onto a rail, then shot up past the crest of the mountain. The heat-seeking rocket locked onto the fighter circling above the volcano.

"Crap!"

Geir saw the missile coming. Risking getting hit by the steam, he dived toward the caldera 2,000 feet below. The missile reversed course and plunged after him. The smell of sulfur, rising from the fuming crater, filled Geir's nose and throat. Not since Judgment Day had he been so close to hell.

This had better work.

Just as he'd prayed, the heat pouring off the volcano acted as a decoy, much more appealing to the missile than his own insignificant signature. It veered away from

Thunderbird to strike one of the venting craters below. The explosion rattled the caldera like a tremor, causing its gray-black andesite walls to crumble inward. Billowing gouts of smoke and fire made it look as though the mountain was erupting for real. Shattered rock opened up fresh fumaroles at the base of the crater, unleashing even larger discharges of scalding vapor.

A sizzling pillar of steam shot up directly in Geir's path, forcing him to bank hard to the right to keep from flying right through it. Yet another plume jetted past the plane's tail, missing it by only a few feet. He suddenly found himself flying an obstacle course made up of fire, smoke, and steam. Two close calls in as many minutes convinced him that the airspace above Mount Wrangell had suddenly become way too hot to handle.

So he accelerated away from the volcano, abandoning whatever safety it had provided. The P-51 Mustang flew north over tracks of densely wooded forest. Frozen lakes and rivers gleamed like mirrors beneath him, reflecting the shifting colors of the aurora. Forgotten logging roads, on the verge of being reclaimed by the wilderness, connected ghost towns and campsites.

Can't complain about the scenery, he thought. Despite Skynet's best efforts, it was still beautiful country to live in. *Or die in*.

Not at all unexpectedly, the HK instantly noted his departure and resumed its pursuit. It circled past one side of the volcano—taking the long way around the unpredictable caldera—before picking up *Thunderbird*'s trail. Geir sweated in the cockpit, and not just because of the steam bath he had left behind.

He was running out of tricks.

He undid his seatbelt. A fully-packed and prepared

parachute was strapped to his back, just in case he needed to make a hasty exit. It would kill him to abandon
Thunderbird after all his work restoring it, but he wasn't
an old-time sea captain. He wasn't going down with his
ship—not if he could avoid it.

The HK grew larger and larger in his rear-view mirror.
He looked ahead of him, seeing nothing but mile after
mile of wintry wilderness with no place to hide. As if to
emphasize his plight, a rattle in the plane's engine gave
new cause for concern. *Thunderbird* was showing her age.

Aren't we all, he thought.

Then again, it was starting to look like getting older
wasn't exactly something he needed to worry about.
Maybe arthritis and rheumatism weren't on the cards.

He adjusted his parachute, getting ready to bail out
before the inevitable plasma blast, when, to his surprise, the Hunter-Killer dropped back in the mirror.
Just as he was almost within range of its weapons, the
HK paused in midair.

What the hell? Geir didn't get it. At first, he thought he
must be mistaken, that it was some sort of optical illusion,
but as he watched the fearsome aircraft shrink behind
him, he realized that his first impression had been correct.
The HK had come to a definite halt. It didn't change
course, or try to outmaneuver him, but just hung there.

Not that I'm complaining, he thought, *but what is it
waiting for?*

An urgent transmission reached the Hunter-Killer's CPU,
informing it that the supply train had encountered resistance. Something had prevented it from completing its run.
Analysis indicated that human insurgents were attempting
to divert valuable strategic minerals.

Immediate action was required.

The HK's advanced neural network processed the data in an instant. It swiftly assessed the value of terminating the fleeing aircraft versus the need to defend the crashed train. It was a simple calculation. The primitive aircraft and its pilot posed a minimal threat. Its primary imperative was to safeguard the uranium required by Skynet for future operations.

PURSUIT OF ENEMY AIRCRAFT: CANCELLED.

It switched off its targeting lasers and reversed course.

Geir watched the HK zoom away. An overwhelming sense of relief was swiftly followed by the terrifying realization that he knew exactly where it was going.

After Molly and the others.

He glanced at his watch. *11:10.* No way could the train robbers have made off with the uranium by now. They'd be sitting ducks for the HK's plasma cannons.

There was only one thing to do.

Crap, he thought. *I must be out of my mind....*

He turned around and chased after the Hunter-Killer. Throwing caution to the north wind, he ignored the worrisome rattle coming from the Mustang's failing engine and came up behind the HK, catching up with it before it even got back to the volcano. He switched on his landing lights, strobes, and nav lights in order to reclaim the machine's attention. He activated the control panel's built-in CD player and turned the volume up to the max. Wagner's *Die Walkure* rocked the cockpit. The stirring music fitted his mood. His inner Viking surfaced.

"Don't you turn your back on me," he muttered over the blaring music. "We're not done yet."

He opened fire with the Gatling gun.

But still the HK ignored him, its cybernetic mind on more important matters. *Thunderbird* dipped beneath it, firing up at its vulnerable turbofans, while zig-zagging back and forth to evade the rear-mounted guns and cannons. The plane darted in and out, stinging and retreating like an angry wasp. Geir yanked the control stick back and forth, relying on his wits and reflexes, like a teenager fighting the toughest level of a particularly challenging computer game.

Only this game was for his own life, and the lives of the people he loved.

That gives me the edge, he thought. *It has to!*

A lucky shot sparked off the spinning blades of the HK's starboard turbofan. It barely scratched the engine, but it did what it was supposed to: convince the machine that the annoying fighter plane constituted a legitimate threat, one that needed to be dealt with.

The machine rotated to face *Thunderbird*. Blinding floodlights bathed the interior of the plane's cockpit with a harsh white radiance.

But Geir wasn't ready to go into the light just yet. *Thunderbird* looped upward to get away. Steam hissed from its overhead engines. Plasma blasts seared the air behind it. The Mustang fled again for its life, but Geir knew it wasn't going to get far.

End of the line, he realized. He popped the canopy, which went flying off into the sky. A freezing gust of wind invaded the cockpit. He heard the HK swooping in for the kill.

'The Ride of the Valkyries' hit its crescendo.

"*Geronimo!*"

Pushing against the gale, he threw the plane into a roll, flinging himself from the cockpit. At the last minute, his boot got stuck between the seat and the rail, but the fierce slipstream tore him loose. Gravity seized him and he plummeted toward the snowbound wilderness thousands of feet below. Freefall sent his heart racing. His aviator's jacket, helmet, and scarf provided scant protection from the frigid wind that was biting into his bones. Forests, lakes, and mountains seemed to lunge toward him at a breath-stealing clip. It was a risky jump. There was a good chance that he'd break his neck or end up impaled on a treetop.

Not that he'd had much choice.

Above him, a plasma blast finally blew *Thunderbird* apart. A boom worthy of its name momentarily drowned out the wind rushing past as he fell. Chunks of burning debris rained down from the sky, chasing after the falling pilot, who raced them to the ground below. A pang stabbed him in the heart as the venerable fighter plane was lost forever. Unlike the fabled phoenix, *Thunderbird* would not be reborn from its ashes.

He held his breath, waiting to see if the HK would come after him next, but apparently the tiny figure had proved beneath its notice. Turning on its axis, it headed south once more—toward Molly and the bridge. He could only hope that he had delayed it long enough to make a difference. His fellow Resistance fighters were on their own now.

Give 'em hell, chief.

All sense of falling vanished as he reached terminal velocity, roughly 120 miles per hour. He fought to maintain a stable arch position, his belly parallel to the earth, but vicious winter winds buffeted him, making it all but impossible to control his descent. He felt like a leaf being tossed about by a hurricane—or maybe an out-of-control Aerostat with a defective gyro.

Estimating his rate of fall, he waited until the HK was entirely out of sight.

Then he pulled the ripcord.

Even though he was expecting it, the chute's deployment was a jolt. The canopy billowed above him, yanking him upward. His gloved hands tugged on the risers. He peered downward, trying to spot a safe drop zone somewhere in the forbidding wilderness. A homing beacon attached to the chute would help Molly and the others find him if he ended up breaking his leg or something, assuming he didn't freeze to death first. Or get eaten by wolves.

Ebony shadows cloaked the forest, hiding its secrets. He searched in vain for an open clearing or meadow. A lake or pond even, if the ice wasn't too thin. If his canopy got fouled in the upper branches of a tree, he was in for a beating, but maybe he wouldn't smack into anything too hard.

I can do this, he thought. *If I can survive fifteen years of Terminators, I'm not going to let a rough landing do me in. I still have a chance.*

The flaming debris caught up with him. Red-hot shards of metal tore through the nylon canopy, shredding it to ribbons. A jagged fragment, twisted and charred beyond recognition, struck him in the leg. It burned and cut at the same time, digging deep into the muscle. He let out an agonized howl even as his controlled descent turned into a sheer terror dive.

This isn't good.

Geir's life passed before his eyes. He remembered fishing and hunting with his folks, back before Judgment Day. His father teaching him how to fly and—more importantly—how to land. Breaking out of that Skynet prison camp years ago. Hanging out with Doc and Sitka and the rest of the Resistance. Scoping out the Skynet Express. Ducking enemy fire as the Terminators chased them across the snow. Making love to Molly in their cabin in the hills....

Thirty-five years, he thought. *Fifteen after Judgment Day*. He had lasted a whole lot longer than most of the world. Not a bad score.

The trees rushed up to meet him.

CHAPTER TWENTY-SIX

Molly finished rigging the explosives. Blocks of C-4, mined from her own backpack, were placed and wired all around the cramped service vestibule. She wasn't the demolitions ace Tammi was, but she knew how to blow things up. Once triggered, the plastic explosives would tear the train apart from the inside out, scattering the precious uranium all over the Alaskan countryside. It would be lost to Skynet forever.

Works for me.

She connected the last wire and took a second to inspect her handiwork. Everything appeared in order. She tucked the detonator into her pocket. Turning to check on Sitka, she found the girl staring mournfully at Doc Rathbone's body.

"Don't look at it," Molly advised her. "Don't think about it now."

Sitka wiped a tear from her eye. A backpack full of yellowcake rested on her shoulders.

"Should have paid more attention to his stories."

"You listened to them. You know you did."

Taking Sitka's hand, she guided the girl away from the body toward the breach in the outer wall. Molly didn't hear any snowmachines nearby. Now might be their only chance to get away.

She crept up to the gap, and raised a finger to her lips. "Fast but quiet, you got that?"

Sitka nodded.

Before they could sneak out of the car, however, a harsh white light flooded the chamber from above. The light invaded the railcar through the cleft in the ceiling. The roar of powerful engines rattled the wreckage. Molly recognized the distinctive thrum of an HK's turbofans.

Fuck! It's back!

She tried not to think about what this meant for Geir. Chances were, the Hunter-Killer was responding to a distress signal from the train or the Aerostats. It had probably just given up on the fighter plane. That had to be it.

Sitka wasn't so sure.

"Geir?"

"He's fine," Molly insisted. She forced herself to focus on their own predicament instead. How the hell were they supposed to get away, with that Hunter-Killer hovering right over their heads? She doubted that it would blast the uranium stores, for fear of destroying the valuable ore, but she and Sitka would be sitting ducks the moment they stepped outside the train.

They were trapped... again.

Molly fingered the detonator in her pocket. If she had to, she'd set off the charges with both of them inside.

If we have to die, we'll go out with a bang.

Her biggest regret was that Sitka would never live to see a world free of the machines.

"This it?" the girl asked. She looked back at the C-4 rigged all around the railcar. She knew what their options were. "Game over?"

"Maybe," Molly admitted.

They needed a miracle.

The A-10 Thunderbolt, with boxy, ungainly contours that had gained it the affectionate nickname "Warthog," controlled like a dream. The single-seat jet fighter zoomed above the sprawling Alaskan wilderness. In the cockpit, Alexei Ivanov was impressed by the aircraft's abilities.

There was something to be said, he mused, for soaring high above the Earth instead of being stuck in a smelly underwater tube hundreds of feet beneath the sea. Despite the urgency of his mission, he savored the privacy of the cockpit. After spending so much of his adult life crammed aboard boats with more than a hundred other sweaty bodies, it was good to be flying solo at last. Who could have suspected that—late in life—he would discover that he was a pilot at heart?

The A-10 had departed Canada the moment he got Losenko's signal. The jet's colorful decor attested to the defiant spirit of the Resistance. Painted flames and lightning-bolts adorned its wings and fins. A porcine snout and tusks embellished its nose. Stenciled silver Terminators, lined up along the plane's side, recorded its kill count. Ivanov hoped to rack up a few more kills before the night was over. His trigger finger was itchy.

To hell with the Americans, he thought. *Just give me a chance to trash some more machines.*

He had been destroying Terminators for fifteen years now. It never seemed to be enough.

Pushing the Warthog to nearly 400 kilometers per hour, he reached the battlefield in less than forty-five minutes. His eyes quickly took in the scene. The shattered bridge. The derailed train at the bottom of the gorge. Dead bodies strewn across the snowy hills and riverbank. A Hunter-Killer hovering above the carnage, searching for fresh targets. From the look of things, the Resistance cell had already been slaughtered.

He caught brief glimpses of motion as unmanned snowmachines chased the survivors through the surrounding woodlands. He wondered if Dmitri's new friend, the Eskimo woman, was still alive. Ivanov had never dealt with Kookesh directly, but he knew Losenko thought highly of her. Admiring the destruction of the bridge, and the crumpled Terminator train lying in ruins, he could see why.

Not bad... for an American. Then again, she was a native of this land, so she likely held a few grudges of her own.

He didn't wait for the HK to come after him. Swooping down from the sky, he fired the Warthog's formidable Avenger anti-tank cannon. The aircraft was literally built around the Gatling-style rotary cannon, making it a flying gun. A burst of depleted uranium slugs strafed the enemy aircraft, scoring its armored carapace. For the moment, Ivanov avoided hitting any vital systems. He didn't want to bring down the massive HK on top of any survivors who might be sheltering in the wreckage below.

A wry smile lifted his lips. He snorted derisively at his own restraint.

Since when did he worry about Yankee casualties?

The HK didn't take his assault lying down. Abandoning its search for Earthbound saboteurs, the Terminator shot skyward on its impellers. It fired back with its plasma cannons, narrowly missing the swiftly moving fighter. A small flock of Aerostats joined the dogfight, trailing after the HK like baby birds. Ivanov paid them little heed. The unarmed surveillance drones were hardly worth killing.

The HK was another story....

He pulled back on his stick. The Warthog climbed to get out of range of the machine's weapons, then circled back to confront the enemy. Besides its central gun, the A-10 was also armed with two Sidewinder air-to-air missiles. He locked the HK in his sights and unleashed the first one. The missile rocketed toward its target.

Just like firing a torpedo, he thought.

Maybe this would be a short battle after all.

Such hopes were dashed when the HK blasted the oncoming missile with its plasma cannon. The Sidewinder exploded in midair, halfway between the two aircraft, too far away to do any damage.

Ivanov cursed under his breath. The shock wave jolted his plane. He dodged flying debris. Acrid black smoke obscured his view of the aurora overhead.

One missile... wasted!

Aerostats swarmed the Warthog, getting in his way. They threw themselves against his windscreen, bouncing harmlessly off the bulletproof plexiglass. He blew them apart with his gun, expending precious ammo. He scowled at the loss. The A-10 carried nearly 1200 rounds of ammo, but at seventy rounds a second that went pretty fast. At this rate, his gun would be empty in no time.

All the more reason to finish things quickly.

He closed on the Hunter-Killer, firing his remaining missile.

Eat this, you bloodthirsty machine.

The Sidewinder zoomed toward the HK, but was intercepted by a suicidal Aerostat instead. Ivanov seethed in frustration. The explosion went off only a few meters away from him, sending the Warthog into a spin. The out-of-control jet dove toward the bottom of the canyon. The rugged landscape whirled vertiginously before his eyes. A field of corpses waited for him to join them.

"No!" he blurted. Straining against killer g-forces, he pulled out of the spin only seconds before he would have crashed into the wreckage below. He gasped, but his relief was short-lived. Catching him by surprise, the demolished train opened fire on him as well. Gunports opened up along the top of the piled railcars. Ground fire slammed into the underside of the Warthog, perforating its thick armor plating. Ivanov was suddenly very grateful for the titanium "bathtub" protecting the cockpit area. The plane shuddered around him.

He fired back at the train with his own cannon. The barrage tore into the exposed gunports.

Meanwhile, the HK circled menacingly above the canyon. Ivanov wondered briefly what it was waiting for, then realized it didn't want to risk blowing apart the train full of uranium. It intended to resume their duel when and if the Warthog climbed back up to meet it. It could afford to be patient.

It wasn't running low on ammo.

A warning light on his instrument panel flashed, informing him that he was losing fuel.

"Hell!"

He glared angrily at the gauge. The Warthog's fuel lines and tanks were supposed to reseal themselves if hit, but apparently the back-up systems had malfunctioned. That was the trouble with twenty-year-old warplanes and equipment. Nothing worked quite the way it used to.

Shoddy American craftsmanship!

Ivanov conducted a quick inventory. He had no more missiles, only a few more rounds of ammunition, and he was leaking fuel by the bucketload. The HK was still waiting for him. Retreat was the only sensible option. If he was lucky—and managed to evade his pursuer—he might make it back to Canada alive.

I've done my part, he reasoned. The Alaskans would have to fend for themselves. *If any of them are still alive.*

Before departing, he swooped over the battlefield one last time, just so he could give Losenko an accurate report. His eyes widened at the sight of two small humans darting out from one of the wrecked railcars. He couldn't be sure, but it looked like a pair of women, one slightly smaller than the other.

Just like his long-lost wife and daughter.

Yelena. Nadia. An ancient scab tore off his heart, leaving it bleeding afresh. The women below were nothing to him. Americans, no less. But they were still mortal, still flesh-and-blood.

Like his own family.

He could not leave them to the HK's tender mercies.

Climbing upward, he spied the Hunter-Killer circling above him, ready to pick up where they had left off. His eyes narrowed. A long-simmering anger boiled over. A muscle twitched beneath his cheek. Let this greedy vulture kill those women?

Not on his life.

He aimed the Warthog's snout directly at the HK's impellers. He unleashed the last of his ammo to keep its own guns at bay. Opening up the throttle, he zoomed toward the unsuspecting HK at top speed, turning the forty-ton aircraft into one enormous missile. White knuckles held the control stick steady. Yelena and Nadia had been waiting for him for fifteen years. It was past time he joined them.

For the Motherland!

Without hesitation, the kamikaze fighter collided with the Hunter-Killer at 400 kilometers an hour. Alexei Ivanov's world ended for the second time, in a storm of fire and thunder.

He had no regrets.

CHAPTER
TWENTY-SEVEN

Gunfire sounded above their heads. Explosions lit up the sky. Staring up in shock through the sundered ceiling of the storage car, Molly caught a glimpse of a Resistance warplane taking on the surprised Hunter-Killer. The noisy aerial combat was the answer to her prayers.

She knew at once who to thank for this unexpected stroke of luck

Losenko, you old sea dog! She punched the air with her fist. *I should have known I could count on you!*

She wasn't about to let this gift horse go to waste.

"Out!" she hollered at Sitka. "Now!"

The women rushed out of the railcar, leaving Doc Rathbone's lifeless body behind, along with several kilos of primed plastic explosive. They scrambled down the piled wooden trestles, which were now riddled with bullet holes. Averting their eyes from the grisly remains of their comrades, they sprinted alongside the river toward the woods. Snowmobile tracks crisscrossed the bloody snow. The icy spray of water pelted their faces. Molly gripped her pistol in one hand, the detonator remote in the other. She looked about anxiously for the snowmachines, but there were none in sight. She counted her blessings.

Maybe our luck is changing....

Sitka kept pace beside her. She nodded at the detonator. "Forget something?"

"Not for a moment." Molly glanced back at the plundered train. It was maybe sixty yards behind her. *Far enough*, she decided. She spotted a fractured concrete pier thrown clear by the train crash and explosions. It was lying sideways at the edge of the river, only a few yards to their right. They weren't going to find any better shelter.

"Cover your ears!"

Sitka recklessly turned to take in the fireworks, but Molly grabbed her and tossed her behind the uprooted pier instead. "Duck your head, you loon. Unless you want those freckles blown off your skull."

She clicked the detonator button.

The C-4 charges went off in unison. A tremendous explosion shook the valley, ripping out the train's guts. More of the cliff gave way. Rockslides crashed down on the Skynet Express, hammering it to a pulp. A cloud of smoke and dust, liberally mixed with yellowcake, billowed up into the sky. Uranium scattered like snowflakes in a blizzard. They'd be digging radioactive powder out of the soil for years to come, but, after Judgment Day, what was a little more fall-out?

The important thing was: Skynet would have to do without.

We did it, Molly thought. *Despite everything, we did it.*

"Bye, Doc," Sitka whispered. The blast had surely vaporized the old man's body. "Never forget you."

They lifted their heads cautiously. Ears ringing, Molly surveyed the aftermath of the blast. Mangled machinery and charred body parts were strewn all over the terrain. It was like Judgment Day all over again. She spied one of the train's bullet-shaped heads lying smoking on the other side of the river. Its demonic red eyes flickered briefly, then went out for good. The Skynet Express was well and truly dead at last.

About time.

A second explosion, coming from further up the canyon, startled her. The ground quaked as something heavy crashed to earth a few miles away, beyond the demolished train and bridge. A churning pillar of smoke rose on the horizon. Molly searched the sky, realizing that she had lost track of the aerial dogfight that had saved their butts before. She wondered who had gone down in flames. The fighter? The HK?

Both?

Sitka stared at the smoke, too.

"Think the pilot made it?"

"Who knows?" Molly said. "We need to get out of here if we're ever going to find out."

They weren't out of the woods yet. Or *into* the woods, to be more exact. Taking Sitka by the hand, she turned away from the dismembered train and started thinking about the fastest way back to camp. They had a long, scary hike ahead of them.

Wish I knew where those fucking Snowminators were.

The ear-pounding roar of a two-stroke engine provided an answer faster than she would have liked. A snowmachine barreled out of the woods in front of them, spraying a roostertail of white powder behind it. Fresh blood glistened on its front skis. A second machine appeared on the other side of the river. Another engine growled in the hills around them. The damn machines were closing in on them. Evil red optical sensors fixed the women in their sights. The muzzles of their mini-guns flashed.

"Down!"

Molly and Sitka dived behind the other side of the concrete pier. A furious barrage of bullets chipped away at the sideways foundation. Molly heard the snowmachine roaring toward them. She remembered what had happened to Tom Jensen. The crumbling concrete block wasn't going to shield them for long.

She looked around frantically, trying to find some way out. The spray from the rushing river sprinkled her face again. Molly's gaze seized on the frothing white water and rapids.

It's our only chance.

Thrusting her pistol into her belt, she yanked the heavy pack off Sitka's shoulders. It was only going to weigh her down.

"Hey!" the girl protested. "What's that for?"

There was no time to explain. The Snowminators would be on them in a second.

"Shut up and follow me!"

Keeping low, she dived into the freezing river. Bullets whizzed over her head, but she could barely hear them over the crash of the rapids. The current gripped her and sent her hurtling downstream at a breakneck pace, far from the deadly machines. Tossed about like flotsam and jetsam, she fought to keep her head above the water. Churning white froth invaded her mouth and nostrils. She kicked and sputtered, swallowing a mouthful of ice water, then spitting it out again. The sudden, frigid immersion shocked her to her marrow. Her heart skipped a beat.

She tumbled over the deep rapids.

There was another loud splash behind her.

"Molly!"

Twisting her head, she caught a glimpse of Sitka bobbing in the water not far away.

"Where are you?"

Molly reached out for the teen, but the relentless current tore them apart. The river carried them away.

Molly tried to remember if Sitka knew how to swim.

CHAPTER TWENTY-EIGHT

Gasping for breath, they dragged themselves to shore, many miles downstream from the battle at the bridge. Molly guessed that they'd been in the water for maybe ten minutes, tops, but it felt like hours had passed since they'd thrown themselves into the freezing current. Her entire body felt black and blue from bouncing over the rapids. She shivered from head to foot. Her legs were wobbly.

She leaned against Sitka, the two women clinging to each other for support as they staggered away from the water, splashing through the thin ice and slush at the edge of the riverbank. Slowing as it rounded a rocky shoal, the river had slackened just enough to give them a chance to break free from the current. It was shallower and narrower here, too.

Another lucky break.

Thank God they hadn't gone over any waterfalls!

Exhausted, they collapsed onto the snow. Molly coughed up a gallon of water. She listened intently for the roar of the snowmachines, but heard only the river continuing on its way. If nothing else, they had escaped the vicious killers, who were presumably far behind them now, and in no position to follow them down the river. *Sure, they can ski*, she gloated, reveling for the moment in their unlikely escape. *But they damn well can't swim!*

Icy water dripped from her hair and clothes. Tremors shook her body. Forget the machines, she thought. Hypothermia was their enemy now. If anything, it felt colder on the shore than it had been in the water. The bitter wind chill could kill them just as surely as a Terminator's bullets. At best, they had maybe a couple of hours before they froze to death. Probably less, given how drenched they were. She could feel her sodden clothing freezing already.

Fuck, it was cold!

"Up!" she ordered Sitka, resisting the temptation to sink forever into the soft white drifts. She hauled herself to her feet and turned her thoughts to survival. Years of wilderness training came to her rescue. *Shelter*, she realized. That was their top priority. She nudged Sitka with her toe. Water slushed inside the boot. "Up and at 'em." Her teeth chattered. "We've g-got work to do."

It took a couple of prods, but the grumbling teen finally got up.

"Always so b-b-bossy." Her soggy red mane was plastered to her head. Her lips were blue. She fumbled in her fanny pack for a cigarette lighter. Shaking fingers tried to get a spark going. "F-fire?"

Molly shook her head. The snow and frost had left any available tinder too damp to kindle; by the time they got a fire going, it would be too late. Besides, they couldn't risk the Terminators seeing the smoke or flames.

"Sh-shelter." She hugged herself to keep warm. It didn't work. "F-follow me."

There was nothing to work with by the river's edge, so

they had to trek deeper into the woods before they found enough timber and debris to construct a crude shelter. While Sitka gathered as many fallen branches, leaves, ferns, and pine needles as she could rustle up, Molly got to work on the basic construction. First, she dug a shallow depression in the snow, barely big enough to hold both her and Sitka. She spread the branches and ground cover over the frozen earth like a carpet, then built a simple wooden framework over the ditch. Two crossed sticks, thrust upright into the dirt and snow supported a longer, diagonal ridgeline

Working together, they leaned the extra branches and debris against the central pole, forming a crude lean-to whose narrow opening rose less than a foot above the surface. The rest of the structure tapered to the ground behind the opening. Packed snow, heaped up against the angled sides of the shelter, provided an additional level of insulation. Given time, it would freeze solid, hopefully keeping the two women from doing the same.

Panting, Molly paused long enough to inspect their work. It wasn't much to look at, but it might keep them alive until the sun came up. She shivered in the wind, taking shelter behind a nearby pine. The heavy exertion had warmed her up some, but had also left her dangerously soaked in sweat. Sitka looked just as cold. They had to get out of the wind before it was too late.

"Y-you first," Molly said. "H-hurry."

For once, the feral teen didn't put up a fight. Getting down on the ground in front of the narrow opening, she wriggled feet-first into the shelter. Molly gave her a five-second head start, then squeezed in after her. It was a tight fit, but there was just enough room for both of them. Their faces were only inches apart.

Molly could practically hear the girl's heartbeat.

"S-still cold," Sitka complained. "Brrr."

"It'll warm up," Molly promised. "Soon."

They stripped off their wet clothes at last, then stuffed the wadded fabric in the mouth of the shelter to keep out the cold. They huddled together, sharing whatever body heat they could still muster. The packed branches and snow kept the warmth inside, just like it was supposed to. For the first time since she had dived into the river, Molly started to feel less like an icicle.

"Uh, Molly," Sitka murmured. "Wrong time to mention that I think I might be gay?"

"Yeah," Molly said firmly. "Wrong time."

Later on in the night, she thought she heard the girl crying.

"I know," Molly said. "I miss Doc, too."

She wondered what had become of Geir and the others.

The next morning, they crouched around a modest campfire. They'd had to strip the damp bark from the kindling to get to its dry, flammable core, but it had been worth the effort. Their frozen parkas and boots were finally starting to dry out. They shared some scraps of smoked meat that had somehow survived their trip down the river. Molly decided she'd never again tease Sitka about being a packrat.

The sound of a helicopter's blades chopping up the air electrified both campers. They knew rescue was at hand. Skynet didn't bother with helicopters. Hunter-Killers were its aircraft of choice. So they leaped to their feet and ran down to the shore, where they jumped up and down like maniacs, waving their arms in the air.

Molly would have killed for another roman candle, but

it turned out she didn't need one. A Chinook transport chopper touched down on the riverbed. A door in its side slid open. A Resistance pilot sporting a red armband called out to them.

"You Kookesh? General Losenko sent me."

Within moments, they were safe and warm aboard the chopper. Molly quickly briefed the pilot on their experiences, then pumped him for information.

"Any other survivors?"

"Not yet," the pilot said. A nametag on his uniform identified him as CARLINO. He had a Brooklyn accent. He looked nothing like Geir. "But we're still looking."

Molly flinched. A sinking feeling came over her.

"Any other aircraft in the vicinity? An old World War II fighter maybe?"

"No, ma'am." The chopper prepared to take off again. "My orders are to ferry you to the base in the Yukon. You'll be safe there." He shrugged. "Well, as much as any place is safe these days."

Molly shook her head.

"Take her." She stepped away from Sitka. "I'm not going anywhere. All I need from you are dry clothes, some ammo, and a survival kit." She looked out the window of the chopper. "I'm not done here yet."

"Going with you then," Sitka insisted. She crossed her arms atop her chest. "Sticking together all the way."

"Not this time." Molly figured the girl knew why Molly needed to stay behind, but that didn't matter. "This is personal. You go with these pilots. Be safe." She played her trump card. "It's what Doc would have wanted."

Sitka couldn't argue with that. Pouting, she slumped into her seat.

"Not fair. Sucks."

Molly wasn't sure if she was referring to the invocation of Doc Rathbone or just the situation in general.

She peeled the red armband off her sleeve. It was a bit soggy and faded, but still intact.

"Here," she said. "I think I promised you this."

The girl's face lit up a little. She eagerly claimed the token.

"Earned it?"

"You bet."

A half-hour later, after wrangling some fresh clothes and supplies, Molly stood upon the shore and watched the Chinook take off into the sky. Sitka waved at her from a window. Molly waved back until the chopper was too high up to see anything.

Give my regards to the old Russian, she had told the pilot right before she got out of the 'copter. *I owe him one.*

The Chinook disappeared, leaving her alone in the wilderness.

She started walking.

CHAPTER
TWENTY-NINE

"To Alexei Mikhalyovich Ivanov, a hero of the Resistance."

Losenko raised a cup in memory of his friend and former officer. A few survivors of K-115 had gathered in the general's private stateroom to honor their fallen comrade. Pushkin. Komarov. Aleksin. Pavlinko. He had uncorked a rare bottle of Massandra wine for the occasion. The good stuff, much better than the rotgut the enlisted men brewed when they thought the officers weren't looking.

The rosy vintage reminded him of the red wine they had consumed to combat radiation sickness in those terrible weeks and months immediately after Judgment Day. In retrospect, it was amazing that any of them had lived through those days, let alone for another fifteen years.

"To Ivanov," the men toasted in unison. "May he rest in peace."

The charred remains of a borrowed A-10 Thunderbolt had been sighted in the Alaskan wilderness, not far from where a railway bridge had once been employed by the enemy. The wreckage of the Warthog had been hopelessly fused and entangled with

a downed Hunter-Killer. All evidence suggested that
Ivanov had died striking a blow against the machines,
just as he would have wanted to. Losenko had also
been informed that Molly Kookesh and a handful of
other Alaskan fighters had survived Operation
Ravenwing. By all accounts, Ivanov had played a key
role in keeping them alive.

Well done, Alexei. Losenko mourned his comrade's
death, but found himself deeply moved as well. In the end,
Ivanov had sacrificed his life to save some of the
Americans he had hated so vehemently all these years.
Perhaps John Connor was right all along. As long as
mankind could stick together, overcoming old feuds and
hatreds, maybe they still had a chance to win this war. If
even Ivanov could learn that, anything was possible.

Losenko raised his glass again.

"To the future—and victory."

There you are, flyboy.

Molly had been hiking for days, living off the land. A
GPS tracking device, procured from the chopper pilots,
had led her to an isolated stretch of densely-wooded forest north of the Wrangell Mountains. Several miles
behind her, steam rose from the fuming crater of the volcano, which seemed far more active than usual. Molly
was tired and hungry. Her feet hurt. An invisible toe
itched. But she had found her missing lover at last.

The body of Geir Svenson hung from the upper
branches of a tall pine. The shredded remains of a parachute were hopelessly fouled in the branches. He had
obviously had a hard landing, without ever hitting the
ground. His head was crooked to one side, and his neck
looked broken. Limp arms and legs dangled high above

the ground. She was grateful for the tangled nylon cords suspending him in the air. That alone had probably kept the body from being carried off and devoured by some large predator. If a bear or wolf had found him first, she might still be searching for him.

"I hope it was quick," she whispered hoarsely. Moist eyes gazed up at him. Her throat tightened. She wasn't surprised by her discovery. Deep in her heart, she had somehow known that he hadn't survived that final sortie. But still....

I loved you. You knew that, right?

Climbing the tree wasn't easy, but it had to be done. Her hunting knife cut through the nylon cords. A fresh layer of deep snow muffled the sound of the body hitting the earth as he finally completed his jump, many days after bailing out of *Thunderbird.*

Molly descended to the ground, albeit much more slowly. She cut him free of the rest of the cords and laid him out gently upon the ground. She considered taking off his helmet and goggles, then reconsidered. She wanted to remember his face the way it was the last time she saw it, right after those feverish moments in the shack. Had they known then that they were never going to see each other again?

Looking back, she thought maybe they had.

She wasn't going to bury him. She had given it a lot of thought while hiking through the woods by herself, and she'd decided that a Viking funeral—befitting his Nordic roots—would be in order. She would send him to Valhalla on wings of flame.

First, though, there was one more thing to do. She unzipped his jacket and rummaged through his pockets. Thick gloves and numb fingers frustrated her efforts.

"C'mon," she muttered irritably. "It's gotta be here somewhere. I know it."

She found the grenade ring in the front pocket of his flannel shirt. Right over his heart, just like she should have known. A sob tore itself from her lungs. A wave of emotion, even stronger than she had anticipated, hit her hard.

She gripped it tightly in her palm, warming it, before she peeled off her left glove.

"I hope you can fucking see this."

She slipped the ring on her finger.

Later, she built a pyre and set it ablaze. As the rising flames consumed Geir's body, she turned and started the long trek home.

She still had a war to fight.

EPILOGUE

Losenko reported to the command center aboard the *Wilmington*. A messenger had informed him that General Ashdown required his presence. As he entered the compartment, Losenko wondered if this was about Ivanov's unauthorized flight to Alaska. That deployment had cost the Resistance a valuable warplane and a veteran officer. Ashdown had yet to raise the matter, but Losenko expected to face the music eventually.

He was prepared to take full responsibility for his decision.

But Ashdown had more important affairs on his mind.

"We've found it," he announced jubilantly, as though he couldn't wait to inform Losenko of the news. He gripped a rolled-up computer printout. Losenko had seldom seen him so enthusiastic. He thrust the paper at the Russian.

"Read it."

Losenko skimmed the document. It was a classified intelligence report suggesting that Skynet's top-secret shutdown code could be obtained at an underground enemy communications complex in the sector of North America not far from the bombed-out ruins of Los Angeles. A substantial array of satellite dishes was the machine's primary shortwave transmission hub for the entire region. If the hidden code was recorded anywhere, it was there.

"This looks very promising," he agreed. The implications of the discovery—if they could be verified—were enormous. They might finally be able to win the war, just as John Connor had always said they could. He wondered if it was just a coincidence that the code was hiding in the very same territory in which Connor was now serving. There were those who believed that Connor was destined to be the one who ultimately found the key to victory over the machines.

An idea occurred to him.

"I suggest we send in General Olsen's forces to secure the code."

Which would include John Connor's Tech Comm unit.

"My thoughts exactly," Ashdown said. "Contact Olsen and get this thing done."

Losenko smiled. A sudden renewal of hope dispelled whatever melancholy had lingered in him after Ivanov's death. He could hardly believe his long voyage might at last be nearing its end. It was a shame that Alexei, and so many others, had not lived to see it.

After fifteen long and brutal years, it seemed as if salvation was at hand....

The End

ACKNOWLEDGMENTS

I still remember being blown away by the original Terminator movie when I first caught it at a multiplex outside Seattle way back in 1984. Three exciting sequels and a TV series later, it's tremendously exciting to finally get to write a little bone-crushing, killer robot action of my own.

Many thanks to my editor, Cath Trechman, for thinking of me and helping me throughout the writing and editing of this book, thanks as well to Steve Saffel and designer Louise Brigenshaw at Titan Books. Many thanks to James Middleton of The Halycon Company for graciously letting me pick his brains on all things Terminator. I also want to thank my agents, Russ Galen and Ann Behar, for handling the business end of things.

Finally, as always, I could not have written this book without the unwavering support and assistance of my girlfriend, Karen Palinko, who kept the household together while I chained myself to my keyboard despite near-daily Pennsylvania thunderstorms that kept knocking out our computers. Karen also looked after our growing family of four-legged children, Alex, Churchill, Henry, Sophie, and Lyla, who often kept me company while I was working. Here's hoping Skynet never goes after our pets, as well.

BIBLIOGRAPHY

The following books were invaluable in my research for this novel.

Submarines

Clancy, Tom with John Gresham. *Submarine: A Guided Tour Inside a Nuclear Warship*. New York: Berkley Books, 1993.
Huchthausen, Peter. *K-19 the Widow Maker: The Secret Story of the Soviet Nuclear Submarine*. Washington, D.C.: National Geographic Society, 2002.
DiMercurio, Michael with Michael Benson. *The Complete Idiot's Guide to Submarines*. Indianapolis: Alpha Books, 2003.
Waller, Douglas C. *Big Red: Three Months on Board a Trident Nuclear Submarine*. New York: HarperCollins, 2001.

Terminator

Bennett, Tara. *Terminator Salvation: The Official Movie*

Companion. London: Titan Books, 2009.

Bennett, Tara. *The Art of Terminator Salvation*. London: Titan Books, 2009.

Foster, Alan Dean. *Terminator Salvation: The Official Movie Novelization*. London: Titan Books, 2009.

Hagberg, David. *Terminator 3: Rise of the Machines* (official movie novelization). New York: Tor Books, 2003.

Naraghi, Dara with art by Alan Robinson. *Terminator Salvation: Sand in the Gears* (graphic novel). San Diego: IDW Publishing, 2009.

Sterling, S. M. *T2: The Future War*. New York: HarperEntertainment, 2003.

Zahn, Timothy. *Terminator Salvation: From the Ashes*. London: Titan Books, 2009.

ABOUT THE AUTHOR

GREG COX is the *New York Times* bestselling author of numerous novels and short stories. He has written the official movie novelizations of such films as *Daredevil*, *Death Defying Acts*, *Ghost Rider*, and all three *Underworld* movies. He has also written books and stories based on such popular series as *Alias*, *Batman*, *Buffy the Vampire Slayer*, *Countdown*, *C.S.I.*, *Fantastic Four*, *Farscape*, *The 4400*, *52*, *Infinite Crisis*, *Iron Man*, *Roswell*, *Spider-Man*, *Star Trek*, *Xena*, *X-Men*, and *Zorro*. He lives in Oxford, Pennsylvania.

His official website is: www.gregcox-author.com.